Turkish Folktales

Turkish Folktales

Introduction by Nathan Young

General Editor: Jake Jackson

FLAME TREE
PUBLISHING

This is a FLAME TREE Book

FLAME TREE PUBLISHING
6 Melbray Mews
Fulham, London SW6 3NS
United Kingdom
www.flametreepublishing.com

First published 2023
Copyright © 2023 Flame Tree Publishing Ltd

23 25 27 26 24
1 3 5 7 9 8 6 4 2

ISBN: 978-1-80417-332-9

The cover artwork is © copyright 2022 Flame Tree Publishing Ltd,
featuring an image courtesy of MBALyon, licensed under the Creative
Commons Attribution-Share Alike 4.0 International license.

All inside images courtesy of Shutterstock.com and the
following: Artstockerillustrator, irmairma.

Contributors, authors, editors and sources for this book include:
Cyrus Adler and Allan Ramsay (collected and translated); R. Nisbet Bain
(translator); Hartwell James; Dr. Ignácz Kúnos; Andrew Lang; Kate Douglas
Wiggin and Nora A. Smith; Dr. Nathan Young (compiled and translated).

Printed and bound in the UK by Clays Ltd, Elcograf S.p.A

Contents

Series Foreword

STRETCHING BACK to the oral traditions of thousands of years ago, tales of heroes and disaster, creation and conquest have been told by many different civilizations in many different ways. Their impact sits deep within our culture even though the detail in the tales themselves are a loose mix of historical record, transformed narrative and the distortions of hundreds of storytellers.

Today the language of mythology lives with us: our mood is jovial, our countenance is saturnine, we are narcissistic and our modern life is hermetically sealed from others. The nuances of myths and legends form part of our daily routines and help us navigate the world around us, with its half truths and biased reported facts.

The nature of a myth is that its story is already known by most of those who hear it, or read it. Every generation brings a new emphasis, but the fundamentals remain the same: a desire to understand and describe the events and relationships of the world. Many of the great stories are archetypes that help us find our own place, equipping us with tools for self-understanding, both individually and as part of a broader culture.

For Western societies it is Greek mythology that speaks to us most clearly. It greatly influenced the mythological heritage of the ancient Roman civilization and is the lens through which we still see the Celts, the Norse and many of the other great peoples and religions. The Greeks themselves learned much from their neighbours, the Egyptians, an older culture that became weak with age and incestuous leadership.

It is important to understand that what we perceive now as mythology had its own origins in perceptions of the divine and the rituals of the sacred. The earliest civilizations, in the crucible of the Middle East, in the Sumer of the third millennium BC, are the source to which many of the mythic archetypes can be traced. As humankind collected together in cities for the first time, developed writing and industrial scale agriculture, started to irrigate the rivers and attempted to control rather than be at the mercy of its environment, humanity began to write down its tentative explanations of natural events, of floods and plagues, of disease.

Early stories tell of Gods (or god-like animals in the case of tribal societies such as African, Native American or Aboriginal cultures) who are crafty and use their wits to survive, and it is reasonable to suggest that these were the first rulers of the gathering peoples of the earth, later elevated to god-like status with the distance of time. Such tales became more political as cities vied with each other for supremacy, creating new Gods, new hierarchies for their pantheons. The older Gods took on primordial roles and became the preserve of creation and destruction, leaving the new gods to deal with more current, everyday affairs. Empires rose and fell, with Babylon assuming the mantle from Sumeria in the 1800s BCE, then in turn to be swept away by the Assyrians of the 1200s BCE; then the Assyrians and the Egyptians were subjugated by the Greeks, the Greeks by the Romans and so on, leading to the spread and assimilation of common themes, ideas and stories throughout the world.

The survival of history is dependent on the telling of good tales, but each one must have the 'feeling' of truth, otherwise it will be ignored. Around the firesides, or embedded in a book or a computer, the myths and legends of the past are still the living materials of retold myth, not restricted to an exploration of origins. Now we have devices and global communications that give us unparalleled access to a diversity of traditions. We can find out about Native American, Indian, Chinese and tribal African mythology in a way that was denied to our ancestors, we can find connections, match the archaeology, religion and the mythologies of the world to build a comprehensive image of the human experience that is endlessly fascinating.

The stories in this book provide an introduction to the themes and concerns of the myths and legends of their respective cultures, with a short introduction to provide a linguistic, geographic and political context. This is where the myths have arrived today, but undoubtedly over the next millennia, they will transform again whilst retaining their essential truths and signs.

Jake Jackson
General Editor

Introduction to Turkish Folktales

T HE CORPUS of Turkish folk literature undeniably inhabits an essential place in the imaginative world of everyday Turks. The formation of national identity in Turkey, as is true elsewhere, has been accompanied by the ardent collection of folktales, a constellation of oral and textual materials known, shared and claimed by a significant portion of the population. To be sure, not every citizen knows every fable, but when outsiders like us read, hear or otherwise pay attention to this body of work, we encounter that which has shaped, and continues to shape, the larger Turkish community.

Episodes and Epics

The folktale genre is an elastic one. Several Turkish words are used broadly, though each carries a unique connotation: *masal* (fairytale), *fikra* (anecdote), *öykü* (fable), *efsane* (legend), *söylence* (myth), and *hikâye* (story). These terms denote varying literary subgenres, with collections of folktales employing all of them, often and interchangeably. Such material may vary in length from aphorisms of just a few sentences, to epics requiring several hours or days for a telling, as eminent folktale collector Ahmet Edip Uysal notes in *Selections from Living Turkish Folktales*. Like the episodic *1001 Nights*, it is reasonable to surmise that a given Turkic epic may comprise shorter narratives that have been spliced together in the production of a greater, coherent whole. For example, we find individual pieces that can be comprehended as standalone works as well as integral strands of a broader raiment. The editorial decision to include 'The Story of Delu Dumrul' from *The Book of Dede Korkut* and 'The Story of the Blind Baba-Abdalla' from *The Blind Man's Son* in this collection underscores that a segment extracted from a longer work can be regarded as a discrete folk narrative possessing its own merit. Further, component parts may be separated, conjoined and strung together in various forms. Regardless, these enticing, independent vignettes may encourage readers to seek out additional installments or tackle the entire work.

Tacit Resistance

Folktales are often counterhegemonic. That is, they push against established powers, against systems that maintain forces and authorities. Through wit, magic and a propitious sprinkling of good fortune, the young, poor and hopeless routinely outmaneuvre the old, wealthy and powerful. Innocuous Nasreddin Hodja comes up clever and cagey, matching wits with the mighty Tamerlane, ruthless ruler of Central Asia and beyond. In a series of tales, the boy Keloğlan overcomes a parade of fierce warriors, exacting sultans and terrorizing giants. The minuscule and defenseless in the animal kingdom outwit their predators. Women and girls subvert a matrix of patriarchal relationships, demonstrating not just agency but efficacy. As Turkish scholar Mark Glazer deftly points out, '...When the hero of the tale takes the advice of women or feminine magical beings seriously and behaves in accordance... he is successful in his endeavors.' In contexts where contemporary notions of universal human rights were absent (and still may be), their recitation becomes an act of resistance – and perhaps an exercise in hope. The voiceless are heard, the marginalized centred. Certainly, there is a gruff, gruesome brutality in many renditions, such as when Keloğlan and his master scheme for the right to flay skin off the other's back to make a pair of sandals in 'Keloğlan and the Köse' (not included in this collection). However, a kind of moral order prevails, even when the folktale itself is not a morality tale. And when there is little possibility of upending entrenched hierarchies, at least their hypocrisy can be exposed amid a few tragicomic laughs.

Young Republic, Old Tales

The richness of our deep dive into the folktales that follow will be enhanced by a brief look at their historical contexts. The year of this volume's publication, 2023, is also the year of Turkey's centennial, marking one hundred years since its phoenix-inception as a republic after Ottoman dissolution following the First World War. Significant interest and attention have been given to collecting, recording and studying Turkish folklore because that is what you do when you become a nation. You demarcate that which imparts a sense of national identity (and pride). Though foreign scholars had issued brief anthologies of Turkish stories during the Ottoman Empire, within two decades of the 1928 republican establishment, folktale scholarship was earnestly undertaken by in-country Turkish academics – and vigorously continues into the twenty-first century. To claim a body of tales as Turkish is to assert that a Turkish people exist; moreover, it is to declare that beyond cosmopolitan Istanbul, officious Ankara or secular Izmir, there remains an 'essential' Turk – rooted in the landscape, connected to the community and ensconced in tradition.

Steles and Steppes

Many of the tales included in this book have been told and retold for ages, in varying iterations. The comparatively recent scholarly emphasis belies the existence of Turkic 'proto-epics' inscribed on several steles dating back to the eighth century CE and excavated in the Orkhon Valley of present-day Mongolia. The Turkic tribes inhabiting Transoxiana (beyond the Oxus River) presumably brought pieces and fragments of plots, narratives, characters and rhetorical devices over the steppes with them as they began their conquest towards the eastern shores of the Mediterranean over a millennium ago.

Swapping Stories

During the generations in which such tribal communities made their way to Anatolia from Central Asia, they encountered many groups – Persians, Arabs, Armenians, Laz, Kurds, Jews, Greeks (to name a few) – with whom they inevitably shared and fought over goods, flocks, wives, religion and traditions... and with whom they swapped stories. So, while it is nearly impossible to ascertain how, when and where a current folktale originated, what can be said with confidence is that wherever it may be told, heard or otherwise encountered, it has travelled. As if transcontinental migrations weren't enough, the multi-cultural, multi-ethnic and multi-confessional composition of the Ottoman Empire continued to press this point. Furthermore, Turkic communities settled at intersections – in the crux, as it were – of Asia, Europe and Africa. Because tales migrate and neighbours lend, borrow and steal, the Tepegöz chapter from the Dede Korkut epic (while not included here) bears uncanny similarities to the cyclops Polyphemus in book nine of Homer's Odyssey. And we are not surprised when Turkish trickster Nasreddin Hodja shows up in Arabic, but is called Juha, or when we find him in Persian, known as Mullah Nasruddin. Thus, while the fables and foibles of this irreverent holy man are central to Turkish cultural identity, he does not remain exclusively Turkish.

Imbrications, Local and Global

The ambulation of Turkish folktales renders them both specific to a given people and part of a much broader socio-cultural milieu. Long since contested as an apt theory, certain early story collectors (such as the Brothers Grimm) surmised that the folktale conveyed the 'soul of the folk,' the essence of ordinary peoples whose ways of life were apparently disappearing against the backdrop of urbanization and industrialization. A collection of tales, it was believed, could reveal what it meant for Germans to be German and by extension, Turks to be Turkish. This understanding of ethnic identity is undeniably problematic and reductionistic. Yet when reading a Turkish tale, one can look for traces, insights and clues that help to interpret what an outsider, perhaps a non-Muslim Westerner, might be noticing in contemporary Turkey. Case in point: within the corpus of Turkish folktales more than a few explore hospitality and interactions and obligations with neighbours. This brings to mind a Turkish adage, 'Don't buy a house, buy a neighbour [Ev alma, komşu al].' Anyone who has spent a little time in a Turkish neighbourhood (not a hotel) knows this to be true: neighbours keep up with each other in ways that the denizens of Western suburbia usually do not.

But folktales are also deep and wide, their scope broader and more extensive than the realms of the people to whom they are attributed; a significant part of their terrain includes the contours of the human heart. The satisfaction in reading one of Aesop's fables is not that we glimpse ancient Greek ways of being and thinking, rather that the dramatic unfolding tells us something about ourselves. A flicker of recognition flashes when the resonant truth to which the tale points is discovered or uncovered.

The Shared 'Aha!' Moment

When I earnestly set out to learn Turkish, a notoriously difficult language for English-speakers, one of my favourite activities was to study a Turkish folktale. Specifically, I would choose from one of the hundreds of anecdotes featuring Nasreddin Hodja, the impertinent, wisecracking central character in popular Turkish tales. Deciphering the tale required two main tasks. First, I had to ascertain what was happening – the basic narrative elements: setting, characters, actions and resolution. The second – and more formidable – task, several orders of magnitude above, delved into hard-to-define concepts: meaning and significance, context and applicability, revelations about how a particular people at a particular time in a particular place within a particular cultural milieu thought about family, community, marriage, religion, authority, life and death. And what present-day circumstances, whether ordinary or extraordinary, might induce a Turk to recall the moral of a certain tale? Once I had approximated answers to these questions, I would take the story to the streets, where among my community of new friends I would stumble through a retelling of Nasreddin Hodja's perils and pitfalls, manipulations and masterful escapes – a foreigner reciting the 'core' of how Turks understood themselves as Turks.

The power of a good folktale is often delivered in the final sentence or final phrase. Through the telling, a tale can produce anxiety and expectation. Something is odd, something out of place, something doesn't fit, something won't coalesce. Seeming opposites are brought together with little hope of reconciliation. Tension mounts as does anticipation. And when the last line is articulated, something satisfying happens. The denouement miraculously unites disparate entities but achieves much more. It reveals what had been there all along, if only the listener had known what to listen for – a structure of cohesiveness hidden in plain sight. 'Cohesiveness' does not imply rationality or reasonableness; rather, a kind of phenomenon produced by the brief narrative that points to a suprarational reality. The ironic, the absurd, the incongruous, the ostensibly contradictory, elucidate some part of the human experience that we rather suspected was true. Understand the basics of the story, yes, but listen for this line, and let it retroactively fuse the tale's seemingly disparate features into an integrated whole. As I discovered, it was this line that resonated with my Turkish friends, usually provoking a chuckle, an expression of recognition, a sigh of satisfaction. This last line of a Nasreddin Hodja story, then, can become an aphorism, a one-liner exposing the heart, the soul, the crux of a given situation. A distillation to its critical, irreducible essence when the one who speaks and the one who hears are in tacit agreement – yes, that's it!

An Emerging Folktale?

During my fieldwork research in a Turkish village about a decade ago, I heard a historical account recognized and repeated by all the villagers. It depicted a time prior to the population exchanges of the 1930s, when the nascent Turkish government, in conjunction with its Greek counterpart, sought to homogenize their respective nations. At that time, the story goes, Greeks and Turks resided in the village in beneficent coexistence.

'A hundred years ago, Turks and Greeks lived together peacefully. Uncle Süleyman (of a Turkish family) and Uncle Yorgi (of a Greek family) were neighbours. One day, Yorgi was over at Süleyman's house. One of Süleyman's daughters asked, 'Who is inside?' Her younger sister answered, 'There is an unbeliever (*gavur*) here.' The girl turned and saw that it was only their neighbour Yorgi, and chided her little sister, 'You don't know *gavur*, and you don't know Yorgi; this is our Yorgi.' Meanwhile, Greek forces had landed in nearby Izmir. Some of the Greek villagers saw their chance to gain liberation from centuries of Ottoman rule. They began to seize land belonging to their Turkish neighbours. However, when Mustafa Kemal, the commanding Turkish general, mounted a successful counterattack against the invading army, both the Greeks who had attempted to take advantage of the situation and the Greeks who had lived amicably among their Turkish neighbours realized that their days in the village had come to an end. For the most part, they fled. Years later, Yorgi returned to the village for a visit. Someone who did not remember Yorgi announced, 'There is an unbeliever (*gavur*) here!' However, a villager who did replied, 'You don't know *gavur*, and you don't know Yorgi; this is our Yorgi.' From then on, the phrase, 'You don't know *gavur*, you don't know Yorgi,' became commonplace in the village, invoked when someone has no idea what is going on.'

Had I been privy to the beginning of the lifecycle of a folktale? Every telling seemed to carry the not-so-distant past to the collective memory of villagers. And similar to my favourite Nasreddin Hodja anecdotes, this tale had been distilled to a final line; when uttered, knowing looks passed between glinting eyes. There is something else here as well. The narrative points to the fact that locals wistfully regret that the contingencies of historical events had displaced their Greek neighbours. It thus not only explains why no Greeks remain, but also allows villagers to voice and implicitly lament the status quo.

Tell Me a Story, Papa

A popular Turkish Istanbul-based television series from the 1990s, 'Super Dad' (Turkish: *Süper Baba*) begins with a lilting soundtrack floating this line, 'Tell me a story, papa,' the bedtime plea of a young boy being raised by his widowed father. The boy lists the requisite elements to weave into the tale: his games, toys, favourite foods, the celestial bodies – sun, moon and stars – plus a few animals sprinkled in for good measure. These snippets of the child's imaginative world, or rather, the commingling of the imaginative with the material, tug at the viewers' heartstrings, uncovering the pathos of a motherless child seeking to wrap himself in a blanket knitted together by what he loves, all that lends security to his life. But even this vulnerable child hopes for more. In the guise of a folktale, the figures of his little world expand and grow, charged with the mystical and magical, providing comfort while calling him out to a more expansive existence.

When this easily recognizable opening song by the popular 1970s and 1980s folk ensemble *Yeni Türkü* washes over the Turkish audience of a certain generation, they are simultaneously ushered into the boy's childhood along with their own. By overlaying the everyday and ordinary with the fantastical, the soundtrack, like a good fairy tale, both tethers one to the tangible present and impels to the numinous elsewhere. The boy not only wants his father, but also an emerging world in which the best aspects of his life are gathered, at once imparting the safety of familiarity with the excitement of an enchanted future. This is the unique province of folktales: the here and now combines with the there and then. Viewers and readers want this too.

Who Knows... What If It Does?

During the process of writing this introduction, I have been submitting applications to secure my next academic position. I've been at this business long enough to know that my chances of being selected are slim. To make matters worse, a particular position is at one of the most prestigious universities in the world. I am almost certain that I will not win this fellowship, despite my qualifications. But, I do hold on to a sliver of hope, because... what if I do? A stint at this renowned university, along with enough time to write a publication-worthy monograph, might be just the thing to slingshot my career. As I lay in bed one night contemplating this potential, the last line from a Nasreddin Hodja story flitted into my mind, 'But what if it does...?' You see, after finishing his noontime meal, our indefatigable character went down to the bank of a lake to rinse the remnants of yogurt from his bowl. As he was absorbed in his task, a passerby chanced upon him. When the visitor saw the creamy, milk-white remnants rippling out into the water, he couldn't reckon what Nasreddin Hodja could possibly be doing. 'Hodja,' he called out, 'What are you doing?' 'Oh, I'm just trying to get this lake to turn into yogurt,' Hodja remarked nonchalantly. 'But that's impossible,' came the retort, 'that gigantic lake will never ferment!' 'You're right, of course,' Hodja shot back. 'But who knows... what if it does?' We attempt 'the impossible' because one never knows if 'the impossible' just might happen after all. And in folktales, sometimes it does.

Nathan Young completed his master's degree in Turkish Folklore at Ege University in Izmir, Turkey (2014) and his PhD in the Department of Near Eastern Languages and Cultures at the Ohio State University (2020). Based on ethnographic fieldwork at several locations in Turkey, his dissertation evaluated how notions of the 'Turkish village' shape personal and national identity. His current research considers nostalgic visions of Turkish history that will accompany Turkey's 2023 centennial celebrations. He is presently a lecturer at the Ohio State University.

Tales of Cunning & Humour

IN A WORLD before television, radio, printing press, and even widespread literacy, everyday folk found entertainment in the verbal arts. Whether in public settings like the coffee shops of pre-modern Ottoman Aleppo or small private sitting rooms restricted to family and friends, the recitation of a tale, aphorism or anecdote was a welcome diversion. The social-cultural milieu of such tales was only too familiar to teller and listener alike. Enmeshed within the hierarchal systems of the times, clever repartee and honeyed sayings might be the best – and only – options for vindicating the powerless.

Enter the wise fool Nasreddin Hodja, who, depending on the day, must navigate the oppressive demands of his neighbours or face down ferocious Tamerlane. Armed only with a well-tuned wit, he negotiates Middle Eastern hospitality obligations, fends off local gossip and extricates himself from life-threatening power differentials. Underneath the audience's laughter lies a more sober sense of solidarity. We too have found ourselves in similar conundrums and after the moment slides by, wish our tongues had been quick enough to smooth over the vicissitudes of the day.

The Silent Princess
(Turkish)

THERE WAS ONCE a Padishah who had a son, and the little Prince had a golden ball with which he was never tired of playing. One day as he sat in his kiosk, playing as usual with his favourite toy, an old woman came to draw water from the spring which bubbled up in front of the mansion.

The Shahzada, merely for a jest, threw his ball at the old woman's jug and broke it. Without a word she fetched another jug and came again to the spring. For the second time the Prince threw his ball at the jug and broke it. The old woman was now angry, yet, fearing the Padishah, she dared not say a word, but went away and bought a third jug on credit, as she had no money. Returning a third time to the spring, she was in the very act of drawing water when again the young Prince's ball struck her jug and shattered it to pieces. Her anger could no longer be suppressed, and, turning toward the Shahzada, she cried: "I will say only this, my Prince: may you fall in love with the Silent Princess." With these words she went her way.

The Prince ere long found himself brooding on the old dame's words and wondering what they could mean. The more he dwelt upon them the more they took possession of his mind, until his health began to suffer; he grew thin and pale, he had no appetite, and in a few days he was so ill that he had to remain in bed. The Padishah could not understand his son's malady; physicians and hodjas were summoned, but none could do any good.

One day the Padishah asked his son whether he could throw any light on the strange complaint from which he was suffering. Then the boy described how three times in succession he had broken an old woman's jug, and related what she had said to him, finally expressing his conviction that neither physicians nor hodjas could effect his cure. He asked his father's permission to set out in quest of the Silent Princess, for he felt that only in this way could he be freed from his affliction. The Padishah saw that the boy would not live long unless his mysterious disease were cured; so, after considerable hesitation, he gave his permission and appointed his lala to accompany the young Prince on his journey.

Toward evening they set out, and as they took no care of their appearance, in six months they looked more like wild savages than a noble prince and his lala. They had quite forgotten rest and sleep; the thought of eating and drinking never occurred to them. At last they arrived at the summit of a mountain. Here they noticed that the rocks and earth glistened like the sun. Looking round, they saw that an old man approached them. The travellers inquired the name of that region. The old man informed them that they stood on the mountain of the Silent Princess. The Princess herself wore a sevenfold veil, but that fact notwithstanding, the glitter they observed around them was caused by the extraordinary brilliance of her countenance. The travellers now inquired where the Princess resided. The old man answered that if they proceeded straight on for six months longer they would reach her serai. Hitherto many men had lost their lives in vain attempts to elicit a word from the Princess. This news, however, did not dismay the Prince, who with his lala again set off on the journey.

After long wanderings they found themselves at the summit of another mountain, which they noticed was blood-red on every side. Going forward, they presently entered a village. Here the Prince said to his lala, "I am very tired; let us rest a while in this place and at the same time make some inquiries." Accordingly they entered a coffeehouse, and when it became known in the village that travellers from a distant land were in their midst, the inhabitants came up one after the other to offer their greetings. The Prince inquired of them why the mountain was blood-red. He was informed that three months' journey distant lived the Silent Princess, whose red lips reflected their hue on the mountain before them; she wore seven veils, spoke not a word, and it was said that many men had sacrificed their lives on her account. On hearing this the youth was impatient to put his fate to the test; he and his lala accordingly set out to continue their journey.

After many days they saw another great mountain in the distance, and concluded it must be the dwelling-place of the object of their quest. In due time they arrived at the foot of the mountain and began the ascent. Above them towered a proud castle, the residence of the Silent Princess; and as they approached near enough to see, they observed that it was built entirely of human skulls. The Prince remarked to his lala, "These are the heads of those who have perished in the attempt to make the Princess speak. Either we attain our object, or our skulls will be used for a similar purpose."

Before attempting to enter the castle they took up their lodgings in a hân for a few days. All this time they heard nothing but weeping and lamentation: "Oh my brother!" "Oh my son!" Inquiring the cause of the general grief, the travellers were answered: "Why do you ask? It appears you also are come to die. This town belongs to the father of the Silent Princess. Whoever wishes to attempt to make her speak must first go to the Padishah, who, if he permits it, will send an escort with the hero to the Princess." When the youth heard this he said to his lala: "We are nearly at the end of our journey. We will rest a few days longer and then see what fate has in store for us." They continued their sojourn at the hân, and took daily walks about the tscharschi. While thus occupied one day the Prince saw a man with a nightingale in a cage.

The bird caught his fancy so much that he resolved to buy it. The lala remonstrated, reminding the youth that they had a more weighty affair on hand. The Prince, however, refused to listen, and finally purchased the bird for a thousand piasters, took it to his lodging, and hung up the cage in his room. Once, when the Prince was alone and wondering by what means he could make the Princess speak, somewhat saddened by the gloomy reflection that failure meant death, he was startled to hear the nightingale thus address him: "Why so gloomy, my Prince? What troubles you?" The Prince trembled, not being sure whether it was the bird or a spirit that spoke to him. Growing calmer, he thought that perhaps it was the manifestation of Allah's grace, and accordingly told the nightingale the story of his love for the Silent Princess, and that he was at his wits' end to think how he should get into her presence. The bird replied: "There is nothing to worry about. It is as easy as can be. Go this evening to the serai, and take me with you. The Sultana wears seven veils; no one has ever seen her face, and she sees no one. Put me in my cage under the lamp-stand, and ask the Sultana how she is. She will vouchsafe no answer, however. Then say that as she will not condescend to speak, you will converse with the lamp-stand. So begin to speak, and I will reply."

The Prince followed this counsel and went direct to the Padishah's palace. When the Shah was informed that the newcomer wished to go to his daughter, he received the Prince and endeavoured to dissuade him from his intention. He represented that thousands already had tried in vain to make the Princess speak. He had vowed, however, to give her in marriage to the one who could succeed in eliciting a word from her; on the other hand, he who tried and failed forfeited his head. As the Prince might see for himself, his daughter's castle was built entirely of human skulls.

The hardy youth could not be moved from his purpose; he cast himself at the feet of the Padishah and vowed either to accomplish his object or perish in the attempt. Thus there was no more to be said: the Padishah ordered the Prince to be taken into the presence of his daughter.

It was evening when the youth found himself in the Princess's apartment, He put down his cage under the lamp-stand, bowed himself low before the Princess, inquired after her health, and spoke also on matters of less importance. No answer came. Then said the Prince to the Princess: "It is getting rather late, and you have not yet favoured me with a single word. I will now address the lamp-stand. Even though it has no soul it may have more feeling than you." At these words he turned to the lamp-stand and asked: "How are you?" And the answer came directly: "Quite well; though it is many years since anyone spoke to me. Allah sent you to me this day, and I feel as glad as if the whole world were mine. May I entertain you with a story?"

The Prince nodding assent, the voice proceeded: "Once there was a Shah who had a daughter, whom three Princes desired to marry. The father said to the wooers: 'Whichever of you excels the others in enterprise shall have my daughter.' The young men accordingly set off together, and coming to a spring they resolved to take different directions, in order to avoid any collision with each other's pursuits. They agreed, however, to leave their rings under a stone at the spring, each to take his own up again when he returned to the spot, thus furnishing an intimation to him who returned last of all that the others had already reached home.

"The first learnt how to go a six months' journey in an hour, the second how to make himself invisible, the third how to bring the dead to life again. All three arrived back simultaneously at the spring. He who could make himself invisible said the Padishah's daughter was very ill and would die in two hours; the other said he would prepare a medicine that would restore her to life again; the third volunteered to deliver the medicine. Quicker than lightning he was at the palace, in the chamber where the Princess lay dead. Hardly had the medicine touched her lips than she sat up as well as ever she had been. Meanwhile both the others came in and the Shah commanded all three to relate their experiences.

The nightingale paused for a few moments and then resumed: "Oh my Shahzada, which of the three Princes thinkest thou best deserved the maiden?" The Prince answered: "In my opinion, he who prepared the medicine." The nightingale contended for him who acquainted the others of the Princess's condition, and so they hotly disputed the matter. The Silent Princess thought to herself: "They are quite forgetting him who could go a six months' journey in an hour." As the dispute continued, she could endure it no longer, and, lifting her sevenfold veil, she cried: "You fools! I would give the maiden to him who brought the medicine. But for him she would have remained dead."

The Padishah was immediately informed that his daughter had at length broken her silence. But the Princess protested that, as she had been the victim of a ruse, the youth should not be considered to have succeeded in his task until he had induced her to speak three times. Now said the Shah to the Prince: "If you can make her speak twice more she shall belong to you."

The youth left the monarch's presence, went to his lodgings, and began to ponder the matter. While deep in thought, the nightingale said: "The Sultana is angry at having broken her silence, and has smashed the lamp-stand, so tonight put me on the other stand by the wall."

Accordingly, when evening was come, the Prince repaired with his nightingale to the serai. Entering the Princess's apartment, he put the birdcage on the stand by the wall, and addressed the Sultana. As she disdained to answer, he turned to the stand and said: "The Princess refuses to speak; therefore I will converse with you. How are you?" "Quite well, thank you," came the answer at once. "I am glad the Sultana would not speak, otherwise you would not have spoken to me. As it is, I will tell you a story, if you will listen." "With great pleasure," returned the Prince. "Let me hear it."

So the nightingale commenced: "In a certain town there once lived a woman with whom three men were in love – Baldji-Oglu the Honey-maker's Son, Jagdji-Oglu the Tallow-maker's Son, and Tiredji-Oglu the Tanner's Son. Each used to visit the woman in such wise that neither knew of the others' visits. While brushing her hair one day, the woman discovered a grey strand, and said to herself, 'Alas! I am growing old. The time will soon come when my friends will become tired of me. I must make up my mind to get married.' Next day she invited the three lovers to visit her, at different hours. The first arrival was Jagdji, who found the woman in tears. Asking the cause of her grief, he was answered: 'My father is dead, and I have buried him in the garden; but his spirit appears to torment me. If you love me wrap yourself in the winding-sheet and go and lie for three hours in the grave; then my father's spirit will haunt me no more.' Saying this, the woman led him to the open grave which she had made, and as Jagdji would have drowned himself for her sake he cheerfully donned the winding-sheet and lay down in it.

"In the meantime came Baldji, who inquired of the woman why she wept. She repeated the story of her father's death and burial, and giving him a large stone, told him to go to the grave, and when the ghost appeared, to hit him with it. No sooner had Baldji taken his leave and gone to the grave than Tiredji came in. He also sympathized with the woman and inquired what was the trouble. 'How can I help but weep,' said the woman, 'when my father is dead and buried in the garden. One of his enemies is a sorcerer; he is now lying in wait to carry off the body; as you may see he has already opened the grave with that intention. If you can bring me the corpse out of the grave all will be well; if not, I am lost.' The words were scarcely uttered before Tiredji had gone to the grave to take up Jagdji and bring him into her presence. But Baldji, thinking there were two ghosts instead of one, endeavoured to hit both with the stone. Meanwhile, Jagdji, believing the ghost had struck him, sprang out of the grave and dropped the winding-sheet. Then the three men recognised each other and explanations were demanded.

"Now, my Prince," said the nightingale, "which of the three most deserved the woman? I think Tiredji." But the Prince was for Baldji, who had put himself to so much trouble; and so they commenced to argue as before, taking care to avoid mentioning Jagdji. The Princess, who had been listening attentively to the narrative, was disappointed that the deserts of Jagdji were not taken into consideration, and she delivered her opinion with some warmth.

The news that the Silent Princess had again spoken was carried to the Padishah in his palace. Yet once more must she be compelled to speak. As the youth was sitting in his room the nightingale informed him that the Princess was so furious for having been tricked into speaking again that she had broken the wall-stand to pieces. Next evening, therefore, he must put the birdcage behind the door.

The third and final interview found the Princess no more amiable than usual; and as she refused to open her mouth the Prince tried his conversational powers on the door. The door (or rather the bird behind it) related the following story:

"There once were a carpenter, a tailor, and a softa travelling together. Coming to a certain town, they hired a common dwelling and opened business. One night when the others were asleep the carpenter got up, drank coffee, lit his chibouque, and formed an image of a charming maiden out of the small pieces of wood lying about the room. Having finished, he lay down again and fell asleep. Shortly afterwards the tailor woke up, and, seeing the image, made suitable clothing for it, put it on, and went to sleep again. About dawn the softa awoke, and, seeing the image of the lovely girl, prayed to Allah to grant it life. The softa's prayer was heard, and the image was transformed into an incomparably beautiful living maiden, who opened her eyes as one waking from a dream. When the others rose all three men set to disputing as to the possession of the lovely creature. Now to which, in justice, should she belong? In my opinion, to the carpenter." Thus the nightingale broke off.

The Prince thought the maiden should belong to the tailor, and as on the previous occasions a lively debate ensued. The Princess's ire was aroused at the softa's claim being neglected, and she exclaimed: "you fools! the softa should have her. She owed her life to him; she therefore belonged to him and to no one else."

Hardly had she finished speaking than the news was carried to the Padishah. The Prince had now rightfully won the Princess – silent no longer. The whole town put on a festive appearance and began preparations for the wedding. The Prince, however, wished his marriage to take place in his father's palace; and great was the rejoicing when he arrived home with his bride. Forty days and forty nights were the festivities kept up; and the old woman whose jugs had been broken was installed in the palace as dady, a post she filled happily to the end of her days.

Kara Mustafa the Hero
(Turkish)

THERE WAS ONCE a woman who had a husband who was so timid that he never dared to go out alone. On one occasion the woman was invited to a party, and as she was about to set out her husband implored her to make haste back, as he would be forced to remain in the house until her return. She promised to do so; and had hardly been with her friends half an hour when she got up to take leave. "Why must you go home so soon?" asked her hosts. She answered that her husband was at home waiting for her. "Why does he wait?" they asked.

"He dare not go out without me," was the reply. "That is strange," observed the women, and prevailed upon her to remain a little longer. They advised her that next time she went out with her husband after dark, she should slip away from him, and leave him alone in the darkness. By that means he would be cured.

The woman followed this advice, and on the first opportunity that offered, she left her husband alone in the darkness. The man cried out in his terror until at last he fell asleep where he waited. At daybreak he awoke, and went angrily into the house.

Among his possessions was a rusty old knife bequeathed him by his father. He took it up and while cleaning it uttered a resolution not to live with his wife anymore. He accordingly set out and came to a place where honey had been spilt, on which a swarm of flies were regaling themselves. Drawing his knife across the sticky mass, he found that he had killed sixty of the flies. He drew it across a second time and counted seventy victims. Immediately he went to a cutler and ordered him to engrave on the knife: "At a single stroke Kara Mustafa, the great hero, has killed sixty, and at the second stroke seventy." The inscription finished, the knife was returned to its owner, who went his way.

Presently he came to a wilderness, and when night fell he lay down and slept, sticking his knife into the earth. Now in this locality dwelt forty Dews, one of whom took an early walk every morning. The Dew saw the sleeping man and the knife, and as he read the inscription upon the latter he was seized with terror. Seeing that Mustafa was now waking up, the Dew, with a view to appeasing this redoubtable person, begged him to join his brothers' company. "Who are you?" asked the hero. "We are Dews to the number of forty, and if you will deign to join us we shall be forty one." "I am willing," said Mustafa; "go and tell the others." Hearing this, the Dew hastened to his fellows and said: "My brothers, a hero desires to join us. His immense strength may be gathered from the inscription on his knife: 'At a single stroke Kara Mustafa, the great hero, has killed sixty, and at the second stroke seventy.' Let us put everything in order, for he will be here directly."

But the Dews hastened to meet Mustafa, who when he saw them felt his courage sink. However, he managed to address them. "God greet you, comrades!" he exclaimed. The Dews modestly returned his greeting and offered him a place among them. By and by he inquired: "Is there among you any fellow like me?" The Dews assured him that there was not. Thus satisfied, Mustafa proceeded: "Because, if so, let him step forth and try his strength with me." "Where shall his equal be found?" exclaimed the Dews, as they walked home.

The Dews were obliged to carry their water from a long distance, and this duty was performed in turn by each of their number. Being of gigantic stature and strength, they were of course able to carry a quantity impossible for a mere mortal. On the following day one of the Dews accosted Mustafa: "It is your turn to fetch the water, and we are sorry to say the well is far away." Being afraid of the hero, the Dews naturally addressed him somewhat apologetically. Mustafa reflected, and then asked for a rope. It was given him, and he proceeded with it to the well. The Dews, full of curiosity to know what he intended to do with the rope, looked on from a distance, and saw him attach it to the stonework of the well. Astonished, they ran up and shouted to him to know what he was about. "Oh," he answered, "I am only going to put the well on my back and bring it home, so that none of us need go so far for water again!" They begged him for Allah's sake to desist, and he promised to do so on the understanding that they would not trouble him again with the duty of water-carrying.

A few days afterwards it was Mustafa's turn to fetch wood from the forest. Again he asked for the rope, and went. The Dews hid themselves and watched him. On the edge of the forest they saw him drive a peg into the ground and fix the rope, which he then drew round the trees. By chance the wind rose and shook the trees to and fro. "What are you doing, Mustafa?" shouted one of the Dews. "Oh, I am only going to take home the forest all at once instead of piecemeal, to save trouble." "Don't shake the trees!" cried all the Dews. "You will destroy the whole forest. We would rather fetch the wood ourselves."

The Dews were now more afraid of Mustafa than ever, and they called a council to deliberate on the best means of getting rid of their formidable associate. It was eventually decided to pour boiling water upon him during the night while he slept, and thus kill him. Fortunately for himself, however, he overheard the conversation, and prepared accordingly. When evening came he went to bed as usual. The Dews heated the water and poured it through the roof of his dwelling. But

Mustafa had laid a bolster in the place where he should have been; on the bolster he had placed his fez, and he had drawn up the bedcover. Then he betook himself to a corner of the room, where he lay down and slept soundly out of harm's way. When morning broke the Dews came in the belief that he was dead, and knocked at the door. "Who's there?" came a voice from the inside. The astonished and affrighted Dews called to him to get up, as it was already nearly midday. "It was very hot last night," he observed. "I lay bathed in perspiration." The astonishment of the Dews that boiling water had no further effect upon him than to make him perspire may be imagined.

The Dews next resolved to drop forty iron balls upon Mustafa while he slept: those would surely kill him. This plan also our hero overheard. When bedtime came he entered his room and arranged the bolster as before, putting his fez upon it and drawing up the cover, after which he retired to his corner to await developments. The Dews mounted the roof, and lifting some of the tiles, looked down upon what appeared to be their sleeping companion. "Look, there is his chest; there is his head," they whispered, and thud came the balls one after the other.

Next morning the Dews went to Mustafa's house and knocked at the door. This time no answer came, and they began to congratulate themselves that the hero would trouble them no more. But as a measure of precaution they knocked again and also uttered loud shouts. Then they found their rejoicing had been premature, for Mustafa's voice was heard: "I couldn't sleep last night for the mice gambolling over me; let me rest a little longer." The Dews were now nearly crazy. What manner of man was this, who thought heavy iron balls were mice?

A few days afterwards the Dews said to Mustafa: "In the adjoining country we have a Dew-brother: will you fight a duel with him?" Mustafa inquired whether the Dew were a strong fellow. "Very," was the reply. "Then he may come." In saying this, however, our hero was ready to die of fright. When the gigantic Dew appeared on the scene, he proposed to preface the duel by a wrestling bout. This being agreed to, they repaired to the field. The Dew caught Mustafa by the throat and held him in such a mighty grasp that his eyes started from their sockets. "What are you staring at?" demanded the Dew, as he relaxed his grip on Mustafa's neck.

"I was looking to see how high I should have to throw you so that all your limbs would be broken by your fall," answered our hero in well-simulated contempt. Hearing this, all the Dews fell upon their knees before him and begged him to spare their brother. Mustafa accordingly graciously pardoned his adversary; and the Dews further entreated him to accept a large number of gold-pieces and go home. Secretly rejoicing, he accepted the proffered money and expressed his willingness to go. Taking a cordial farewell of them all, he set out in the company of a Dew, who had been deputed to act as his escort.

When he arrived in sight of his home, Mustafa saw his wife looking out of the window; and as her gaze rested upon him she cried, "Here comes my coward of a husband with a Dew!" Mustafa made a sign to her, behind the Dew's back, to say nothing, and then began to run toward the house. "Where are you going in such a hurry?" demanded the Dew. "Into the house to get a bow and arrow to shoot you," was the answer of the flying hero. On hearing this the Dew made off back again to rejoin his brothers.

Mustafa had hardly had time to rest in his home when news was brought of a fierce bear that was playing havoc in the district.

The inhabitants went to the vali and begged him to order the hero to slay the depredator. "He has already encountered forty Dews," they said. "It is a pity that the bear should kill so many poor people."

The vali sent for Mustafa and informed him that it was unseemly that the people should be terrorized by a bear while the province held such a valorous man as himself. Then spake Mustafa: "Show me the place where the bear is, and let forty horsemen go with me." His request was granted. Mustafa went into the stable, took a handful of small pebbles, and flung them among the horses. The creatures, all with the exception of one, began to rear. This Mustafa himself took. When the horsemen saw what he did, they remarked to the vali that the man was mad and they were not disposed to help him to hunt the bear. The vali advised them: "As soon as you hear the bear, go away and leave him to it, to do what he will." So the cavalcade set out, and when presently they came to the bear's hiding-place, the mounted escort left our hero in the lurch and rode back. Mustafa spurred his steed, but the animal would not move, and the bear came at him with ungainly strides. Seeing a tree close at hand, our hero sprang on to the back of his horse, clutched at the overhanging branches, and pulled himself up. The bear came underneath the tree and was preparing to ascend when Mustafa, letting go his hold, alighted on its back, and boxed bruin's ears so severely that he set off in the direction the horsemen had taken. Catching sight of them, he yelled: "Kara Mustafa, the hero, is coming!" Whereon they all wheeled round, and, understanding the situation, dispatched the bear with their lances.

After this the fame of Kara Mustafa spread far and wide. The vali conferred upon him various marks of honour, and he enjoyed the respect of his neighbours to his long life's end.

How the Devil Lost His Wager
(Turkish)

A PEASANT, PLOUGHING HIS FIELD, was panting with fatigue, when the devil appeared before him and said: "Oh, poor man! you complain of your lot, and with justice; for your labor is not that of a man, but is as heavy as that of a beast of burden. Now I have made a wager that I shall find a contented man; so give me the handle of your plough and the goad of your oxen, that I may do the work for you."

The peasant consenting, the devil touched the oxen and in one turn of the plough all the furrows of the field were opened up and the work finished.

"Is it well done?" asked the devil.

"Yes," replied the man, "but seed is very dear this year."

In answer to this, the devil shook his long tail in the air, and lo, little seeds began to fall like hail from the sky.

"I hope," said the devil, "that I have gained my wager."

"Bah," answered the peasant, "what's the good of that? These seeds might be lost. You do not take into consideration frost, blighting winds, drought, damp, storms, diseases of plants, and other things. How can I judge as yet?"

"Behold," said the devil, "in this box are both sun and rain, take it and use it as you please."

The peasant did so and to very good purpose, for his corn soon ripened and up to that time he had never seen so good a harvest. But the corn of his neighbours had also prospered from the rain and sun.

At harvest time the devil came, and saw that the man was looking with envious eyes at his neighbour's fields where the corn was as good as his own.

"Have you been able to obtain what you desired?" asked the devil.

"Alas!" answered the man, "all the barns will break down under the weight of the sheaves. The grain will be sold at a low price. This fine harvest will make me sit on ashes."

While he was speaking, the devil had taken an ear of corn from the ground and was crushing it in his hand, and as soon as he blew on the grains they all turned into pure gold. The peasant took up one and examined it attentively on all sides, and then in a despairing tone cried out: "Oh, my God! I must spend money to melt all these and send them to the mint."

The devil wrung his hands in despair. He had lost his wager. He could do everything, but he could not make a contented man.

The Metamorphosis
(Turkish)

HUSSEIN AGHA WAS MUCH TROUBLED in spirit and mind. He had saved a large sum of money in order that he might make the pilgrimage to Mecca. What troubled him was, that after having carefully provided for all the expenses of this long journey there still remained a few hundred piasters over and above. What was he to do with these? True, they could be

distributed amongst the poor, but then, might not he, on his return, require the money for even a more meritorious purpose?

After much consideration, he decided that it was not Allah's wish that he should at once give this money in charity. On the other hand, he felt convinced that he should not give it to a brother for safe keeping, as he might be inspired, during Hussein's pilgrimage, to spend it on some charitable purpose. After a time he thought of a kindly Jew who was his neighbour, and decided to leave his savings in the hands of this man, to whom Allah had been good, seeing that his possessions were great. After mature thought he decided not to put temptation in the way of his neighbour. He therefore secured a jar, at the bottom of which he placed a small bag containing his surplus of wealth, and filled it with olives. This he carried to his neighbour, and begged him to take care of it for him. Ben Moïse of course consented, and Hussein Agha departed on his pilgrimage, contented.

On his return from the Holy Land, Hussein, now a Hadji, repaired to Ben Moïse and asked for his jar of olives, and at the same time presented Ben Moïse with a rosary of Yemen stones, in recognition of the service rendered him in the safe keeping of the olives, which, he said, were exceptionally palatable. Ben Moïse thanked him, and Hadji Hussein departed with his jar, well satisfied.

During the absence of Hussein Agha, it happened that Ben Moïse had some distinguished visitors, to whom, as is the Eastern custom, he served raki. Unfortunately, however, he had no mézé (appetizer) to offer, as is also the custom in the East. Ben Moïse bethought him of the olives and immediately went to the cellar, opened the jar, and extracted some of them, saying: "Olives are not rare; Hussein will never know the difference if I replace them."

The olives were found excellent, and Ben Moïse again and again helped his friends to them. Great was his surprise when he found that instead of olives, he brought forth a bag containing a quantity of gold. Ben Moïse could not understand this phenomenon, but appropriated the gold and held his peace.

Arriving home, poor Hussein Agha was distracted to find that his jar contained nothing but olives. Vainly did he protest to Ben Moïse.

"My friend," he would reply, "you gave me the jar, saying it contained olives. I believed you and kept the jar safe for you. Now you say that in the jar you had put some money together with the olives; perhaps you did, but is not that the jar you gave me? If, as you say, there was gold in the jar and it is now gone, all I can say is, the stronger has overcome the weaker, and that in this case the gold has either been converted into olives or into oil. What can I do? The jar you gave me I returned to you."

Hadji Hussein admitted this, and fully appreciated that he had no case against the Jew, so saying: "Chok shai!" he returned to his home.

That night Hussein mingled in his prayers a vow to recover his gold at no matter what cost or trouble.

In his younger days Hadji Hussein had been a pipe-maker, and many were the chibooks of exceptional beauty that he had made. Go but to the potters' lane at Tophane, and the works of art displayed by the majority of them have been fashioned by the hands of Hussein. The art that had fed him for years was now to be the means of recovering his money.

Hadji Hussein daily met Ben Moïse but he never again referred to the money, and further, Hussein's sons were always in company with Ben Moïse's only son, a lad of ten.

Time passed, and Ben Moïse entirely forgot about the jar, olives, and gold; not so Hadji Hussein. He had been working. First he had made an effigy of Ben Moïse. When he had completed this image to his satisfaction, he dressed it in the identical manner and costume the Jew habitually wore. He then purchased a monkey. This monkey was kept in a cage opposite the effigy of Ben Moïse. Twice a day regularly the monkey's food was placed on the shoulders of the Jew, and Hussein would open the cage, saying: "Babai git" (go to your father). At a bound the monkey would plant himself on the shoulders of the Jew, and would not be dislodged until its hunger had been satisfied.

In the meantime Hadji Hussein and Ben Moïse were greater friends than ever, and their children were likewise playmates. One day Hussein took Ben Moïse's son to his Harem and told him, much to the lad's joy, that he was to be their guest for a week. Later on Ben Moïse called on

Hadji Hussein to know the reason of his son's not returning as usual at sundown.

"Ah, my friend," said Hussein, "a great calamity has befallen you! Your son, alas! has been converted into a monkey, a furious monkey! So furious that I was compelled to put him into a cage. Come and see for yourself."

No sooner did Ben Moïse enter the room in which the caged monkey was, than it set up a howl, not having had any food that day. Poor Ben Moïse was thunderstruck, and Hadji Hussein begged him to take the monkey away.

Next day Hussein was summoned to the court, the case of Ben Moïse was heard, and the Hadji was ordered to return the child at once. This he vowed he could not do, and to convince the judges he offered to bring the monkey caged as it was to the court, and, Inshallah, they would see for themselves that the child of the Jew had been converted into a monkey. This was ultimately agreed to, and the monkey was brought. Hadji Hussein took special care to place the cage opposite Ben Moïse, and no sooner did the monkey catch sight of him than it set up a scream, and the judges said: "Chok shai!" Hussein Agha then opened the cage door, saying: "Go to your father," and the monkey with a bound and a yell embraced Ben Moïse, putting his head, in search of food, first on one shoulder of the Jew and then on the other. The judges were thunderstruck, and declared their incompetency to give judgment in such a case. Ben Moïse protested, saying that it was against the laws of nature for such a metamorphosis to take place, whereupon Hadji Hussein told the judges of an analogous instance of some gold pieces turning into olives, and called upon Ben Moïse to witness the veracity of his statement. The judges, much perplexed, dismissed the case, declaring that provision had not been made in the law for it, and there being no precedent to their knowledge they were incompetent to give judgment.

Leaving the court, Hadji Hussein informed Ben Moïse that there would still be pleasure and happiness in this world for him, provided he could reconvert the olives into gold. Needless to add that Ben Moïse handed the money to Hadji Hussein, and the heir of Ben Moïse returned to his home none the worse for his transformation.

Mahomet, the Bald-Head
(A Turkish Keloğlan Tale)

WHEN THE CAMEL was a messenger, when frogs could fly, and when I used to roam up hill and down dale, there lived two brothers together. Besides their mother and poverty they had a little livestock which they had inherited from their father.

Now the younger brother, who was bald, conceived one day the idea of dividing their little property; so he went to his elder brother and said: "You see these two stalls; the one is quite new, the other almost worn out. Let us turn all the cows loose, and those that return to the new stall shall be mine, the others yours." "Oh, no, Mahomet," answered the other, "those that return to the old stall shall be yours." Mahomet agreed. The cows were let loose, and all returned to the new stall except a miserable old blind one. Mahomet uttered not a word of complaint or dissatisfaction, but daily drove his blind cow to pasture, returning regularly every evening.

One day as Mahomet was sitting by the roadside, the wind blowing violently through the trees made the branches bend and creak. Mahomet accosted the tree thus: "Eh, creaker, have you seen my brother?" The tree apparently not hearing, creaked all the louder. Mahomet repeated his question, and as again the tree did not reply the bald-head became furious, took his axe and proceeded to cut it down. But lo! an avalanche of gold-pieces fell out of the hollow trunk through the incisions he had made. Making use of what little sense he had, Mahomet went home and borrowed an ox from his elder brother, yoked it to a cart, procured sacks, which he filled with earth, and went therewith to the tree. Arrived at the spot, he emptied the sacks and refilled them with the gold. On his return home he amazed his brother with the sight of so much wealth.

The younger brother was again seized with a desire to divide – the elder, we may be sure, having no objection this time. He borrowed a measure from a neighbour, exciting that worthy man's curiosity as to what that stupid fellow Mahomet could have to measure. The neighbour smeared the inside of the measure with bird lime, and when the bald-head returned the article a gold-piece was found adhering to it. This neighbour related his discovery to another, that one to a third, and in a short time the whole village knew of Mahomet's luck.

The possession of so much gold occasioned the two brothers much perplexity. They did not know what to do with it. Eventually they took spades, dug a deep trench, buried the money, and hastened to leave their native place. After setting off, however, the elder bethought himself that he had not locked the house-door, and he dispatched the younger to see to it. On reaching home it occurred to Mahomet that he ought to secure his mother's silence; so he heated a boiler of water, put the old lady in, and kept her there until she uttered no further sound. He then took her out, supported her against the wall with a broom, put the door on his back and went with it to his brother in the forest.

When the elder saw the door and understood what had happened to his mother he became very angry with the bald-head, who flattered himself that he had done something extremely clever in bringing away the door to prevent anyone opening it. The elder took the younger by the scruff of his neck and shook him violently. While reflecting what he should do further he saw three horsemen riding along the road. In their fright the brothers thought the cavaliers were pursuing them, and anxious to escape they climbed up a tree, carrying the door with them. As it was already dark they were not discovered. Mahomet reflected that they were lucky to have escaped with their lives, and in this grateful frame of mind he let the door fall on the head of one of the cavaliers who was just passing beneath.

The rider whom it struck put spurs to his horse and galloped quickly away with the cry: "Mercy on us! It is the end of the world!" A few days after this adventure the elder brother had had enough of the younger's vagaries, and secretly forsook him. What could Mahomet do now? He was alone in the world. He wandered on, weary and hungry, till at length he reached a village. He took up his position at the door of the djâmi and begged paras and food from the passersby.

A little man with a thin beard came out of the djâmi, and on seeing Mahomet asked him if he would like to become his servant. "Yes," answered Mahomet, "if you promise never to be angry with me whatever happens. If ever you become angry with me, I have the right to kill you; if, on the other hand, I ever become angry with you, you have the right to kill me." As it was very difficult to obtain a servant in this locality, the man agreed to this extraordinary condition.

The bald-head commenced his duties by slaughtering all his master's fowls and sheep. "Are you angry with me, master?" he asked. "No, of course not. Why should I be angry?" returned the affrighted man. Henceforth, however, Mahomet's duties consisted of sitting in the house doing nothing.

The master's wife was afraid that soon it might be her turn to follow the fowls and sheep, so in order to escape from the madman she persuaded her husband to go away with her secretly by night. But Mahomet, hearing of their intention, hid himself in the luggage, and when it was opened in another village he stepped out. Now the husband and wife took counsel together, and as a measure of safety resolved that all should sleep at night on the seashore; Mahomet should go with them, and they would seize the opportunity while he slept to cast him into the sea and drown him. Mahomet, however, had so much cunning that he threw in the woman instead, and she was drowned. "Are you angry with me, master?" he asked. "Why should I not be angry with thee, thou wretch!" cried the man. "Thou hast not only ruined me in fortune and brought me to beggary, but now thou hast bereft me of my wife!" Upon this the bald-head seized him, and, reminding him of the condition of his employment, cast him also into the sea after his wife.

Mahomet, once more alone in the world, tramped about, drank coffee, and smoked his pipe. One day he found a five-para piece, with which he bought leblebi. While eating them he accidentally dropped one, which fell into the well and was lost. Now Mahomet began to cry: "I want my leblebi! I want my leblebi!" and this loud bellowing brought to the surface an Arab with two such immense lips that one swept the sky and the other the earth. "What willst thou?" he demanded of Mahomet. "I want my leblebi! I want my leblebi!" the bald-head continued to scream. The Arab disappeared in the well, and presently came up again holding in his hands a small table. Giving it to the bald-head, he said: "When thou art hungry say, 'Table, be laid!' and when thou art satisfied say, 'Table, enough!'"

Mahomet took the table and went to the village. When hungry he had only to say, "Table, be laid!" and the most expensive dishes were set before him; the food was so delicious he hardly knew of what to partake first. In his conceit he thought, "I should like the villagers to see this," so he invited them all to supper. When they arrived and saw neither fire nor food, they concluded their host was jesting with them. But when the fellow brought in his little table and pronounced the words, "Table, be laid!" the feast was ready in a moment. All ate their fill, and went home envying their bald neighbour and devising various schemes to deprive him of his wonderful piece of furniture. Finally it was settled that one of their number should creep into Mahomet's house during his absence and steal the magic table.

Thus it came about that Mahomet felt the pangs of hunger once more. What should he do? He went to the well and began to cry: "I want my leblebi! I want my leblebi!" and the Arab appeared. "Where is the table?" "It has been stolen!" The Arab with the thick lips popped down into the well and reappeared with a hand-mill. Giving it to the bald-head, he said: "Turn to the right – gold; turn to the left – silver." So the fellow took the mill home, and turned so many times right and left that his floor was strewn with money. He was now a richer man than ever had been in the village before.

Somehow the villagers got wind of the precious mill, and one fine day it was missing. "I want my leblebi! I want my leblebi!" was again the cry at the well. The Arab came up and demanded: "Where are the table and the mill?" "Both have been stolen from me," lamented the bald-head. The Arab went down again and appeared with two sticks, which he gave to our hero, cautioning him strictly against saying other than the words, "Cudgels, come together!"

Mahomet took the sticks and examined them. Desiring to put their efficacy to the test, he pronounced the words, "Cudgels, come together!" and immediately they flew out of his hands and commenced to beat him most mercilessly. "Stop, cudgels!" he exclaimed as soon as he had overcome his surprise, and they ceased belabouring him. Though sore from his chastisement, Mahomet was glad nevertheless, for he had already thought of the use to which he should apply his sticks.

Hastening home, he invited all the villagers to his house, though without divulging his reason for calling them thus together. They came eagerly, full of curiosity to see what other wonderful thing he had to show them. At the auspicious moment Mahomet introduced his couple of sticks, and at the words "Cudgels, come together!" fearful strokes descended on the heads and bodies of the guests. They began to cry out for mercy, but Mahomet declined to utter the formula by which the punishment ceased until all had promised to return him the table and the mill. The articles were brought back without loss of time, and peace was restored.

The bald-head took his three magic gifts and went to his native village, where he rejoined his brother. Being now wise and wealthy, our hero, as well as his brother, married and lived a merry life. Henceforth there was no more prudent man in the village than Mahomet the Bald-head.

Paradise Sold by the Yard
(Turkish)

THE CHIEF IMAM of the Vilayet of Broussa owed to a Jew money-lender the sum of two hundred piasters. The Jew wanted his money and would give no rest to the Imam. Daily he came to ask for it, but without success. The Jew was becoming very anxious and determined to make a great effort. Not being able to take the Imam to court, he decided to try and shame him into paying the sum due; and to effect this, he came, sat on his debtor's doorstep and bewailed his sad fate in having fallen into the hands of a tyrant. The Imam saw that if this continued, his reputation as a man of justice would be considerably impaired,

so he thought of a plan by which to pay off his creditor. Calling the Jew into his house, he said: "Friend, what wilt thou do with the money if I pay thee?"

"Get food, clothe my children, and advance in my business," answered the Jew.

"My friend," said the Imam, "thy pitiful position awakens my compassion. Thou art gathering wealth in this world at the cost of thy soul and peace in the world to come; and I wish I could help thee. I will tell thee what I will do for thee. I would not do the same thing for any other Jew in the world, but thou hast awakened my commiseration. For the debt I owe thee, I will sell thee two hundred yards of Paradise, and being owner of this incomparable possession in the world to come, thou canst fearlessly go forth and earn as much as possible in this world, having already made ample provision for the next."

What could the Jew do but take what the Imam was willing to give him? So he accepted the deed for the two hundred yards of Paradise. A happy thought now struck the Jew. He set off and found the tithe-collector of the revenues of the mosque, and made friends with him. He then explained to him, when the intimacy had developed, how he was the possessor of a deed entitling him to two hundred yards of Paradise, and offered the collector a handsome commission if he would help him in disposing of it. When the money had been gathered for the quarter, the collector came and discounted the Imam's document, returning it to him as two hundred piasters of the tithes collected, with the statement that this document had been given to him by a peasant, and that bearing his holy seal, he dared not refuse it.

The Imam was completely deceived, and thought that the Jew had sold the deed at a discount to some of his subjects who were in arrears, and of course had to receive it as being as good as gold. Nevertheless the Jew was not forgotten, and the Imam determined to have him taken into court and sentenced if possible. His charge against the Jew was that he, the chief priest of the province, had taken pity on this Jew, thinking what a terrible thing it was to know no future, and as the man hitherto had an irreproachable character, in consideration of a small debt he had against the church, which it was desirable to balance, he thought he would give this Jew two hundred yards of Paradise, which he did.

"Now, gentlemen, this ungrateful dog sold this valuable document, and it was brought back to me as payment of taxes in arrears due to the church. Therefore, I say that this Jew has committed a great sin and ought to be punished accordingly."

The Cadis now turned to hear the Jew, who, the personification of meekness, stood as if awaiting his death sentence. With the most innocent look possible, the Jew replied, when the Cadis asked him what he had to say for himself:

"Effendim, it is needless to say how I appreciate the kindness of our Imam, but the reason that I disposed of that valuable document was this: When I went to Paradise I found a seat, and measured out my two hundred yards, and took possession of the further inside end of the bench. I had not been there long when a Turk came and sat beside me. I showed him my document and protested against his taking part of my seat; but, gentlemen, I assure you it was altogether useless; the Turks came and came, one after the other, till, to make a long story short, I fell off at the other end of the seat, and here I am. The Turks in Paradise will take no heed of your document, and either will not recognize the authority of the Imam, or will not let the Jews enter therein.

"Effendim, what could I do but come back and sell the document to men who could enter Paradise, and this I did."

The Cadis, after consulting, gave judgment as follows:

"We note that you could not have done anything else but sell the two hundred yards of Paradise, and the fact that you cannot enter there is ample punishment for the wrong committed; but there is still a grievous charge against you, which, if you can clear to our satisfaction, you will at once be dismissed. How much did the document cost you and what did you sell it for?"

"Effendim, it cost me two hundred piasters, and I sold it for two hundred piasters."

This statement having been proved by producing the deed in question, and the tithe-collector who had given it to the Imam for two hundred piasters, the Jew was acquitted.

The Rabbit's Broth
(A Nasreddin Hodja Tale)

NASREDDIN HODJA was the kind of person who looked out for the needs of others. When he saw someone hungry, he offered to feed them. When someone had a need, he offered to help them.

One day, Nasreddin Hodja heard a knock on his door and looked out the window to see who it was. He noted a man standing at the door with a dead rabbit tucked under his arm. When Hodja opened the door, the man politely said, "Hodja, I'm from the next village, and I'm wondering if, by the mercy of God, I could stay the night at your place. I've brought a rabbit with me for your wife to cook." Hodja accepted the villager as his guest, and invited him in. That evening, they enjoyed a fine meal together, with succulent rabbit a tasty part of their feast. The villager spent the night at Hodja's house and departed the next morning, though not before sitting down to a respectable breakfast provided by Hodja's hardworking wife. Later that day just before evening, a second visitor came by. "Hodja!" he called, "I'm a townsperson from the same village as last night's guest; I'm his fellow villager. I was hoping, in the name of God, that you might show me the kindness of allowing me to stay this night in your home." Hodja agreed and welcomed the man inside. They passed a pleasant evening and Hodja and his wife generously served the man a sumptuous meal. The man left the next morning, after first enjoying a leisurely breakfast with several glasses of steaming-hot tea. Later that day, Hodja was greeted by yet more guests, but this time there were not one, but three men gathered at his doorstep. "Hodja!" they called. "In the name of God, would you be willing to accommodate us for the evening? We are friends of the guest that you hosted just last night." Neither of these men had anything in their hands, certainly no rabbits or bread or anything else. Hodja accepted them in, and as he had done with the previous guests, fed them dinner and provided them lodging for the night. The next morning, the guests woke and Hodja served them breakfast. They continued to talk throughout the day, and late into the evening, with Hodja dutifully serving them meal after meal, tea glass after tea glass, and even baklava and coffee. Finally, around dinner time, when it was clear the guests had no intentions of leaving, Hodja ran out of patience – and he had nearly run out of food. His guests, however, now accustomed to the cooking skills of Hodja and his wife, eagerly looked forward to their next meal. They were quite excited when Hodja asked his wife to bring a pot out to them. They could only imagine what it might be! Based on the other dishes that had been served, they had high expectations. Perhaps kebap? Generous portions of köfte? Yet when they uncovered it, their eagerness turned to sheer bewilderment. The pot had simply been filled with water. "What is this, Hodja? What are you giving us?" they exclaimed, more than a little irritated. "Well," replied the Hodja, "you all told me, when you first knocked on my door, that you were the friends of the friend of the first villager who stayed with me. This, then, is the broth of the broth of the broth of the rabbit!"

On Borrowing Pots
(A Nasreddin Hodja Tale)

ONE DAY, NASREDDIN HODJA was in need of a big cauldron in which to cook a stew. He went to his neighbour's house and asked if he could borrow one. The neighbour kindly obliged and lent Hodja his best pot, a huge cauldron.

The next day, Hodja returned the cauldron to his neighbour, placing a smaller pot inside it. "What's this, Hodja?" the neighbour exclaimed. "I only gave you one pot, and you are now returning two." "Well," explained the Hodja, "it seems as though your pot had a baby." The neighbour was very pleased and accepted both pots gladly. A month later, Hodja returned to this same neighbour, and again requested to borrow his large cauldron.

The neighbour was only too happy to lend it out to Hodja once again. A couple of days later, Hodja hadn't yet returned the pot. A week passed, and the neighbour began to wonder when Hodja would bring it back. A month passed, and Hodja still hadn't given it back. Finally, when the neighbour's patience ran out, he went to Hodja's house and knocked on the door. When Hodja answered he exclaimed, "Hodja, why haven't you returned my pot to me? I'd really like to use it again!" Hodja's face filled with sorrow. "I'm so sorry," he replied, "I should have told you sooner. I'm afraid that your pot has died. I hate to break the news to you." The neighbour burst out with laughter. "That's impossible, Hodja, you know pots can't die!" "Well," said the Hodja, "since you believed me when I told you your pot had a baby, how come you won't believe me now when I tell you that your pot has died?"

Hodja at Friday Prayers
(A Nasreddin Hodja Tale)

ONE DAY, HODJA ENTERED the mosque on Friday. He walked to the front of those who had gathered for Friday prayers, waiting for the imam to come and offer an enlightening sermon. "O people!" he exclaimed, "do you have any idea what I'm about to say to you today?" Hodja was greeted by a chorus of "No's". Hodja looked exasperated. "You don't, do you? Well, if you are so foolish as to have no idea about what I'm going say, I'm not even going to waste my time." He stomped out angrily.

The next Friday, the gathered faithful were back at the mosque. Hodja entered, and again posed the question, "My people, do you have any idea what I'm going to explain to you today?" This time, he was greeted by a chorus of "Yeses". "Yes, yes, we do, Hodja," various people shouted. Hodja responded, "Very well, in that case, since you already know, there is no need for me to take the time to explain it again." And he left. On the third Friday, Hodja once again entered the mosque and stood before the community. "Good people," he called, "do you have any idea what I'm about to say to you?" This time, the responses were varied; some said "Yes, yes," others said, "No, no," and still others merely sat silently with confused looks on their faces. After the cacophony died down, Hodja said, "Let the ones who know explain it to the ones who don't," and quickly exited the mosque.

Who Do You Believe?
(A Nasreddin Hodja Tale)

ONE DAY, NASREDDIN HODJA'S NEIGHBOUR came over and asked if he could borrow Hodja's donkey for the day. "I'm very sorry," said Hodja. "The donkey is not here. My wife just left and took him to the bazaar."

Just then, both men heard the loud bray of a donkey come from inside the barn. "Hodja!" exclaimed the neighbour. "You're not telling me the truth! Your donkey is right there, inside the barn!" Without blinking an eye, the Hodja responded, "What kind of friend are you, to trust the voice of a donkey above the voice of your neighbour?"

Hodja on His Donkey
(A Nasreddin Hodja Tale)

ONE DAY, HODJA WAS RIDING his donkey down the road. He encountered a group of his students. When they began to follow him, Hodja turned around on his donkey and started to ride the animal facing backwards. To the surprise of his students, Hodja continued in this manner through the town, even as the townspeople laughed at him. "Hodja has really lost it!" they chuckled amongst themselves.

Finally, the students couldn't stand it any longer. "Hodja," exclaimed one, "why are you riding like this? Can't you see that everyone is mocking you?" Hodja replied, "If I faced forward, all you would see is my back and we wouldn't be able to discuss important matters. But if you walked in front of me, that would be disrespectful, because students shouldn't be in front of their teachers. So, you see, this is clearly the best way for me to ride my donkey!"

What If I'd Been Wearing It?
(A Nasreddin Hodja Tale)

IN THE MIDDLE OF THE NIGHT, Hodja was awakened by a sound coming from outside his house. He grabbed his bow and arrow and ran to the garden where he saw the dim outline of a thief. Without hesitation, Hodja drew back the string of his bow and let an arrow fly. It pierced the thief's heavy cloak, and he dropped to the ground. Satisfied that the criminal had been thwarted, Hodja went back to bed.

The next morning, in the light of the day, Hodja returned to his garden expecting to find the dead thief. When he got there, however, he noticed that his own garment lay on the ground, having fallen from the laundry line where his wife had hung it to dry. The arrow he shot the night before was firmly lodged in the cloak's collar. Upon seeing this, Hodja knelt down on his knees, thanking and praising God. "Why are you giving thanks to God?" asked Hodja's surprised wife. "You've ruined your best cloak." Hodja retorted, "Shouldn't I praise God? After all, what if I'd been wearing it last night?"

Tamerlane's Elephants
(A Nasreddin Hodja Tale)

AFTER CONQUERING GREAT SWATHES of land with his overpowering elephants, who trampled everything in their path and caused great fear and trepidation among his enemies, Tamerlane began to settle down. He dispersed these great beasts among various villages and towns. The elephants enjoyed a break from the rigours of warfare, and drank and ate to their hearts' content, consuming gallons of water from village fountains and tons of grain from nearby fields. One community of villagers grew tired of their elephant's appetite and commissioned a delegation to go to Tamerlane and beg him to take back the insatiable animal. Nasreddin Hodja was part of this entourage, and together they made their way to the ruler's court.

As the villagers got closer and closer to their audience with Tamerlane, they became increasingly fearful. One by one, they started to abandon their journey and return to the village. The group got smaller and smaller, but Nasreddin Hodja, who was walking in the front, didn't notice until he had finally reached Tamerlane's throne. Looking to the right and to the left and realizing that he was alone, he faced the great and terrible warrior all by himself.

Tamerlane addressed him, "What do you request of me?" Hodja replied, "Great ruler, on behalf of my fellow villagers, we want to thank you for the gift of the elephant. But we do have one request. You see, it seems that this elephant is quite lonely, and we ask, in your beneficence, that you grant us another, to keep it company." Tamerlane was pleased to hear that the villagers appreciated the elephant so much that they wanted another. "It shall be given," he declared, and promptly made arrangements for a second elephant to be sent as soon as possible. Delighted by Nasreddin Hodja, Tamerlane gave him a new set of garments, invited him to a sumptuous feast that evening, and sent him back home with a sack each of gold and silver and a skin of his best wine.

"Well," asked the villagers when Hodja returned, "what happened? What did you say to Tamerlane?" They couldn't avoid noticing Hodja's new garb and bulging sacks, and were sure that Tamerlane had responded most positively to their request. Hodja replied, "I felt so alone by the time I got to Tamerlane's courts that I couldn't help but think about our poor, lonely elephant. I asked Tamerlane to give us a second one to keep it company… and…" Hodja paused for a moment. "What's that sound? I think it has just arrived!"

God's Guest
(A Nasreddin Hodja Tale)

A TRAVELLER CAME TO HODJA'S VILLAGE one day and knocked at his door. "Please," he said, "I am the guest of God, and I beg you, take me in and let me stay with you this night!" "Well," said Hodja, "you are the guest of God? Let me show you something then." Hodja stepped outside and led the villager down the road. The villager was confused – this was exactly the road he had just been on, and it was getting late.

Hodja pointed towards the village square, where, in the light of the moon, they could just make out the minaret of the local mosque towering above the other buildings. "Since you are God's guest, over there you'll find God's house. Feel free to stay with him!"

40-Year-Old Vinegar
(A Nasreddin Hodja Tale)

O NE OF HODJA'S NEIGHBOURS was sick and in need of a little vinegar with which to mix a healing elixir. He knew that Hodja possessed a bottle of high-quality, 40-year-aged vinegar, and stopped by his home to see if he might get some. "Hodja, may I have some of your 40-year vinegar?" he requested. "No, you may not," Hodja replied. "I will not give you any."

The neighbour was shocked and stunned by this terse refusal. After recovering himself, he implored, "Hodja, everyone knows you have a bottle of 40-year-old vinegar. Why won't you give me just a little?" Hodja retorted, "If I gave everyone who asked me just a little, I wouldn't have vinegar that was 40-years-old, would I?"

The King and the Fisherman
(Persian)

THE COUNTRIES washed by the great rivers Tigris and Euphrates were once ruled by a certain King who was passionately fond of fish.

He was seated one day with Sherem, his wife, in the royal gardens that stretch down to the banks of the Tigris, at the point where it is spanned by the wonderful bridge of boats; and looking up spied a boat gliding by, in which was seated a fisherman having a large fish.

Noticing that the King was looking closely at him, and knowing how much the King liked this particular kind of fish, the fisherman made his obeisance, and skilfully bringing his boat to the shore, came before the King and begged that he would accept the fish as a present. The King was greatly pleased at this, and ordered that a large sum of money be given to the fisherman.

But before the fisherman had left the royal presence, the Queen turned towards the King and said: "You have done a foolish thing." The King was astonished to hear her speak in this way, and asked how that could be. The Queen replied:

"The news of your having given so large a reward for so small a gift will spread through the city and it will be known as the fisherman's gift. Every fisherman who catches a big fish will bring it to the palace, and should he not be paid in like manner, he will go away discontented, and secretly speak evil of you among his fellows."

"Thou speakest the truth, light of my eyes," said the King, "but can not you see how mean it would be for a King, if for that reason he were to take back his gift?" Then perceiving that the Queen was ready to argue the matter, he turned away angrily, saying: "The matter is closed."

However, later in the day, when he was in a more amiable frame of mind, the Queen again approached him, and said that if that was his only reason for not taking back his gift, she would arrange it. "You must summon the fisherman," she said, "and then ask him, 'Is this fish male or female?' If he says male, then you will tell him that you wanted a female fish; but if he should say female, your reply will be that you wanted a male fish. In this way the matter will be properly adjusted."

The King thought this an easy way out of the difficulty, and commanded the fisherman to be brought before him. When the fisherman, who, by the way, was a most intelligent man, stood before the King, the King said to him: "O fisherman, tell me, is this fish male or female?"

The fisherman replied, "The fish is neither male nor female." Whereupon the King smiled at the clever answer, and to add to the Queen's annoyance, directed the keeper of the royal purse to give the fisherman a further sum of money.

Then the fisherman placed the money in his leather bag, thanked the King, and swinging the bag over his shoulder, hurried away, but not so quickly that he did not notice that he had dropped one small coin. Placing the bag on the ground, he stooped and picked up the coin, and again went on his way, with the King and Queen carefully watching his every action.

"Look! what a miser he is!" said Sherem, triumphantly. "He actually put down his bag to pick up one small coin because it grieved him to think that it might reach the hands of one of the King's servants, or some poor person, who, needing it, would buy bread and pray for the long life of the King."

"Again thou speakest the truth," replied the King, feeling the justice of this remark; and once more was the fisherman brought into the royal presence. "Are you a human being or a beast?" the King asked him. "Although I made it possible for you to become rich without toil, yet the miser within you could not allow you to leave even one small piece of money for others." Then the King bade him to go forth and show his face no more within the city.

At this the fisherman fell on his knees and cried: "Hear me, O King, protector of the poor! May God grant the King a long life. Not for its value did thy servant pick up the coin, but because on one side it bore the name of God, and on the other the likeness of the King. Thy servant feared that someone, not seeing the coin, would tread it into the dirt, and thus defile both the name of God and the face of the King. Let the King judge if by so doing I have merited reproach."

This answer pleased the King beyond all measure, and he gave the fisherman another large sum of money. And the Queen's wrath was turned away, and she looked kindly upon the fisherman as he departed with his bag laden with money.

The Arabian Nights
(From One Thousand and One Arabian Nights, of Arabic, Egyptian, Sanskrit, Persian, and Mesopotamian origins)

IN THE CHRONICLES of the ancient dynasty of the Sassanidae, who reigned for about four hundred years, from Persia to the borders of China, beyond the great river Ganges itself, we read the praises of one of the kings of this race, who was said to be the best monarch of his time. His subjects loved him, and his neighbours feared him, and when he died he left his kingdom in a more prosperous and powerful condition than any king had done before him.

The two sons who survived him loved each other tenderly, and it was a real grief to the elder, Schahriar, that the laws of the empire forbade him to share his dominions with his brother Schahzeman. Indeed, after ten years, during which this state of things had not ceased to trouble him, Schahriar cut off the country of Great Tartary from the Persian Empire and made his brother king.

Now the Sultan Schahriar had a wife whom he loved more than all the world, and his greatest happiness was to surround her with splendour, and to give her the finest dresses and the most beautiful jewels. It was therefore with the deepest shame and sorrow that he accidentally discovered, after several years, that she had deceived him completely, and her whole conduct turned out to have been so bad, that he felt himself obliged to carry out the law of the land, and order the grand-vizir to put her to death. The blow was so heavy that his mind almost gave way, and he declared that he was quite sure that at bottom all women were as wicked as the sultana, if you could only find them out, and that the fewer the world contained the better. So every evening he married a fresh wife and had her strangled the following morning before the grand-vizir, whose duty it was to provide these unhappy brides for the Sultan. The poor man fulfilled his task with reluctance, but there was no escape, and every day saw a girl married and a wife dead.

This behaviour caused the greatest horror in the town, where nothing was heard but cries and lamentations. In one house was a father weeping for the loss of his daughter, in another perhaps a mother trembling for the fate of her child; and instead of the blessings that had formerly been heaped on the Sultan's head, the air was now full of curses.

The grand-vizir himself was the father of two daughters, of whom the elder was called Scheherazade, and the younger Dinarzade. Dinarzade had no particular gifts to distinguish her from other girls, but her sister was clever and courageous in the highest degree. Her father had given her the best masters in philosophy, medicine, history and the fine arts, and besides all this, her beauty excelled that of any girl in the kingdom of Persia.

One day, when the grand-vizir was talking to his eldest daughter, who was his delight and pride, Scheherazade said to him, "Father, I have a favour to ask of you. Will you grant it to me?"

"I can refuse you nothing," replied he, "that is just and reasonable."

"Then listen," said Scheherazade. "I am determined to stop this barbarous practice of the Sultan's, and to deliver the girls and mothers from the awful fate that hangs over them."

"It would be an excellent thing to do," returned the grand-vizir, "but how do you propose to accomplish it?"

"My father," answered Scheherazade, "it is you who have to provide the Sultan daily with a fresh wife, and I implore you, by all the affection you bear me, to allow the honour to fall upon me."

"Have you lost your senses?" cried the grand-vizir, starting back in horror. "What has put such a thing into your head? You ought to know by this time what it means to be the sultan's bride!"

"Yes, my father, I know it well," replied she, "and I am not afraid to think of it. If I fail, my death will be a glorious one, and if I succeed I shall have done a great service to my country."

"It is of no use," said the grand-vizir, "I shall never consent. If the Sultan was to order me to plunge a dagger in your heart, I should have to obey. What a task for a father! Ah, if you do not fear death, fear at any rate the anguish you would cause me."

"Once again, my father," said Scheherazade, "will you grant me what I ask?"

"What, are you still so obstinate?" exclaimed the grand-vizir. "Why are you so resolved upon your own ruin?"

But the maiden absolutely refused to attend to her father's words, and at length, in despair, the grand-vizir was obliged to give way, and went sadly to the palace to tell the Sultan that the following evening he would bring him Scheherazade.

The Sultan received this news with the greatest astonishment.

"How have you made up your mind," he asked, "to sacrifice your own daughter to me?"

"Sire," answered the grand-vizir, "it is her own wish. Even the sad fate that awaits her could not hold her back."

"Let there be no mistake, vizir," said the Sultan. "Remember you will have to take her life yourself. If you refuse, I swear that your head shall pay forfeit."

"Sire," returned the vizir. "Whatever the cost, I will obey you. Though a father, I am also your subject." So the Sultan told the grand-vizir he might bring his daughter as soon as he liked.

The vizir took back this news to Scheherazade, who received it as if it had been the most pleasant thing in the world. She thanked her father warmly for yielding to her wishes, and, seeing him still bowed down with grief, told him that she hoped he would never repent having allowed her to marry the Sultan. Then she went to prepare herself for the marriage, and begged that her sister Dinarzade should be sent for to speak to her.

When they were alone, Scheherazade addressed her thus:

"My dear sister, I want your help in a very important affair. My father is going to take me to the palace to celebrate my marriage with the Sultan. When his Highness receives me, I shall beg him, as a last favour, to let you sleep in our chamber, so that I may have your company during the last night I am alive. If, as I hope, he grants me my wish, be sure that you wake me an hour before the dawn, and speak to me in these words: 'My sister, if you are not asleep, I beg you, before the sun rises, to tell me one of your charming stories.' Then I shall begin, and I hope by this means to deliver the people from the terror that reigns over them." Dinarzade replied that she would do with pleasure what her sister wished.

When the usual hour arrived the grand-vizir conducted Scheherazade to the palace, and left her alone with the Sultan, who bade her raise her veil and was amazed at her beauty. But seeing her eyes full of tears, he asked what was the matter. "Sire," replied Scheherazade, "I have a sister who loves me as tenderly as I love her. Grant me the favour of allowing her to sleep this night in the same room, as it is the last we shall be together." Schahriar consented to Scheherazade's petition and Dinarzade was sent for.

An hour before daybreak Dinarzade awoke, and exclaimed, as she had promised, "My dear sister, if you are not asleep, tell me I pray you, before the sun rises, one of your charming stories. It is the last time that I shall have the pleasure of hearing you."

Scheherazade did not answer her sister, but turned to the Sultan. "Will your highness permit me to do as my sister asks?" said she.

"Willingly," he answered. So Scheherazade began.

The Uncanny & the Divine

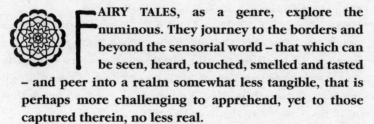

AIRY TALES, as a genre, explore the numinous. They journey to the borders and beyond the sensorial world – that which can be seen, heard, touched, smelled and tasted – and peer into a realm somewhat less tangible, that is perhaps more challenging to apprehend, yet to those captured therein, no less real.

For Turkic peoples, such tales include fragments drawn from Sufi Islam, Shamanistic practices and even Christian traditions, eschewing a commitment to any single doctrine. For the scientifically schooled twenty-first-century reader, the nonchalant ease with which the mystical and the mundane or the fantastical and the familiar coexist in fairy tales can be jarring, even awkward. However, this is all the more reason to be immersed in them. Staunch physical materialists notwithstanding, most of us acknowledge not only the reality of a spiritual world, but also its necessity. Modernity and associated technologies have achieved much for human beings in the world, though stop short of explicating ultimate meaning, proscribing absolute morality or opening up intimations of life on the other side. It may be overly hopeful to place those burdens on the lowly folktale, but only something that makes no apologies for stitching together existential interstices can attempt such explorations.

The Horse-Devil and the Witch
(Turkish)

THERE WAS ONCE UPON A TIME a Padishah who had three daughters. One day the old father made him ready for a journey, and calling to him his three daughters straightly charged them to feed and water his favourite horse, even though they neglected everything else. He loved the horse so much that he would not suffer any stranger to come near it.

So the Padishah went on his way, but when the eldest daughter brought the fodder into the stable the horse would not let her come near him. Then the middling daughter brought the forage, and he treated her likewise. Last of all the youngest daughter brought the forage, and when the horse saw her he never budged an inch, but let her feed him and then return to her sisters. The two elder sisters were content that the youngest should take care of the horse, so they troubled themselves about it no more.

The Padishah came home, and the first thing he asked was whether they had provided the horse with everything. "He wouldn't let us come near him," said the two elder sisters; "it was our youngest sister here who took care of him."

No sooner had the Padishah heard this than he gave his youngest daughter to the horse to wife, but his two other daughters he gave to the sons of his Chief Mufti and his Grand Vizier, and they celebrated the three marriages at a great banquet, which lasted forty days. Then the youngest daughter turned into the stable, but the two eldest dwelt in a splendid palace. In the daytime the youngest sister had only a horse for a husband and a stable for a dwelling; but in the night-time the stable became a garden of roses, the horse-husband a handsome hero, and they lived in a world of their own. Nobody knew of it but they two. They passed the day together as best they could, but eventide was the time of their impatient desires.

One day the Padishah held a tournament in the palace. Many gallant warriors entered the lists, but none strove so valiantly as the husbands of the Sultan's elder daughters.

"Only look now!" said the two elder daughters to their sister who dwelt in the stable, "only look now! how our husbands overthrow all the other warriors with their lances; our two lords are not so much lords as lions! Where is this horse-husband of thine, prythee?"

On hearing this from his wife, the horse-husband shivered all over, turned into a man, threw himself on horseback, told his wife not to betray him on any account, and in an instant appeared within the lists. He overthrew everyone with his lance, unhorsed his two brothers-in-law, and re-appeared in the stable again as if he had never left it.

The next day, when the sports began again, the two elder sisters mocked as before, but then the unknown hero appeared again, conquered and vanished. On the third day the horse-husband said to his wife: "If ever I should come to grief or thou shouldst need my help, take these three wisps of hair, burn them, and it will help thee wherever thou art." With that he hastened to the games again and triumphed over his brothers-in-law. Everyone was amazed at his skill, the two elder sisters likewise, and again they said to their younger sister: "Look how these heroes excel in prowess! They are very different to thy dirty horse-husband!"

The girl could not endure standing there with nothing to say for herself, so she told her sisters that the handsome hero was no other than her horse-husband – and no sooner had she pointed at him than he vanished from before them as if he had never been. Then only did she call to mind her lord's command to her not to betray her secret, and away she hurried off to the stable. But 'twas all in vain, neither horse nor man came to her, and at midnight there was neither rose nor rose-garden.

"Alas!" wept the girl, "I have betrayed my lord, I have broken my word, what a crime is mine!" She never closed an eye all that night, but wept till morning. When the red dawn appeared she went to her father the Padishah, complained to him that she had lost her horse-husband, and begged that she might go to the ends of the earth to seek him. In vain her father tried to keep her back, in vain he pointed out to her that her husband was now most probably among devils, and she would never be able to find him – turn her from her resolution he could not. What could he do but let her go on her way?

With a great desire the damsel set out on her quest. She went on and on till her tender body was all aweary, and at last she sank down exhausted at the foot of a great mountain. Then she called to mind the three hairs, and she took out one and set fire to it – and lo! her lord and master was in her arms again, and they could not speak for joy.

"Did I not bid thee tell none of my secret?" cried the youth sorrowfully. "And now if my hag of a mother see thee she will instantly tear thee to pieces. This mountain is our dwelling-place. She will be here immediately, and woe to thee if she see thee!"

The poor Sultan's daughter was terribly frightened, and wept worse than ever at the thought of losing her lord again, after all her trouble in finding him. The heart of the devil's son was touched at her sorrow: he struck her once, changed her into an apple, and put her on the shelf. The hag flew down from the mountain with a terrible racket, and screeched out that she smelt the smell of a man, and her mouth watered for the taste of human flesh. In vain her son denied that there was any human flesh there, she would not believe him one bit.

"If thou wilt swear by the egg not to be offended, I'll show thee what I've hidden," said her son. The hag swore, and her son gave the apple a tap, and there before them stood the beautiful damsel. "Behold my wife!" said he to his mother. The old mother said never a word, what was done could not be undone. "I'll give the bride something to do all the same," thought she.

They lived a couple of days together in peace and quiet, but the hag was only waiting for her son to leave the house. At last one day the youth had work to do elsewhere, and scarcely had he put his foot out of doors when the hag said to the damsel: "Come, sweep and sweep not!" and with that she went out and said she should not be back till evening. The girl thought to herself again and again: "What am I to do now? What did she mean by 'sweep and sweep not'?" Then she thought of the hairs, and she took out and burned the second hair also. Immediately her lord stood before her and asked her what was the matter, and the girl told him of his mother's command: "Sweep and sweep not!" Then her lord explained to her that she was to sweep out the chamber, but not to sweep the ante-chamber.

The girl did as she was told, and when the hag came home in the evening she asked the girl whether she had accomplished her task. "Yes, little mother," replied the bride, "I have swept and I have not swept." – "Thou daughter of a dog," cried the old witch, "not thine own wit but my son's mouth hath told thee this thing."

The next morning when the hag got up she gave the damsel vases, and told her to fill them with tears. The moment the hag had gone the damsel placed the three vases before her, and wept and wept, but what could her few teardrops do to fill them? Then she took out and burned the third hair.

Again her lord appeared before her, and explained to her that she must fill the three vases with water, and then put a pinch of salt in each vase. The girl did so, and when the hag came home in the evening and demanded an account of her work, the girl showed her the three vases full of tears. "Thou daughter of a dog!" chided the old woman again, "that is not thy work; but I'll do for thee yet, and for my son too."

The next day she devised some other task for her to do; but her son guessed that his mother would vex the wench, so he hastened home to his bride. There the poor thing was worrying herself about it all alone, for the third hair was now burnt, and she did not know how to set about doing the task laid upon her. "Well, there is now nothing for it but to run away," said her lord, "for she won't rest now till she hath done thee a mischief." And with that he took his wife, and out into the wide world they went.

In the evening the hag came home, and saw neither her son nor his bride. "They have flown, the dogs!" cried the hag, with a threatening voice, and she called to her sister, who was also a witch, to make ready and go in pursuit of her son and his bride. So the witch jumped into a pitcher, snatched up a serpent for a whip, and went after them.

The demon-lover saw his aunt coming, and in an instant changed the girl into a bathing-house, and himself into a bath-man sitting down at the gate. The witch leaped from the pitcher, went to the bath-keeper, and asked him if he had not seen a young boy and girl pass by that way.

"I have only just warmed up my bath," said the youth, "there's nobody inside it; if thou dost not believe me, thou canst go and look for thyself." The witch thought: "'Tis impossible to get a sensible word out of a fellow of this sort," so she jumped into her pitcher, flew back, and told her sister that she couldn't find them. The other hag asked her whether she had exchanged words with anyone on the road. "Yes," replied the younger sister, "there was a bath-house by the roadside, and I asked the owner of it about them; but he was either a fool or deaf, so I took no notice of him."

"'Tis thou who wert the fool," snarled her elder sister. "Didst thou not recognize in him my son, and in the bath-house my daughter-in-law?" Then she called her second sister, and sent her after the fugitives.

The devil's son saw his second aunt flying along in her pitcher. Then he gave his wife a tap and turned her into a spring, but he himself sat down beside it, and began to draw water out of it with a pitcher. The witch went up to him, and asked him whether he had seen a girl and a boy pass by that way.

"There's drinkable water in this spring," replied he, with a vacant stare. "I am always drawing it." The witch thought she had to do with a fool, turned back, and told her sister that she had not met with them. Her sister asked her if she had not come across anyone by the way. "Yes, indeed," replied she. "A half-witted fellow was drawing water from a spring, but I couldn't get a single sensible word out of him."

"That half-witted fellow was my son, the spring was his wife, and a pretty wiseacre thou art," screeched her sister. "I shall have to go myself, I see," and with that she jumped into her pitcher, snatched up a serpent to serve her as a whip, and off she went.

Meanwhile the youth looked back again, and saw his mother coming after them. He gave the girl a tap and changed her into a tree, but he himself turned into a serpent, and coiled himself round the tree. The witch recognized them, and drew near to the tree to break it to pieces; but when she saw the serpent coiled round it, she was afraid to kill her own son along with it, so she said to her son: "Son, son! show me, at least, the girl's little finger, and then I'll leave you both in peace." The son saw that he could not free himself from her any other way, and that she must have at least a little morsel of the damsel to nibble at. So he showed her one of the girl's little fingers, and the old hag wrenched it off, and returned to her domains with it. Then the youth gave the girl a tap and himself another tap, put on human shape again, and away they went to the girl's father, the Padishah. The youth, since his talisman had been destroyed, remained a mortal man, but the diabolical part of him stayed at home with his witch-mother and her kindred. The Padishah rejoiced greatly in his children, gave them a wedding-banquet with a wave of his finger, and they inherited the realm after his death.

The Magic Turban, the Magic Whip, and the Magic Carpet
(Turkish)

ONCE UPON A TIME that was no time there were two brothers. Their father and mother had died and divided all their property between them. The elder brother opened a shop, but the younger brother, who was but a feather-brain, idled about and did nothing; so that at last, what with eating and drinking and gadding abroad, the day came when he had no more money left. Then he went to his elder brother and begged a copper or two of him, and when that all was spent he came to him again, and so he continued to live upon him.

At last the elder brother began to grow tired of this waste, but seeing that he could not be quit of his younger brother, he turned all his possessions into sequins, and embarked on a ship in order to go into another kingdom. The younger brother, however, had got wind of it, and before the ship started he managed to creep on board and conceal himself without anyone observing him. The elder brother suspected that if the younger one heard of his departure he would be sure to follow after, so he took good care not to show himself on deck. But scarcely had they unfurled the sails when the two brothers came face to face, and the elder brother found himself saddled with his younger brother again.

The elder brother was not a little angry, but what was the use of that! – for the ship did not stop till it came to Egypt. There the elder brother said to the younger brother: "Thou stay here, and I will go and get two mules that we may go on further." The youth sat down on the shore and waited for his brother, and waited, but waited in vain. "I think I had better look for him," thought he, and up he got and went after his elder brother.

He went on and on and on, he went a short distance and he went a long distance, six months was he crossing a field; but once as he looked over his shoulder, he saw that for all his walking he walked no further than a barley-stalk reaches. Then he strode still more, he strode still further, he strode for half a year continuously; he kept plucking violets as he went along, and as he went striding, striding, his feet struck upon a hill, and there he saw three youths quarrelling with one another about something. He soon made a fourth, and asked them what they were tussling about.

"We are the children of one father," said the youngest of them, "and our father has just died and left us, by way of inheritance, a turban, a whip, and a carpet. Whoever puts the turban on his head is hidden from mortal eyes. Whoever extends himself on the carpet and strikes it once with the whip can fly far away, after the manner of birds; and we are eternally quarrelling among ourselves as to whose shall be the turban, whose the whip, and whose the carpet."

"All three of them must belong to one of us," cried they all. "They are mine, because I am the biggest," said one. – "They are mine by right, because I am the middling-sized brother," cried the second. – "They are mine, because I am the smallest," cried the third. From words they speedily came to blows, so that it was as much as the youth could do to keep them apart.

"You can't settle it like that," said he. "I'll tell you what we'll do. I'll make an arrow from this little piece of wood, and shoot it off. You run after it, and he who brings it to me here soonest shall have all three things." Away flew the dart, and after it pelted the three brothers, helter-skelter; but the wise youth knew a trick worth two of that, for he stuck the turban on his head, sat down on the carpet, tapped it once with the whip, and cried:

"Hipp-hopp! let me be where my elder brother is!" and when he awoke a large city lay before him.

He had scarce taken more than a couple of steps through the street, when the Padishah's herald came along, and proclaimed to the inhabitants of the town that the Sultan's daughter disappeared every night from the palace. Whoever could find out what became of her should receive the damsel and half the kingdom. "Here am I!" cried the youth. "Lead me to the Padishah, and if I don't find out, let them take my head!"

So they brought the fool into the palace, and in the evening there lay the Sultan's daughter watching, with her eyes half-closed, all that was going on. The damsel was only waiting for him to go to sleep, and presently she stuck a needle into her heel, took the candle with her, lest the youth should awake, and went out by a side door.

The youth had his turban on his head in a trice, and no sooner had he popped out of the same door than he saw a black efrit standing there with a golden buckler on his head, and on the buckler sat the Sultan's daughter, and they were just on the point of starting off. The lad was not such a fool as to fancy that he could keep up with them by himself, so he also leaped onto the buckler, and very nearly upset the pair of them in consequence. The efrit was alarmed, and asked the damsel in Allah's name what she was about, as they were within a hair's-breadth of falling. "I never moved," said the damsel. "I am sitting on the buckler just as you put me there."

The black efrit had scarcely taken a couple of steps, when he felt that the buckler was unusually heavy. The youth's turban naturally made him invisible, so the efrit turned to the damsel and said: "My Sultana, thou art so heavy today that I all but break down beneath thee!" – "Darling Lala!" replied the girl, "thou art very odd tonight, for I am neither bigger nor smaller than I was yesterday."

Shaking his head the black efrit pursued his way, and they went on and on till they came to a wondrously beautiful garden, where the trees were made of nothing but silver and diamonds. The youth broke off a twig and put it in his pocket, when straightway the trees began to sigh and weep and say: "There's a child of man here who tortures us! there's a child of man here who tortures us!"

The efrit and the damsel looked at each other. "They sent a youth in to me today," said the damsel. "Maybe his soul is pursuing us."

Then they went on still further, till they came to another garden, where every tree was sparkling with gold and precious stones. Here too the youth broke off a twig and shoved it into his pocket, and immediately the earth and the sky shook, and the rustling of the trees said: "There's a child of man here torturing us, there's a child of man here torturing us," so that both he and the damsel very nearly fell from the buckler in their fright. Not even the efrit knew what to make of it.

After that they came to a bridge, and beyond the bridge was a fairy palace, and there an army of slaves awaited the damsel, and with their hands straight down by their sides they bowed down before her till their foreheads touched the ground. The Sultan's daughter dismounted from the efrit's head, the youth also leaped down; and when they brought the princess a pair of slippers covered with diamonds and precious stones, the youth snatched one of them away, and put it in his pocket. The girl put on one of the slippers, but being unable to find the other, sent for another pair, when, presto! one of these also disappeared. At this the damsel was so annoyed that she walked on without slippers; but the youth, with the turban on his head and the whip and the carpet in his hand, followed her everywhere like her shadow. So the damsel went on before, and he followed her into a room, and there he saw the black Peri, one of whose lips touched the sky, while the other lip swept the ground. He angrily asked the damsel where she had been all the time, and why she hadn't come sooner. The damsel told him about the youth who had arrived the evening before, and about what had happened on the way, but the Peri comforted her by saying that the whole thing was fancy, and she was not to trouble herself about it anymore. After that he sat down with the damsel, and ordered a slave to bring them sherbet. A black slave brought the noble drink in a lovely diamond cup, but just as he was handing it to the Sultan's daughter the invisible youth gave the hand of the slave such a wrench that he dropped and broke the cup to pieces. A piece of this also the youth concealed in his pocket.

"Now didn't I say that something was wrong?" cried the Sultan's daughter. "I want no sherbet nor anything else, and I think I had better get back again as soon as possible." – "Tush! tush!" said the efrit, and he ordered other slaves to bring them something to eat. So they brought a little table covered with many dishes, and they began to eat together; whereupon the hungry youth also set to work, and the viands disappeared as if three were eating instead of two.

And the black Peri himself began to be a little impatient, when not only the food but also the forks and spoons began to disappear, and he said to his sweetheart, the Sultan's daughter, that perhaps it would be as well if she did make haste home again. First of all the black efrit wanted to kiss the girl, but the youth slipped in between them, pulled them asunder, and one of them fell to the right and the other to the left. They both turned pale, called the Lala with his buckler, the damsel sat upon it, and away they went. But the youth took down a sword from the wall, bared his arm, and with one blow he chopped off the head of the black Peri. No sooner had his head rolled from his shoulders than the heavens roared so terribly, and the earth groaned so horribly, and a voice cried so mightily: "Woe to us, a child of man hath slain our king!" that the terrified youth knew not whether he stood on his head or his heels.

He seized his carpet, sat upon it, gave it one blow with his whip, and when the Sultan's daughter returned to the palace, there she found the youth snoring in his room. "Oh, thou wretched bald-pate," cried the damsel viciously, "what a night I've had of it. So much the worse for thee!" Then she took out a needle and pricked the youth in the heel, and because he never stirred she fancied he was asleep, and lay down to sleep herself also.

Next morning when she awoke she bade the youth prepare for death, as his last hour had come. "Nay," replied he, "not to thee do I owe an account of myself; let us both come before the Padishah."

Then they led him before the father of the damsel, but he said he would only tell them what had happened in the night if they called all the people of the town together. "In that way I shall find my brother, perhaps," thought he. So the town-crier called all the people together, and the youth stood on a high daïs beside the Padishah and the Sultana, and began to tell them the whole story, from the efrit's buckler to the Peri king. "Believe him not, my lord Padishah and father; he lies, my lord

68

father and Padishah!" stammered the damsel; whereupon the youth drew from his pocket the diamond twig, the twig of gems, the golden slipper, the precious spoons and forks. Then he went on to tell them of the death of the black Peri, when all at once he caught sight of his elder brother, whom he had been searching for so long. He had now neither eyes nor ears for anything else, but leaping off the daïs, he forced his way on and on through the crowd to his brother, till they both came together.

Then the elder brother told *their* story, while the younger brother begged the Padishah to give his daughter and half the kingdom to his elder brother. He was quite content, he said, with the magic turban and the magic whip and carpet to the day of his death, if only he might live close to his elder brother.

But the Sultan's daughter rejoiced most of all when she heard of the death of the Peri king. He had carried her off by force from her room one day, and so enchanted her with his power that she had been unable to set herself free. In her joy she agreed that the youth's elder brother should be her lord; and they made a great banquet, at which they feasted forty days and forty nights with one another. I also was there, and I begged so much pilaw from the cook, and I got so much in the palm of my hand, that I limp to this day.

The Wizard Dervish
(Turkish)

A LONG TIME AGO lived a Padishah who had no son. As he was taking a walk with his lala one day, they came to a well, near which they stopped to wish.

A dervish suddenly appeared and cried: "All hail, my Padishah!" upon which the latter made answer: "If you know that I am the Padishah, then can you tell me the cause of my sorrow?" The dervish drew an apple from his breast and said: "Your sorrow is that you have no son. Take this apple; eat half yourself and give the other half to your wife; then in due time you shall have a son. He shall belong to you till his twentieth year; afterwards he is mine." With these words he vanished.

The Padishah went home to his palace, and cut the apple, sharing it with his wife according to the instructions of the dervish. Some time later, as the wizard had promised, a little prince came to the palace and the Padishah, in his great joy, ordered the happy event to be celebrated throughout his dominions.

When the boy was five years old a tutor was appointed to teach him reading and writing. In his thirteenth year he began to take walks and go on journeys, and soon after wards he took part in the hunting excursions also. When he was nearing his twentieth year his father began to think of finding him a wife. A suitable maiden being discovered, the young couple were betrothed, but on the very day of the wedding, when all the guests had assembled in readiness for the ceremony, the dervish came and carried off the bridegroom to the foot of a mountain. With the words "Remain in peace" he went away. In great fear the young Prince looked around him, but saw nothing more alarming than three white doves flying towards the river on whose bank he was resting.

As they alighted, they were transformed into three beautiful maidens, who entered the water to bathe. Presently two of them came out, resumed their bird forms, and flew away. As the third maiden left the water, she caught sight of the young Prince. Much astonished at his presence, she inquired how he had come there.

"A dervish carried me hither," he answered, whereon the girl rejoined: "That dervish is my father. When he comes, he will take you by your hair, hang you on that tree, and flog you with a whip. 'Dost know?' he will ask, and to this question you must answer, 'I know not.'" Having given this advice, the girl, transforming herself into a white dove, flew quickly away.

Presently the young Prince saw the dervish approaching with a whip in his hand. He hung the youth by his hair to a tree, flogged him soundly, and asked, "Dost know?" When the young Prince answered "I know not," the dervish went away. For three days in succession the youth was beaten black and blue; but when the dervish had satisfied himself that his victim understood nothing at all, he set him free.

When the youth was out walking one day the dove came to him and said: "Take this bird and hide it. When my father asks which of the three maidens you desire, point to me; if, however, you do not recognise me, produce the bird and answer: 'I desire the maiden to whom this bird shall fly.'"

Saying this the dove flew away.

The next day the dervish brought with him the three maidens and asked the youth which of them pleased him best. The youth accordingly produced the bird and said that he desired her to whom the bird should fly. The bird was set free and alighted on the maiden who had instructed him. She was given in marriage to the youth, but without the consent of her mother, who was a witch.

While the youth and the maiden were walking together, they saw the mother coming after them. The maiden, giving the youth a knock, changed him into a large garden, and by another knock changed herself into a gardener. When the woman came up she inquired: "Gardener, did not a maiden and a youth pass this way?" The gardener answered: "My red turnips are not yet ripe – they are still small." The witch retorted: "My dear Gardener, I do not ask about your turnips, but about a youth and a maiden." But the gardener only replied: "I have set no spinach, it will not be up for a month or two." Seeing she was not understood, the woman turned and went away. When the woman was no longer in sight, the gardener knocked the garden, which became a youth again, and knocked herself and became a maiden once more.

They now walked on. The woman, turning back and seeing them together, hastened to overtake them. The maiden also turned round and saw her mother hurrying after them. Quickly she gave the youth a knock and turned him into an oven, knocked herself and became a baker. The mother came up and asked: "Baker, have not a youth and a maiden passed this way?" "The bread is not yet baked – I have just put it in; come again in half an hour, then you may have some," was the answer. At this the woman said: "I did not ask you for bread; I inquired whether a youth and a maiden had passed this way." The reply was as little to the point as before. "Wait a while; when the bread is ready we will eat." When the woman saw she was not understood she went away again. As soon as the coast was clear the baker knocked the oven, which became a youth, and knocked herself back into a maiden; then they pursued their way.

Looking back once more, the woman again saw the youth and the maiden.

She now realised that the oven and the baker were the runaways in disguise, and hurried after them. Seeing that her mother was coming, the maiden again knocked the youth and changed him into a pond; herself she changed into a duck swimming upon the water. When the woman arrived at the pond she ran to and fro seeking a place whence she could reach the opposite side. At length, seeing she could go no further, she turned round and went home again. The danger over, the duck struck the pond and changed it into the youth; and transformed herself into a maiden as before; upon which they resumed their journey.

Wandering onward, they came at length to the birthplace of the youth, where they entered an inn. Then said he to the maiden: "Remain here while I fetch a carriage to take you away." On the road he encountered the dervish, who seized him and transported him immediately to his father's palace, and set him down in the great hall where the wedding-guests were still waiting. The Prince looked round at them all, and rubbed his eyes. Had he been dreaming? "What can it all mean?" he said to himself.

Meanwhile, the maiden at the inn, seeing that the youth returned not, said to herself: "The faithless one has forsaken me." Then she transformed herself into a dove, and flew to the palace. Through an open window she entered the great hall, and alighted on the Prince's shoulder. "Faithless one!" she said reproachfully, "to leave me alone at the inn whilst you are making merry here!" Saying this, she flew back immediately to the inn.

When the youth realised that it was no dream, but fact, he took a carriage and returned without delay to the inn, put the maiden into the coach, and took her to the palace. By this time the first bride had grown tired of waiting for so eccentric a bridegroom and had gone home. So the Prince married the dervish's daughter, and the wedding festivities lasted forty days and forty nights.

The Magic Hairpins
(Turkish)

THERE WAS ONCE a Padishah whose daughter was so beautiful that her loveliness was without equal in the world.

Now the Padishah's wife had an Arab slave whom she kept locked up in a room, and to whom every day she put the following questions: "Is the moon beautiful? Am I beautiful? Are you beautiful?" "Everything and everybody is beautiful," was invariably the answer. After this entertaining dialogue the Sultana would lock the door again and go away.

One day, as the Padishah's daughter, by name Nar-tanesi or little Pomegranate, was making a tour of the serai, the Arab caught a glimpse of her and immediately fell in love with her. Thus on the next day the Arab modified his usual answer as follows: "The moon is beautiful, you are beautiful, I am beautiful, but Nar-tanesi is the most beautiful of all."

The Sultana was exceedingly angry. Now that the Arab had seen her daughter, probably he would no longer admire the mother. So she went to the Princess and proposed that they should take a walk together. During the promenade they came to a meadow, where the maiden, being fatigued, lay down in the shade of a tree. When she fell asleep the mother left her there and hastened back to the palace.

When the Princess awoke and could not see her mother she began to weep, running hither and thither in fear, seeking her mother everywhere. It was of no avail, however, and soon her cries of despair echoed through wood and field.

Three brothers were by chance hunting in the forest, and came upon the distressed maiden. When she saw them she was still more afraid, and implored their grace and protection, requesting them to accept her as a sister. Overcome with pity the three hunters agreed to be her brothers, and she accompanied them to their home.

Henceforth the three youths went hunting every day, and when they brought home the game, the Princess prepared it for eating. Thus the days passed merrily away.

But the news of the maiden's extraordinary loveliness spread far and wide. The story was told of her discovery by the three brothers in the forest, and how they had taken her home to be their sister. This came to the ears of the Sultana, her mother, who was enraged to find her daughter still living. She thought the girl had long ago been torn to pieces and devoured by wild beasts.

She went accordingly to a witch and asked what she should do further to get rid of her daughter. The witch gave the Sultana two magic hairpins, saying that if she stuck them in the Princess's head the girl would surely die. The woman took the hairpins, and disguised herself as a poor beggar by means of an old feredje. Packing various articles in a bundle, she went to the maiden.

Whenever the three brothers were away hunting, the Princess kept the door locked; and when the woman knocked she made no answer. "Oh, my child," cried the woman, "why do you not open the door? I have come all the way from Anatolia with presents for my sons; at least receive them from me." Then the maiden answered through a crack in the door: "The door is locked." "My daughter," returned the woman, "having heard that you are their sister, I have brought you also a present of some hair pins; hold your head close to the keyhole that I may stick them in." Suspecting no evil, the girl put her head to the keyhole. The woman stuck the pins into the Princess's head, and she fell down dead immediately. Having thus accomplished her revenge, the Sultana went straight back to the serai.

When towards evening the brothers returned from hunting and entered the house, they saw the dead body of the maiden lying by the door. They raised loud lamentation and wrung their hands in despair. When their grief was somewhat calmed they began to prepare for the funeral. Laying their sister in a golden casket, they took it up a hill and hung it between two trees.

It came to pass soon after this that the son of a Padishah went hunting and saw the golden casket hanging from the trees. Taking it down, he opened it, and when he saw the lovely maiden lying within he fell deeply in love with her. The casket was carried to his home and put into his own apartment, and whenever he went out he took care to lock the door. The

Prince spent his days in hunting, and the nights in looking at and sighing over the dead maiden.

In the meantime the Padishah intended to take part in a war that had broken out; but the Vezir dissuaded him, advising him to send his son the Shahzada instead. Therefore the King called his son and ordered him to go to the battlefield. The youth returned to his apartment, opened the casket and took a last fond look at the serene countenance of the maiden. He then locked up the room, and ordering that none should enter it during his absence, he departed for the war.

We have omitted to state that the Shahzada was betrothed. The Princess he was going to marry chanced to hear of the Shahzada's locked apartment, and she determined to discover what secret he hid therein. It availed nothing to tell her that the Prince had forbidden anyone to enter it during his absence. She shook the door with such force that it opened, and she entered the room. Seeing the dead girl in the casket, she exclaimed in great irritation: "Who is this maiden that the Prince guards day and night!" Looking at her more closely, she saw the hairpins sticking in her head. Putting forth her hand, she drew them out; and hardly had she done so than the maiden was transformed into a bird and flew away.

A long time passed; the war was over, and the Shahzada came home again. Hastening to his apartment, he found to his sorrow and dismay that the casket was open and empty. In great wrath he asked his slave: "Who has dared to enter my apartment?" "The Princess who is to be your bride," was the reply. "What can she have done to her!" groaned the Prince, and from that time he became ill and grew worse every day.

Now that the war was ended the Padishah began to make preparations for his son's marriage, and in due time the wedding took place.

Every morning the bird came to the palace garden, and sitting on a tree said to the gardener, "How is my Shahzada?" "He sleeps," was the answer. "May he sleep and enjoy good health," said the bird, "and may the tree, on which I sit, wither!" This dialogue continued daily for several days, and every day a tree withered. The gardener called the attention of the Shahzada to the matter, observing that if the thing went on much longer there would not be a tree alive in the whole garden. The Prince's curiosity being excited, he set a trap to catch the bird. The bird being duly caught, the Prince put it in a golden cage and took a delight in regarding its wonderful plumage.

When first the Prince's wife saw the bird, she recognised it as the maiden of the casket, and made up her mind to destroy it as soon as possible. Her opportunity came when one day the Shahzada had to go on a journey. No sooner had he set off than she wrung the bird's neck and threw it into the garden; and on his return home she told her husband the cat had devoured it. The Shahzada was very sorry for the accident, but it could not be helped. When the dead bird was flung into the garden, rose bushes sprang up wherever its blood-drops fell. One day the gardener's wife came for some flowers, and among those the gardener plucked was one of these roses. They were put all together in a vase, but soon faded, with the exception of the rose, which remained as fresh as when it was growing on its stalk. "What wonderful flower is this?" exclaimed the woman. "It does not fade!" And while she was sniffing its delightful odour it suddenly changed into a bird, and flew hither and thither about the room. The woman was startled, thinking it must be either an in or a jin. However, after she had recovered herself somewhat, she took the beautiful creature and caressed it, and in doing so she remarked on its head something resembling a diamond. Examining it, she saw it was a pin. She drew it out, and behold! the bird was transformed into a maiden, who related to the astounded woman the story of her adventures.

Without delay the old woman went to the serai, stole into the private apartment of the Shahzada and told him all. His joy was unutterable; he bade the woman go home and take care of the maiden until he himself should come in the evening.

Twilight was scarcely past when the Shahzada was on the spot. At sight of the maiden he swooned away, and when he came to himself he requested her to relate her story with her own lips. When he left the gardener's house he took the maiden with him, but while on the road to the palace a monkey sprang out upon them. The Prince started in pursuit of it, and he was away so long that the maiden, being tired, fell fast asleep. Now it had come to the knowledge of the maiden's mother that she had disappeared from the casket, and in order to make certain that she would not annoy her again, the Sultana left the serai in search of her, meaning to kill her. After long wandering the woman chanced upon the spot where her daughter lay sleeping. With suppressed glee she muttered: "Oh! you have fallen into my hands once more!"

Meanwhile, failing to catch the monkey, the Prince hurried back to the maiden, anxious lest any further harm should come to her. On arriving at the spot, he saw the maiden asleep and a woman by her side. When the Prince demanded her intention, the woman said she was only keeping watch over the girl, who might otherwise have suffered some ill.

Suddenly a thought struck the Shahzada, and he asked the woman who and what she was. She replied that she was a poor forsaken creature, who had nothing, and who was alone in the world. Then said the Prince, "Come with me, and I will repay your kindness." The maiden, however, being now awake, recognised her mother, and secretly informed the Prince.

All three set off together towards the serai, the woman rejoicing over the opportunity thus afforded her of putting her daughter out of the way forever. But as soon as they arrived at the palace the Prince ordered the woman, as well as his wife, to be hanged, as a punishment for their treacherous cruelty, and made preparations for his wedding with the maiden of the golden casket. Thus they lived happily ever afterwards.

The Rose Beauty
(Turkish)

IN OLDEN TIMES, when the camel was a horse-dealer, the mouse a barber, the cuckoo a tailor, the tortoise a baker, and the ass still a servant, there was a miller who had a black cat. Besides this miller, there was a Padishah who had three daughters, aged respectively forty, thirty, and twenty years. The eldest went to the youngest and made her write a letter to her father in these terms:

"Dear father, one of my sisters is forty, the other thirty, and they have not yet married. Take notice that I will not wait so long before I get a husband."

The Padishah, on reading the letter, sent for his daughters and thus addressed them: "Here are a bow and arrow for each of you; go and shoot, and wherever your arrows fall, there you will find your future husbands."

Taking the weapons from their father, the three maidens went forth. The eldest shot first, and her arrow fell in the palace of the Vezir's son; she was accordingly united to him. The second daughter's arrow fell in the palace of the son of the Sheikh-ul-Islam, and him she got for a husband. When the youngest shot, however, her arrow fell into the hut of a wood-cutter. "That doesn't count," cried everybody; and she shot again. The second time the arrow fell in the same spot; and a third attempt met no better success.

The Shah was wrathful with his daughter on account of her letter, and exclaimed: "You foolish creature, that serves you right. Your elder sisters have waited patiently and are rewarded. You, the youngest, have dared to write me that impertinent letter: you are justly punished. Take your woodcutter and be off with you." So the poor girl left her father's palace to be the wife of the woodcutter.

In the course of time a beautiful girl-baby was born to them. The wood-cutter's wife bitterly lamented the fact that her child must have so poor a home, but even while she wept, three wonderful fairies stepped through the wall of the hut into the dismal room where the child lay. Standing by her cot, each in turn stretched out a hand over the sleeping infant.

Said the first fairy: "Rose-Beauty shall she be called; and instead of tears, pearls shall she shed."

Said the second fairy: "When she smiles, roses shall blossom." Said the third: "Wherever her foot falls shall grass spring up!" Then the three disappeared as they had come.

Years passed away. The child grew and attained her twelfth year, developing such loveliness as none had ever seen before. To gaze once upon her was to be filled with love for her. When she smiled roses blossomed; when she wept pearls fell from her eyes, and grass grew wherever her feet trod. The fame of her beauty spread far and wide.

The mother of a certain Prince heard of Rose-Beauty and resolved that this maiden and no other should become her son's bride. She called her son to her and told him that in the town was a maiden who smiled roses, wept pearls, and under whose feet grass grew; he must see her.

The fairies had already shown the maid to the Prince in a dream, and thus kindled in him the fire of love; but before his mother he was shy and refused to seek the object of his passion. The Sultana therefore insisted, and finally ordered a lady of the palace to accompany him on his quest. They entered the hut, explained the purpose of their visit, and in the name of Allah demanded the maiden for the Shahzada. The poor people were overcome with joy at their good fortune; they promised their daughter, and commenced preparations for her departure.

Now this palace-dame had a daughter, who somewhat resembled the Rose-Beauty, and she was displeased that the Prince should marry a poor girl instead of her own daughter. Accordingly she concocted a scheme to deceive the people and bring about the Prince's marriage to her own child. On the wedding-day she gave the woodcutter's daughter salt food to eat, and took a jug of water and a large basket and put them in the bridal coach wherein the Rose-Beauty, herself, and her daughter were about to set out for the palace.

On the way the maiden, complaining of thirst, asked for a drink of water. The palace-dame answered: "I shall give you no water unless you give me an eye in exchange." Nearly dying of thirst, the maiden took out one of her eyes and gave it to the cruel woman for a drink of water.

As they proceeded the torments of thirst again overcame the poor maiden, and again she asked for water. "I will give you drink, but only in exchange for your other eye," answered the woman. So great was her agony that the victim yielded her other eye. No sooner had the woman got it in her possession than she took the now sightless Rose-Beauty, bound her in the basket, and had her carried to the top of a mountain.

The woman now hastened to the palace and presented her daughter, clad in a gorgeous wedding garment, to the Prince, saying: "Here is your bride." The marriage was accordingly celebrated with great festivity;

but when the Prince came to lift his wife's veil he saw that she was not the one revealed to him in his dream. As, however, she resembled the dream-bride somewhat, he held his peace.

The Prince knew that the maiden of his dream wept pearls, smiled roses, and that the grass grew under her feet; from this one, however, came neither pearls, roses, nor grass. He suspected more than ever that he had been deceived, but "I will soon find out," he thought to himself, and spoke no word on the subject to anyone.

Meanwhile the poor Rose-Beauty on the mountaintop wept and moaned, pearls rolling down her cheeks from her sightless eye-sockets until the basket in which she lay bound was filled to overflowing. A scavenger at work on the road heard the sounds of grief and cried out in fear: "Who is that, a spirit or a fairy?" The maiden answered: "Neither a spirit nor a fairy, but a human being like yourself."

The scavenger, reassured, approached the basket, opened it, and saw the blind girl and the pearls she had shed. He took her home to his miserable hovel, and being alone in the world, adopted her as his own child. But the maiden constantly bemoaned the loss of her eyes, and as she was always weeping, the man now had nothing else to do but gather the pearls she shed and go out and sell them. Time rolled on. In the palace was merriment, in the scavenger's hovel grief and pain. One day as the Rose-Beauty was sitting at the door, she smiled at some pleasant recollection, and forthwith a rose appeared. Said the maiden to the scavenger: "Father, here is a rose; take it to the Prince's palace and say thou hast a rose of a rare kind to sell. When the palace dame appears, say it cannot be sold for money, but for a human eye." The man took the rose, went to the palace and cried aloud: "A rose for sale; the only one of its kind in the world."

Indeed, it was not the season for roses. The palace-dame, hearing the scavenger's cry, resolved to buy the rose for her daughter, thinking that when the Prince saw the flower in his wife's possession his suspicions would be set at rest. Calling the poor man aside, she inquired the price of the rose. "Money cannot buy it," replied the scavenger, "but I will part with it for a human eye." Hereupon the woman produced one of the Rose-Beauty's eyes and gave it in exchange for the rose. Carrying the flower immediately to her daughter, she fixed it in her hair, and when the Prince saw her he began to fancy that she might after all be the maiden the fairies had showed him in his dream, though he was by no means sure. He consoled himself with the thought that soon the matter would be cleared up.

The old man took the eye and gave it to the Rose-Beauty. Praising Allah, she fixed it in its place, and had the joy of being able to see quite well once more. In her newfound happiness the maiden smiled so much that ere long there were quite a number of roses. One of these she gave to the scavenger that he might go with it to the palace and secure her remaining eye. Scarcely had he arrived at the palace than the woman saw him with the rose and thought to herself: "All is coming right; the Prince is already beginning to love my daughter. I will buy this other rose, and as his love strengthens he will soon forget the woodcutter's child." She called the scavenger and demanded the rose, which the man said could only be sold on the same terms as the first. The woman willingly gave him the other eye and hastened with the flower to her daughter, while the old man went home with his prize.

The Rose-Beauty, now in possession of both her eyes, was even lovelier than before. As now she smilingly took her walks abroad, roses and grass transformed the barren hillside into a veritable Eden. One day while the maiden was walking in the neighbourhood, the palace-dame saw her and was dismayed. What would be her daughter's fate if the truth became known? She inquired for the scavenger's dwelling, hastened to him, and frightened the old man out of his wits by accusing him of harbouring a witch. In his fright he asked the woman what he should do. "Ask her about her talisman," she advised; "then I can soon settle the matter." So when the girl came in, the first thing her foster-father did was to ask her how it was that, being human, she could work such magic.

Suspecting no harm, she informed him that at her birth the fairies gave her a talisman whereby she could bring forth pearls, roses, and grass as long as the talisman lived. "What is your talisman?" inquired the old man. "A young stag that lives on the mountain; when it dies I must die too," answered the maiden.

Next day the palace-dame came secretly to the scavenger, and learned from him what the talisman was. With this precious knowledge she hastened joyfully home, imparted the information to her daughter, and advised her to ask the Prince for the stag. Without delay the young wife complained to her lord of indisposition, saying she must have the heart of a certain mountain stag to eat. The Prince sent out his hunters, who ere long returned with the animal, slaughtered it and took out its heart, which was cooked for the pretended invalid.

At that same instant the Rose-Beauty also died. The scavenger buried her, and mourned for her long and sincerely.

Now in the stag's heart was a red coral, that escaped observation; and when the Prince's wife was eating, it fell to the floor and rolled under the stairs.

A year later there was born to the Prince a daughter who wept pearls, smiled roses, and under whose tiny feet grass grew. When the Prince saw that his child was a Rose-Beauty, he easily persuaded himself that his wife was really the right one. But one night in a dream the Rose-Beauty appeared to him and said: "Oh, Prince, my own bridegroom, my soul is under the palace-stairs, my body in the cemetery, thy daughter is my daughter, my talisman the little coral."

As soon as the Prince awoke he went to the stairs and searched for and found the coral. He carried it to his room and laid it on the table. When his little daughter came in she took up the coral, and hardly had her fingers touched it than both vanished. The three fairies conveyed the child to her mother, the Rose-Beauty, who, as the coral fell into her mouth, awakened to a new life.

The Prince, in his restless state, went to the cemetery. Behold! there he found the Rose-Beauty of his dreams with his child in her arms. They cordially embraced, and as mother and daughter wept for joy, pearls streamed from the eyes of both; when they smiled roses blossomed, and grass sprang up wherever their feet touched.

The palace-dame and her daughter were severely punished, and the old scavenger was invited to live with the Rose-Beauty and the Prince at their palace. The reunited lovers had a magnificent wedding-feast and their happiness lasted forever.

Aladdin and the Wonderful Lamp
(From One Thousand and One Arabian Nights, of Arabic, Egyptian, Sanskrit, Persian, and Mesopotamian origins)

THERE ONCE LIVED a poor tailor, who had a son called Aladdin, a careless, idle boy who would do nothing but play all day long in the streets with little idle boys like himself. This so grieved the father that he died; yet, in spite of his mother's tears and prayers, Aladdin did not mend his ways. One day, when he was playing in the streets as usual, a stranger asked him his age, and if he were not the son of Mustapha the tailor.

"I am, sir," replied Aladdin; "but he died a long while ago."

On this the stranger, who was a famous African magician, fell on his neck and kissed him, saying: "I am your uncle, and knew you from your likeness to my brother. Go to your mother and tell her I am coming."

Aladdin ran home, and told his mother of his newly found uncle.

"Indeed, child," she said, "your father had a brother, but I always thought he was dead."

However, she prepared supper, and bade Aladdin seek his uncle, who came laden with wine and fruit. He presently fell down and kissed the place where Mustapha used to sit, bidding Aladdin's mother not to be surprised at not having seen him before, as he had been forty years out of the country. He then turned to Aladdin, and asked him his trade, at which the boy hung his head, while his mother burst into tears. On learning that Aladdin was idle and would learn no trade, he offered to take a shop for him and stock it with merchandise. Next day he bought Aladdin a fine suit of clothes, and took him all over the city, showing him the sights, and brought him home at nightfall to his mother, who was overjoyed to see her son so fine.

Next day the magician led Aladdin into some beautiful gardens a long way outside the city gates. They sat down by a fountain, and the magician pulled a cake from his girdle, which he divided between them. They then journeyed onwards till they almost reached the mountains. Aladdin was so tired that he begged to go back, but the magician beguiled him with pleasant stories, and led him on in spite of himself.

At last they came to two mountains divided by a narrow valley.

"We will go no farther," said the false uncle. "I will show you something wonderful; only do you gather up sticks while I kindle a fire."

When it was lit, the magician threw on it a powder he had about him, at the same time saying some magical words. The earth trembled a little and opened in front of them, disclosing a square flat stone with a brass ring in the middle to raise it by. Aladdin tried to run away, but the magician caught him and gave him a blow that knocked him down.

"What have I done, uncle?" he said piteously; whereupon the magician said more kindly: "Fear nothing, but obey me. Beneath this stone lies a treasure which is to be yours, and no one else may touch it, so you must do exactly as I tell you."

At the word treasure, Aladdin forgot his fears, and grasped the ring as he was told, saying the names of his father and grandfather. The stone came up quite easily and some steps appeared.

"Go down," said the magician. "At the foot of those steps you will find an open door leading into three large halls. Tuck up your gown and go through them without touching anything, or you will die instantly. These halls lead into a garden of fine fruit trees. Walk on till you come to a niche in a terrace where stands a lighted lamp. Pour out the oil it contains and bring it to me."

He drew a ring from his finger and gave it to Aladdin, bidding him prosper.

Aladdin found everything as the magician had said, gathered some fruit off the trees, and, having got the lamp, arrived at the mouth of the cave. The magician cried out in a great hurry: "Make haste and give me the lamp." This Aladdin refused to do until he was out of the cave. The magician flew into a terrible passion, and throwing some more powder on the fire, he said something, and the stone rolled back into its place.

The magician left Persia forever, which plainly showed that he was no uncle of Aladdin's, but a cunning magician who had read in his magic books of a wonderful lamp, which would make him the most powerful man in the world. Though he alone knew where to find it, he could only receive it from the hand of another. He had picked out the foolish Aladdin for this purpose, intending to get the lamp and kill him afterwards.

For two days Aladdin remained in the dark, crying and lamenting. At last he clasped his hands in prayer, and in so doing rubbed the ring, which the magician had forgotten to take from him. Immediately an enormous and frightful genie rose out of the earth, saying: "What wouldst thou with me? I am the Slave of the Ring, and will obey thee in all things."

Aladdin fearlessly replied: "Deliver me from this place!" whereupon the earth opened, and he found himself outside. As soon as his eyes could bear the light he went home, but fainted on the threshold. When he came to himself he told his mother what had passed, and showed her the lamp and the fruits he had gathered in the garden, which were in reality precious stones. He then asked for some food.

"Alas! child," she said, "I have nothing in the house, but I have spun a little cotton and will go and sell it."

Aladdin bade her keep her cotton, for he would sell the lamp instead. As it was very dirty, she began to rub it, that it might fetch a higher price. Instantly a hideous genie appeared, and asked what she would have. She fainted away, but Aladdin, snatching the lamp, said boldly: "Fetch me something to eat!"

The genie returned with a silver bowl, twelve silver plates containing rich meats, two silver cups, and two bottles of wine. Aladdin's mother, when she came to herself, said: "Whence comes this splendid feast?"

"Ask not, but eat," replied Aladdin.

So they sat at breakfast till it was dinner-time, and Aladdin told his mother about the lamp. She begged him to sell it, and have nothing to do with devils.

"No," said Aladdin. "Since chance has made us aware of its virtues, we will use it and the ring likewise, which I shall always wear on my finger." When they had eaten all the genie had brought, Aladdin sold one of the silver plates, and so on till none were left. He then had recourse to the genie, who gave him another set of plates, and thus they lived for many years.

One day Aladdin heard an order from the Sultan proclaimed that everyone was to stay at home and close his shutters while the princess, his daughter, went to and from the bath. Aladdin was seized by a desire to see her face, which was very difficult, as she always went veiled. He hid himself behind the door of the bath, and peeped through a chink. The princess lifted her veil as she went in, and looked so beautiful that Aladdin fell in love with her at first sight. He went home so changed that his mother was frightened. He told her he loved the princess so deeply that he could not live without her, and meant to ask her in marriage of her father. His mother, on hearing this, burst out laughing, but Aladdin at last prevailed upon her to go before the Sultan and carry his request. She fetched a napkin and laid in it the magic fruits from the enchanted garden, which sparkled and shone like the most beautiful jewels. She took these with her to please the Sultan, and set out, trusting in the lamp. The grand-vizir and the lords of council had just gone in as she entered the hall and placed herself in front of the Sultan. He, however, took no notice of her. She went every day for a week, and stood in the same place.

When the council broke up on the sixth day, the Sultan said to his vizir: "I see a certain woman in the audience-chamber every day carrying something in a napkin. Call her next time, that I may find out what she wants."

Next day, at a sign from the vizir, she went up to the foot of the throne, and remained kneeling till the Sultan said to her: "Rise, good woman, and tell me what you want."

She hesitated, so the Sultan sent away all but the vizir, and bade her speak freely, promising to forgive her beforehand for anything she might say. She then told him of her son's violent love for the princess.

"I prayed him to forget her," she said, "but in vain; he threatened to do some desperate deed if I refused to go and ask your Majesty for the hand of the princess. Now I pray you to forgive not me alone, but my son Aladdin."

The Sultan asked her kindly what she had in the napkin, whereupon she unfolded the jewels and presented them.

He was thunderstruck and, turning to the vizir, said: "What sayest thou? Ought I not to bestow the princess on one who values her at such a price?"

The vizir, who wanted her for his own son, begged the Sultan to withhold her for three months, in the course of which he hoped his son would contrive to make him a richer present. The Sultan granted this, and told Aladdin's mother that, though he consented to the marriage, she must not appear before him again for three months.

Aladdin waited patiently for nearly three months, but after two had elapsed, his mother, going into the city to buy oil, found everyone rejoicing, and asked what was going on.

"Do you not know," was the answer, "that the son of the grand-vizir is to marry the Sultan's daughter tonight?"

Breathless, she ran and told Aladdin, who was overwhelmed at first, but presently bethought him of the lamp. He rubbed it, and the genie appeared, saying: "What is thy will?"

Aladdin replied: "The Sultan, as thou knowest, has broken his promise to me, and the vizir's son is to have the princess. My command is that tonight you bring hither the bride and bridegroom."

"Master, I obey," said the genie.

Aladdin then went to his chamber, where, sure enough at midnight the genie transported the bed containing the vizir's son and the princess.

"Take this new-married man," he said, "and put him outside in the cold, and return at daybreak."

Whereupon the genie took the vizir's son out of bed, leaving Aladdin with the princess.

"Fear nothing," Aladdin said to her. "You are my wife, promised to me by your unjust father, and no harm shall come to you."

The princess was too frightened to speak, and passed the most miserable night of her life, while Aladdin lay down beside her and slept soundly. At the appointed hour the genie fetched in the shivering bridegroom, laid him in his place, and transported the bed back to the palace.

Presently the Sultan came to wish his daughter good morning. The unhappy vizir's son jumped up and hid himself, while the princess would not say a word, and was very sorrowful.

The Sultan sent her mother to her, who said: "How comes it, child, that you will not speak to your father? What has happened?"

The princess sighed deeply, and at last told her mother how, during the night, the bed had been carried into some strange house, and what had passed there. Her mother did not believe her in the least, but bade her rise and consider it an idle dream.

The following night exactly the same thing happened, and next morning, on the princess's refusing to speak, the Sultan threatened to cut off her head. She then confessed all, bidding him ask the vizir's son if it were not so. The Sultan told the vizir to ask his son, who owned the truth, adding that, dearly as he loved the princess, he had rather die than go through another such fearful night, and wished to be separated from her. His wish was granted, and there was an end of feasting and rejoicing.

When the three months were over, Aladdin sent his mother to remind the Sultan of his promise. She stood in the same place as before, and the Sultan, who had forgotten Aladdin, at once remembered him, and sent for her. On seeing her poverty, the Sultan felt less inclined than ever to keep his word, and asked the vizir's advice, who counselled him to set so high a value on the princess that no man living could come up to it.

The Sultan then turned to Aladdin's mother, saying: "Good woman, a Sultan must remember his promises, and I will remember mine, but your son must first send me forty basins of gold brimful of jewels, carried by forty black slaves, led by as many white ones, splendidly dressed. Tell him that I await his answer." The mother of Aladdin bowed low and went home, thinking all was lost.

She gave Aladdin the message, adding: "He may wait long enough for your answer!"

"Not so long, mother, as you think," her son replied. "I would do a great deal more than that for the princess."

He summoned the genie, and in a few moments the eighty slaves arrived, and filled up the small house and garden.

Aladdin made them set out to the palace, two and two, followed by his mother. They were so richly dressed, with such splendid jewels in their girdles, that everyone crowded to see them and the basins of gold they carried on their heads.

They entered the palace, and, after kneeling before the Sultan, stood in a half-circle round the throne with their arms crossed, while Aladdin's mother presented them to the Sultan.

He hesitated no longer, but said: "Good woman, return and tell your son that I wait for him with open arms."

She lost no time in telling Aladdin, bidding him make haste. But Aladdin first called the genie.

"I want a scented bath," he said, "a richly embroidered habit, a horse surpassing the Sultan's, and twenty slaves to attend me. Besides this, six slaves, beautifully dressed, to wait on my mother; and lastly, ten thousand pieces of gold in ten purses."

No sooner said than done. Aladdin mounted his horse and passed through the streets, the slaves strewing gold as they went. Those who had played with him in his childhood knew him not, he had grown so handsome.

When the Sultan saw him he came down from his throne, embraced him, and led him into a hall where a feast was spread, intending to marry him to the princess that very day.

But Aladdin refused, saying, "I must build a palace fit for her," and took his leave.

Once home he said to the genie: "Build me a palace of the finest marble, set with jasper, agate, and other precious stones. In the middle you shall build me a large hall with a dome, its four walls of massy gold and silver, each side having six windows, whose lattices, all except one, which is to be left unfinished, must be set with diamonds and rubies. There must be stables and horses and grooms and slaves; go and see about it!"

The palace was finished by next day, and the genie carried him there and showed him all his orders faithfully carried out, even to the laying of a velvet carpet from Aladdin's palace to the Sultan's. Aladdin's mother then dressed herself carefully, and walked to the palace with her slaves, while he followed her on horseback. The Sultan sent musicians with trumpets and cymbals to meet them, so that the air resounded with music and cheers. She was taken to the princess, who saluted her and treated her with great honour. At night the princess said good-bye to her father, and set out on the carpet for Aladdin's palace, with his mother at her side, and followed by the hundred slaves. She was charmed at the sight of Aladdin, who ran to receive her.

"Princess," he said, "blame your beauty for my boldness if I have displeased you."

She told him that, having seen him, she willingly obeyed her father in this matter. After the wedding had taken place Aladdin led her into the hall, where a feast was spread, and she supped with him, after which they danced till midnight.

Next day Aladdin invited the Sultan to see the palace. On entering the hall with the four-and-twenty windows, with their rubies, diamonds, and emeralds, he cried: "It is a world's wonder! There is only one thing that surprises me. Was it by accident that one window was left unfinished?"

"No, sir, by design," returned Aladdin. "I wished your Majesty to have the glory of finishing this palace."

The Sultan was pleased, and sent for the best jewelers in the city. He showed them the unfinished window, and bade them fit it up like the others.

"Sir," replied their spokesman, "we cannot find jewels enough."

The Sultan had his own fetched, which they soon used, but to no purpose, for in a month's time the work was not half done. Aladdin, knowing that their task was vain, bade them undo their work and carry the jewels back, and the genie finished the window at his command. The Sultan was surprised to receive his jewels again and visited Aladdin, who showed him the window finished. The Sultan embraced him, the envious vizir meanwhile hinting that it was the work of enchantment.

Aladdin had won the hearts of the people by his gentle bearing. He was made captain of the Sultan's armies, and won several battles for him, but remained modest and courteous as before, and lived thus in peace and content for several years.

But far away in Africa the magician remembered Aladdin, and by his magic arts discovered that Aladdin, instead of perishing miserably in the cave, had escaped, and had married a princess, with whom he was living in great honour and wealth. He knew that the poor tailor's son could only have accomplished this by means of the lamp, and travelled night and day till he reached the capital of China, bent on Aladdin's ruin. As he passed through the town he heard people talking everywhere about a marvellous palace.

"Forgive my ignorance," he asked, "what is this palace you speak of?"

"Have you not heard of Prince Aladdin's palace," was the reply, "the greatest wonder of the world? I will direct you if you have a mind to see it."

The magician thanked him who spoke, and having seen the palace knew that it had been raised by the genie of the lamp, and became half mad with rage. He determined to get hold of the lamp, and again plunge Aladdin into the deepest poverty.

Unluckily, Aladdin had gone a-hunting for eight days, which gave the magician plenty of time. He bought a dozen copper lamps, put them into a basket, and went to the palace, crying: "New lamps for old!" followed by a jeering crowd.

The princess, sitting in the hall of four-and-twenty windows, sent a slave to find out what the noise was about, who came back laughing, so that the princess scolded her.

"Madam," replied the slave, "who can help laughing to see an old fool offering to exchange fine new lamps for old ones?"

Another slave, hearing this, said: "There is an old one on the cornice there which he can have."

Now this was the magic lamp, which Aladdin had left there, as he could not take it out hunting with him. The princess, not knowing its value, laughingly bade the slave take it and make the exchange.

She went and said to the magician: "Give me a new lamp for this."

He snatched it and bade the slave take her choice, amid the jeers of the crowd. Little he cared, but left off crying his lamps, and went out of the city gates to a lonely place, where he remained till nightfall, when he pulled out the lamp and rubbed it. The genie appeared, and at the magician's command carried him, together with the palace and the princess in it, to a lonely place in Africa.

Next morning the Sultan looked out of the window towards Aladdin's palace and rubbed his eyes, for it was gone. He sent for the vizir, and asked what had become of the palace. The vizir looked out too, and was lost in astonishment. He again put it down to enchantment, and this time the Sultan believed him, and sent thirty men on horseback to fetch

Aladdin in chains. They met him riding home, bound him, and forced him to go with them on foot. The people, however, who loved him, followed, armed, to see that he came to no harm. He was carried before the Sultan, who ordered the executioner to cut off his head. The executioner made Aladdin kneel down, bandaged his eyes, and raised his scimitar to strike.

At that instant the vizir, who saw that the crowd had forced their way into the courtyard and were scaling the walls to rescue Aladdin, called to the executioner to stay his hand. The people, indeed, looked so threatening that the Sultan gave way and ordered Aladdin to be unbound, and pardoned him in the sight of the crowd.

Aladdin now begged to know what he had done.

"False wretch!" said the Sultan, "come hither," and showed him from the window the place where his palace had stood.

Aladdin was so amazed that he could not say a word.

"Where is my palace and my daughter?" demanded the Sultan. "For the first I am not so deeply concerned, but my daughter I must have, and you must find her or lose your head."

Aladdin begged for forty days in which to find her, promising if he failed to return and suffer death at the Sultan's pleasure. His prayer was granted, and he went forth sadly from the Sultan's presence. For three days he wandered about like a madman, asking everyone what had become of his palace, but they only laughed and pitied him. He came to the banks of a river, and knelt down to say his prayers before throwing himself in. In so doing he rubbed the magic ring he still wore.

The genie he had seen in the cave appeared, and asked his will.

"Save my life, genie," said Aladdin, "and bring my palace back."

"That is not in my power," said the genie. "I am only the slave of the ring; you must ask the slave of the lamp."

"Even so," said Aladdin "but thou canst take me to the palace, and set me down under my dear wife's window." He at once found himself in Africa, under the window of the princess, and fell asleep out of sheer weariness.

He was awakened by the singing of the birds, and his heart was lighter. He saw plainly that all his misfortunes were owing to the loss of the lamp, and vainly wondered who had robbed him of it.

That morning the princess rose earlier than she had done since she had been carried into Africa by the magician, whose company she was forced to endure once a day. She, however, treated him so harshly that he dared not live there altogether. As she was dressing, one of her women looked out and saw Aladdin. The princess ran and opened the window, and at the noise she made Aladdin looked up. She called to him to come to her, and great was the joy of these lovers at seeing each other again.

After he had kissed her, Aladdin said: "I beg of you, Princess, in God's name, before we speak of anything else, for your own sake and mine, tell me what has become of an old lamp I left on the cornice in the hall of four-and-twenty windows, when I went a-hunting."

"Alas!" she said, "I am the innocent cause of our sorrows," and told him of the exchange of the lamp.

"Now I know," cried Aladdin, "that we have to thank the African magician for this! Where is the lamp?"

"He carries it about with him," said the princess. "I know, for he pulled it out of his breast to show me. He wishes me to break my faith with you and marry him, saying that you were beheaded by my father's command. He is forever speaking ill of you, but I only reply by my tears. If I persist, I doubt not that he will use violence."

Aladdin comforted her, and left her for a while. He changed clothes with the first person he met in the town, and having bought a certain powder returned to the princess, who let him in by a little side door.

"Put on your most beautiful dress," he said to her, "and receive the magician with smiles, leading him to believe that you have forgotten me. Invite him to sup with you, and say you wish to taste the wine of his country. He will go for some, and while he is gone I will tell you what to do."

She listened carefully to Aladdin and, when he left her, arrayed herself gaily for the first time since she left China. She put on a girdle and head-dress of diamonds, and seeing in a glass that she looked more beautiful than ever, received the magician, saying to his great amazement: "I have made up my mind that Aladdin is dead, and that all my tears will not bring him back to me, so I am resolved to mourn no more, and have therefore invited you to sup with me; but I am tired of the wines of China, and would fain taste those of Africa."

The magician flew to his cellar, and the princess put the powder Aladdin had given her in her cup. When he returned, she asked him to drink her health in the wine of Africa, handing him her cup in exchange for his as a sign she was reconciled to him.

Before drinking, the magician made her a speech in praise of her beauty, but the princess cut him short, saying: "Let me drink first, and you shall say what you will afterwards." She set her cup to her lips and kept it there, while the magician drained his to the dregs and fell back lifeless.

The princess then opened the door to Aladdin, and flung her arms round his neck, but Aladdin put her away, bidding her to leave him, as he had more to do. He then went to the dead magician, took the lamp out of his vest, and bade the genie carry the palace and all in it back to China. This was done, and the princess in her chamber only felt two little shocks, and little thought she was at home again.

The Sultan, who was sitting in his closet, mourning for his lost daughter, happened to look up, and rubbed his eyes, for there stood the palace as before! He hastened thither, and Aladdin received him in the hall of the four-and-twenty windows, with the princess at his side. Aladdin told him what had happened, and showed him the dead body of the magician, that he might believe. A ten days' feast was proclaimed, and it seemed as if Aladdin might now live the rest of his life in peace; but it was not to be.

The African magician had a younger brother, who was, if possible, more wicked and more cunning than himself. He travelled to China to avenge his brother's death, and went to visit a pious woman called Fatima, thinking she might be of use to him. He entered her cell and clapped a dagger to her breast, telling her to rise and do his bidding on pain of death. He changed clothes with her, coloured his face like hers, put on her veil and murdered her, that she might tell no tales. Then he went towards the palace of Aladdin, and all the people thinking he was the holy woman, gathered round him, kissing his hands and begging his blessing. When he got to the palace there was such a noise going on round him that the princess bade her slave look out of the window and ask what was the matter. The slave said it was the holy woman, curing people by her touch of their ailments, whereupon the princess, who had long desired to see Fatima, sent for her. On coming to the princess, the magician offered up a prayer for her health and prosperity. When he had done, the princess made him sit by her, and begged him to stay with her always. The false Fatima, who wished for nothing better, consented, but kept his veil down for fear of discovery. The princess showed him the hall, and asked him what he thought of it.

"It is truly beautiful," said the false Fatima. "In my mind it wants but one thing."

"And what is that?" said the princess.

"If only a roc's egg," replied he, "were hung up from the middle of this dome, it would be the wonder of the world."

After this the princess could think of nothing but a roc's egg, and when Aladdin returned from hunting he found her in a very ill humour. He begged to know what was amiss, and she told him that all her pleasure in the hall was spoilt for the want of a roc's egg hanging from the dome.

"If that is all," replied Aladdin, "you shall soon be happy."

He left her and rubbed the lamp, and, when the genie appeared, commanded him to bring a roc's egg. The genie gave such a loud and terrible shriek that the hall shook.

"Wretch!" he cried, "is it not enough that I have done everything for you, but you must command me to bring my master and hang him up in the midst of this dome? You and your wife and your palace deserve to be burnt to ashes; but this request does not come from you, but from the brother of the African magician whom you destroyed. He is now in your palace disguised as the holy woman – whom he murdered. He it was who put that wish into your wife's head. Take care of yourself, for he means to kill you." So saying, the genie disappeared.

Aladdin went back to the princess, saying his head ached, and requesting that the holy Fatima should be fetched to lay her hands on it. But when the magician came near, Aladdin, seizing his dagger, pierced him to the heart.

"What have you done?" cried the princess. "You have killed the holy woman!"

"Not so," replied Aladdin, "but a wicked magician," and told her of how she had been deceived.

After this, Aladdin and his wife lived in peace. He succeeded the Sultan when he died, and reigned for many years, leaving behind him a long line of kings.

The Talking Bird, the Singing Tree, and the Golden Water

(From One Thousand and One Arabian Nights, of Arabic, Egyptian, Sanskrit, Persian, and Mesopotamian origins)

THERE WAS AN EMPEROR of Persia named Kosrouschah, who, when he first came to his crown, in order to obtain a knowledge of affairs, took great pleasure in night excursions, attended by a trusty minister. He often walked in disguise through the city, and met with many adventures, one of the most remarkable of which happened to him upon his first ramble, which was not long after his accession to the throne of his father.

After the ceremonies of his father's funeral rites and his own inauguration were over, the new sultan, as well from inclination as from duty, went out one evening attended by his grand vizier, disguised like himself, to observe what was transacting in the city. As he was passing through a street in that part of the town inhabited only by the meaner sort, he heard some people talking very loud; and going close to the house whence the noise proceeded, and looking through a crack in the door, perceived a light, and three sisters sitting on a sofa, conversing together after supper. By what the eldest said he presently understood the subject of their conversation was wishes: "For," said she, "since we are talking about wishes, mine shall be to have the sultan's baker for my husband, for then I shall eat my fill of that bread, which by way of excellence is called the sultan's; let us see if your tastes are as good as mine." "For my part," replied the second sister, "I wish I was wife to the sultan's chief cook, for then I should eat of the most excellent dishes; and as I am persuaded that the sultan's bread is common in the palace, I should not want any of that; therefore you see," addressing herself to her eldest sister, "that I have a better taste than you." The youngest sister, who was very beautiful, and

96

had more charms and wit than the two elder, spoke in her turn: "For my part, sisters," said she, "I shall not limit my desires to such trifles, but take a higher flight; and since we are upon wishing, I wish to be the emperor's queen-consort. I would make him father of a prince, whose hair should be gold on one side of his head, and silver on the other; when he cried, the tears from his eyes should be pearls; and when he smiled, his vermilion lips should look like a rosebud fresh-blown."

The three sisters' wishes, particularly that of the youngest, seemed so singular to the sultan, that he resolved to gratify them in their desires; but without communicating his design to his grand vizier, he charged him only to take notice of the house, and bring the three sisters before him the following day.

The grand vizier, in executing the emperor's orders, would but just give the sisters time to dress themselves to appear before his majesty, without telling them the reason. He brought them to the palace, and presented them to the emperor, who said to them, "Do you remember the wishes you expressed last night, when you were all in so pleasant a mood? Speak the truth; I must know what they were." At these unexpected words of the emperor, the three sisters were much confounded. They cast down their eyes and blushed, and the colour which rose in the cheeks of the youngest quite captivated the emperor's heart. Modesty, and fear lest they might have offended by their conversation, kept them silent. The emperor, perceiving their confusion, said to encourage them, "Fear nothing, I did not send for you to distress you; and since I see that without my intending it, this is the effect of the question I asked, as I know the wish of each, I will relieve you from your fears. You," added he, "who wished to be my wife, shall have your desire this day; and you," continued he, addressing himself to the two elder sisters, "shall also be married to my chief baker and cook."

As soon as the sultan had declared his pleasure, the youngest sister, setting her elders an example, threw herself at the emperor's feet to express her gratitude. "Sir," said she, "my wish, since it is come to your majesty's knowledge, was expressed only in the way of conversation and amusement. I am unworthy of the honour you do me, and supplicate your pardon for my presumption." The other two sisters would have excused themselves also, but the emperor, interrupting them, said, "No, no; it shall be as I have declared; the wishes of all shall be fulfilled." The nuptials were all celebrated that day, as the emperor had resolved, but in a different manner. The youngest sister's were solemnized with all the rejoicings usual at the marriages of the emperors of Persia; and those of the other two sisters according to the quality and distinction of their husbands; the one as the sultan's chief baker, and the other as head cook.

The two elder felt strongly the disproportion of their marriages to that of their younger sister. This consideration made them far from being content, though they were arrived at the utmost height of their late wishes, and much beyond their hopes. They gave themselves up to an excess of jealousy, which not only disturbed their joy, but was the cause of great trouble and affliction to the queen-consort, their younger sister. They had not an opportunity to communicate their thoughts to each other on the preference the emperor had given her, but were altogether employed in preparing themselves for the celebration of their marriages. Some days afterward, when they had an opportunity of seeing each other at the public baths, the eldest said to the other: "Well, what say you to our sister's great fortune? Is not she a fine person to be a queen!" "I must own," said the other sister, "I cannot conceive what charms the emperor could discover to be so bewitched by her. Was it a reason sufficient for him not to cast his eyes on you, because she was somewhat younger? You were as worthy of his throne, and in justice he ought to have preferred you."

"Sister," said the elder, "I should not have regretted if his majesty had but pitched upon you; but that he should choose that little simpleton really grieves me. But I will revenge myself; and you, I think, are as much concerned as I; therefore, I propose that we should contrive measures and act in concert: communicate to me what you think the likeliest way to mortify her, while I, on my side, will inform you what my desire of revenge shall suggest to me." After this wicked agreement, the two sisters saw each other frequently, and consulted how they might disturb and interrupt the happiness of the queen. They proposed a great many ways, but in deliberating about the manner of executing them, found so many difficulties that they durst not attempt them. In the meantime, with a detestable dissimulation, they often went together to make her visits, and every time showed her all the marks of affection they could devise, to persuade her how overjoyed they were to have a sister raised to so high a fortune. The queen, on her part, constantly received them with all the demonstrations of esteem they could expect from so near a relative. Some time after her marriage, the expected birth of an heir gave great joy to the queen and emperor, which was communicated to all the court, and spread throughout the empire. Upon this news the two sisters came to pay their compliments, and proffered their services, desiring her, if not provided with nurses, to accept of them.

The queen said to them most obligingly: "Sisters, I should desire nothing more, if it were in my power to make the choice. I am, however, obliged to you for your goodwill, but must submit to what the emperor shall order on this occasion. Let your husbands employ their friends to make interest, and get some courtier to ask this favour of his majesty, and if he speaks to me about it, be assured that I shall not only express the pleasure he does me but thank him for making choice of you."

The two husbands applied themselves to some courtiers, their patrons, and begged of them to use their interest to procure their wives the honour they aspired to. Those patrons exerted themselves so much in their behalf that the emperor promised them to consider of the matter, and was as good as his word; for in conversation with the queen he told her that he thought her sisters were the most proper persons to be about her, but would not name them before he had asked her consent. The queen, sensible of the deference the emperor so obligingly paid her, said to him, "Sir, I was prepared to do as your majesty might please to command. But since you have been so kind as to think of my sisters, I thank you for the regard you have shown them for my sake, and therefore I shall not dissemble that I had rather have them than strangers." The emperor therefore named the queen's two sisters to be her attendants; and from that time they went frequently to the palace, overjoyed at the opportunity they would have of executing the detestable wickedness they had meditated against the queen.

Shortly afterward a young prince, as bright as the day, was born to the queen; but neither his innocence nor beauty could move the cruel hearts of the merciless sisters. They wrapped him up carelessly in his cloths and put him into a basket, which they abandoned to the stream of a small canal that ran under the queen's apartment, and declared that she had given birth to a puppy. This dreadful intelligence was announced to the emperor, who became so angry at the circumstance, that he was likely to have occasioned the queen's death, if his grand vizier had not represented to him that he could not, without injustice, make her answerable for the misfortune.

In the meantime, the basket in which the little prince was exposed was carried by the stream beyond a wall which bounded the prospect of the queen's apartment, and from thence floated with the current down the gardens. By chance the intendant of the emperor's gardens, one of the principal officers of the kingdom, was walking in the garden by the side of this canal, and, perceiving a basket floating, called to a gardener who was not far off, to bring it to shore that he might see what it contained. The gardener, with a rake which he had in his hand, drew the basket to the side of the canal, took it up, and gave it to him. The intendant of the gardens was extremely surprised to see in the basket a child, which, though he knew it could be but just born, had very fine features. This officer had been married several years, but though he had always been desirous of having children, Heaven had never blessed him with any. This accident interrupted his walk: he made the gardener follow him with the child, and when he came to his own house, which was situated at the entrance to the gardens of the palace, went into his wife's apartment. "Wife," said he, "as we have no children of our own, God has sent us one. I recommend him to you; provide him a nurse, and take as much care of him as if he were our own son; for, from this moment, I acknowledge him as such." The intendant's wife received the child with great joy, and took particular pleasure in the care of him. The intendant himself would not inquire too narrowly whence the infant came. He saw plainly it came not far off from the queen's apartment, but it was not his business to examine too closely into what had passed, nor to create disturbances in a place where peace was so necessary.

The following year another prince was born, on whom the unnatural sisters had no more compassion than on his brother, but exposed him likewise in a basket and set him adrift in the canal, pretending, this time, that the sultana had given birth to a cat. It was happy also for this child that the intendant of the gardens was walking by the canal side, for he had it carried to his wife, and charged her to take as much care of it as of the former, which was as agreeable to her inclination as it was to his own.

The emperor of Persia was more enraged this time against the queen than before, and she had felt the effects of his anger if the grand vizier's remonstrances had not prevailed. The third year the queen gave birth to a princess, which innocent babe underwent the same fate as her brothers, for the two sisters, being determined not to desist from their detestable schemes till they had seen the queen cast off and humbled, claimed that a log of wood had been born and exposed this infant also on the canal. But the princess, as well as her brothers, was preserved from death by the compassion and charity of the intendant of the gardens.

Kosrouschah could no longer contain himself, when he was informed of the new misfortune. He pronounced sentence of death upon the wretched queen and ordered the grand vizier to see it executed.

The grand vizier and the courtiers who were present cast themselves at the emperor's feet, to beg of him to revoke the sentence. "Your majesty, I hope, will give me leave," said the grand vizier, "to represent to you, that the laws which condemn persons to death were made to punish crimes; the three extraordinary misfortunes of the queen are not crimes, for in what can she be said to have contributed toward them? Your majesty may abstain from seeing her, but let her live. The affliction in which she will spend the rest of her life, after the loss of your favour, will be a punishment sufficiently distressing."

The emperor of Persia considered with himself, and, reflecting that it was unjust to condemn the queen to death for what had happened, said: "Let her live then; I will spare her life, but it shall be on this condition: that she shall desire to die more than once every day. Let a wooden shed be built for her at the gate of the principal mosque, with iron bars to the windows, and let her be put into it, in the coarsest habit; and every Mussulman that shall go into the mosque to prayers shall heap scorn upon her. If any one fail, I will have him exposed to the same punishment; and that I may be punctually obeyed, I charge you, vizier, to appoint persons to see this done." The emperor pronounced his sentence in such a tone that the grand vizier durst not further remonstrate; and it was executed, to the great satisfaction of the two envious sisters. A shed was built, and the queen, truly worthy of compassion, was put into it and exposed ignominiously to the contempt of the people, which usage she bore with a patient resignation that excited the compassion of those who were discriminating and judged of things better than the vulgar.

The two princes and the princess were, in the meantime, nursed and brought up by the intendant of the gardens and his wife with the tenderness of a father and mother; and as they advanced in age, they all showed marks of superior dignity, which discovered itself every day by a certain air which could only belong to exalted birth. All this increased the affections of the intendant and his wife, who called the eldest prince Bahman, and the second Perviz, both of them names of the most ancient emperors of Persia, and the princess, Periezade, which name also had been borne by several queens and princesses of the kingdom.

As soon as the two princes were old enough, the intendant provided proper masters to teach them to read and write; and the princess, their sister, who was often with them, showing a great desire to learn, the intendant, pleased with her quickness, employed the same master to teach her also. Her vivacity and piercing wit made her, in a little time, as great a proficient as her brothers. From that time the brothers and sister had the same masters in geography, poetry, history, and even the secret sciences, and made so wonderful a progress that their tutors were amazed, and frankly owned that they could teach them nothing more. At the hours of recreation, the princess learned to sing and play upon all sorts of instruments; and when the princes were learning to ride she would not permit them to have that advantage over her, but went through all the exercises with them, learning to ride also, to bend the bow, and dart the reed or javelin, and oftentimes outdid them in the race and other contests of agility.

The intendant of the gardens was so overjoyed to find his adopted children so accomplished in all the perfections of body and mind, and that they so well requited the expense he had been at in their education, that he resolved to be at a still greater; for, as he had until then been content simply with his lodge at the entrance of the garden, and kept no country-house, he purchased a mansion at a short distance from the city, surrounded by a large tract of arable land, meadows, and woods. As the house was not sufficiently handsome nor convenient, he pulled it down, and spared no expense in building a more magnificent residence. He went every day to hasten, by his presence, the great number of workmen he employed, and as soon as there was an apartment ready to receive him, passed several days together there when his presence was not necessary at court; and by the same exertions, the interior was furnished in the richest manner, in consonance with the magnificence of the edifice. Afterward he made gardens, according to a plan drawn by himself. He took in a large extent of ground, which he walled around, and stocked with fallow deer, that the princes and princess might divert themselves with hunting when they chose.

When this country seat was finished and fit for habitation, the intendant of the gardens went and cast himself at the emperor's feet, and, after representing how long he had served, and the infirmities of age which he found growing upon him, begged that he might be permitted to resign his charge into his majesty's disposal and retire. The emperor gave him leave, with the more pleasure, because he was satisfied with his long services, both in his father's reign and his own, and when he granted it, asked what he should do to recompense him. "Sir," replied the intendant of the gardens, "I have received so many obligations from your majesty and the late emperor, your father, of happy memory, that I desire no more than the honour of dying in your favour." He took his leave of the emperor and retired with the two princes and the princess to the country retreat he had built. His wife had been dead some years, and he himself had not lived above six months with his charges before he was surprised by so sudden a death that he had not time to give them the least account of the manner in which he had discovered them. The Princes Bahman and Perviz, and the Princess Periezade, who knew no other father than the intendant of the emperor's gardens, regretted and bewailed him as such, and paid all the honours in his funeral obsequies which love and filial gratitude required of them. Satisfied with the plentiful fortune he had left them, they lived together in perfect union, free from the ambition of distinguishing themselves at court, or aspiring to places of honour and dignity, which they might easily have obtained.

One day when the two princes were hunting, and the princess had remained at home, a religious old woman came to the gate, and desired leave to go in to say her prayers, it being then the hour. The servants asked the princess's permission, who ordered them to show her into the oratory, which the intendant of the emperor's gardens had taken care to fit up in his house, for want of a mosque in the neighbourhood. She bade them, also, after the good woman had finished her prayers, to show her the house and gardens and then bring her to the hall.

The old woman went into the oratory, said her prayers, and when she came out two of the princess's women invited her to see the residence, which civility she accepted, followed them from one apartment to another, and observed, like a person who understood what belonged to furniture, the nice arrangement of everything.

They conducted her also into the garden, the disposition of which she found so well planned, that she admired it, observing that the person who had formed it must have been an excellent master of his art. Afterward she was brought before the princess, who waited for her in the great hall, which in beauty and richness exceeded all that she had admired in the other apartments.

As soon as the princess saw the devout woman, she said to her: "My good mother, come near and sit down by me. I am overjoyed at the happiness of having the opportunity of profiting for some moments by the example and conversation of such a person as you, who have taken the right way by dedicating yourself to the service of God. I wish everyone were as wise."

The devout woman, instead of sitting on a sofa, would only sit upon the edge of one. The princess would not permit her to do so, but rising from her seat and taking her by the hand, obliged her to come and sit by her. The good woman, sensible of the civility, said: "Madam, I ought not to have so much respect shown me; but since you command, and are mistress of your own house, I will obey you." When she had seated herself, before they entered into any conversation, one of the princess's women brought a low stand of mother-of-pearl and ebony, with a china dish full of cakes upon it, and many others set round it full of fruits in season, and wet and dry sweetmeats.

The princess took up one of the cakes, and presenting her with it, said: "Eat, good mother, and make choice of what you like best; you had need to eat after coming so far." "Madam," replied the good woman, "I am not used to eat such delicacies, but will not refuse what God has sent me by so liberal a hand as yours."

While the devout woman was eating, the princess ate a little too, to bear her company, and asked her many questions upon the exercise of devotion which she practised and how she lived; all of which she answered with great modesty. Talking of various things, at last the princess asked her what she thought of the house, and how she liked it.

"Madam," answered the devout woman, "I must certainly have very bad taste to disapprove anything in it, since it is beautiful, regular, and magnificently furnished with exactness and judgment, and all its ornaments adjusted in the best manner. Its situation is an agreeable spot, and no garden can be more delightful; but yet, if you will give me leave to speak my mind freely, I will take the liberty to tell you that this house would be incomparable if it had three things which are wanting to complete it." "My good mother," replied the Princess Periezade, "what are those? I entreat you to tell me what they are; I will spare nothing to get them."

"Madam," replied the devout woman, "the first of these three things is the Talking Bird, so singular a creature, that it draws round it all the songsters of the neighbourhood which come to accompany its voice. The second is the Singing Tree, the leaves of which are so many mouths which form a harmonious concert of different voices and never cease. The third is the Golden Water, a single drop of which being poured into a vessel properly prepared, it increases so as to fill it immediately, and rises up in the middle like a fountain, which continually plays, and yet the basin never overflows."

"Ah! my good mother," cried the princess, "how much am I obliged to you for the knowledge of these curiosities! I never before heard there were such rarities in the world; but as I am persuaded that you know, I expect that you should do me the favour to inform me where they are to be found."

"Madam," replied the good woman, "I should be unworthy the hospitality you have shown me if I should refuse to satisfy your curiosity on that point, and am glad to have the honour to tell you that these curiosities are all to be met with in the same spot on the confines of this kingdom, toward India. The road lies before your house, and whoever you send needs but follow it for twenty days, and on the twentieth only let him ask the first person he meets where the Talking Bird, the Singing Tree, and the Golden Water are, and he will be informed." After saying this, she rose from her seat, took her leave, and went her way.

The Princess Periezade's thoughts were so taken up with the Talking Bird, Singing Tree, and Golden Water, that she never perceived the devout woman's departure, till she wanted to ask her some questions for her better information; for she thought that what she had been told was not a sufficient reason for exposing herself by undertaking a long journey. However, she would not send after her visitor, but endeavoured to remember all the directions, and when she thought she had recollected every word, took real pleasure in thinking of the satisfaction she should have if she could get these curiosities into her possession; but the difficulties she apprehended and the fear of not succeeding made her very uneasy.

She was absorbed in these thoughts when her brothers returned from hunting, who, when they entered the great hall, instead of finding her lively and gay, as she was wont to be, were amazed to see her so pensive and hanging down her head as if something troubled her.

"Sister," said Prince Bahman, "what is become of all your mirth and gaiety? Are you not well? Or has some misfortune befallen you? Tell us, that we may know how to act, and give you some relief. If anyone has affronted you, we will resent his insolence."

The princess remained in the same posture some time without answering, but at last lifted up her eyes to look at her brothers, and then held them down again, telling them nothing disturbed her.

"Sister," said Prince Bahman, "you conceal the truth from us; there must be something of consequence. It is impossible we could observe so sudden a change if nothing was the matter with you. You would not have us satisfied with the evasive answer you have given; do not conceal anything, unless you would have us suspect that you renounce the strict union which has hitherto subsisted between us."

The princess, who had not the smallest intention to offend her brothers, would not suffer them to entertain such a thought, but said: "When I told you nothing disturbed me, I meant nothing that was of importance to you, but to me it is of some consequence; and since you press me to tell you by our strict union and friendship, which are so dear to me, I will. You think, and I always believed so too, that this house was so complete that nothing was wanting. But this day I have learned that it lacks three rarities which would render it so perfect that no country seat in the world could be compared with it. These three things are the Talking Bird, the Singing Tree, and the Golden Water." After she had informed them wherein consisted the excellency of these rarities, "A devout woman," added she, "has made this discovery to me, told me the place where they are to be found, and the way thither. Perhaps you may imagine these things of little consequence; that without these additions our house will always be thought sufficiently elegant, and that we can do without them. You may think as you please, but I cannot help telling you that I am persuaded they are absolutely necessary, and I shall not be easy without them. Therefore, whether you value them or not, I desire you to consider what person you may think proper for me to send in search of the curiosities I have mentioned."

"Sister," replied Prince Bahman, "nothing can concern you in which we have not an equal interest. It is enough that you desire these things to oblige us to take the same interest; but if you had not, we feel ourselves inclined of our own accord and for our own individual satisfaction. I am persuaded my brother is of the same opinion, and therefore we ought to undertake this conquest, for the importance and singularity of the undertaking deserve that name. I will take the charge upon myself; only tell me the place and the way to it, and I will defer my journey no longer than till tomorrow."

"Brother," said Prince Perviz, "it is not proper that you, who are the head of our family, should be absent. I desire my sister should join with me to oblige you to abandon your design, and allow me to undertake it. I hope to acquit myself as well as you, and it will be a more regular proceeding." "I am persuaded of your goodwill, brother," replied Prince Bahman, "and that you would succeed as well as myself in this journey;

but I have resolved and will undertake it. You shall stay at home with our sister, and I need not recommend her to you."

The next morning Bahman mounted his horse, and Perviz and the princess embraced and wished him a good journey. But in the midst of their adieus, the princess recollected what she had not thought of before. "Brother," said she, "I had quite forgotten the accidents which attend travellers. Who knows whether I shall ever see you again? Alight, I beseech you, and give up this journey. I would rather be deprived of the sight and possession of the Talking Bird, the Singing Tree, and the Golden Water, than run the risk of never seeing you more."

"Sister," replied Bahman, smiling at her sudden fears, "my resolution is fixed. The accidents you speak of befall only those who are unfortunate; but there are more who are not so. However, as events are uncertain, and I may fail in this undertaking, all I can do is to leave you this knife."

Bahman, pulling a knife from his vestband and presenting it to the princess in the sheath, said: "Take this knife, sister, and give yourself the trouble sometimes to pull it out of the sheath; while you see it clean as it is now, it will be a sign that I am alive; but if you find it stained with blood, then you may believe me dead and indulge me with your prayers."

The princess could obtain nothing more of Bahman. He bade adieu to her and Prince Perviz for the last time and rode away. When he got into the road, he never turned to the right hand nor to the left, but went directly forward toward India. The twentieth day he perceived on the roadside a hideous old man, who sat under a tree near a thatched house, which was his retreat from the weather.

His eyebrows were as white as snow, as was also the hair of his head; his whiskers covered his mouth, and his beard and hair reached down to his feet. The nails of his hands and feet were grown to an extensive length, while a flat, broad umbrella covered his head. He had no clothes, but only a mat thrown round his body. This old man was a dervish for so many years retired from the world to give himself up entirely to the service of God that at last he had become what we have described.

Prince Bahman, who had been all that morning very attentive, to see if he could meet with anybody who could give him information of the place he was in search of, stopped when he came near the dervish, alighted, in conformity to the directions which the devout woman had given the Princess Periezade, and leading his horse by the bridle, advanced toward him and saluted him, saying: "God prolong your days, good father, and grant you the accomplishment of your desires."

The dervish returned the prince's salutation, but so unintelligibly that he could not understand one word he said, and Prince Bahman, perceiving that this difficulty proceeded from the dervish's whiskers hanging over his mouth, and unwilling to go any further without the instructions he wanted, pulled out a pair of scissors he had about him, and having tied his horse to a branch of the tree, said: "Good dervish, I want to have some talk with you, but your whiskers prevent my understanding what you say; and if you will consent, I will cut off some part of them and of your eyebrows, which disfigure you so much that you look more like a bear than a man."

The dervish did not oppose the offer, and when the prince had cut off as much hair as he thought fit, he perceived that the dervish had a good complexion, and that he was not as old as he seemed. "Good dervish," said he, "if I had a glass I would show you how young you look: you are now a man, but before, nobody could tell what you were."

The kind behaviour of Prince Bahman made the dervish smile and return his compliment. "Sir," said he, "whoever you are, I am obliged by the good office you have performed, and am ready to show my gratitude by doing anything in my power for you. You must have alighted here upon some account or other. Tell me what it is, and I will endeavour to serve you."

"Good dervish," replied Prince Bahman, "I am in search of the Talking Bird, the Singing Tree, and the Golden Water; I know these three rarities are not far from hence, but cannot tell exactly the place where they are to be found; if you know, I conjure you to show me the way, that I may not lose my labour after so long a journey."

The prince, while he spoke, observed that the dervish changed countenance, held down his eyes, looked very serious, and remained silent, which obliged him to say to him again: "Good father, tell me whether you know what I ask you, that I may not lose my time, but inform myself somewhere else."

At last the dervish broke silence. "Sir," said he to Prince Bahman, "I know the way you ask of me; but the regard which I conceived for you the first moment I saw you, and which is grown stronger by the service you have done me, kept me in suspense as to whether I should give you the satisfaction you desire." "What motive can hinder you?" replied the prince; "and what difficulties do you find in so doing?" "I will tell you," replied the dervish; "the danger to which you are going to expose yourself is greater than you may suppose. A number of gentlemen of as much bravery as you can possibly possess have passed this way, and asked me the same question. When I had used all my endeavours to persuade them to desist, they would not believe me; at last I yielded to their importunities; I was compelled to show them the way, and I can assure you they have all perished, for I have not seen one come back. Therefore, if you have any regard for your life, take my advice, go no farther, but return home."

Prince Bahman persisted in his resolution. "I will not suppose," said he to the dervish, "but that your advice is sincere. I am obliged to you for the friendship you express for me; but whatever may be the danger, nothing shall make me change my intention: whoever attacks me, I am well armed, and can say I am as brave as anyone." "But they who will attack you are not to be seen," replied the dervish; "how will you defend yourself against invisible persons?" "It is no matter," answered the prince; "all you say shall not persuade me to do anything contrary to my duty. Since you know the way, I conjure you once more to inform me."

When the dervish found he could not prevail upon Prince Bahman, and that he was obstinately bent to pursue his journey, notwithstanding his friendly remonstrance, he put his hand into a bag that lay by him and pulled out a bowl, which he presented to him. "Since I cannot prevail on you to attend to my advice," said he, "take this bowl and when you are on horseback throw it before you, and follow it to the foot of a mountain, where it will stop. As soon as the bowl stops, alight, leave your horse with the bridle over his neck, and he will stand in the same place till you return. As you ascend you will see on your right and left a great number of large black stones, and will hear on all sides a confusion of voices, which will utter a thousand abuses to discourage you, and prevent your reaching the summit of the mountain. Be not afraid; but, above all things, do not turn your head to look behind you, for in that instant you will be changed into such a black stone as those you see, which are all youths who have failed in this enterprise. If you escape the danger of which I give you but a faint idea, and get to the top of the mountain, you will see a cage, and in that cage is the bird you seek; ask him which are the Singing Tree and the Golden Water, and he will tell you. I have nothing more to say; this is what you have to do, and if you are prudent you will take my advice and not expose your life. Consider once more while you have time that the difficulties are almost insuperable."

"I am obliged to you for your advice," replied Prince Bahman, after he had received the bowl, "but cannot follow it. However, I will endeavour to conform myself to that part of it which bids me not to look behind me, and I hope to come and thank you when I have obtained what I am seeking." After these words, to which the dervish made no other answer than that he should be overjoyed to see him again, the prince mounted his horse, took leave of the dervish with a respectful salute, and threw the bowl before him.

The bowl rolled away with as much swiftness as when Prince Bahman first hurled it from his hand, which obliged him to put his horse to the same pace to avoid losing sight of it, and when it had reached the foot of the mountain it stopped. The prince alighted from his horse, laid the bridle on his neck, and having first surveyed the mountain and seen the black stones, began to ascend, but had not gone four steps before he heard the voices mentioned by the dervish, though he could see nobody.

Some said: "Where is that fool going? Where is he going? What would he have? Do not let him pass." Others: "Stop him, catch him, kill him:" and others with a voice like thunder: "Thief! assassin! murderer!" while some in a gibing tone cried: "No, no, do not hurt him; let the pretty fellow pass, the cage and bird are kept for him."

Notwithstanding all these troublesome voices, Prince Bahman ascended with resolution for some time, but the voices redoubled with so loud a din, both behind and before, that at last he was seized with dread, his legs trembled under him, he staggered, and finding that his strength failed him, he forgot the dervish's advice, turned about to run down the hill, and was that instant changed into a black stone; a metamorphosis which had happened to many before him who had attempted the ascent. His horse, likewise, underwent the same change.

From the time of Prince Bahman's departure, the Princess Periezade always wore the knife and sheath in her girdle, and pulled it out several times in a day, to know whether her brother was alive. She had the consolation to understand he was in perfect health and to talk of him frequently with Prince Perviz. On the fatal day that Prince Bahman was transformed into a stone, as Prince Perviz and the princess were talking together in the evening, as usual, the prince desired his sister to pull out the knife to know how their brother did. The princess readily complied, and seeing the blood run down the point was seized with so much horror that she threw it down. "Ah! my dear brother," cried she, "I have been the cause of your death, and shall never see you more! Why did I tell you of the Talking Bird, Singing Tree, and Golden Water; or rather, of what importance was it to me to know whether the devout woman thought this house ugly or handsome, or complete or not? I wish to Heaven she had never addressed herself to me!"

Prince Perviz was as much afflicted at the death of Prince Bahman as the princess, but not to waste time in needless regret, as he knew that she still passionately desired possession of the marvellous treasures, he interrupted her, saying: "Sister, our regret for our brother is vain; our lamentations cannot restore him to life; it is the will of God; we must submit and adore the decrees of the Almighty without searching into them. Why should you now doubt of the truth of what the holy woman told you? Do you think she spoke to you of three things that were not in being, and that she invented them to deceive you who had received her with so much goodness and civility? Let us rather believe that our brother's death is owing to some error on his part, or some accident which we cannot conceive. It ought not therefore to prevent us from pursuing our object. I offered to go this journey, and am now more resolved than ever; his example has no effect upon my resolution; tomorrow I will depart."

The princess did all she could to dissuade Prince Perviz, conjuring him not to expose her to the danger of losing two brothers; but he was obstinate, and all the remonstrances she could urge had no effect upon him. Before he went, that she might know what success he had, he left her a string of a hundred pearls, telling her that if they would not run when she should count them upon the string, but remain fixed, that would be a certain sign he had undergone the same fate as his brother; but at the same time told her he hoped it would never happen, but that he should have the delight of seeing her again.

Prince Perviz, on the twentieth day after his departure, met the same dervish in the same place as his brother Bahman had done before him. He went directly up to him, and after he had saluted, asked him if he could tell him where to find the Talking Bird, the Singing Tree, and the Golden Water. The dervish urged the same remonstrances as he had done to Prince Bahman, telling him that a young gentleman, who very much resembled him, was with him a short time before; that, overcome by his importunity, he had shown him the way, given him a guide, and told him how he should act to succeed, but that he had not seen him since, and doubted not but he had shared the same fate as all other adventurers.

"Good dervish," answered Prince Perviz, "I know whom you speak of; he was my elder brother, and I am informed of the certainty of his death, but know not the cause." "I can tell you," replied the dervish; "he was changed into a black stone, as all I speak of have been; and you must expect the same transformation, unless you observe more exactly than he has done the advice I gave him, in case you persist in your resolution, which I once more entreat you to renounce."

"Dervish," said Prince Perviz, "I cannot sufficiently express how much I am obliged for the concern you take in my life, who am a stranger to you, and have done nothing to deserve your kindness; but I thoroughly considered this enterprise before I undertook it; therefore I beg of you to do me the same favour you have done my brother. Perhaps I may have better success in following your directions." "Since I cannot prevail with you," said the dervish, "to give up your obstinate resolution, if my age did not prevent me, and I could stand, I would get up to reach you a bowl I have here, which will show you the way."

Without giving the dervish time to say more, the prince alighted from his horse and went to the dervish, who had taken a bowl out of his bag, in which he had a great many, and gave it him, with the same directions he had given Prince Bahman; and after warning him not to be discouraged by the voices he should hear, however threatening they might be, but to continue his way up the hill till he saw the cage and bird, he let him depart.

Prince Perviz thanked the dervish, and when he had remounted and taken leave, threw the bowl before his horse, and spurring him at the same time, followed it. When the bowl came to the bottom of the hill it stopped, the prince alighted, and stood some time to recollect the dervish's directions. He encouraged himself, and began to walk up with a resolution to reach the summit; but before he had gone above six steps, he heard a voice, which seemed to be near, as of a man behind him, say in an insulting tone: "Stay, rash youth, that I may punish you for your presumption."

Upon this affront the prince, forgetting the dervish's advice, clapped his hand upon his sword, drew it, and turned about to revenge himself; but had scarcely time to see that nobody followed him before he and his horse were changed into black stones.

In the meantime the Princess Periezade, several times a day after her brother's departure, counted her chaplet. She did not omit it at night, but when she went to bed put it about her neck, and in the morning when she awoke counted over the pearls again to see if they would slide.

The day that Prince Perviz was transformed into a stone she was counting over the pearls as she used to do, when all at once they became immovably fixed, a certain token that the prince, her brother, was dead. As she had determined what to do in case it should so happen, she lost no time in outward demonstrations of grief, which she concealed as much as possible, but having disguised herself in man's apparel, she mounted her horse the next morning, armed and equipped, having told her servants she should return in two or three days, and took the same road that her brothers had done.

The princess, who had been used to ride on horseback in hunting, supported the fatigue of so long a journey better than most ladies could have done; and as she made the same stages as her brothers, she also met with the dervish on the twentieth day. When she came near him, she alighted from her horse, leading him by the bridle, went and sat down by the dervish, and after she had saluted him, said: "Good dervish, give me leave to rest myself; and do me the favour to tell me if you have not heard that there are somewhere in this neighbourhood a Talking Bird, a Singing Tree, and Golden Water."

"Princess," answered the dervish, "for so I must call you, since by your voice I know you to be a woman disguised in man's apparel, I know the place well where these things are to be found; but what makes you ask me this question?"

"Good dervish," replied the princess, "I have had such a flattering relation of them given me, that I have a great desire to possess them." "Madam," replied the dervish, "you have been told the truth. These curiosities are more singular than they have been represented, but you have not been made acquainted with the difficulties which must be surmounted in order to obtain them. If you had been fully informed of these, you would not have undertaken so dangerous an enterprise. Take my advice, return, and do not urge me to contribute toward your ruin."

"Good father," said the princess, "I have travelled a great way, and should be sorry to return without executing my design. You talk of difficulties and danger of life, but you do not tell me what those difficulties are, and wherein the danger consists. This is what I desire to know, that I may consider and judge whether I can trust my courage and strength to brave them."

The dervish repeated to the princess what he had said to the Princes Bahman and Perviz, exaggerating the difficulties of climbing up to the top of the mountain, where she was to make herself mistress of the Bird, which would inform her of the Singing Tree and Golden Water. He magnified the din of the terrible threatening voices which she would hear on all sides of her, and the great number of black stones alone sufficient to strike terror. He entreated her to reflect that those stones were so many brave gentlemen, so metamorphosed for having omitted to observe the principal condition of success in the perilous undertaking, which was not to look behind them before they had got possession of the cage.

When the dervish had done, the princess replied: "By what I comprehend from your discourse, the difficulties of succeeding in this affair are, first, the getting up to the cage without being frightened at the terrible din of voices I shall hear; and, secondly, not to look behind me. For this last, I hope I shall be mistress enough of myself to observe it; as to the first, I own that voices, such as you represent them to be, are capable of striking terror into the most undaunted; but as in all enterprises and dangers everyone may use stratagem, I desire to know of you if I may use any in one of so great importance." "And what stratagem is it you would employ?" said the dervish. "To stop my ears with cotton," answered the princess, "that the voices, however terrible, may make the less impression upon my imagination, and my mind remain free from that disturbance which might cause me to lose the use of my reason."

"Princess," replied the dervish, "of all the persons who have addressed themselves to me for information, I do not know that ever one made use of the contrivance you propose. All I know is that they all perished. If you persist in your design, you may make the experiment. You will be fortunate if it succeeds, but I would advise you not to expose yourself to the danger."

"My good father," replied the princess, "I am sure my precaution will succeed, and am resolved to try the experiment. Nothing remains for me but to know which way I must go, and I conjure you not to deny me that information." The dervish exhorted her again to consider well what she was going to do; but finding her resolute, he took out a bowl, and presenting it to her, said: "Take this bowl, mount your horse again, and when you have thrown it before you, follow it through all its windings, till it stops at the bottom of the mountain; there alight and ascend the hill. Go, you know the rest."

After the princess had thanked the dervish, and taken her leave of him, she mounted her horse, threw the bowl before her, and followed it till it stopped at the foot of the mountain.

She then alighted, stopped her ears with cotton, and, after she had well examined the path leading to the summit, began with a moderate pace and walked up with intrepidity. She heard the voices and perceived the great service the cotton was to her. The higher she went, the louder and more numerous the voices seemed, but they were not capable of making any impression upon her. She heard a great many affronting speeches and raillery very disagreeable to a woman, which she only laughed at. "I mind not," said she to herself, "all that can be said, were it worse; I only laugh at them and shall pursue my way." At last, she climbed so high that she could perceive the cage and the Bird which endeavoured, in company with the voices, to frighten her, crying in a thundering tone, notwithstanding the smallness of its size: "Retire, fool, and approach no nearer."

The princess, encouraged by this sight, redoubled her speed, and by effort gained the summit of the mountain, where the ground was level; then running directly to the cage and clapping her hand upon it, cried: "Bird, I have you, and you shall not escape me."

While Periezade was pulling the cotton out of her ears the Bird said to her: "Heroic princess, be not angry with me for joining with those who exerted themselves to preserve my liberty. Though in a cage, I was content with my condition; but since I am destined to be a slave, I would rather be yours than any other person's, since you have obtained me so courageously. From this instant, I swear entire submission to all your commands. I know who you are. You do not; but the time will come when I shall do you essential service, for which I hope you will think yourself obliged to me. As a proof of my sincerity, tell me what you desire and I am ready to obey you."

The princess's joy was the more inexpressible, because the conquest she had made had cost her the lives of two beloved brothers, and given her more trouble and danger than she could have imagined. "Bird," said she, "it was my intention to have told you that I wish for many things which are of importance, but I am overjoyed that you have shown your goodwill and prevented me. I have been told that there is not far off a Golden Water, the property of which is very wonderful; before all things, I ask you to tell me where it is." The Bird showed her the place, which was just by, and she went and filled a little silver flagon which she had brought with her. She returned at once and said: "Bird, this is not enough; I want also the Singing Tree; tell me where it is." "Turn about," said the Bird, "and you will see behind you a wood where you will find the tree." The princess went into the wood, and by the harmonious concert she heard, soon knew the tree among many others, but it was very large and high. She came back again and said: "Bird, I have found the Singing Tree, but I can neither pull it up by the roots nor carry it." The Bird replied: "It is not necessary that you should take it up; it will be sufficient to break off a branch and carry it to plant in your garden; it will take root as soon as it is put into the earth, and in a little time will grow to as fine a tree as that you have seen."

When the princess had obtained possession of the three things for which she had conceived so great a desire, she said again: "Bird, what you have yet done for me is not sufficient. You have been the cause of the death of my two brothers, who must be among the black stones I saw as I ascended the mountain. I wish to take the princes home with me."

The Bird seemed reluctant to satisfy the princess in this point, and indeed made some difficulty to comply. "Bird," said the princess, "remember you told me that you were my slave. You are so; and your life is in my disposal." "That I cannot deny," answered the bird; "but although what you now ask is more difficult than all the rest, yet I will do it for you. Cast your eyes around," added he, "and look if you can see a little pitcher." "I see it already," said the princess. "Take it then," said he, "and as you descend the mountain, sprinkle a little of the water that is in it upon every black stone."

The princess took up the pitcher accordingly, carried with her the cage and Bird, the flagon of Golden Water, and the branch of the Singing Tree, and as she descended the mountain, threw a little of the water on every black stone, which was changed immediately into a man; and as she did not miss one stone, all the horses, both of her brothers and of the other gentlemen, resumed their natural forms also. She instantly recognised Bahman and Perviz, as they did her, and ran to embrace her. She returned their embraces and expressed her amazement. "What do you here, my dear brothers?" said she, and they told her they had been asleep. "Yes," replied she, "and if it had not been for me, perhaps you might have slept till the day of judgment. Do not you remember that you came to fetch the Talking Bird, the Singing Tree, and the Golden Water, and did not you see, as you came along, the place covered with black stones? Look and see if there be any now. The gentlemen and their horses who surround us, and you yourselves, were these black stones. If you desire to know how this wonder was performed," continued she, showing the pitcher, which she set down at the foot of the mountain, "it was done by virtue of the water which was in this pitcher, with which I sprinkled every stone. After I had made the Talking Bird (which you see in this cage) my slave, by his directions I found out the Singing Tree, a branch of which I have now in my hand; and the Golden Water, with which this flagon is filled; but being still unwilling to return without taking you with me, I constrained the Bird, by the power I had over him, to afford me the means. He told me where to find this pitcher, and the use I was to make of it."

The Princes Bahman and Perviz learned by this relation the obligation they had to their sister, as did all the other gentlemen, who expressed to her that, far from envying her happiness in the conquest she had made, and which they all had aspired to, they thought they could not better express their gratitude for restoring them to life again, than by declaring themselves her slaves, and that they were ready to obey her in whatever she should command.

"Gentlemen," replied the princess, "if you had given any attention to my words, you might have observed that I had no other intention in what I have done than to recover my brothers; therefore, if you have received any benefit, you owe me no obligation, and I have no further share in your compliment than your politeness toward me, for which I return you my thanks. In other respects, I regard each of you as quite as free as you were before your misfortunes, and I rejoice with you at the happiness which has accrued to you by my means. Let us, however, stay no longer in a place where we have nothing to detain us, but mount our horses and return to our respective homes."

The princess took her horse, which stood in the place where she had left him. Before she mounted, Prince Bahman desired her to give him the cage to carry. "Brother," replied the princess, "the Bird is my slave and I will carry him myself; if you will take the pains to carry the branch of the Singing Tree, there it is; only hold the cage while I get on horseback." When she had mounted her horse, and Prince Bahman had given her the cage, she turned about and said to Prince Perviz: "I leave the flagon of Golden Water to your care, if it will not be too much trouble for you to carry it," and Prince Perviz accordingly took charge of it with pleasure.

When Bahman, Perviz, and all the gentlemen had mounted their horses, the princess waited for some of them to lead the way. The two princes paid that compliment to the gentlemen, and they again to the princess, who, finding that none of them would accept the honour, but that it was reserved for her, addressed herself to them and said: "Gentlemen, I expect that some of you should lead the way:" to which one who was nearest to her, in the name of the rest, replied: "Madam, were we ignorant of the respect due to your sex, yet after what you have done for us there is no deference we would not willingly pay you, notwithstanding your modesty; we entreat you no longer to deprive us of the happiness of following you."

"Gentlemen," said the princess, "I do not deserve the honour you do me, and accept it only because you desire it." At the same time she led the way, and the two princes and the gentlemen followed.

This illustrious company called upon the dervish as they passed, to thank him for his reception and wholesome advice, which they had all found to be sincere. He was dead, however; whether of old age, or because he was no longer necessary to show the way to obtaining the three rarities, did not appear. They pursued their route, but lessened in their numbers every day. The gentlemen who, as we said before, had come from different countries, after severally repeating their obligations to the princess and her brothers, took leave of them one after another as they approached the road by which they had come.

As soon as the princess reached home, she placed the cage in the garden, and the Bird no sooner began to warble than he was surrounded by nightingales, chaffinches, larks, linnets, goldfinches, and every species of birds of the country. The branch of the Singing Tree was no sooner set in the midst of the parterre, a little distance from the house, than it took root and in a short time became a large tree, the leaves of which gave as harmonious a concert as those of the parent from which it was gathered. A large basin of beautiful marble was placed in the garden, and when it was finished, the princess poured into it all the Golden Water from the flagon, which instantly increased and swelled so much that it soon reached up to the edges of the basin, and afterward formed in the middle a fountain twenty feet high, which fell again into the basin perpetually, without running over.

The report of these wonders was presently spread abroad, and as the gates of the house and those of the gardens were shut to nobody, a great number of people came to admire them.

Some days after, when the Princes Bahman and Perviz had recovered from the fatigue of their journey, they resumed their former way of living; and as their usual diversion was hunting, they mounted their horses and went for the first time since their return, not to their own demesne, but two or three leagues from their house. As they pursued their sport, the emperor of Persia came in pursuit of game upon the same ground. When they perceived, by the number of horsemen in different places, that he would soon be up, they resolved to discontinue their chase, and retire to avoid encountering him; but in the very road they took they chanced to meet him in so narrow a way that they could not retreat without being seen. In their surprise they had only time to alight and prostrate themselves before the emperor, without lifting up their heads to look at him. The emperor, who saw they were as well mounted and dressed as if they had belonged to his court, had a curiosity to see their faces. He stopped and commanded them to rise. The princes rose up and stood before him with an easy and graceful air, accompanied with modest countenances. The emperor took some time to view them before he spoke, and after he had admired their good air and mien, asked them who they were and where they lived.

"Sir," said Prince Bahman, "we are the sons of the late intendant of your majesty's gardens, and live in a house which he built a little before he died, till we should be fit to serve your majesty and ask of you some employ when opportunity offered."

"By what I perceive," replied the emperor, "you love hunting." "Sir," replied Prince Bahman, "it is our common exercise, and what none of your majesty's subjects who intend to bear arms in your armies, ought, according to the ancient custom of the kingdom, to neglect." The emperor, charmed with so prudent an answer, said: "Since it is so, I should be glad to see your expertness in the chase; choose your own game."

The princes mounted their horses again and followed the emperor, but had not gone far before they saw many wild beasts together. Prince Bahman chose a lion and Prince Perviz a bear, and pursued them with so much intrepidity that the emperor was surprised. They came up with their game nearly at the same time, and darted their javelins with so much skill and address that they pierced the one the lion and the other the bear so effectually that the emperor saw them fall one after the other. Immediately afterward Prince Bahman pursued another bear, and Prince Perviz another lion, and killed them in a short time, and would have beaten out for fresh game, but the emperor would not let them, and sent to them to come to him. When they approached he said: "If I had given you leave, you would soon have destroyed all my game; but it is not that which I would preserve, but your persons; for I am so well assured your bravery may one time or other be serviceable to me, that from this moment your lives will be always dear to me."

The emperor, in short, conceived so great a kindness for the two princes, that he invited them immediately to make him a visit, to which Prince Bahman replied: "Your majesty does us an honour we do not deserve, and we beg you will excuse us."

The emperor, who could not comprehend what reason the princes could have to refuse this token of his favour, pressed them to tell him why they excused themselves. "Sir," said Prince Bahman, "we have a sister younger than ourselves, with whom we live in such perfect union, that we undertake nothing before we consult her, nor she anything without asking our advice." "I commend your brotherly affection," answered the emperor. "Consult your sister, meet me tomorrow, and give me an answer."

The princes went home, but neglected to speak of their adventure in meeting the emperor and hunting with him, and also of the honour he had done them, yet did not the next morning fail to meet him at the place appointed. "Well," said the emperor, "have you spoken to your sister, and has she consented to the pleasure I expect of seeing you?" The two princes looked at each other and blushed. "Sir," said Prince Bahman, "we beg your majesty to excuse us, for both my brother and I forgot." "Then remember today," replied the emperor, "and be sure to bring me an answer tomorrow."

The princes were guilty of the same fault a second time, and the emperor was so good-natured as to forgive their negligence; but to prevent their forgetfulness the third time, he pulled three little golden balls out of a purse, and put them into Prince Bahman's bosom. "These balls," said he, smiling, "will prevent your forgetting a third time what I wish you to do for my sake; since the noise they will make by falling on the floor when you undress will remind you, if you do not recollect it before." The event happened just as the emperor foresaw; and without these balls the princes had not thought of speaking to their sister of this affair, for as Prince Bahman unloosed his girdle to go to bed the balls dropped on the floor, upon which he ran into Prince Perviz's chamber, when both went into the Princess Periezade's apartment, and after they had asked her pardon for coming at so unseasonable a time, they told her all the circumstances of their meeting the emperor.

The princess was somewhat surprised at this intelligence. "Your meeting with the emperor," said she, "is happy and honourable and may in the end be highly advantageous to you, but it places me in an awkward position. It was on my account, I know, you refused the emperor, and I am infinitely obliged to you for doing so. I know by this that you would rather be guilty of incivility toward the emperor than violate the union we have sworn to each other. You judge right, for if you had once gone you would insensibly have been engaged to devote yourselves to him. But do you think it an easy matter absolutely to refuse the emperor what he seems so earnestly to desire? Monarchs will be obeyed in their desires, and it may be dangerous to oppose them; therefore, if to follow my inclination I should dissuade you from obeying him, it may expose you to his resentment, and may render myself and you miserable. These are my sentiments; but before we conclude upon anything let us consult the Talking Bird and hear what he says; he is penetrating, and has promised his assistance in all difficulties."

The princess sent for the cage, and after she had related the circumstances to the Bird in the presence of her brothers, asked him what they should do in this perplexity. The Bird answered: "The princes, your brothers, must conform to the emperor's pleasure, and in their turn invite him to come and see your house."

"But, Bird," replied the princess, "my brothers and I love one another, and our friendship is yet undisturbed. Will not this step be injurious to that friendship?" "Not at all," replied the Bird; "it will tend rather to cement it." "Then," answered the princess, "the emperor will see me." The Bird told her it was necessary he should, and that everything would go better afterward.

Next morning the princes met the emperor hunting, who asked them if they had remembered to speak to their sister. Prince Bahman approached and answered: "Sir, we are ready to obey you, for we have not only obtained our sister's consent with great ease, but she took it amiss that we should pay her that deference in a matter wherein our duty to your majesty was concerned. If we have offended, we hope you will pardon us." "Do not be uneasy," replied the emperor. "I highly approve of your conduct, and hope you will have the same deference and attachment to my person, if I have ever so little share in your friendship." The princes, confounded at the emperor's goodness, returned no other answer but a low obeisance.

The emperor, contrary to his usual custom, did not hunt long that day. Presuming that the princes possessed wit equal to their courage and bravery, he longed with impatience to converse with them more at liberty. He made them ride on each side of him, an honour which was envied by the grand vizier, who was much mortified to see them preferred before him.

When the emperor entered his capital, the eyes of the people, who stood in crowds in the streets, were fixed upon the two Princes Bahman and Perviz; and they were earnest to know who they might be.

All, however, agreed in wishing that the emperor had been blessed with two such handsome princes, and said that his children would have been about the same age, if the queen had not been so unfortunate as to lose them.

The first thing the emperor did when he arrived at his palace was to conduct the princes into the principal apartments, who praised without affectation the beauty and symmetry of the rooms, and the richness of the furniture and ornaments. Afterward a magnificent repast was served up, and the emperor made them sit with him, which they at first refused; but finding it was his pleasure, they obeyed.

The emperor, who had himself much learning, particularly in history, foresaw that the princes, out of modesty and respect, would not take the liberty of beginning any conversation. Therefore, to give them an opportunity, he furnished them with subjects all dinner-time. But whatever subject he introduced, they shewed so much wit, judgment, and discernment, that he was struck with admiration. "Were these my own children," said he to himself, "and I had improved their talents by suitable education, they could not have been more accomplished or better informed." In short, he took such great pleasure in their conversation, that, after having sat longer than usual, he led them into his closet, where he pursued his conversation with them, and at last said: "I never supposed that there were among my subjects in the country youths so well brought up, so lively, so capable; and I never was better pleased with any conversation than yours; but it is time now we should relax our minds with some diversion; and as nothing is more capable of enlivening the mind than music, you shall hear a vocal and instrumental concert which may not be disagreeable to you."

The emperor had no sooner spoken than the musicians, who had orders to attend, entered, and answered fully the expectations the princes had been led to entertain of their abilities. After the concerts, an excellent farce was acted, and the entertainment was concluded by dancers of both sexes.

The two princes, seeing night approach, prostrated themselves at the emperor's feet; and having first thanked him for the favours and honours he had heaped upon them, asked his permission to retire; which was granted by the emperor, who, in dismissing them, said: "I give you leave to go; but remember, you will be always welcome, and the oftener you come the greater pleasure you will do me."

Before they went out of the emperor's presence, Prince Bahman said: "Sir, may we presume to request that your majesty will do us and our sister the honour to pass by our house, and refresh yourself after your fatigue, the first time you take the diversion of hunting in that neighbourhood? It is not worthy of your presence; but monarchs sometimes have vouchsafed to take shelter in a cottage." "My children," replied the emperor, "your house cannot be otherwise than beautiful and worthy of its owners. I will call and see it with pleasure, which will be the greater for having for my hosts you and your sister, who is already dear to me from the account you give me of the rare qualities with which she is endowed: and this satisfaction I will defer no longer than tomorrow. Early in the morning I will be at the place where I shall never forget that I first saw you. Meet me, and you shall be my guides."

When the Princes Bahman and Perviz had returned home, they gave the princess an account of the distinguished reception the emperor had given them, and told her that they had invited him to do them the honour, as he passed by, to call at their house, and that he had appointed the next day.

"If it be so," replied the princess, "we must think of preparing a repast fit for his majesty; and for that purpose I think it would be proper we should consult the Talking Bird, who will tell us, perhaps, what meats the emperor likes best." The princes approved of her plan, and after they had retired she consulted the Bird alone. "Bird," said she, "the emperor will do us the honour tomorrow to come and see our house, and we are to entertain him; tell us what we shall do to acquit ourselves to his satisfaction."

"Good mistress," replied the Bird, "you have excellent cooks, let them do the best they can; but above all things, let them prepare a dish of cucumbers stuffed full of pearls, which must be set before the emperor in the first course before all the other dishes."

"Cucumbers stuffed full of pearls!" cried Princess Periezade with amazement; "surely, Bird, you do not know what you say; it is an unheard-of dish. The emperor may admire it as a piece of magnificence, but he will sit down to eat, and not to admire pearls; besides, all the pearls I possess are not enough for such a dish."

"Mistress," said the Bird, "do what I say, and be not uneasy about what may happen. Nothing but good will follow. As for the pearls, go early tomorrow morning to the foot of the first tree on your right hand in the park, dig under it, and you will find more than you want."

That night the princess ordered a gardener to be ready to attend her, and the next morning early, led him to the tree which the Bird had told her of, and bade him dig at its foot. When the gardener came to a certain depth, he found some resistance to the spade, and presently discovered a gold box about a foot square, which he showed the princess. "This," said she, "is what I brought you for; take care not to injure it with the spade."

When the gardener took up the box, he gave it into the princess's hands, who, as it was only fastened with neat little hasps, soon opened it, and found it full of pearls of a moderate size, but equal and fit for the use that was to be made of them. Very well satisfied with having found this treasure, after she had shut the box again, she put it under her arm and went back to the house, while the gardener threw the earth into the hole at the foot of the tree as it had been before.

The Princes Bahman and Perviz, who, as they were dressing themselves in their own apartments, saw their sister in the garden earlier than usual, as soon as they could get out went to her, and met her as she was returning with a gold box under her arm, which much surprised them. "Sister," said Bahman, "you carried nothing with you when we saw you before with the gardener, and now we see you have a golden box; is this some treasure found by the gardener, and did he come and tell you of it?" "No, brother," answered the princess, "I took the gardener to the place where this casket was concealed, and showed him where to dig; but you will be more amazed when you see what it contains."

The princess opened the box, and when the princes saw that it was full of pearls, which, though small, were of great value, they asked her how she came to the knowledge of this treasure. "Brothers," said she, "come with me and I will tell you." The princess, as they returned to the house, gave them an account of her having consulted the Bird, as they had agreed she should, and the answer he had given her; the objection she had raised to preparing a dish of cucumbers stuffed full of pearls, and how he had told her where to find this box. The sister and brothers formed many conjectures to penetrate into what the Bird could mean by ordering them to prepare such a dish; but after much conversation, they agreed to follow his advice exactly.

As soon as the princess entered the house, she called for the head cook; and after she had given him directions about the entertainment for the emperor, said to him: "Besides all this, you must dress an extraordinary dish for the emperor's own eating, which nobody else must have anything to do with besides yourself. This dish must be of cucumbers stuffed with these pearls:" and at the same time she opened him the box, and showed him the jewels.

The chief cook, who had never heard of such a dish, started back, and showed his thoughts by his looks; which the princess penetrating, said: "I see you take me to be mad to order such a dish, which one may say with certainty was never made. I know this as well as you; but I am not mad, and give you these orders with the most perfect recollection. You must invent and do the best you can, and bring me back what pearls are left." The cook could make no reply, but took the box and retired; and afterward the princess gave directions to all the domestics to have everything in order, both in the house and gardens, to receive the emperor.

Next day the two princes went to the place appointed, and as soon as the emperor of Persia arrived, the chase began and lasted till the heat of the sun obliged him to leave off. While Prince Bahman stayed to conduct the emperor to their house, Prince Perviz rode before to show the way, and when he came in sight of the house, spurred his horse, to inform the princess that the emperor was approaching; but she had been told by some servants whom she had placed to give notice, and the prince found her waiting ready to receive him.

When the emperor had entered the courtyard and alighted at the portico, the princess came and threw herself at his feet, and the two princes informed him she was their sister, and besought him to accept her respects.

The emperor stooped to raise her, and after he had gazed some time on her beauty, struck with her fine person and dignified air, he said: "The brothers are worthy of the sister, and she worthy of them; since, if I may judge of her understanding by her person, I am not amazed that the brothers would do nothing without their sister's consent; but," added he, "I hope to be better acquainted with you, my daughter, after I have seen the house."

"Sir," said the princess, "it is only a plain country residence, fit for such people as we are, who live retired from the great world. It is not to be compared with the magnificent palaces of emperors." "I cannot perfectly agree with you in opinion," said the emperor very obligingly, "for its first appearance makes me suspect you; however, I will not pass my judgment upon it till I have seen it all; therefore be pleased to conduct me through the apartments."

The princess led the emperor through all the rooms except the hall; and, after he had considered them very attentively, and admired their variety, "My daughter," said he to the princess, "do you call this a country house? The finest and largest cities would soon be deserted if all country houses were like yours. I am no longer surprised that you despise the town. Now let me see the garden, which I doubt not is answerable to the house."

The princess opened a door which led into the garden, and the first object which presented itself to the emperor's view was the golden fountain. Surprised at so rare an object, he asked from whence that wonderful water, which gave so much pleasure to behold, had been procured; where was its source, and by what art it was made to play so high. He said he would presently take a nearer view of it.

The princess then led him to the spot where the harmonious tree was planted; and there the emperor heard a concert, different from all he had ever heard before; and stopping to see where the musicians were, he could discern nobody far or near, but still distinctly heard the music which ravished his senses. "My daughter," said he to the princess, "where are the musicians whom I hear? Are they underground, or invisible in the air? Such excellent performers will hazard nothing by being seen; on the contrary, they would please the more."

"Sir," answered the princess, smiling, "they are not musicians, but the leaves of the tree your majesty sees before you, which form this concert; and if you will give yourself the trouble to go a little nearer, you will be convinced, and the voices will be the more distinct."

The emperor went nearer and was so charmed with the sweet harmony that he would never have been tired with hearing it, but that his desire to have a nearer view of the fountain of golden water forced him away. "Daughter," said he, "tell me, I pray you, whether this wonderful tree was found in your garden by chance, or was a present made to you, or have you procured it from some foreign country? It must certainly have come from a great distance, otherwise curious as I am after natural rarities I should have heard of it. What name do you call it by?"

"Sir," replied the princess, "this tree has no other name than that of the Singing Tree, and is not a native of this country. It would at present take up too much time to tell your majesty by what adventures it came here; its history is connected with the Golden Water and the Talking Bird, which came to me at the same time, and which your majesty may presently see. But if it be agreeable to your majesty, after you have rested yourself and recovered the fatigue of hunting, which must be the greater because of the sun's intense heat, I will do myself the honour of relating it to you."

"My daughter," replied the emperor, "my fatigue is so well recompensed by the wonderful things you have shown me, that I do not feel it in the least. Let me see the Golden Water, for I am impatient to see and admire afterward the Talking Bird."

When the emperor came to the Golden Water, his eyes were fixed so steadfastly upon the fountain, that he could not take them off. At last, addressing himself to the princess, he said: "As you tell me, daughter, that this water has no spring or communication, I conclude that it is foreign, as well as the Singing Tree."

"Sir," replied the princess, "it is as your majesty conjectures; and to let you know that this water has no communication with any spring, I must inform you that the basin is one entire stone, so that the water cannot come in at the sides or underneath. But what your majesty will think most wonderful is that all this water proceeded but from one small flagon, emptied into this basin, which increased to the quantity you see, by a property peculiar to itself, and formed this fountain." "Well," said the emperor, going from the fountain, "this is enough for one time. I promise myself the pleasure to come and visit it often; but now let us go and see the Talking Bird."

As he went toward the hall, the emperor perceived a prodigious number of singing birds in the trees around, filling the air with their songs and warblings, and asked why there were so many there and none on the other trees in the garden. "The reason, sir," answered the princess, "is because they come from all parts to accompany the song of the Talking Bird, which your majesty may see in a cage in one of the windows of the hall we are approaching; and if you attend, you will perceive that his notes are sweeter than those of any of the other birds, even the nightingale's."

The emperor went into the hall; and as the Bird continued singing, the princess raised her voice, and said, "My slave, here is the emperor, pay your compliments to him." The Bird left off singing that instant, when all the other birds ceased also, and said: "The emperor is welcome; God prosper him and prolong his life!" As the entertainment was served on the sofa near the window where the Bird was placed, the sultan replied, as he was taking his seat: "Bird, I thank you, and am overjoyed to find in you the sultan and king of birds."

As soon as the emperor saw the dish of cucumbers set before him, thinking they were prepared in the best manner, he reached out his hand and took one; but when he cut it, was in extreme surprise to find it stuffed with pearls. "What novelty is this?" said he; "and with what design were these cucumbers stuffed thus with pearls, since pearls are not to be eaten?" He looked at his hosts to ask them the meaning when the Bird interrupting him, said: "Can your majesty be in such great astonishment at cucumbers stuffed with pearls, which you see with your own eyes, and yet so easily believe that the queen, your wife, gave birth to a dog, a cat, and a piece of wood?" "I believed those things," replied the emperor, "because the attendants assured me of the facts." "Those attendants, sir," replied the Bird, "were the queen's two sisters, who, envious of her happiness in being preferred by your majesty before them, to satisfy their envy and revenge, have abused your majesty's credulity. If you interrogate them, they will confess their crime. The two brothers and the sister whom you see before you are your own children, whom they exposed, and who were taken in by the intendant of your gardens, who provided nurses for them, and took care of their education."

This speech presently cleared up the emperor's understanding. "Bird," cried he, "I believe the truth which you discover to me. The inclination which drew me to them told me plainly they must be of my own blood. Come then, my sons, come, my daughter, let me embrace you, and give you the first marks of a father's love and tenderness." The emperor then rose, and after having embraced the two princes and the princess, and mingled his tears with theirs, said: "It is not enough, my children; you must embrace each other, not as the children of the intendant of my gardens, to whom I have been so much obliged for preserving your lives, but as my own children, of the royal blood of the monarchs of Persia, whose glory, I am persuaded you will maintain."

After the two princes and princess had embraced mutually with new satisfaction, the emperor sat down again with them, and finished his meal in haste; and when he had done, said: "My children, you see in me your father; tomorrow I will bring the queen, your mother, therefore prepare to receive her."

The emperor afterward mounted his horse, and returned with expedition to his capitol. The first thing he did, as soon as he had alighted and entered his palace, was to command the grand vizier to seize the queen's two sisters. They were taken from their houses separately, convicted, and condemned to death; which sentence was put in execution within an hour.

In the meantime, the Emperor Kosrouschah, followed by all the lords of his court who were then present, went on foot to the door of the great mosque; and after he had taken the queen out of the strict confinement she had languished under for so many years, embracing her in the miserable condition to which she was then reduced, said to her with tears in his eyes: "I come to entreat your pardon for the injustice I have done you, and to make you the reparation I ought; which I have begun, by punishing the unnatural wretches who put the abominable cheat upon me; and I hope you will look upon it as complete, when I present to you two accomplished princes and a lovely princess, our children. Come and resume your former rank, with all the honours which are your due." All this was done and said before great crowds of people who flocked from all parts at the first news of what was passing, and immediately spread the joyful intelligence through the city.

Next morning early the emperor and queen, whose mournful humiliating dress was changed for magnificent robes, went with all their court to the house built by the intendant of the gardens, where the emperor presented the Princes Bahman and Perviz, and the Princess Periezade to their enraptured mother. "These, much injured wife," said he, "are the two princes your sons, and the princess your daughter; embrace them with the same tenderness I have done, since they are worthy both of me and you." The tears flowed plentifully down their cheeks at these tender embraces, especially the queen's, from the comfort and joy of having two such princes for her sons, and such a princess for her daughter, on whose account she had so long endured the severest afflictions.

The two princes and the princess had prepared a magnificent repast for the emperor and queen and their court. As soon as that was over, the emperor led the queen into the garden, and shewed her the Harmonious Tree and the beautiful effect of the Golden Fountain. She had seen the Bird in his cage, and the emperor had spared no panegyric in his praise during the repast.

When there was nothing to detain the emperor any longer, he took horse, and with the Princes Bahman and Perviz on his right hand, and the queen consort and the princess at his left, preceded and followed by all the officers of his court, according to their rank, returned to his capital. Crowds of people came out to meet them, and with acclamations of joy ushered them into the city, where all eyes were fixed not only upon the queen, and her royal children, but also upon the Bird, which the princess carried before her in his cage, admiring his sweet notes, which had drawn all the other birds about him, and followed him flying from tree to tree in the country, and from one house top to another in the city. The Princes Bahman and Perviz and the Princess Periezade were at length brought to the palace with pomp, and nothing was to be seen or heard all that night but illuminations and rejoicings both in the palace and in the utmost parts of the city, which lasted many days, and were continued throughout the empire of Persia, as intelligence of the joyful event reached the several provinces.

Tales of Animals & Mythical Creatures

IN TURKISH FAIRY TALES, clear divisions between humans, animals and spiritual beings are blurred. Humans learn the language of birds, fish become marriageable maidens, and good and evil spirits alternatively bless and thwart those with whom they interact.

It is not the diversity of these beings that is so surprising as much as the ease by which they move from one plane of existence to another. The worlds they inhabit, as becomes apparent, are not segmented, demarcated or otherwise kept apart. The rhetorical move to anthropomorphize creatures may be rooted in human-centricity and narcissism. It is, nevertheless, still a rummaging for what is true and real in overlooked places among alternative forms. Phantasmagoric monsters are the substance of nightmares, as well as a modality of communication. What people refuse to learn from each other might be better accepted when it comes from a non-human voice.

The Cinder-Youth
(Turkish)

ONCE UPON A TIME that was no time, in the days when the servants of Allah were many and the misery of man was great, there lived a poor woman who had three sons and one daughter. The youngest son was half-witted, and used to roll about all day in the warm ashes.

One day the two elder brothers went out to plough, and said to their mother: "Boil us something, and send our sister out with it into the field." – Now the three-faced devil had pitched his tent close to this field, and in order that the girl might not come near them, he determined to persuade her to go all round about instead of straight to them.

The mother cooked the dinner and the girl went into the field with it, but the devil contrived to make her lose her road, so that she wandered further and further away from the place where she wanted to go. At last, when her poor head was quite confused, the devil's wife appeared before her and asked the terrified girl what she meant by trespassing there. Then she talked her over and persuaded her to come home with her, that she might hide her from the vengeance of the devil, her husband.

But the three-faced devil had got home before them, and when they arrived the old woman told the girl to make haste and get something ready to eat while her maid-servant stirred up the fire. But scarcely had she begun to get the dish ready than the devil crept stealthily up behind her, opened his mouth wide, and swallowed the girl whole, clothes and all.

Meanwhile her brothers were waiting in the field for their dinner, but neither the damsel nor the victuals appeared. Afternoon came and went and evening too, and then the lads went home, and when they heard from their mother that their sister had gone to seek them early in the morning, they suspected what had happened – their little sister must have fallen into the hands of the devil. The two elder brothers did not think twice about it, but the elder of them set off at once to seek his sister.

He went on and on, puffing at his chibook, sniffing the perfume of flowers and drinking coffee, till he came to an oven by the wayside. By the oven sat an old man, who asked the youth on what errand he was bent. The youth told him of his sister's case, and said he was going in search of the three-faced devil, and would not be content till he had killed him. "Thou wilt never be able to slay the devil," said the man, "till thou hast eaten of bread that has been baked in this oven." The youth thought this no very difficult matter, took the loaves out of the oven, but scarcely had he bitten a piece out of one of them than the oven, the man, and the loaves all disappeared before his eyes, and the bit he had taken swelled within him so that he nearly burst.

The youth hadn't gone two steps further on when he saw on the highway a large cauldron, and the cauldron was full of wine. A man was sitting in front of the cauldron, and he asked him the way, and told him the tale of the devil. "Thou wilt never be able to cope with the devil," said the man, "if thou dost not drink of this wine." The youth drank, but: "Woe betide my stomach, woe betide my bowels!" for so plagued was he that he could not have stood upright if he had not seen two bridges before him. One of these bridges was of wood and the other was of iron, and beyond the two bridges were two apple trees, and one bore unripe bitter apples and the other sweet ripe ones.

The three-faced devil was waiting on the road to see which bridge he would choose, the wooden or the iron one, and which apples he would eat, the sour or the sweet ones. The youth went along the iron bridge, lest the wooden one might break down, and plucked the sweet apples, because the green ones were bitter. That was just what the devil wanted him to do, and he at once sent his mother to meet the youth and entice him into his house as he had done his sister, and it was not long before he also found his way into the devil's belly.

And next in order, the middling brother, not wishing to be behind-hand, also went in search of his kinsmen. He also could not eat of the bread his inside also was plagued by the wine, he went across the iron bridge and ate of the sweet apples, and so he also found his way into the devil's belly. Only the youngest brother who lay among the ashes remained. His mother besought him not to forsake her in her old age.

If the others had gone he at least could remain and comfort her, she said. But the youth would not listen. "I will not rest," said Cinderer, "till I have found the three lost ones, my two brothers and my sister, and slain the devil." Then he rose from his chimney corner, and no sooner had he shaken the ashes from off him than such a tempest arose that all the labourers at work in the fields left their ploughs where they stood, and ran off as far as their eyes could see. Then the youngest son gathered together the ploughshares and bade a blacksmith make a lance of them, but a lance of such a kind as would fly into the air and come back again to the hand that hurled it without breaking its iron point. The smith made the lance, and the youth hurled it. Up into the air flew the lance, but when it came down again on to the tip of his little finger it broke to pieces. Then the youth shook himself still more violently in the ashes, and again the labourers in the field fled away before the terrible tempest which immediately arose, and the youth gathered together a still greater multitude of ploughshares and took them to the smith. The smith made a second lance, and that also flew up into the air and broke to pieces when it came down again. Then the youth shook himself in the ashes a third time, and such a hurricane arose that there was scarce a ploughshare in the whole countryside that was not carried away. It was only with great difficulty that the smith could make the third lance, but when that came down on the youth's finger it did not break in pieces like the others. "This will do pretty well," said the youth, and catching up the lance he went forth into the wide world.

He went on and on and on till he also came to the oven and the cauldron. The men who guarded the oven and the cauldron stopped him and asked him his business, and on finding out that he was going to kill the devil, they told the youth that he must first eat the bread of the oven and then drink the wine in the cauldron if he could. The son of the cinders wished for nothing better. He ate the loaves that were baked in the oven, drank all the wine, and further on he saw the wooden bridge and the iron bridge, and beyond the bridges the apple-trees.

The devil had observed the youth from afar, and his courage began to ooze out of him when he saw the deeds of the son of the ashes. "Any fool can go across the iron bridge," thought the youth. "I'll go across the wooden one." And as it was no very great feat to eat the sweet apples, he ate the sour ones. "There will be no joking with this one," said the devil. "I see I must get ready my lance and measure my strength with him."

The son of the ashes saw the devil from afar and, full of the knowledge of his own valour, went straight up to him.

"If thou doest not homage to me, I'll swallow thee straight off," cried the devil.

"And if thou doest not homage to me, I'll knock thee to pieces with my lance," replied the youth.

"Oh ho! if we're so brave as all that," cried the three-faced monster, "let us out with our lances without losing any more time."

So the devil out with his lance, whirled it round his head, and aimed it with all his might at the youth, who gave but one little twist with his finger, and crick-crack! the devil's lance broke all to bits. "Now it's my turn," cried the son of the cinders; and he hurled his lance at the devil with such force that the devil's first soul flew out of his nose. "At it again once more, if thou art a man," yelled the devil, with a great effort. "Not I," cried the youth, "for my mother only bore me once," whereupon the devil breathed forth his last soul also. Then the youth went on to seek the devil's wife. Her also he chased down the road after her husband, and when he had cut them both in two, lo and behold! all three of his kinsfolk stood before him, so he turned back home and took them with him. Now his brothers and sister had grown very thirsty in the devil's belly, and when they saw a large well by the wayside, they asked their brother Cinder-son to draw them a little water. Then the youths took off their girdles, tied them together, and let down the biggest brother, but he had scarcely descended more than half-way down when he began to shriek unmercifully: "Oh, oh, draw me up, I have had enough," so that they had to pull him up and let the second brother try. And with him it fared the same way. "Now 'tis my turn," cried Cinder-son, "but mind you do not pull me up, however loudly I holloa." So they let down the youngest brother, and he too began to holloa and bawl, but they paid no heed to it, and let him down till he stood on the dry bottom of the well. A door stood before him, he opened it, and there were three lovely damsels sitting in a room together, and each of them shone like the moon when she is only fourteen days old. The three damsels were amazed at the sight of the youth. How durst he come into the devil's cavern? they asked – and they begged and besought him to escape as he valued dear life. But the youth would not budge at any price, till he had got the better of this devil also. The end of the matter was that he slew the devil and released the three damsels, who were Sultans' daughters, and had been stolen from their fathers and kept here for the last seven years. The two elder princesses he intended for his two brothers, but the youngest, who was also the loveliest, he chose for himself and, filling the pitcher with water, he brought the damsels to the bottom of the well, right below the mouth of it.

First of all he let them draw up the eldest princess for his eldest brother, then he made them pull up the middling princess for his middling brother, and then it came to the youngest damsel's turn. But she desired that the youth should be drawn up at all hazards and herself afterwards. "Thy brethren," she explained, "will be wroth with thee for keeping the loveliest damsel for thyself, and will not draw thee out of the well for sheer jealousy."

"I'll find my way out even then," answered the youth, and though she begged and besought him till there was no more soul in her, he would not listen to her. Then the damsel drew from her breast a casket and said to the youth: "If any mischief befall thee, open this casket. Inside it is a piece of flint, and if thou strike it once a black efrit will appear before thee and fulfil all thy desires. If thy brethren leave thee in the well, go to the palace of the devil and stand by the well. Two rams come there every day, a black one and a white one; if thou cling fast to the white one, thou wilt come to the surface of the earth, but if thou cling on to the black one, thou wilt sink down into the seventh world."

Then he let them draw up the youngest damsel, and no sooner did his brethren see their brother's bride and perceive that she was the loveliest of all, than jealousy overtook them, and in their wrath they left him in the well and went home with the damsels.

So what else could the poor youth at the bottom of the well do than go back to the devil's palace, stand by the well, and wait for the two rams? Not very long afterwards a white ram came bounding along before him, and after that a black ram, and the youth, instead of catching hold of the white ram, seized the black one and immediately perceived that he was at the bottom of the seventh world…He went on and on, he went for a long time and he went for a short time, he went by day and he went by night, he went up hill and down dale till he could do no more, and stopped short by a large tree to take a little rest. But what was that he saw before him? A large serpent was gliding up the trunk of the tree and would have devoured all the young birds on the tree if Cinder-son had let him. But the youth quickly drew forth his lance and cut the serpent in two with a single blow. Then, like one who has done his work well, he lay down at the foot of the tree, and inasmuch as he was tired and it was warm he fell asleep at once.

Now while he slept, the emerald Anka, who is the mother of the birds and the Padishah of the Peris, passed by that way, and when she saw the sleeping youth she fancied him to be her enemy, who was wont to destroy her children year by year. She was about to cut him to pieces, when the birds whispered to her not to hurt the youth, because he had killed their enemy the serpent. It was only then that the Anka perceived the two halves of the serpent. And now, lest anything should harm the sleeping youth, she hopped round and round him, and touched him softly and sheltered him with both her wings lest the sun should scorch him, and when he awoke from his sleep the wing of the bird was spread over him like a tent. And now the Anka approached him and said she would fain reward him for his good deed, and he might make a request of her. Then replied the youth: "I would fain get to the surface of the earth again."

"Be it so," said the emerald bird, "but first thou must get forty tons of ox-flesh and forty pitchers of water and sit on my back with them, so that when I say 'Gik!' thou mayest give me to eat, and when I say 'Gak!' thou mayest give me to drink."

Then the youth bethought him of his casket, took the flint-stone out of it, and struck it once, and immediately a black efrit with a mouth as big as the world stood before him and said: "What dost thou command, my Sultan?" – "Forty tons of ox-flesh, and forty pitchers of water," said the youth. In a short time the efrit brought the flesh and the water, and the youth packed it all up together and mounted on the wing of the bird. Off they went, and whenever the Anka cried "Gik!" he gave her flesh, and whenever she cried "Gak!" he gave her water. They flew from one layer of worlds to the next, till in a short time they got above the surface of the earth again, and he dismounted from the bird's back and said to her: "Wait here a while, and in a short time I shall be back."

Then the youth took out his coffer, struck the flint-stone, and bade the black bounding efrit get him tidings of the three sisters. In a short time the efrit reappeared with the three damsels, who were preparing a banquet for the brothers. He made them all sit on the bird's back, took with him again forty tons of ox-flesh and forty pitchers of water, and away they all went to the land of the three damsels. Every time the Anka said "Gik!" he gave her flesh to eat, and every time she said "Gak!" he gave her water to drink. But as the youth now had three with him besides himself, it came to pass that the flesh ran short, so that when the Anka said "Gik!" once more he had nothing to give her. Then the youth drew his knife, cut a piece of flesh out of his thigh, and stuffed it into the bird's mouth. The Anka perceived that it was human flesh and did not eat it, but kept it in her mouth, and when they had reached the realm of the three damsels, the bird told him that he might now go in peace.

But the poor youth could not move a step because of the smart in his leg. "Thou go on first," he said to the bird, "but I will first rest me here a while."

"Nay, but thou art a droll rogue," quoth the bird, and with that it spit out of its mouth the piece of human flesh and put it back in its proper place just as if it had never been cut out.

The whole city was amazed at the sight of the return of the Sultan's daughters. The old Padishah could scarce believe his own eyes. He looked and looked and then he embraced the first princess; he looked and looked and then he kissed the second princess, and when they had told him the story he gave his whole kingdom and his three daughters to Cinder-son. Then the youth sent for his mother and his sister, and they all sat down to the banquet together. Moreover, he found his sister a husband who was the son of the Vizier, and for forty days and forty nights they were full of joyfulness.

The Forty Princes and the
Seven-Headed Dragon
(Turkish)

THERE WAS ONCE UPON A TIME a Padishah, and this Padishah had forty sons. All day long they disported themselves in the forest, snaring birds and hunting beasts, but when the youngest of them was fourteen years old, their father wished to marry them. So he sent for them all and told them his desire. "We will marry," said the forty brothers, "but only when we find forty sisters who are the daughters of the same father and the same mother." Then the Padishah searched the whole realm through to find forty such sisters, but though he found families of thirty-nine sisters, families of forty sisters he could never find.

"Let the fortieth of you take another wife," said the Padishah to his sons. But the forty brothers would not agree thereto, and they begged their father to allow them to go and search if haply they might find what they wanted in another empire. What could the Padishah do? He could not refuse them their request, so he gave them his permission. But before they departed, he summoned them into his presence, and this is what their father the Padishah said to them: "I have three things to say to you, which bear ye well in mind. When ye come in your journey to a large spring, take heed not to pass the night near it. Beyond the spring is a caravanserai; there also ye must not abide. Beyond the caravanserai is a vast desert; and there also ye must not take a moment's rest." The sons promised their father that they would keep his words, and with baggage light of weight but exceedingly precious, they took horse and set out on their journey.

They went on and on, they smoked their chibooks and drank forty cups of coffee, and when evening descended the large spring was right before them. "Verily," began the elder brethren, "we will not go another step further. We are weary, and the night is upon us, and what need forty men fear?" And with that they dismounted from their horses, ate their suppers, and laid them down to rest. Only the youngest brother, who was fourteen years of age, remained awake.

It might have been near midnight when the youth heard a strange noise. He caught up his arms and, turning in the direction of the sound, saw before him a seven-headed dragon. They rushed towards each other, and thrice the dragon fell upon the prince, but could do him no harm. "Well, now it is my turn," cried the youth. "Wilt thou be converted to the true faith?" And with these words he struck the monster such a blow that six of his seven heads came flying down.

"Strike me once more," groaned the dragon.

"Not I," replied the youth. "I myself only came into the world once." Immediately the dragon fell to pieces, but his one remaining head began to roll and roll and roll till it stood on the brink of the well. "Whoever can take my soul out of this well," it said, "shall have my treasure also," and with these words the head bounded into the well.

The youth took a rope, fastened one end of it to a rock and, seizing the other end himself, lowered himself into the well. At the bottom of the well he found an iron door. He opened it, passed through, and there right before him stood a palace compared with which his father's palace was a hovel. Into this palace he went, and in it were forty rooms, and in each room was a damsel sitting by her embroidery frame with enormous treasures behind her. "Art thou a man or a spirit?" cried the terrified damsels. "A man am I, and the son of a man," replied the prince. "I have just slain a seven-headed dragon, and have followed its rolling head hither."

Oh, how the forty damsels rejoiced at hearing these words. They embraced the youth, and begged and prayed him not to leave them there. They were the children of one father and one mother, they said. The dragon had killed their parents and carried them off, and they had nobody to look to in the whole wide world.

"We also are forty," said the youth, "and we are seeking forty damsels." Then he told them that he would first of all ascend to his brethren, and then he would come for them again. So he ascended out of the well, went to the spring, lay down beside it and fell asleep.

Early in the morning the forty brothers arose and laughed at their father for trying to frighten them with the well. Again they set out on their way, and went on and on till evening overtook them, when they perceived a caravanserai before them. "Not a step further will we go," said the elder brothers. The youngest brother indeed insisted that it would be well to remember their father's words, for his speech could surely not have been in vain. But they laughed at their youngest brother, ate and drank, said their prayers, and lay down to sleep. Only the youngest brother remained wide awake.

About midnight he again heard a noise. The youth snatched up his arms, and again he saw before him a seven-headed dragon, but much larger than the former one. The dragon rushed at him first of all, but could not overcome him, then the youth dealt him one blow and off went six of the dragon's heads. Then the dragon wished him to take one more blow, but he would not; the head rolled into a well, the youth went after it, and came upon a palace larger than the former one, and with ever so much more treasures and precious things in it. He marked the well so that he should know it again, returned to his brothers and, wearied out with his great combat, slept so soundly that his brothers had to wake him up with blows next morning.

Again they arose, took horse, went up hill and down dale, and just as the sun was setting, behold! a vast desert stood before them. They fell to eating straightway, drank their fill also, and were just going to lie down to sleep when all at once such a roaring, such a bellowing arose that the very mountains fell down from their places.

The princes were horribly afraid, especially when they saw coming against them a gigantic seven-headed dragon. He vomited forth venomous fire in his wrath, and roared furiously: "Who killed my two brothers? Hither with him! I'll try conclusions with him also!"

The youngest brother saw that his brethren were more dead than alive from fear, so he gave them the keys of the two wells, in one of which was the vast heap of treasure, and in the other the forty damsels. Let them take everything home, he said; as for himself, he must first slay the dragon and then he would follow after them. The thirty-nine brothers lost no time in mounting their horses and galloping off. They drew the treasure out of one well and the forty damsels out of the other, and so returned home to their father. But now we will see what happened to the youngest brother.

He fought the dragon and the dragon fought him, but neither could get the better of the other. The dragon perceived that it was vain to try and vanquish the youth, so he said to him: "If thou wilt go to the Empire of Chin-i-Machin and fetch me thence the Padishah's daughter, I will not worry the life out of thee." To this the prince readily agreed, for he could not have sustained the conflict much longer.

Then Champalak, for that was the dragon's name, gave the prince a bridle and said to him: "A good steed comes hither to feed every day; seize him, put this bridle in his mouth, and bid him take thee to the Empire of Chin-i-Machin!" So the youth took the bridle and waited for the good charger. Presently a golden-maned charger came flying through the air, and the moment the prince had put the bridle in its mouth, the charger said: "What dost thou command, little Sultan?" and before you could wink your eyes, the Empire of Chin-i-Machin stood before him. Then he dismounted from his horse, took off the bridle, and went into the town. There he entered into an old woman's hut and asked her whether she received guests. "Willingly," answered the old woman. Then she made ready a place for him, and while he was sipping his coffee he asked her all about the talk of the town. "Well," said the old woman, "a seven-headed dragon is very much in love with our Sultan's daughter. A war has been raging between them on that account these many years, and the monster presses us so hardly that not even a bird can fly into our realm."

"Then where is the Sultan's daughter?" asked the youth. "In a little palace in the Padishah's garden," replied the old woman, "and the poor thing dare not put her foot outside it."

The next day the youth went to the Padishah's garden, and asked the gardener to take him as a servant, and he begged and prayed till the gardener had not the heart to refuse him. "Very well, I will take thee," said he, "and thou wilt have nought to do but water the flowers of the garden."

Now the Sultan's daughter saw the youth, called him to her window, and asked him how he had managed to reach that realm. Then the youth told her that his father was a Padishah, that he had fought with the dragon

Champalak on his travels, and had promised to bring him the Sultan's daughter. "Yet fear thou nothing," added the youth. "My love is stronger than the love of the serpent, and if thou wilt only have the courage to come with me, trust me to find a way of disposing of him."

The damsel was so much in love with the prince, and so eager to escape from her captivity, that she consented to trust herself to him, and one night they escaped from her palace and went straight towards the desert, where dwelt the dragon Champalak. They agreed on the way that the girl should find out what the dragon's talisman was, that they might destroy him that way if they could do it no other.

Imagine the joy of Champalak when he perceived the princess! "What joy, what rapture, that thou hast come!" cried Champalak; but fondle her and caress her as he might, the damsel did nothing but weep. Days passed by, weeks passed by, and yet the tears never left the damsel's eyes. "Tell me at least what thy talisman is," said the damsel to him one day, "if thou wouldst see me happy and not wretched with thee all thy days."

"Alas, my soul!" said the dragon. "My talisman is guarded in a place whither it is impossible ever to come. It is in a large palace in a neighbouring realm, and though one may venture thither for it, no one has ever been able to get back again."

The prince needed no more; that was quite good enough for him. He took his bridle, went with it to the seashore, and summoned his golden-maned steed. "What dost thou command me, little Sultan?" said the steed. "I desire thee to convey me to the neighbouring realm, to the palace of the talisman of the dragon Champalak," cried the youth – and in no more time than it takes to wink an eye, the palace stood before him.

Then the steed said to the youth: "When we reach the palace thou wilt tie the bridle to two iron gates, and when I neigh once and strike my iron hoofs together, a door will open. In this open door thou wilt see a lion's throat, and if thou canst not kill that lion at one stroke, escape, or thou art a dead man." With that they went up to the palace, he tied the horse to the two iron gates by his bridle, and when he neighed the door flew open. The youth struck with all his might at the gaping throat of the lion in the doorway and split it right in two. Then he cut open the lion's belly, and drew out of it a little gold cage with three doves in it, so beautiful that the like of them is not to be found in the wide world. He took one of them and began softly stroking and caressing it, when all at once – pr-r-r-r! – away it flew out of his hand. The steed galloped swiftly after it, and if he had not caught it and wrung its neck it would have gone hard with the good youth.

Then he mounted his steed again, and in the twinkling of an eye he stood once more before Champalak's palace. In the gateway of the palace he killed the second dove, so that when the youth entered the dragon's room, there the monster lay quite helpless, and there was no more spirit in him at all. When he saw the dove in the youth's hand he implored him to let him stroke it for the last time before he died. The youth's heart felt for him, and he was just about to hand the bird to him when the princess rushed out, snatched the dove from his hand, and killed it, whereupon the dragon expired before their very eyes. "'Twas well for thee," said the steed, "that thou didst not give him the dove, for if he had got it, fresh life would have flowed into him." And with that the steed disappeared, bridle and all.

Then they got together the dragon's treasures, and went with them to the Empire of Chin-i-Machin. The Padishah was sick for grief at the loss of the damsel, and after searching for her in all parts of the kingdom in vain, was persuaded that she had fallen into the hands of the dragon. And lo! there she stood before him now, hand in hand with the King's son. Then there was such a marriage-feast in that city that it seemed as if there was no end to it. After the marriage they set out on their journey again, and travelled with a great escort of soldiers to the prince's father. There they had long held the King's son to be dead, and would not believe that it was he even now till he had told them the tale of the three seven-headed dragons and the forty damsels.

The fortieth damsel was waiting patiently for him there, and the prince said to his wife: "Behold now my second bride!" – "Thou didst save my life from the dragon," replied the Princess of Chin-i-Machin. "I therefore give her to thee; do as thou wilt with her!" So they made a marriage-feast for the second bride also, and they spent half their days in the Empire of the prince's father, and the other half in the Empire of Chin-i-Machin, and their lives flowed away in happiness.

The Wind-Demon
(Turkish)

THERE WAS ONCE UPON A TIME an old Padishah who had three sons and three daughters. One day the old man fell ill, and though they called all the leeches together to help him, his disease would not take a turn for the better. "I already belong to Death," he thought, and calling to him his sons and daughters, he thus addressed them: "If I die, he among you shall be Padishah who watches three nights at my tomb. As for my daughters, I give them to him who first comes to woo them." And with that he died, and was buried as became a Padishah.

Now, as the realm could have a Padishah in no other way, the eldest son went to his father's tomb and sat there for half the night, said his prayers upon his carpet, and awaited the dawn. But all at once a horrible din arose in the midst of the darkness, and so frightened was he that he snatched up his slippers and never stopped till he got home. The next night the middling son also went out to the tomb, and he also sat there for half the night, but no sooner did he hear the great din than he too caught up his slippers and hurried off homewards. So it now came to the turn of the third and youngest son.

The third son took his sword, stuck it in his girdle, and went off to the tomb. Sure enough, when he had sat there till midnight, he heard the horrible din, and so horrible was it that the very earth trembled. The youth pulled himself together, went straight towards the spot from whence the noise came loudest, and behold! right in front of him stood a huge dragon. Drawing his sword, the youth fell upon the dragon so furiously that at last the monster had scarcely strength enough left to say: "If thou art a man, put thy heel upon me and strike me with thy sword but once more!"

"Not I," cried the King's son. "My mother only bore me into the world once" – whereupon the dragon yielded up its filthy soul. The King's son would have cut off the beast's ears and nose, but he could not see very well in the dark, and began groping about for them, when all at once he saw afar off a little shining light. He went straight towards it, and there in the midst of the brightness he saw an old man. Two globes were in his hand, one black and the other white; the black globe he was turning round and round, and from the white globe proceeded the light.

"What art thou doing, old father?" asked the King's son.

"Alas! my son," replied the old man, "my business is my bane. I hold fast the nights and let go the days." – "Alas! my father," replied the King's son, "my task is even greater than thine." With that he tied together the old man's arms, so that he might not let go the days, and went on still further to seek the light. He went on and on till he came to the foot of a castle wall, and forty men were taking counsel together beneath it.

"What's the matter?" inquired the King's son. "We should like to go into the castle to steal the treasure," said the forty men, "but we don't know how."

"I would very soon help you if you only gave me a little light," said the King's son. This the robbers readily promised to do, and after that he took a packet of nails, knocked them into the castle wall, row after row, right up to the top, clambered up himself, and then shouted down to them: "Now you come up one by one, just as I have done."

So the robbers caught hold of the nails and began to clamber up, one after another, the whole forty of them. But the youth was not idle. He drew his sword, and the moment each one of them reached the top, he chopped off his head and pitched his body into the courtyard, and so he did to the whole forty. Then he leaped down into the courtyard himself, and there right before him was a beautiful palace; and no sooner had he opened the door than a serpent glided past him, and crawled up a column close by the staircase. The youth drew his sword to strike the serpent; he struck and cut the serpent in two, but his sword remained in the stone wall, and he forgot to draw it out again. Then he mounted the staircase and went into a room, and there lay a lovely damsel asleep. So he went out again, closed the door very softly behind him, and ascended to the second flight, and went into a room there, and before him lay a still lovelier damsel on a bed. This door he also closed, and went up to the third and topmost flight, and opened a door there also, and lo! the whole room was piled up with nothing but steel, and such a splendid damsel lay asleep there that, if the King's son had had a thousand hearts, he would have loved her with them all. This door he also closed, remounted the castle wall, re-descended on the other side by means of the nails, which he took out as he descended, and so reached the ground again. Then he went straight up to the old man whose arms he had tied together. "Oh, my son!" cried he from afar, "thou hast remained a long time away. Everybody's side will be aching from so much lying down." Then the youth untied his arms, the old man let the white globes of day move round again, and the youth went up to the dragon, cut off its ears and nose, and put them in his knapsack. Then he went back to the palace, and when he drew nigh to it, he found that they had made his eldest brother Padishah. However, he let it be and said nothing.

Not very long afterwards a lion came to the palace, and went straight up to the Padishah. "What dost thou want?" asked the Padishah. "I want thy eldest sister to wife," replied the lion. "I give not my sister to a brute beast," said the Padishah, and forthwith they began chasing the lion away; but now the King's son appeared and said: "Such was not our father's will, but he said we were to give her to whomsoever asked for her." With that they brought the damsel and gave her to the lion, and he took her and was gone.

The next day came a tiger, and demanded the middling daughter from the Padishah. The two elder brethren would by no means give her up, but again the youngest brother insisted that they should do so, as it was their father's wish. So they sent for the damsel and gave her to the tiger.

On the third day a bird alighted in the palace, and said that he must have the youngest of the Sultan's daughters. The Padishah and the second brother were again unwilling to agree to it, but the youngest brother stood them out that the bird ought to be allowed to fly back with his sister. Now this bird was the Padishah of the Peris, the emerald Anka. But now let us see what happened in that castle of which we have before spoken.

In this castle there dwelt just about this time a Padishah and his three daughters. Rising one morning and going out, he saw a man walking in the palace. He went out into the courtyard, and saw a serpent cut in two on the staircase, and a sword sticking in the stone column, and going on still further, and searching in all directions, he perceived the bodies of the forty robbers in his castle moat. "Not an enemy, but only the hand of a friend could have done this," thought he, "and he has saved me from the robbers and the serpent. The sword is my good friend's, but where is the sword's master?" And he took counsel with his Vizier.

"Oh, we'll soon get to the bottom of that," said the Vizier. "Let us make a great bath, and invite everyone to come and bathe in it for nothing. We will watch carefully each single man, and whosoever has a sheath without a sword will be the man who has saved us." And the Padishah did so. He made ready a big bath, and the whole realm came and bathed in it.

Next day the Vizier said to him: "Everyone has been here to bathe save only the King's three sons; they still remain behind." Then the Padishah sent word to the King's three sons to come and bathe, and, looking closely at their garments, he perceived that the youngest of the three wore a sheath without a sword.

Then the Padishah called the King's son to him and said: "Great is the good thou hast done to me; ask me what thou wilt for it!" – "I ask nought from thee," replied the King's son, "but thy youngest daughter."

"Alas! my son, ask me anything but that," sighed the Padishah. "Ask my crown, my kingdom, and I'll give them to thee, but my daughter I cannot give thee."

"If thou givest me thy daughter, I will take her," replied the King's son, "but nought else will I take from thy hand."

"My son," groaned the Padishah, "I will give thee my eldest daughter, I'll give thee my second daughter, nay, I'll give thee the pair of them if thou wilt. But my youngest daughter has a deadly enemy, the Wind-Demon. Because I would not give her to him, I must needs fence her room about with walls of steel, lest any of the devil race draw near to her. For the Wind-Demon is such a terrible monster that eye cannot see nor dart overtake him; like the tempest he flies, and his coming is like the coming of a whirlwind."

But whatever the Padishah might say to turn him from seeking after the damsel fell on deaf ears. He begged and pleaded so hard for the damsel that the Padishah was wearied by his much speaking, and promised him the damsel, nay they held the bridal banquet. The two elder brothers received the two elder damsels, and returned to their kingdom, but the youngest brother remained behind to guard his wife against the Wind-Demon.

Time came and went, and the King's son avoided the light of day for the sake of his lovely Sultana. One day, however, the King's son said to his wife: "Behold now, my Sultana, all this time I have never moved from thy side; methinks I will go a-hunting, though it only be for a little hour or so."

"Alas! my King," replied his wife, "if thou dost depart from me, I know that thou wilt never see me more." But as he begged her for leave again and again, and promised to be back again immediately, his wife consented. Then he took his weapons and went forth into the forest.

Now the Wind-Demon had been awaiting this chance all along. He feared the famous prince, and durst not snatch his wife from his arms; but as soon as ever the King's son had put his foot out of doors, the Wind-Demon came in and vanished with the wife of the King's son.

Not very long afterwards the King's son came back, and could find his wife nowhere. He went to the Padishah to seek her, and came back again, for it was certain that the Demon must have taken her; no other living soul could have got near her. Bitterly did he weep, fiercely did he dash himself against the floor, but then he quickly rose up again, took horse, and galloped away into the wide world, determined to find either death or his consort.

He went on for days, he went on for weeks; in his trouble and anguish he gave himself no rest. All at once a palace sprang up before him, but it seemed to him like a mirage, which baffles the eye that looks upon it. It was the palace of his eldest sister. The damsel was just then looking out of the window, and lo! she caught sight of a man wandering there where never a bird had flown and never a caravan had travelled. Then she recognized him as her brother, and so great was their mutual joy that they could not come to words for hugging and kissing.

Towards evening the damsel said to the King's son: "The lion will be here shortly, and although he is very good to me, he is only a brute beast for all that, and may do thee a mischief." And she took her brother and hid him.

In the evening the lion came home sure enough, and when they had sat down together and begun to talk, the girl asked him what he would do if any of her brothers should chance to come there. "If the eldest were to come," said the lion, "I would strike him dead with one blow, if the second came I would slay him also, but if the youngest came, I would let him go to sleep on my paws if he liked."

"Then he has come," said his wife.

"Where is he – where is he? Bring him out, let me see him!" cried the lion; and when the King's son appeared, the lion did not know what to do with himself for joy. Then they began to talk, and the lion asked him why he had come there, and whither he was going. The youth told him what had happened, and said he was going to seek the Wind-Demon.

"I know but the rumour of him," said the lion, "but take my word for it: thou hadst better have nothing to do with him, for there is none that can cope with the Wind-Demon." But the King's son would not listen to reason, remained there that night, and next morning mounted his horse again. The lion accompanied him to show him the right way, and then they parted, one going to the right and the other to the left.

Again he went on and on, till he saw another palace, and this was the palace of his middling sister. The damsel saw from the window that a man was on the road, and no sooner did she recognize him than she rushed out to meet him, and led him into the palace. Full of joy, they conversed together till the evening, and then the damsel said to the youth: "In a short time my tiger-husband will be here, I'll hide thee from him, lest a mischief befall thee," and she took her brother and hid him.

In the evening the tiger came home, and while they talked together his wife asked him what he would do if any of her brothers should chance to look in upon them.

"If the elder were to come," said the tiger, "I would strike them dead, but if the youngest came, I would go down on my knees before him." Whereupon the damsel called to her youngest brother, the King's son, to come forth. The tiger was overjoyed to see him, welcomed him as a brother, and asked him whence he came and whither he was going. Then the King's son told the tiger of all his trouble, and asked him whether he knew the Wind-Demon. "Only by hearsay," replied the tiger; and then he tried to persuade the King's son not to go, for the danger was great. But the red dawn had no sooner appeared than the King's son was ready to set out again. The tiger showed him the way, and the one went back and the other went forward.

He pursued his way, and it was endlessly long, but time passes quickly in a fairy tale, and at last a dark object stood out against him. "What can it be?" thought he, but when he drew nearer he saw that it was a palace. It was the abode of his youngest sister. The damsel was just then looking out of the window. "Alas! my brother!" cried she, and very nearly fell out of the window for pure joy. Then she led him into the house. The youth rejoiced that he had found all his sisters so well, but the lack of his wife was still a weight upon his heart.

Now when evening was drawing nigh the girl said to her brother: "My bird-husband will be here anon; conceal thyself from him, for if he see thee he will tear thy heart out," and with that she took her brother and hid him.

And now there was a great clapping of wings, and the Anka had scarce rested a while when his wife asked him what he would do if any of her brothers came to see them.

"As to the two elder," said the bird, "I would take them in my mouth, fly up to the sky with them, and cast them down from thence; but if the youngest were to come, I would let him sit down on my wings and go to sleep there if he liked." Then the girl called forth her youngest brother.

"Alas! my dear little child," cried the bird, "how didst thou find thy way hither? Wert thou not afraid of the long journey?"

The youth told what had happened to him, and asked the Anka whether he could help him to get to the Wind-Demon.

"It is no easy matter," said the bird, "but even if thou couldst get to him, I would counsel thee to let it alone and stay rather among us."

"Not I," replied the resolute youth. "I will either release my wife or perish there!" Then the Anka saw that he could not turn him from his purpose, and began to explain to him all about the palace of the Wind-Demon. "He is now asleep," said the Anka, "and thou mayest be able to carry off thy wife; but if he should awake and see thee, he will without doubt grind thee to atoms. Guard against him thou cannot, for eye cannot see and fire cannot harm him, so look well to thyself!"

So next day the youth set out on his journey, and when he had gone on and on for a long, long time, he saw before him a vast palace that had neither door nor chimney, nor length nor breadth. It was the palace of the Wind-Demon. His wife chanced just then to be sitting at the window, and when she saw her husband she leaped clean out of the window to him. The King's son caught his wife in his arms, and there were no bounds to their joy and their tears, till at last the girl bethought her of the terrible demon.

"This is now the third day that he has slept," cried she. "Let us hasten away before the fourth day is spent also." So they mounted, whipped up their horses, and were already well on their way when the Wind-Demon awoke on the fourth day. Then he went to the girl's door and bade her open, that he might at least see her face for a brief moment. He waited, but he got no answer. Then, auguring some evil, he beat in the door, and lo! the place where the damsel should have lain was cold.

"So-ho, Prince Mehmed!" cried he, "thou hast come here, eh, and stolen away my Sultana? Well, wait a while! go thy way, whip up thy fleet steed! for I'll catch thee up in the long run." And with that he sat down at his ease, drank his coffee, smoked his chibook, and then rose up and went after them.

Meanwhile the King's son was galloping off with the girl with all his might, when all at once the girl felt the demon's breath, and cried out in her terror: "Alas, my King, the Wind-Demon is here!" Like a whirlwind the invisible monster was upon them, caught up the youth, tore off his arms and legs, and smashed his skull and all his bones till there was not a bit of him left.

The damsel began to weep bitterly. "Even if thou hast killed him," sobbed she, "let me at least gather together his bones and pile them up somewhere, for if thou suffer it, I would fain bury him." – "I care not what thou dost with his bones!" cried the Demon.

So the damsel took the bones of the King's son, piled them up together, kissed the horse between the eyes, placed the bones on his saddle, and whispered in his ear: "Take these bones, my good steed, take them to the proper place." Then the Demon took the girl and led her back to the palace, for the power of her beauty was so great that it always kept the Demon close to her. Into her presence, indeed, she never suffered the monster to come. At the door of her chamber he had to stop, but he was allowed to show himself to her now and then.

Meanwhile the good steed galloped away with the youth's bones till he stopped at the door of the palace of the youngest sister, and then he neighed and neighed till the damsel heard him. She rushed out to the horse, and when she perceived the knapsack, and in the knapsack the bones of her brother, she began to weep bitterly, and dashed herself against the ground as if she would have dashed herself to pieces. She could hardly wait for her lord the Anka to come home. At last there was a sound of mighty wings, and the Padishah of the Birds, the emerald Anka, came home, and when he saw the scattered bones of the King's son in the basket, he called together all the birds of the air and asked them, saying: "Which of you goes to the Garden of Paradise?"

"An old owl is the only one that goes there," said the birds, "and he has now grown so old that he has no more strength left for such a journey."

Then the Anka sent a bird to bring the owl on his back. The bird flew away, and in a very short time was back again, with the aged owl on his back.

"Well, my father," said the Bird-Padishah, "hast thou ever been in the Garden of Paradise?"

"Yes, my little son," croaked the aged owl, "a long, long time ago, twelve years or more, and I haven't been there since."

"Well, if thou hast been there," said the Anka, "go again now, and bring me from thence a little glass of water." The old owl kept on saying that it was a long, long way for him to go, and that he would never be able to hold out the whole way. The Anka would not listen to him, but perched him upon a bird's back, and the twain flew into the Garden of Paradise, drew a glass of water, and returned to the Anka's palace.

Then the Anka took the youth's bones and began to put them together. The arms, the legs, the head, the thighs, everything he put in its proper place; and when he had sprinkled it all with the water, the youth fell a-gaping, as if he had been asleep and was just coming to himself again. The youth looked all about him, and asked the Anka where he was, and how he came there.

"Didn't I say that the Wind-Demon would twist thee round his little finger?" replied the Anka. "He ground all thy bones and sinews to dust, and we have only just now picked them all out of the basket. But now thou hadst better leave the matter alone, for if thou gettest once more into the clutches of this demon, I know that we shall never be able to put thee together again."

But the youth was not content to do this, but said he would go seek his consort a second time.

"Well, if thou art bent on going at any price," counselled the Anka, "go first to thy wife and ask her if she knows the Demon's talisman. If only thou canst get hold of that, even the Wind-Demon will be in thy power."

So again the King's son took horse, again he went right up to the Demon's palace, and as the Demon was dreaming dreams just then, the youth was able to find and converse with his wife. After they had rejoiced with a great joy at the sight of each other, the youth told the lady to discover the secret of the Demon's talisman, and win it by wheedling words and soft caresses if she could get at it no other way. Meanwhile the youth hid himself in the neighbouring mountain, and there awaited the good news.

When the Wind-Demon awoke from his forty days' sleep he again presented himself at the damsel's door. "Depart from before my eyes," cried the girl. "Here hast thou been doing nothing but sleep these forty days, so that life has been a loathsome thing to me all the while."

The Demon rejoiced that he was allowed to be in the room along with the damsel, and in his happiness asked her what he should give her to help her to while away the time.

"What canst thou give me," said the girl, "seeing that thou thyself art but wind? Now if at least thou hadst a talisman, that, at any rate, would be something to while away the time with."

"Alas! my Sultana," replied the Demon, "my talisman is far away, in the uttermost ends of the earth, and one cannot fetch it hither in a little instant. If only we had some such brave man as thy Mehmed was, he perhaps might be able to go for it."

The damsel was now more curious than ever about the talisman, and she coaxed and coaxed till at last she persuaded the Demon to tell her about the talisman, but not till she had granted his request that he might sit down quite close to her. The damsel could not refuse him that happiness, so he sat down beside her, and breathed into her ear the secret of the talisman.

"On the surface of the seventh layer of sea," began the Demon, "there is an island, on that island an ox is grazing, in the belly of that ox there is a golden cage, and in that cage there is a white dove. That little dove is my talisman."

"But how can one get to that island?" inquired the Sultana.

"I'll tell thee," said the Demon. "Opposite to the palace of the emerald Anka is a huge mountain, and on the top of that mountain is a spring. Every morning forty sea-horses come to drink at that spring. If anyone can be found to catch one of these horses by the leg (but only while he is drinking the water), bridle him, saddle him, and then leap on his back, he will be able to go wherever he likes. The sea-horse will say to him: 'What dost thou command, my sweet master?' and will carry him whithersoever he bids him."

"What good will the talisman be to me if I cannot get near it?" said the girl. With that she drove the Demon from the room, and when the time of his slumber arrived, she hastened with the news to her lord. Then the King's son made great haste, leaped on his horse, hastened to the palace of his youngest sister, and told the matter to the Anka.

Early next morning the Anka arose, called five birds, and said to them: "Lead the King's son to the spring on the mountain beyond, and wait there till the sea-horses come up. Forty steeds will appear by the running water, and when they begin to drink, seize one of them, bridle and saddle it, and put the King's son on its back."

So the birds took the King's son, carried him up to the mountain close by the spring, and as soon as the horses came up, they did to one of them what the Anka had said. The King's son sat on the horse's back forthwith, and the first thing the good steed said was: "What dost thou command, my sweet master?"

"There is an island on the surface of the seventh ocean," cried the King's son. "There should I like to be!" And the King's son had flown away before you could shut your eyes; and before you could open them again, there he was on the shore of that island.

He dismounted from his horse, took off the bridle, stuck it in his pocket, and went off to seek the ox. As he was walking up and down the shore a Jew met him, and asked him what had brought him there.

"I have suffered shipwreck," replied the youth. "My ship and everything I possess have perished, and only with difficulty did I swim ashore."

"As for me," said the Jew, "I am in the service of the Wind-Demon. Thou must know that there is an ox on this island, and I must watch it night and day. Wouldst thou like to enter the service? Thou wilt have nothing else to do all day but watch this beast."

The King's son took advantage of the opportunity, and could scarce await the moment when he was to see the ox. At watering-time the Jew brought it along, and no sooner did he find himself alone with the beast than he cut open its belly, took out the golden cage, and hastened with it to the seashore. Then he drew the bridle from his pocket, and when he had struck the sea with it, the steed immediately appeared and cried: "What dost thou command, sweet master?" – "I desire to be taken to the palace of the Wind-Demon," cried the youth.

Shut your eyes, open your eyes – and there they were before the palace. Then he took his wife, made her sit down beside him, and when the steed said: "What dost thou command, sweet master?" he bade it fly straight to the emerald Anka.

Away with them flew the steed. It flew right up to the very clouds, and as they were approaching the Anka's palace the Demon awoke from his sleep. He saw that his wife had again disappeared, and immediately set off in pursuit. Already the Sultana felt the breath of the Demon, and he had all but overtaken them when the steed hastily bade them twist the neck of the white dove in the cage. They had barely time to do so, when the Wind died away and the Demon was destroyed.

With great joy they arrived at the Anka's palace, let the horse go his way, and rested themselves awhile. On the next day they went to their second brother, and on the third day to their third brother, and it was only then that the King's son discovered that his lion brother-in-law was the King of the Lions, and his tiger brother-in-law the King of the Tigers. At last they reached their home which was the domain of the damsel's. Here they made a great banquet, and rejoiced their hearts for forty days and forty nights, after which they arose and went to the prince's own empire. There he showed them the tongue of the dragon and its nose, and as he had thus fulfilled the wishes of his father, they chose him to be their Padishah; and their lives were full of joy till the day of their death, and their end was a happy one.

The Language of Birds
(Turkish)

THERE ONCE LIVED a Hodja who, it was said, understood the language of birds, but refused to impart his knowledge. One young man was very persistent in his desire to know the language of these sweet creatures, but the Hodja was inflexible.

In despair, the young man went to the woods at least to listen to the pleasant chirping of the birds. By degrees it conveyed to him a meaning, till, finally, he understood them to tell him that his horse would die. On returning from the woods, he immediately sold his horse and went and told the Hodja.

"Oh Hodja, why will you not teach me the language of birds? Yesterday I went to the woods and they warned me that my horse would die, thus affording me an opportunity of selling it and avoiding the loss."

The Hodja was silent, but would not give way.

The following day the young man again went to the woods, and the chirping of the birds told him that his house would be burned. The young man hurried away, sold his house, again went to the Hodja and told him all that had happened, adding:

"See, Hodja Effendi, you would not teach me the language of the birds, but I have saved my horse and my house by listening to them."

On the following day, the young man again went to the woods, and the birds chirped him the doleful tale, that on the following day he would die. In tears the young man went to the Hodja for advice.

"Oh Hodja Effendi! Alas! What am I to do? The birds have told me that tomorrow I must die."

"My son," answered the Hodja, "I knew this would come, and that is why I refused to teach you the language of birds. Had you borne the loss of your horse, your house would have been saved, and had your house been burned, your life would have been saved."

The Bird of Sorrow
(Turkish)

IN VERY REMOTE TIMES there lived a Padishah whose daughter was so much attached to her governess that she scarcely ever left her side.

One day, seeing the latter deep in thought, the Princess asked: "Of what are you thinking?" "I have sorrow," answered the governess. "What is sorrow?" questioned the Padishah's daughter; "let me also have it." "It is well," said the woman, and went to the tscharschi, where she bought a Bird of Sorrow in a cage. She presented it to the maiden, who was so delighted that she amused herself day and night with the creature.

Some time afterwards the Sultan's daughter, attended by her slaves, paid a visit to the Zoo. She took with her the bird in its cage, which she hung upon the branch of a tree. Suddenly the bird commenced to speak. "Set me free a little while, Sultana," it pleaded, "that I may play with the other birds. I will come back again." The Princess accordingly set her favourite at liberty.

A few hours later, while the Princess was sauntering idly about the park, the bird returned, seized its mistress and flew off with her to the top of a high mountain. "Behold! this is sorrow," said the bird. "I will prepare more of it for you!" Saying this, he flew away. The Princess, now hungry and thirsty, wandered about until she met a herdsman, with whom she exchanged raiment, so that she might disguise herself as a man for her better protection. After long wandering she came to a village where, finding a coffeehouse, she entered, and besought the proprietor to engage her as his assistant. The former, regarding her as a young man in need of employment, accordingly engaged her, and towards evening went home, leaving her in charge of the house. Having closed the shop, the girl lay down to sleep. At midnight, however, the Bird of Sorrow appeared, broke all the cups and saucers and nargiles in the place, woke the maiden from her sleep, and thus addressed her: "Behold! this is sorrow; I will prepare more of it for you!" Having thus spoken, he flew away as before. All night long the poor girl lay thinking what she should say to her master on the morrow. When morning came the proprietor returned, and seeing the woeful damage done, beat his assistant severely and drove her away.

Her eyes filled with bitter tears, she set out once more, and ere many hours arrived at a tailor's shop. As preparations were being made for the great religious feast of Bairam, the tailor was busy in executing orders for the serai. He was therefore in need of an extra hand, and took the youth, as he supposed the girl to be, into his service. After a day or two the tailor went away, leaving the maiden alone in the house. When evening came she closed the shop and retired to rest. At midnight came the bird again, and tore to shreds all the clothes on the premises, and waking up the girl, said: "Behold! this is sorrow; I will prepare still more of it for you!" and flew off again. Next morning brought the master, who seeing the clothing all torn up, called his assistant to account. As the girl answered nothing, the master beat her soundly and sent her away.

Weeping bitterly, she once more set forth, and by and by came to a fringe-maker's, where she was taken in. Being again left alone, she fell asleep. The Bird of Sorrow reappeared, tore up the fringes, woke the girl, made his customary speech, and flew away as on previous occasions.

When the master returned next morning and saw the mischief, he beat his assistant more cruelly than ever, and dismissed her. Overwhelmed with grief, the unhappy maiden again took her lonely way. Feeling sure that the Bird of Sorrow would give her no peace, she went into a mountain pass, where she lived in seclusion for many days, suffering the pangs of hunger and thirst, and in constant fear of the wild beasts that haunted the region. Her nights were spent in the leafy branches of a tree.

One day the son of a Padishah, when out hunting, espied the girl in the tree. Mistaking her for a bird, he shot an arrow at her, but it merely struck one of the branches. On approaching the tree to reclaim his arrow, the Shahzada observed that what he had supposed to be a bird appeared to be a man. "Are you an in or a jin?" he called out. "Neither in nor jin," was the response, "but a human creature like yourself." Where upon the Prince permitted her to descend from the tree, and took the seeming herdsman to the palace. Here, after bathing, she resumed the garments of a maiden. Then the royal youth saw that she was beautiful as the moon at the full, and straightway fell violently in love with her. Without delay he besought his father, the Padishah, to consent to his wedding with her. The Sultan commanded the maiden to be brought into his presence, and as he gazed upon her wonderful beauty, her loveliness and grace won his heart. The betrothal took place forthwith; and after a period of festivity lasting forty days and forty nights the marriage was celebrated. In due time a little daughter was born to the princely pair, a child gentle and fair to look upon, and giving early promise of becoming as lovely as its mother.

One midnight came the bird, stole the babe, and besmeared the mother's lips with blood. Then it woke the Princess, and said: "Behold, I am taking away your child; and still more sorrow will I prepare for you!" So saying, the bird flew off. In the morning the Prince missed his little daughter, and observed that his wife's lips were blood-stained. Going quickly to his father, the Padishah, he related the ominous occurrence.

"From the mountain did you bring the woman," said the Padishah. "She is forsooth a daughter of the mountain and eats human flesh; therefore I counsel you to send her away!" But the devoted Prince pleaded for his young wife and prevailed over his father.

Some time later another daughter was born to them, which also the bird stole away under similar circumstances. This time the Padishah commanded that the mother should be put to death, though yielding at length to the earnest entreaties of his son he grudgingly consented to pardon her.

Time passed away, and eventually a son was born. The Prince, fearing that if this child also should disappear his beloved wife would surely be put to death, determined to lie awake at night and keep watch and ward over his loved ones. Tired nature, however, insisted on her toll, and the Prince slept.

Meanwhile the bird returned, stole the babe, besmeared the Princess's lips with blood as before, and flew away. When the poor mother awoke and discovered her terrible loss, she wept bitterly; and when the Prince also awoke and found the child missing and his wife's mouth and nose dripping with blood, he hastened to his father with the awful intelligence. The Padishah, in a violent rage, again condemned the woman to death. The executioners were summoned; they bound her hands behind her and led her forth to execution. But so smitten were they with her ravishing beauty, and so stricken with pity for her sore affliction, that they said to her: "We cannot find it in our hearts to kill you. Go where you will, only return not again to the palace."

The poor ill-fated woman again sought her mountain refuge, brooding over her sad lot; until one day the bird once more appeared, seized her and carried her off to the garden of a grand palace.

Setting down his burden, the bird shook himself, and lo! he was suddenly transformed into a handsome youth. Taking her by the hand, he led the disconsolate woman upstairs into the palace. Here a wonderful sight met her eyes. Attended by many servants, three beautiful children, all radiant and smiling, approached her. As her astonished gaze fell upon them, her eyes filled with tears of joy and her heart melted with tenderness.

Escorting the now happy and wondering Princess into a stately apartment, richly carpeted and furnished with all the art of the luxurious Orient, the youth thus addressed her: "Sultana, though I afflicted you with much grief and sorrow, robbed you of your precious children, and nearly brought you to an ignominious death, yet have you patiently borne it all and not betrayed me. In reward I have built for you this palace, in which I now restore to you your loved ones. Behold your children! Henceforth, Sultana, I am your slave." The Princess hastened with winged feet to her long-lost children, embraced them, pressed them to her bosom, and covered them with kisses.

How fared it with the Prince? Sorrowing for his children and for his beloved wife, whom he believed to have been put to death, he grew morose and melancholy, passing the time with his old opium smoker, who beguiled the hours with indifferent stories.

One day, having no more opium, the old man requested the Prince's permission to go to the tscharschi in order to buy more. On his way thither he saw something he had never before beheld: a large and magnificent serail! "It is remarkable," thought the old fellow. "I frequent this street daily, yet have I not seen this palace before. When can it have been built? I must inspect it."

The Sultana, whose palace it was, happened to be at one of the windows and caught sight of her husband's opium smoker. The slave – formerly her Bird of Sorrow – being in attendance, he respectfully suggested: "What say you, lady, to playing a trick on the Prince's old storyteller?" At these words he threw a magic rose at the feet of the greybeard. The latter picked it up, inhaled its exquisite perfume, and muttered to himself: "If your rose is so beautiful, how must it be with yourself!" So instead of returning home he entered the palace.

The Prince in the meantime grew concerned over the prolonged absence of the old man and sent his steward to look for him. The steward, arriving before the palace, the door of which had been left open intentionally by the slave, went in to look round. A number of female slaves received him and led the way up the stairs. At the top he was handed over to the magician slave, who requested him to remove his outer robe and precede him. The robe was taken off without difficulty, but the steward was astonished to find that in spite of all his efforts he was quite unable to remove his fez. At this the magician ordered him to be cast out "for refusing to take off his fez." The steward was therefore forcibly ejected. But no sooner was he outside than – wonderful to relate – the fez fell from his head of its own accord! On his way home he overtook the old opium smoker. Meanwhile the Shahzada was troubled at the non-return of his steward and dispatched his treasurer after him. The treasurer met both on the road and demanded to know what had befallen them. The old opium smoker answered somewhat enigmatically: "If a rose be thrown from that palace, take care not to smell it, or the consequences be on your own head." And the steward warned him no less mysteriously: "When you enter that palace, be sure to leave your fez at the door!"

The treasurer considered the behaviour of both his companions somewhat peculiar, but taking their warning lightly, he entered the palace. Inside he was ordered to don a dressing-gown before proceeding upstairs. Commencing to undress for the purpose, he discovered that his schalwar refused to part company with his person. Consequently he was unceremoniously thrown out of the palace. Hardly, however, was he outside than his schalwar came off by itself!

The Prince, becoming unable longer to endure the unaccountable absence of his servants, set out himself to discover, if possible, what had happened to them. On the way he met all three, who counselled him in an excited manner: "If a rose be thrown to you from the palace, be careful not to smell it; when you enter, be sure to leave your fez at the door; and before you arrive there, take off your schalwar and enter without it!"

The Prince was exceedingly puzzled at such extraordinary advice, yet he straightway went to the serail and disappeared from sight within the portal. Unlike his servants, the Prince was received with every mark of honour and respect, and conducted to a noble hall. Here a lady of remarkable beauty, surrounded by three lovely children, awaited him.

The lady gave to her eldest child a stool, to the second a towel, and to the youngest a tray; into the tray she put a bowl, into the bowl a pear, and beside it a spoon. The eldest set the stool on the floor, the second offered the towel to the Prince, while the youngest sat himself down in the bowl. The Prince then inquired of the children: "How long has it been the custom to eat pears with a spoon?" "Since human beings have eaten human flesh," they answered in chorus. The chord of memory was struck; the past flashed before the mind's eye of the Prince. Here the magician appeared and cried: "Oh Prince, behold thy Sultana! Behold also thy children!" Whereat all – father, mother, and children – fell on each other's necks weeping for joy.

The magician continued: "My Shahzada, I am your slave; if, however, you deign to give me my liberty, I will hasten to my own parents." Overflowing with gratitude for their reunion, they immediately set the magician slave free and prepared a new festival, happy in the knowledge that henceforth they would never be parted from each other.

The Fish-Peri
(Turkish)

THERE WAS ONCE a fisherman of the name of Mahomet, who made a living by catching fish and selling them. One day, being seriously ill and having no hope of recovery, he requested that, after his death, his wife should never reveal to their son that their livelihood had been derived from the sale of fish.

The fisherman died; and time passed away until the son reached an age when he should begin to think about an occupation. He tried many things, but in none did he succeed. Soon afterwards his mother also died, and the boy found himself alone in the world and destitute, without food or money. One day he ascended to the lumber-room of the house, hoping to find there something he might be able to sell.

During his search he discovered his father's old fishing-net. The sight of it convinced the youth that his father had been a fisherman; so he took the net and went to the sea. A modest success attended his efforts, for he caught two fish, one of which he sold, purchasing bread and coal with the money. The remaining fish he cooked over the coal he had bought, and having eaten it, he resolved that he would follow the occupation of a fisherman.

It happened one day that he caught a fish so fine that it grieved him either to sell it or to eat it. So he took it home, dug a well, and put the fish therein. He went supperless to bed, and being hungry he got up early next morning to catch more fish.

When he came home in the evening we may imagine his astonishment at finding that his house had been swept and put in order during his absence. Thinking, however, that he owed it to his neighbours' kindness, he prayed for them and called down Allah's blessing upon them.

Next morning he rose as usual, cheered himself with a sight of the fish in the well, and went to his daily work. On returning in the evening, he found that again everything in the house had been made beautifully clean and tidy. After amusing himself for some time by watching the fish, he went to a coffeehouse where he tried to think who it could be that had put his house in order. His reflective mood was noticed by one of his companions, who asked what he was thinking about. When the youth had told the story, his companion inquired where the key was kept, and who remained at home during the fisherman's absence. The youth informed him that he carried the key with him, and that there was no living creature about except the fish. The companion then advised him to remain at home next day and watch in secret.

The youth accordingly went home, and next morning instead of going out, merely made a pretence of doing so. He opened the door and closed it again, then hid himself in the house. All at once he saw the fish jump out of the well and shake itself, when behold! it became a beautiful maiden. The youth quickly seized the fish's skin, which it had shed, and cast it into the fire. "You should not have done that," said the maiden reprovingly, "but as it cannot now be helped, it does not matter."

Being thus set free, the maiden consented to become the youth's wife, and preparations were made for the wedding. All who saw the maiden were bewildered by her beauty and said she was worthy to become the bride of a Padishah. This news reaching the ears of the Padishah, he ordered her to be brought before him. When he saw her he fell in love with her instantly, and determined to marry her.

Therefore he sent for the youth, and said to him: "If in forty days you can build me a palace of gold and diamonds in the middle of the sea, I will not deprive you of the girl; but if you fail, I shall take her away." The youth went home very sadly and wept. "Why do you weep?" asked the maiden. He told her what the Padishah had commanded, but she said cheerfully: "Do not weep; we shall manage it. Go to the spot where you caught me as a fish and cast in a stone. An Arab will appear and utter the words 'your command?' Tell him the lady sends her compliments and requests a cushion. He will give you one; take it, and cast it into the sea where the Padishah wishes his palace built. Then return home."

The youth followed all these instructions, and next day, when they looked toward the place where the cushion had been thrown into the sea, they saw a palace even more beautiful than that the Padishah had described. Rejoicing, they hastened to tell the monarch that his palace was an accomplished fact.

Now the Padishah demanded a bridge of crystal. Again the youth went home and wept. When the maiden heard the cause of his new grief she said: "Go to the Arab as before, and ask him for a bolster. When you get it, cast it in the sea before the palace." The youth did as he was counselled, and looking round, he saw a beautiful bridge of crystal. He went directly to the Padishah and told him that the task was fulfilled.

As a third test, the Padishah now demanded that the youth should prepare such a feast that everyone in the land might eat thereof and yet something should remain over. The young fisherman went home, and while he was absorbed in thought, the maiden inquired what was the matter. On hearing of the new command she advised: "Go to the Arab and ask him for the coffee-mill, but take care not to turn it on the way." The youth obtained the coffee-mill from the Arab without any difficulty. In bringing it home, he began quite unconsciously to turn it, and seven or eight plates of food fell out. Picking them up, he proceeded homewards.

On the appointed day everyone in the land, in accordance with the Padishah's invitation, repaired to the fisherman's house to take part in the feast. Each guest ate as much as he wanted, and yet in the end a considerable portion of food remained over.

Still obdurate, the Padishah ordered the youth to produce a mule from an egg. The youth described to the maiden his latest task, and she told him to fetch three eggs from the Arab and bring them home without breaking them. He obtained the eggs, but on his way back dropped one and broke it. Out of the egg sprang a great mule, which after running to and fro finally plunged into the sea and was seen no more.

The youth arrived home safely with the two remaining eggs. "Where is the third?" asked the maiden. "It is broken," replied the youth.

"You ought to have been more careful," said the maiden, "but as it is done it can't be helped." The youth carried the eggs to the Padishah, and asked permission to mount upon a bench. This being granted, he stood on the bench and threw up the egg. Instantly a mule sprang forth and fell upon the Padishah, who sought in vain to flee. The youth rescued the monarch from his danger, and the mule then ran away and plunged into the sea.

In despair at his inability to find an impossible task for the youth, the Padishah now demanded an infant not more than a day old, who could both speak and walk. Still undaunted, the maiden counselled the youth to go to the Arab with her compliments and inform him that she wished to see his baby nephew. The youth accordingly summoned the Arab and delivered the message. The Arab answered: "He is but an hour old: his mother may not wish to spare him. However, wait a bit, and I will do my best."

To be brief, the Arab went away and soon reappeared with a newly born infant. No sooner did it see the fisherman than it ran up to him and exclaimed: "We are going to Auntie's, are we not?" The youth took the child home, and immediately it saw the maiden; with the word "Auntie!" it embraced her. On this the youth took the child to the Padishah.

When the child was brought into the presence of the monarch, it stepped up to him, struck him on the face, and thus addressed him: "How is it possible to build a palace of gold and diamonds in forty days? To rear a crystal bridge also in the same time? For one man to feed all the people in the land? For a mule to be produced from an egg?" At every sentence the child struck him a fresh blow, until finally the Padishah cried to the youth that he might keep the maiden himself if only he would deliver him from the terrible infant. The youth then carried the child home. He wedded the maiden, and the rejoicings lasted forty days and forty nights.

Three apples fell from the sky: one belongs to me, another to Husni, the third to the storyteller. Which belongs to me?

Kamer-Taj, the Moon-Horse
(Turkish)

THERE WAS ONCE a Padishah who one day found a little insect. The Padishah called his lala and they both examined the tiny creature. What could it be? What could it feed on? Every day an animal was killed for its sustenance, and by thus living it grew and

grew until it was as big as a cat. Then they killed it and skinned it, hanging up the skin on the palace gate.

The Padishah now issued a proclamation that whoever could guess correctly to what animal the skin belonged should receive the Sultan's daughter in marriage.

A great crowd collected and examined the skin from all sides, but no one was found wise enough to answer the question. The story of the skin spread far and wide until it reached the ears of a Dew. "That is exceedingly fortunate for me," thought he to himself. "I have had nothing to eat for three days; now I shall be able to satisfy myself with the Princess." So he went to the Padishah, told him the name of the creature, and immediately demanded the maiden.

"Woe is me," groaned the Padishah "How can I give this Dew my only daughter?" He offered him, in ransom for her, as many slaves as he liked, but all in vain! The Dew insisted on having the Sultan's daughter. Therefore the Padishah called the maiden and told her to prepare for the journey, as her kismet was the Dew. All weeping and wailing were fruitless. The maiden put on her clothes, while the Dew waited for her outside the palace.

The Padishah had a horse that drank attar of roses and ate grapes; Kamer-taj, or Moon-horse, was its name. This was the creature on which the Sultan's daughter was to accompany the Dew to his abode. A cavalcade escorted her a portion of the way and then, turning, rode back. Now the maiden offered up a prayer to Allah to deliver her from the fiend.

Suddenly the Moon-horse began to speak: "Lady, fear not! shut both your eyes and hold my mane firmly." Hardly had she shut her eyes when she felt the horse rise with her, and when she opened her eyes again she found herself in the garden of a lovely palace on an island in the midst of the sea.

The Dew was very angry at the disappearance of the maid. "Still, never mind!" he said, "I will soon find her," and went his way home alone. Not far from the island a Prince sat in a canoe with his lala. The Prince, seeing on the calm surface of the water the reflection of the golden-hued steed, said to his lala that perhaps someone had arrived at his palace. They rode to the island, got out of the canoe, and entered the garden. Here the youth saw the beautiful Princess, who, however much she essayed to veil her face, could not succeed in hiding from him her loveliness.

"Oh, Peri!" said the Prince, "fear me not; I am not an enemy!" "I am only a Sultan's daughter, a child of man and no Peri," announced the Princess, and told the Prince how she had been delivered from the Dew. The Prince assured her that she could not have come to a better place. His father also was a Padishah; with her permission he would take her to him, and by the grace of Allah he would make her his wife. So they went to the Padishah, the Prince told him of the maiden's adventure, and in the end they were married, merriment and feasting lasting forty days and forty nights.

For a time they lived in undisturbed bliss, but war broke out with a neighbouring kingdom and, in accordance with the custom of that period, the Padishah also must set out for the campaign. Hearing of this, the Prince went to his father and asked permission to go to the war. The Padishah was unwilling to consent, saying: "You are young, also you have a wife whom you must not forsake." But the son begged so assiduously that in the end the Padishah agreed to stay at home and let the Prince go in his stead.

The Dew discovered that the Prince would be on the battlefield, and he also made the further discovery that during his absence a son and a daughter had been born to him.

At that time Tartars were employed as messengers and carried letters between the Padishah at home and the Prince at the seat of war. One of these messengers was intercepted by the Dew and invited into a coffeehouse. There the Dew entertained him so long that night came on. The messenger now wished to be off, but was persuaded that it would be better to remain till morning. At midnight, while he was asleep, the Dew searched his letter-bag and found a letter from the Padishah to the Prince informing the latter that a baby son and daughter had come to the palace during his absence. Tearing up this letter, the Dew wrote another to the effect that a couple of dogs had been born. "Shall we destroy them or keep them till your return?" wrote the Dew in the false letter. This missive he placed in the original envelope, and in the morning the Tartar arose, took his sack of letters, and went into the Prince's camp.

When the Prince had read his father's letter, he wrote the following answer: "Shah and father, do not destroy the young dogs, but keep them until I return." This was given to the Tartar, who set out on his return journey.

He was again met by the Dew, who enticed him into a coffeehouse and detained him till next morning. During the night the Dew abstracted the letter and wrote another, which said: "Shah and father, take my wife and her two children and throw them down a precipice, and bind the Moon-horse with a fifty-ton chain."

In the evening of the day following, the Tartar delivered the letter to the Padishah. When the Princess saw the Tartar she hastened joyfully to the monarch that he might show her her husband's letter. The Padishah, having read it, was astonished and dared not show it to the Princess, so he denied that any letter had arrived. The woman answered: "I have indeed seen the letter with my own eyes; perchance some misfortune has happened to him and you are keeping it from me." Then, catching a glimpse of the letter, she put forth her hand quickly and took it. Having read it, the poor woman wept bitterly. The monarch did his best to comfort her, but she refused to remain longer in the palace. Taking her children, she left the city and went forth into the wide world.

Days and weeks passed away and she was without food to appease her hunger or bed on which to rest her tired body, until, worn out with fatigue, she could go no step farther. "Let not my children die of hunger!" she prayed. Behold! instantly water gushed forth from the earth and flour fell from the skies, and, making bread with these, she fed her children.

In the meantime, the Dew heard of the woman's fate and set out immediately to destroy the children. The Princess saw the Dew coming and in her terrible agony she cried: "Hasten, my Kamer-taj, or I die!" In the far-off land the magic horse heard this cry for help; he strained at his fifty-ton fetters but could not break them. The nearer the Dew came, the more the poor Princess's anguish increased. Clasping her children to her breast, she sent up another despairing cry to the Moon-horse. The fettered steed strained still more at his chain, but it was of no avail. The Dew was now quite close upon her, and for the last time the poor mother shrieked with all her remaining strength. Kamer-taj, hearing it, put forth all the force he could muster, broke his chain, and appeared before the

Princess. "Fear not, lady!" he said. "Shut your eyes and grasp my mane," and immediately they were on the other side of the ocean. Thus the Dew went away hungry once more.

The Moon-horse took the Princess to his own country. He felt that his last hour had now come, and told his beloved mistress that he must die. She implored him not to leave her alone with her children. If he did, who would protect them from the evil designs of the Dew? "Fear not," the horse comforted her, "no evil will befall you here. When I am dead, off my head and set it in the earth. Slit up my stomach, and having done this, lay yourself and your children within it." Saying these words, the magic horse breathed his last.

The Princess now cut off his head and stuck it in the ground, then opened his stomach and laid herself and her children in it. Here they fell fast asleep. When she awoke she saw that she was in a beautiful palace; one finer than either her father's or her husband's. She was lying in a lovely bed, and hardly had she risen when slaves appeared with water: one bathed her, others clothed her. The twins lay in a golden cradle, and nurses stood around them, soothing them with sweet songs. At dinnertime, gold and silver dishes appeared laden with delicious food. It was like a dream; but days and weeks passed away, weeks passed into months, and the months into a year, and still the dream – if dream it was – did not come to an end.

Meanwhile the war was over and the Prince hastened home. Seeing nothing of his wife, he asked his father what had become of her and her children. The Padishah was astonished at this strange question. The letters were produced, and the Tartar messenger was sent for. Being closely questioned, he related the account of his meeting with the Dew on both occasions. They now realized that the Dew had tampered with the messenger and the correspondence. There was no more thought of peace for the Prince until he had discovered his wife. With that intention he set out in the company of his lala.

They wandered on and on unceasingly. Six months had passed already, yet they continued their way over hill and down dale, never stopping to rest. One day they reached the foot of a mountain, whence they could see the palace of the Moon-horse. The Prince was entirely exhausted and said to his lala: "Go to that palace and beg a crust of bread and a little water, that we may continue our journey.

When he reached the palace gate, the lala was met by two little children, who invited him in to rest. Entering, he found the floor of the apartment so beautiful that he hardly dared set his foot upon it. But the children pulled him to the divan and made him sit down while food and drink were set before him. The lala excused himself, saying that outside waited his tired son, to whom he wished to take the refreshment.

"Father Dervish," said the children, "eat first yourself, then you can take food to your son." So the lala ate, drank coffee, and smoked, and while he was preparing to return to the Prince, the children went to tell their mother about their guest.

Looking out of the window, the Princess recognized the Prince her husband. She took food with her own hands, and, putting it in golden vessels, sent it out by the lala. On receiving it, the Prince was struck with the richness of the service. He lifted the cover of one of the dishes, set it on the ground, and it rolled back to the palace of its own accord. The same happened with the other dishes, and when the last had disappeared, a slave came to invite the stranger to take coffee in the palace.

While this was happening, the Princess gave each of her children a wooden horse, and sent them to the gate to receive the guests. "When the dervish comes with his son," said their mother, "take them to such and such an apartment." The dervish and his son came up, the two children on their wooden horses greeted them with a salaam and escorted them to their apartments. Again the Princess took dishes of food and said to the children: "Take these to our guests and press them to eat. If they say they have already had sufficient and ask you to partake of the food, answer that you also are satisfied, but perhaps your horses are hungry, and put them to the table. They will then probably ask, how can wooden horses eat? And you must reply—" (here she whispered something into the children's ears).

The children did as their mother had commanded them. The food was so delicious that the guests tried to eat a second time, but becoming satisfied very soon, they asked: "Will you not eat also, children?" "We cannot eat," answered the children, "but perhaps our horses are hungry," so saying they drew them up to the table. "Children," remonstrated the Prince, "wooden horses cannot eat." "That you seem to know," answered the children, "but apparently you do not know that it is impossible for little dogs to become human children such as we are." The Prince sprang up with a cry of joy, kissed and embraced both his children. His wife entering at the moment, he humbly begged her pardon for the suffering she had experienced. They related to each other all that had befallen them during the time of their separation, and their joy knew no bounds. Now the Princess and her children prepared to accompany the Prince back to his own kingdom. After they had gone some distance, they turned to take a farewell look at the palace, and lo! the wind swept over the place as though no building had ever been there.

The Dew was lurking on the wayside, but the Prince caught him and killed him, and after that they arrived home without further adventure. Soon afterwards the old Padishah died, and the Prince became chief of the land.

Three apples have fallen from the sky. One belongs to the storyteller, the second to the listener, the third to me.

The Cat and the Mouse
(Persian)

ACCORDING TO THE DECREE OF HEAVEN, there once lived in the Persian city of Kerman a cat like unto a dragon – a longsighted cat who hunted like a lion; a cat with fascinating eyes and long whiskers and sharp teeth. Its body was like a drum, its beautiful fur like ermine skin.

Nobody was happier than this cat, neither the newly-wedded bride, nor the hospitable master of the house when he looks round on the smiling faces of his guests.

This cat moved in the midst of friends, boon companions of the saucepan, the cup, and the milk jug of the court, and of the dinner table when the cloth is spread.

Perceiving the wine cellar open, one day, the cat ran gleefully into it to see if he could catch a mouse, and hid himself behind a wine jar. At that moment a mouse ran out of a hole in the wall, quickly climbed the jar, and, putting his head into it, drank so long and so deeply that he became drunk, talked very stupidly, and fancied he was as bold as a lion.

"Where is the cat?" shouted he, "that I may off with his head. I would cut off his head as if on the battlefield. A cat in front of me would fare worse than any dog who might happen to cross my path."

The cat ground his teeth with rage while hearing this. Quicker than the eye could follow, he made a spring, seized the mouse in his claws, and said, "Oh, little mouse, now will you take off my head?"

"I am thy servant," replied the mouse. "Forgive my sin. I was drunk. I am thy slave, a slave whose ear is pierced and on whose shoulder the yoke is."

"Tell fewer lies," replied the cat. "Was there ever such a liar? I heard all you said and you shall pay for your sin with your life. I will make your life less than that of a dead dog."

So the cat killed and ate the mouse; but afterwards, being sorry for what he had done, he ran to the Mosque, and passed his hands over his face, poured water on his hands, and anointed himself as he had seen the faithful do at the appointed hours of prayer.

Then he began to recite the beautiful chapter to Allah in the Holy Book of the Persians, and to make his confession in this wise: "I have repented, and will not again tear the body of a mouse with my teeth. I will give bread to the deserving poor. Forgive my sin, O great Forgiver, for have I not come to Thee bowed down with sorrow?"

He repeated this so many times and with so much feeling that he really thought he meant it, and finally wept for grief.

A little mouse happened to be behind the pulpit, and overhearing the cat's vows, speedily carried the glad but surprising news to the other mice. Breathlessly he related how that the cat had become a true Mussulman; how that he had seen him in the Mosque weeping and lamenting, and saying: "Oh, Creator of the world, put away my sin, for I have offended like a big fool." Then the mouse went on to describe how that the cat had a rosary of beads, and made pious reflections in the spirit of a true penitent.

The mice began to make merry when they heard this startling news, for they were exceedingly glad. Seven chosen mice, each the headman of the village, arose and gave thanks that the cat should at last have entered the fold of the true believers.

All danced and shouted, "Ah! Ah! Hu! Hu!" and drank red wine and white wine until they were very merry. Two rang bells, two played castanets, and two sang. One carried a tray behind his back laden with good things, so that all could help themselves; some smoked water-pipes; another acted like a clown; others played various tunes on different instruments of music.

A few days after the feast, the King of the mice said to them, "Oh, friends, all of you bring costly presents worthy of the cat!" Then the mice scattered in search of gifts, but soon returned, each bearing something worthy of presentation, even to a nobleman.

One brought a bottle of wine; another a dish full of raisins; others came with salted nuts and melon seeds, lumps of cheese, basins of sugar-candy, pistachio nuts, little cakes iced with sugar, bottles of lemon juice, Indian shawls, hats, cloaks and many other things.

Discreetly they bore their gifts before the King of the Cats. When in the royal presence, they made humble obeisances, touching their foreheads on the ground, and, saluting him, said: "Oh, master, liberator of the lives of all, we have brought gifts worthy of thy service. We beseech thee to deign to accept of them."

Then the cat thought to himself, "I am rewarded for becoming a pious Mussulman. Though I have endured much hunger, yet this day finds me freely and amply provided for. Not for many days have I broken my fast. It is clear that Allah is appeased."

Then he turned to the mice, and bade them come nearer, calling them his friends. And they went forward trembling. So frightened were they that they were hardly aware of what they were doing. When they were close the cat made a sudden spring upon them.

Five mice he caught, each one the chief of a village; two with his front paws, two with his hind ones, and one in his mouth. The remaining mice barely escaped with their lives.

Picking up one of their murdered brothers, they quickly carried the sad news to the mice, saying: "Why do ye sit still, oh mice? Throw dust on your heads, oh young men, for the cruel cat has seized five of our unsuspecting companions with teeth and claws and has killed them."

Then for the space of five days they rent their clothes as do the mourners, and cast dust on their heads. Then they said: "We must go and tell our King all that has befallen the mice. We must not fail to tell him this calamity."

Whereupon they all rose up and went their way in deep sorrow; one beating the muffled drum, one tolling the bell; all had shawls around their necks; their tears the while running in little streams down their whiskers.

Arrived where the King was sitting on his throne, the mice paid homage to him, saying: "Master, we are subjects and thou art King. Behold the cat has treated us cruelly since he became a pious follower of Mahomet. Whereas, before his conversion he was wont to catch only one of us in a year, now that he is a sincere Mussulman his appetite has so increased that only five at a time will satisfy him."

Whereupon the King fell into such a violent rage that he resembled a saucepan boiling over. But to the deputation of mice he spoke very kindly, calling them his newly-arrived and welcome guests, and to comfort them vowed that he would give the cat such a chastisement that the news of it should circulate through the world.

Then, observing their grief, he commanded that the dead mouse should be buried with all pomp and ceremony. Accordingly they made lamentation for a whole week, as though it had been for one of royal degree; and having prepared delicious sweetmeats, they placed them in baskets and carried them with streaming eyes to the grave.

After the burial service, the King ordered the army to assemble on a given day on the great sandy plain that stretches as far as the eye can see around the city. Then he addressed them, saying: "Oh, men and soldiers, inasmuch as the cat has so cruelly ill-treated our countrymen, he being a heretic and an evil doer, and brutal in nature, we must now go to the city of Kerman and fight him."

So three hundred and thirty thousand mice went forth, armed with swords, guns, and spears; and with flags and pennons bravely flying. A passing Arab from the desert, skilfully balancing himself on the back of a swift-traveling camel by means of a long pole, spied the great army in motion, and was so overcome with astonishment that he lost his balance and fell off. Several regiments of mice were put out of action by his fall; but nothing daunted, the army pressed on.

When the army was ready for battle, the King again addressed them, saying: "O young men, an ambassador must be sent to the cat, one who is able, discreet, and eloquent." Then they all shouted: "The King's orders shall be carried out! Upon our heads be it."

Now, there was present a learned and eloquent mouse, the ruler of a province, and he it was that the King commanded to go as an ambassador to the cat in the city of Kerman. Almost before his name was out of the King's mouth, he had jumped out of his place in the ranks, and, traveling swiftly as the winds of the desert, he went in boldly before the cat and said: "As an ambassador from the King of the Mice am I come, bowed down with grief and fatigue. Know this, my master has determined to wage war, and is even now come with his army to take off your head."

The cat roared out in reply, "Go tell your King to eat dust! I come not out of this city except at my good pleasure!" Then he sent messengers to bring up quickly some fighting and hunting cats from Khorassan – the land of the sun – to Kerman.

As soon as the cat's army was ready, the King of the Cats gave them marching orders, promising to come himself to the battle on the next day. The cats came out on horseback, each one like a hungry tiger. The mice also mounted their steeds, armed to the teeth, and boiling with rage. Shouting "Allah! Allah!" the armies fell upon each other with unsheathed swords.

So many cats and mice were killed that there was no room for the horses' feet. The cats fought valiantly, their fierce attacks carrying them through the first line of the mice, then through the second, and many Ameers and chiefs were killed. The mice, thinking the battle lost, turned to flee, crying out: "Throw dust upon your heads, young men!"

But afterwards, rallying again, they faced their pursuers and attacked the right wing of the cat's army, shouting their battle cry of "Allah! Allah!"

In the thickest of the fray a mounted mouse speared the King of the Cats, so that he fell fainting to the ground. Before he could rise, the mouse leaped upon him and brought him captive to the King. So the cats were defeated on that day and sullenly retreated to the city of Kerman.

Having bound the cat, the mice beat him until he became unconscious. Then the plain echoed with the beating of tom-toms and shouts of joy. Then the King of the Mice seated himself on his throne and ordered the cat to be brought before him.

"Scoundrel!" he said to him. "Why hast thou eaten up my army? Hear now the King of the Mice." The cat hung his head in fear, and remained silent. After a few minutes, he said: "I am thy servant, even to death." Then the King replied: "Carry this black-faced dog to the execution ground. I will come in person without delay to kill him in revenge for the blood of my slaughtered subjects."

So he mounted his elephant, and his guard marched proudly before him. The cat, with his hands tied together, stood weeping. Upon arriving at the execution grounds and discerning that the cat was not yet executed, the King said angrily to the hangman: "Why is it this prisoner is still alive? Hang him immediately!"

At that very moment a horseman came galloping furiously from the city and besought the King, saying: "Forgive this miserable cat; in future he will do us no harm." However, the King turned a deaf ear to his entreaties, ordering that the cat be killed at once. The mice hesitated, being unwilling, through fear, to carry out the order.

Of course, this made the King very angry. "O foolish mice!" he cried. "Ye will all take pity on the cat, in order that he may again make a sacrifice of you."

Directly the cat saw the horseman, his courage revived. With one bound he sprang from his place as does the tiger on his prey, burst his bonds asunder, and seized five unfortunate mice. The other mice, filled with dismay and terror, ran hither and thither, crying wildly: "Allah! Allah! Shoot him! Cut off his head, as did Rastam his enemies on the day of battle!"

When the King of the Mice saw what had happened, he fainted; whereupon the cat leaped on him, pulled off his crown, and, placing the rope over his head, hanged him, so that he died immediately.

Then he darted here and there, seizing and slaying, and dashing mice to the earth, till the whole army of mice was routed, and there was none left to oppose him.

Morality, Justice & Twists of Fate

A TALE WELL TOLD is the best pedagogy. Linear outlines, organized by subject matter with points and subpoints, may have temporarily won the day in Western institutions. But more often it is the plots, narratives and dénouements that we remember... and that we prefer. Great teachers throughout the ages have known this. Rather than posit ethical requirements logically deduced from ontological commitments, they mostly told stories. Moralizing is often met with suspicion and critique, but stories invite participation.

Nasreddin Hodja's experience at the banquet (see 'Eat My Coat, Eat') is quite familiar – we easily identify with each and every one of the characters: the host, the guests and the hodja himself. And as we do, we connect with the moral imperatives underlying this scenario because they cohere to a plot we can vicariously experience. The entries that follow are compelling because they involve the reader by invitation not declaration.

How the Hodja Saved Allah
(Turkish)

NOT FAR FROM THE FAMOUS Mosque Bayezid an old Hodja kept a school, and very skilfully he taught the rising generation the everlasting lesson from the Book of Books. Such knowledge had he of human nature that by a glance at his pupil he could at once tell how long it would take him to learn a quarter of the Koran. He was known over the whole Empire as the best reciter and imparter of the Sacred Writings of the Prophet. For many years this Hodja, famed far and wide as the Hodja of Hodjas, had taught in this little school. The number of times he had recited the Book with his pupils is beyond counting; and should we attempt to consider how often he must have corrected them for some misplaced word, our beards would grow gray in the endeavor.

Swaying to and fro one day as fast as his old age would let him, and reciting to his pupils the latter part of one of the chapters, Bakara, divine inspiration opened his inward eye and led him to pause at the following sentence: "And he that spends his money in the ways of Allah is likened unto a grain of wheat that brings forth seven sheaves, and in each sheaf an hundred grains; and Allah giveth twofold unto whom He pleaseth." As his pupils, one after the other, recited this verse to him, he wondered why he had overlooked its meaning for so many years. Fully convinced that anything either given to Allah, or in the way that He proposes, was an investment that brought a percentage undreamed of in known commerce, he dismissed his pupils, and, putting his hand into his bosom, drew forth from the many folds of his dress a bag, and proceeded to count his worldly possessions.

Carefully and attentively he counted and then recounted his money, and found that if invested in the ways of Allah it would bring a return of no less than one thousand piasters.

"Think of it," said the Hodja to himself, "one thousand piasters! One thousand piasters! Mashallah! a fortune."

So, having dismissed his school, he sallied forth, his bag of money in his hand, and began distributing its contents to the needy that he met in the highways. Ere many hours had passed the whole of his savings was gone. The Hodja was very happy; for now he was the creditor in Allah's books for one thousand piasters.

He returned to his house and ate his evening meal of bread and olives, and was content.

The next day came. The thousand piasters had not yet arrived. He ate his bread, he imagined he had olives, and was content.

The third day came. The old Hodja had no bread and he had no olives. He suffered the pangs of hunger. So when the end of the day had come, and his pupils had departed to their homes, the Hodja, with a full heart and an empty stomach, walked out of the town, and soon got beyond the city walls.

There, where no one could hear him, he lamented his sad fate, and the great calamity that had befallen him in his old age.

What sin had he committed? What great wrong had his ancestors done, that the wrath of the Almighty had thus fallen on him, when his earthly course was well-nigh run?

"Ya! Allah! Allah!" he cried, and beat his breast.

As if in answer to his cry, the howl of the dreaded Fakir Dervish came over across the plain. In those days the Fakir Dervish was a terror in the land. He knocked at the door, and it was opened. He asked, and received food. If refused, life often paid the penalty.

The Hodja's lamentations were now greater than ever; for should the Dervish ask him for food and the Hodja have nothing to give, he would certainly be killed.

"Allah! Allah! Allah! Guide me now. Protect one of your faithful followers," cried the frightened Hodja, and he looked around to see if there was anyone to rescue him from his perilous position. But not a soul was to be seen, and the walls of the city were five miles distant. Just then the howl of the Dervish again reached his ear, and in terror he flew, he knew not whither. As luck would have it, he came upon a tree, up which, although stiff from age and weak from want, the Hodja, with wonderful agility, scrambled and, trembling like a leaf, awaited his fate.

Nearer and nearer came the howling Dervish, till at last his long hair could be seen floating in the air, as with rapid strides he preceded the wind upon his endless journey.

On and on he came, his wild yell sending the blood, from very fear, to unknown parts of the poor Hodja's body and leaving his face as yellow as a melon.

To his utter dismay, the Hodja saw the Dervish approach the tree and sit down under its shade.

Sighing deeply, the Dervish said in a loud voice, "Why have I come into this world? Why were my forefathers born? Why was anybody born? Oh, Allah! Oh, Allah! What have you done! Misery! Misery! Nothing but misery to mankind and everything living. Shall I not be avenged for all the misery my father and my father's fathers have suffered? I shall be avenged."

Striking his chest a loud blow, as if to emphasize the decision he had come to, the Dervish took a small bag that lay by his side, and slowly proceeded to untie the leather strings that bound it. Bringing forth from it a small image, he gazed at it a moment and then addressed it in the following terms:

"You, Job! you bore much; you have written a book in which your history is recorded; you have earned the reputation of being the most patient man that ever lived; yet I have read your history and found that when real affliction oppressed you, you cursed God. You have made men believe, too, that there is a reward in this life for all the afflictions they suffer. You have misled mankind. For these sins no one has ever punished you. Now I will punish you," and taking his long, curved sword in his hand he cut off the head of the figure.

The Dervish bent forward, took another image and, gazing upon it with a contemptuous smile, thus addressed it:

"David, David, singer of songs of peace in this world and in the world to come, I have read your sayings in which you counsel men to lead a righteous life for the sake of the reward which they are to receive. I have learned that you have misled your fellow-mortals with your songs of peace and joy. I have read your history, and I find that you have committed many sins. For these sins and for misleading your fellowmen you have never been punished. Now I will punish you," and taking his sword in his hand he cut off David's head.

Again the Dervish bent forward and brought forth an image which he addressed as follows:

"You, Solomon, are reputed to have been the wisest man that ever lived. You had command over the host of the Genii and could control the legion of the demons. They came at the bidding of your signet ring, and they trembled at the mysterious names to which you gave utterance. You understood every living thing. The speech of the beasts of the field, of the birds of the air, of the insects of the earth, and of the fishes of the sea, was known unto you. Yet when I read your history I found that in spite of the vast knowledge that was vouchsafed unto you, you committed many wrongs and did many foolish things, which in the end brought misery into the world and destruction unto your people; and for all these no one has ever punished you. Now I will punish you," and taking his sword, he cut off Solomon's head.

Again the Dervish bent forward and brought forth from the bag another figure, which he addressed thus:

"Jesus, Jesus, prophet of God, you came into this world to atone, by giving your blood, for the sins of mankind and to bring unto them a religion of peace. You founded a church, whose history I have studied, and I see that it set fathers against their children and brethren against one another; that it brought strife into the world; that the lives of men and women and children were sacrificed so that the rivers ran red with blood unto the seas. Truly you were a great prophet, but the misery you caused must be avenged. For it no one has yet punished you. Now I will punish you," and he took his sword and cut off Jesus' head.

With a sorrowful face the Dervish bent forward and brought forth another image from the bag.

"Mohammed," he said, "I have slain Job, David, Solomon, and Jesus. What shall I do with you? After the followers of Jesus had shed much blood, their religion spread over the world, was acceptable unto man, and the nations were at peace. Then you came into the world, and you brought a new religion, and father rose against father, and brother rose against brother; hatred was sown between your followers and the followers of Jesus, and again the rivers ran red with blood unto the seas; and you have not been punished. For this I will punish you. By the beard of my forefathers, whose blood was made to flow in your cause, you too must die," and with a blow the head of Mohammed fell to the ground.

Then the Dervish prostrated himself to the earth, and after a silent prayer rose and brought forth from the bag the last figure. Reverently he bowed to it, and then he addressed it as follows:

"Oh, Allah! The Allah of Allahs. There is but one Allah, and thou art He. I have slain Job, David, Solomon, Jesus, and Mohammed for the folly that they have brought into the world. Thou, God, art all powerful. All men are thy children, thou createst them and bringest them into the world. The thoughts that they think are thy thoughts. If all these men have brought all this evil into the world, it is thy fault. Shall I punish them and allow thee to go unhurt? No. I must punish thee also," and he raised his sword to strike.

As the sword circled in the air the Hodja, secreted in the tree, forgot the fear in which he stood of the Dervish. In the excitement of the moment he cried out in a loud tone of voice: "Stop! Stop! He owes me one thousand piasters."

The Dervish reeled and fell senseless to the ground. The Hodja was overcome at his own words and trembled with fear, convinced that his last hour had arrived. The Dervish lay stretched upon his back on the grass like one dead. At last the Hodja took courage. Breaking a twig from off the tree, he threw it down upon the Dervish's face, but the Dervish made no sign. The Hodja took more courage, removed one of his heavy outer shoes and threw it on the outstretched figure of the Dervish, but still the Dervish lay motionless. The Hodja carefully climbed down the tree, gave the body of the Dervish a kick, and climbed back again, and still the Dervish did not stir. At length the Hodja descended from the tree and placed his ear to the Dervish's heart. It did not beat. The Dervish was dead.

"Ah, well," said the Hodja, "at least I shall not starve. I will take his garments and sell them and buy me some bread."

The Hodja commenced to remove the Dervish's garments. As he took off his belt he found that it was heavy. He opened it, and saw that it contained gold. He counted the gold and found that it was exactly one thousand piasters.

The Hodja turned his face toward Mecca and, raising his eyes to heaven, said, "Oh God, you have kept your promise, but," he added, "not before I saved your life."

How Cobbler Ahmet Became the Chief Astrologer
(Turkish)

EVERY DAY COBBLER AHMET, year in and year out, measured the breadth of his tiny cabin with his arms as he stitched old shoes. To do this was his Kismet, his decreed fate, and he was content – and why not? his business brought him quite sufficient to provide the necessaries of life for both himself and his wife. And had it not been for a coincidence that occurred, in all probability he would have mended old boots and shoes to the end of his days.

One day cobbler Ahmet's wife went to the Hamam (bath), and while there she was much annoyed at being obliged to give up her compartment, owing to the arrival of the Harem and retinue of the Chief Astrologer to the Sultan. Much hurt, she returned home and vented her pique upon her innocent husband.

"Why are you not the Chief Astrologer to the Sultan?" she said. "I will never call or think of you as my husband until you have been appointed Chief Astrologer to his Majesty."

Ahmet thought that this was another phase in the eccentricity of woman which in all probability would disappear before morning, so he took small notice of what his wife said. But Ahmet was wrong. His wife persisted so much in his giving up his present means of earning a livelihood and becoming an astrologer, that finally, for the sake of peace, he complied with her desire. He sold his tools and collection of sundry old boots and shoes, and, with the proceeds purchased an inkwell and reeds. But this, alas! did not constitute him an astrologer, and he explained to his wife that this mad idea of hers would bring him to an unhappy end. She, however, could not be moved, and insisted on his going to the highway, there to wisely practise the art, and thus ultimately become the Chief Astrologer.

In obedience to his wife's instructions, Ahmet sat down on the highroad, and his oppressed spirit sought comfort in looking at the heavens and sighing deeply. While in this condition a Hanoum in great excitement came and asked him if he communicated with the stars. Poor Ahmet sighed, saying that he was compelled to converse with them.

"Then please tell me where my diamond ring is, and I will both bless and handsomely reward you."

The Hanoum, with this, immediately squatted on the ground, and began to tell Ahmet that she had gone to the bath that morning and that she was positive that she then had the ring, but every corner of the Hamam had been searched, and the ring was not to be found.

"Oh! astrologer, for the love of Allah, exert your eye to see the unseen."

"Hanoum Effendi," replied Ahmet, the instant her excited flow of language had ceased, "I perceive a rent," referring to a tear he had noticed in her shalvars, or baggy trousers.

Up jumped the Hanoum, exclaiming: "A thousand holy thanks! You are right! Now I remember! I put the ring in a crevice of the cold water fountain." And in her gratitude she handed Ahmet several gold pieces.

In the evening he returned to his home, and, giving the gold to his wife, said: "Take this money, wife; may it satisfy you, and in return all I ask is that you allow me to go back to the trade of my father, and not expose me to the danger and suffering of trudging the road shoeless."

But her purpose was unmoved. Until he became the Chief Astrologer she would neither call him nor think of him as her husband.

In the meantime, owing to the discovery of the ring, the fame of Ahmet the cobbler spread far and wide. The tongue of the Hanoum never ceased to sound his praise.

It happened that the wife of a certain Pasha had appropriated a valuable diamond necklace, and as a last resource, the Pasha determined, seeing that all the astrologers, Hodjas, and diviners had failed to discover the article, to consult Ahmet the cobbler, whose praises were in every mouth.

The Pasha went to Ahmet, and, in fear and trembling, the wife who had appropriated the necklace sent her confidential slave to overhear what the astrologer would say. The Pasha told Ahmet all he knew about the necklace, but this gave no clue, and in despair he asked how many diamonds the necklace contained. On being told that there were twenty-four, Ahmet, to put off the evil hour, said it would take an hour to discover each diamond; consequently would the Pasha come on the morrow at the same hour when, Inshallah, he would perhaps be able to give him some news.

The Pasha departed, and no sooner was he out of earshot, than the troubled Ahmet exclaimed in a loud voice: "Oh woman! Oh woman! what evil influence impelled you to go the wrong path, and drag others with you! When the twenty-four hours are up, you will perhaps repent! Alas! Too late. Your husband gone from you forever! Without a hope even of being united in paradise."

Ahmet was referring to himself and his wife, for he fully expected to be cast into prison on the following day as an impostor. But the slave who had been listening gave another interpretation to his words, and hurrying off, told her mistress that the astrologer knew all about the theft. The good man had even bewailed the separation that would inevitably take place. The Pasha's wife was distracted, and hurried off to plead her cause in person with the astrologer. On approaching Ahmet, the first words she said, in her excitement, were:

"Oh learned Hodja, you are a great and good man. Have compassion on my weakness and do not expose me to the wrath of my husband! I will do such penance as you may order, and bless you five times daily as long as I live."

"How can I save you?" innocently asked Ahmet. "What is decreed is decreed!"

And then, though silent, looked volumes, for he instinctively knew that words unuttered were arrows still in the quiver.

"If you won't pity me," continued the Hanoum, in despair, "I will go and confess to my Pasha, and perhaps he will forgive me."

To this appeal Ahmet said he must ask the stars for their views on the subject. The Hanoum inquired if the answer would come before the twenty-four hours were up. Ahmet's reply to this was a long and concentrated gaze at the heavens.

"Oh Hodja Effendi, I must go now, or the Pasha will miss me. Shall I give you the necklace to restore to the Pasha without explanation, when he comes tomorrow for the answer?"

Ahmet now realized what all the trouble was about, and in consideration of a fee, he promised not to reveal her theft on the condition that she would at once return home and place the necklace between the mattresses of her Pasha's bed. This the grateful woman agreed to do, and departed invoking blessings on Ahmet, who in return promised to exercise his influence on her behalf for astral intervention.

When the Pasha came to the astrologer at the appointed time, he explained to him that if he wanted both the necklace and the thief or thieves, it would take a long time, as it was impossible to hurry the stars; but if he would be content with the necklace alone, the horoscope indicated that the stars would oblige him at once. The Pasha said that he would be quite satisfied if he could get his diamonds again, and Ahmet at once told him where to find them. The Pasha returned to his home not a little sceptical, and immediately searched for the necklace where Ahmet had told him it was to be found. His joy and astonishment on discovering the long-lost article knew no bounds, and the fame of Ahmet the cobbler was the theme of every tongue.

Having received handsome payment from both the Pasha and the Hanoum, Ahmet earnestly begged of his wife to desist and not bring down sorrow and calamity upon his head. But his pleadings were in vain. Satan had closed his wife's ear to reason with envy. Resigned to his fate, all he could do was to consult the stars, and after mature thought give their communication, or assert that the stars had, for some reason best known to the applicant, refused to commune on the subject.

It happened that forty cases of gold were stolen from the Imperial Treasury, and every astrologer having failed to get even a clue as to where the money was or how it had disappeared, Ahmet was approached. Poor man, his case now looked hopeless! Even the Chief Astrologer was in disgrace. What might be his punishment he did not know – most probably death. Ahmet had no idea of the numerical importance of forty; but concluding that it must be large, he asked for a delay of forty days to discover the forty cases of gold. Ahmet gathered up the implements of his occult art, and before returning to his home, went to a shop and asked for forty beans – neither one more nor one less. When he got home and laid them down before him, he appreciated the number of cases of gold that had been stolen, and also the number of days he had to live. He knew it would be useless to explain to his wife the seriousness of the case, so that evening he took from his pocket the forty beans and mournfully said: "Forty cases of gold, forty thieves, forty days; and here is one of them," handing a bean to his wife. "The rest remain in their place until the time comes to give them up."

While Ahmet was saying this to his wife, one of the thieves was listening at the window. The thief was sure he had been discovered when he heard Ahmet say, "And here is one of them," and hurried off to tell his companions.

The thieves were greatly distressed, but decided to wait till the next evening and see what would happen then, and another of the number was sent to listen and see if the report would be verified. The listener had not long been stationed at his post when he heard Ahmet say to his wife: "And here is another of them," meaning another of the forty days of his life. But the thief understood the words otherwise, and hurried off to tell his chief that the astrologer knew all about it and knew that he had been there. The thieves consequently decided to send a delegation to Ahmet, confessing their guilt and offering to return the forty cases of gold intact. Ahmet received them, and on hearing their confession, accompanied with their condition to return the gold, boldly told them that he did not require their aid; that it was in his power to take possession of the forty cases of gold whenever he wished, but that he had no special desire to see them all executed, and he would plead their cause if they would go and put the gold in a place he indicated. This was agreed to, and Ahmet continued to give his wife a bean daily – but now with another purpose; he no longer feared the loss of his head, but discounted by degrees the great reward he hoped to receive. At last the final bean was given to his wife, and Ahmet was summoned to the Palace. He went, and explained to his Majesty that the stars refused both to reveal the thieves and the gold, but whichever of the two his Majesty wished would be immediately granted. The Treasury being low, it was decided that, provided the cases were returned with the gold intact, his Majesty would be satisfied. Ahmet conducted them to the place where the gold was buried, and amidst great rejoicing it was taken back to the Palace. The Sultan was so pleased with Ahmet, that he appointed him to the office of Chief Astrologer, and his wife attained her desire.

The Sultan was one day walking in his Palace grounds accompanied by his Chief Astrologer; wishing to test his powers, he caught a grasshopper, and, holding his closed hand out to the astrologer, asked him what it contained. Ahmet, in a pained and reproachful tone, answered the Sultan by a much-quoted proverb: "Alas! Your Majesty! the grasshopper never knows where its third leap will land it," figuratively alluding to himself and the dangerous hazard of guessing what was in the clenched hand of his Majesty. The Sultan was so struck by the reply that Ahmet was never again troubled to demonstrate his powers.

The Merciful Khan
(Turkish)

THERE LIVED ONCE near Ispahan a tailor, a hard-working man, who was very poor. So poor was he that his workshop and house together consisted of a wooden cottage of but one room.

But poverty is no protection against thieves, and so it happened that one night a thief entered the hut of the tailor. The tailor had driven nails in various places in the walls on which to hang the garments that were brought to him to mend. It chanced that in groping about for plunder, the thief struck against one of these nails and put out his eye.

The next morning the thief appeared before the Khan (Judge) and demanded justice. The Khan accordingly sent for the tailor, stated the complaint of the thief, and said that in accordance with the law, "an eye for an eye," it would be necessary to put out one of the tailor's eyes. As usual, however, the tailor was allowed to plead in his own defence, whereupon he thus addressed the court:

"Oh great and mighty Khan, it is true that the law says an eye for an eye, but it does not say my eye. Now I am a poor man, and a tailor. If the Khan puts out one of my eyes, I will not be able to carry on my trade, and so I shall starve. Now it happens that there lives near me a gunsmith. He uses but one eye with which he squints along the barrel of his guns. Take his other eye, oh Khan, and let the law be satisfied."

The Khan was favorably impressed with this idea, and accordingly sent for the gunsmith. He recited to the gunsmith the complaint of the thief and the statement of the tailor, whereupon the gunsmith said:

"Oh great and mighty Khan, this tailor knows not whereof he talks. I need both of my eyes; for while it is true that I squint one eye along one side of the barrel of the gun, to see if it is straight, I must use the other eye for the other side. If, therefore, you put out one of my eyes you will take away from me the means of livelihood. It happens, however, that there lives not far from me a flute-player. Now I have noticed that whenever he plays the flute he closes both of his eyes. Take out one of his eyes, oh Khan, and let the law be satisfied."

Accordingly, the Khan sent for the flute-player, and after reciting to him the complaint of the thief, and the words of the gunsmith, he ordered him to play upon his flute. This the flute-player did, and though he endeavored to control himself, he did not succeed, but, as the result of long habit, closed both of his eyes. When the Khan saw this, he ordered that one of the flute-player's eyes be put out, which being done, the Khan spoke as follows:

"Oh flute-player, I saw that when playing upon your flute you closed both of your eyes. It was thus clear to me that neither was necessary for your livelihood, and I had intended to have them both put out, but I have decided to put out only one in order that you may tell among men how merciful are the Khans."

The Prayer Rug and the Dishonest Steward
(Turkish)

A POOR HAMAL (PORTER) brought to the Pasha of Stamboul his savings, consisting of a small canvas bag of medjidies (Turkish silver dollars), to be kept for him, while he was absent on a visit to his home. The Pasha, being a kind-hearted man, consented, and after sealing the bag, called his steward, instructing him to keep it till the owner called for it. The steward gave the man a receipt, to the effect that he had received a sealed bag containing money.

When the poor man returned, he went to the Pasha and received his bag of money. On reaching his room he opened the bag, and to his horror found that it contained, instead of the medjidies he had put in it, copper piasters, which are about the same size as medjidies. The poor Hamal was miserable, his hard-earned savings gone.

He at last gathered courage to go and put his case before the Pasha. He took the bag of piasters, and with trembling voice and faltering heart he assured the Pasha that though he had received his bag apparently intact, on opening it he found that it contained copper piasters and not the medjidies he had put in it. The Pasha took the bag, examined it closely, and after some time noticed a part that had apparently been darned by a master-hand. The Pasha told the Hamal to go away and come back in a week; in the meantime he would see what he could do for him. The grateful man departed, uttering prayers for the life and prosperity of his Excellency.

The next morning after the Pasha had said his prayers kneeling on a most magnificent and expensive rug, he took a knife and cut a long rent in it. He then left his Konak without saying a word to anyone. In the evening when he returned, he found that the rent had been so well repaired that it was with difficulty that he discovered where it had been. Calling his steward, he demanded who had repaired his prayer rug. The steward told the Pasha that he thought the rug had been cut by accident by some of the servants, so he had sent to the Bazaar for the darner, Mustapha, and had it mended, the steward, by way of apology, adding that it was very well done.

"Send for Mustapha immediately," said the Pasha, "and when he comes, bring him to my room."

When Mustapha arrived, the Pasha asked him if he had repaired the rug. Mustapha at once replied that he had mended it that very morning.

"It is indeed well done," said the Pasha; "much better than the darn you made in that canvas bag."

Mustapha agreed, saying that it was very difficult to mend the bag, as it was full of copper piasters. On hearing this, the Pasha gave him a backsheesh (present) and told him to retire. The Pasha then called his steward, and not only compelled him to pay the Hamal his money, but discharged him from his service, in which he had been engaged for many years.

The Deceiver and the Thief
(Turkish)

THERE WAS ONCE a cunning woman who had two husbands, neither of whom knew of the other's existence. The one got his living by cheating, the other by stealing, each of which excellent industries they had learnt from the woman.

The thief went with his stolen goods to the merchant, sold them, and took the money to the woman. Then came the other to the merchant, gripped him by the collar, and said: "That is my property; that and more besides have been stolen from me – by thee I am certain. I will that thou takest it all back again to the place whence thou hast stolen it." But the other protested: "Woe is me! I am no thief; I have bought these things from others; how sayest thou they are thine? Let me go, and seek the real thief."

There was a great uproar. The thief perceived that they would soon be on his track, so he went home without loss of time. His wife informed him that his theft had been discovered, and advised him to go away for a few days to escape capture by the police.

The woman took a sheep's tail and cut it in two halves, one of which she made into a package with bread and gave to the thief, who soon shook the dust of the town from his feet.

In a short time the cheat came home and told the woman that his game was up; his deception could no longer be hidden. "Give me food," he said, "and I will withdraw myself from public notice until the storm has blown over." So the woman gave him the half loaf and the other half of the sheep's tail, and he quickly took himself off. The first, the thief, weary from long tramping, came to a river, where he sat down to rest. As he was unpacking his food, the deceiver came up, sat down, and, opening his packet, prepared to eat. The former said: "Friend, let us eat together." So they sat face to face. Presently the one called attention to the similarity of their respective pieces of bread, and putting them together they found the two formed a complete loaf. Presently the two pieces of sheep's tail attracted their notice; these were also put together, and a complete sheep's tail was the result.

Astounded, the deceiver said to the thief: "If I may ask, whence comest thou?" "From such and such a town," was the answer. "What street?" "In such and such a street lives a certain woman – she is my wife." The deceiver was almost choking with excitement. "Allah! Allah!" he cried, "that woman is my wife; she has been my wife for a year. Why dost thou lie?"

"Man, art thou out of thy senses, or joking?" returned the thief. "That woman has been my wife for a long time." Knowing not what to make of it, they both scratched their heads. At length the deceiver said: "This is a matter we cannot decide ourselves; let us go to the woman and ask her. Thus shall we know which of us two is her husband." They got up and set forth together. When the woman saw them both coming together, she suspected what was the matter. She greeted them, invited them to take seats, and sat herself opposite them. The deceiver opened the conversation. "Tell us," he said, "whose wife art thou?" "Hitherto," she replied, "I have been the wife of you both; henceforth I intend to be his who is the cleverer of you. I have taught you each a trade; he shall be my husband who plies it most to my satisfaction." Both men confessed themselves content to abide by the lady's decision. Said the deceiver to the thief: "Today I will prove my skill; tomorrow thou canst prove thine." On this they left the house together and went to the marketplace.

Now the deceiver observed a man put a thousand gold-pieces into his wallet, which he then hid in his bosom. The former stole after him, and in the pressure of the crowd, abstracted the wallet from the man's bosom. Going to a secluded spot, he took out nine gold-pieces, slipped his seal-ring from his finger into the wallet, fastened it up, and went back and replaced it without observation in the bosom of its rightful owner.

We have said he did this "without observation"; there was one person, however, by whom the trick was observed – this was the thief. The deceiver now went away, and returned some time after to the owner of the wallet, grasped him by the scruff of the neck, and shouted: "Ah, rascal! thou hast stolen my wallet with the ducats!" The man was embarrassed, not understanding the accusation, but answered: "My friend, go thy way and leave me in peace. I do not know thee." To this the deceiver replied: "It is not necessary for thee to know me; come with me to the judge." There was nothing for it but to go. The deceiver was the accuser. "How many gold-pieces are there here?" demanded the judge of the accused. "A thousand," was the immediate answer. Then the judge turned to the accuser: "And how many have been stolen from thee?" "Nine hundred and ninety-one," readily replied he, "and my seal-ring will also be found in the wallet." The judge counted the ducats, and lo! there were exactly nine hundred and ninety-one and the seal-ring! The rightful owner was beaten severely, and the ducats handed to the deceiver, who went away.

The next evening the thief took a rope, and in company with the deceiver, went to the palace of the Padishah. The thief threw the rope over the wall, where it caught; he climbed up it and his friend followed. They entered the treasure chamber after trying various keys; and now the thief advised the deceiver to take away as many ducats as he could carry. He himself, dazzled by the sight of so much gold, got together as much as he could put on his back, and away they went. The thief went to the fowl-house, caught a goose, wrung its neck, put it on a spit, made a fire under it and set it to cook, ordering his companion to turn it to prevent its burning. This done, he went back to the Padishah's sleeping-chamber. The deceiver called after him: "Stop! Whither goest thou?" "I am going," he answered, "to tell the Padishah what a clever thing I've done, and to ask him whether he thinks the woman should belong to me or to thee." His companion called back: "For God's sake, let us go away from here. I'll give up the woman; thou canst have her." "Oh, yes," was the retort, "now thou sayst thus; tomorrow thou wilt alter thy mind. But if the Padishah decides the matter, thou art bound to agree."

He slid stealthily into the Padishah's bed chamber. From where he hid he had a good view of the interior, and saw the Padishah lying in bed; a slave was chafing his feet and chewing a raisin. Taking a horsehair which lay on the floor, the thief stuck one end in the slave's mouth so that it adhered to the raisin. The slave, being very sleepy, commenced to yawn, and no sooner had he opened his mouth than the thief withdrew the raisin by means of the horse hair and transferred it to his own mouth. The slave now opened his eyes very wide, looked all about the floor, but nowhere could he find his raisin. Shortly afterwards he fell asleep. The thief held a phial of strong spirits under his nose until he lost his senses and fell to the floor like a log. Lifting him gently, the thief put him in a basket, hung the basket from the balcony, and commenced himself to chafe the monarch's feet. (The deceiver, who had followed, saw all this from the door of the apartment.) Suddenly the Padishah stirred, and the thief said in a low tone: "O King, if thou permittest, I will tell thee a story." "It is well," murmured the sleepy Padishah, "let me hear."

On this the thief related all that had happened between him and his companion. (Turning to him at the door, he admonished him to go and turn the goose lest it should burn.) He told of his burglary of the treasure-chamber, of the theft of the slave's raisin from his mouth. (All this time his companion was trembling just outside the door and continually crying in his fear: "Come away; let us go." To which the thief, interrupting his story, would retort: "Go and mind the goose.") "Now, O Padishah," concluded the thief, "whose exploit is the greater, mine or my friend's? Which of us has won the woman?" The King answered that the thief's was certainly the greater, and therefore the woman was rightfully his.

The thief continued to chafe the Padishah's feet a little longer until the latter was fast asleep; he then stole noiselessly away and rejoined his companion. "Hast heard what the Padishah said – that the woman belongs to me?" "Yes, yes, I heard," answered the other. Then the thief pressed the point: "Whose is the woman?" "I have said it, she is thine," answered the other rather testily. "Now let us get away from here, lest we should be discovered. I am nearly dead; I shall soon lose my wits." The deceiver was certainly nearly out of his mind with fright. Then the thief began again: "Thou hast lied; I will go once more and ask the Padishah." Terror-stricken, the other shrieked: "Thou wilt be caught. For all the world, let us go away out of this. Not only shall the woman be thy wife, but I also will be thy bond-slave!" At length they went away and took the money with them. They went directly to the woman, who was so pleased with the thief's prowess that she married him without further delay.

Next morning the Padishah woke up and called for his slaves. Deep silence reigned everywhere. Seeing that no one came, the monarch waited a little, then called again. Still no slave came. Then, his anger rising, the Padishah sprang from his bed and saw the basket suspended from the balcony. "What's this?" he said, and taking down the basket, saw his attendant in a state of insensibility within. Then calling more loudly, a number of slaves ran in and brought back the stupefied man to consciousness. The King demanded to know what was the matter with the man. He was quite unable to say. Now it began to dawn upon the Padishah that he had during the night listened to some story told by a thief. He seated himself at once on his throne and sent for his vezirs. All the vezirs, beys, and mighty men came, and when they were assembled the King related his experience of the previous night. "This thief must be found," he concluded. "Let heralds proclaim in all the city that he may come to me in confidence. I swear by Allah that no harm shall be done him; he may keep the gold he has stolen and he shall have a pension besides."

Thus the heralds proclaimed the will of their lord and master. The thief heard, and when he knew that the Padishah had sworn, he went boldly into his presence and said: "O Shah, thou mayst kill me or reward me: I am the man!"

"Why hast thou done this thing?" demanded the monarch. The thief related all from beginning to end.

True to his oath, the Padishah allowed the thief to keep the stolen treasure, and settled a pension on him for life. But the latter, out of gratitude for the Padishah's clemency, vowed on his heart and soul that he would never steal again; and both he and his wife prayed constantly for the health and happiness of the Padishah as long as they lived.

The Island of Akdamar
(Turkish)

MANY YEARS AGO, in the eastern part of Anatolia, there lived a priest who served God at a little church that was on the island in the middle of Lake Van. He had one daughter named Tamara. She was very lovely, and when she reached the age when most girls of that time would marry, rumours of her beauty had spread far and wide. Yet her father denied any potential suitors, not allowing them even to step foot on the island.

Across the lake lived a boy who happened to be an excellent swimmer. From time to time, he would swim in the lake, and despite the distance, one day, he swam across and reached the island's shore. There, partially hidden among the trees, he glimpsed the girl, and she him. They fell in love immediately. Knowing that her father would never accept a marriage, they devised a plan. When the girl desired to see the boy, she would go down to the shore and light a lantern near the shore. Guided by its rays, the boy would know which way to swim. This he did many nights, and paying no heed to strenuous effort, he would reach the shore safe and sound where his beloved waited. One particularly dark and stormy night, the girl went down to the shore and lit the lantern. Seeing the light, the boy jumped in the lake and began to swim across just as he had many times before. That night, the wind drove the waves against him, but all the more determined, the boy simply doubled his efforts. But unbeknownst to the young lovers, the priest had become wise to their trysts. He came to the shore and extinguished the lantern. Suddenly, the boy had no idea which way to swim. Turning this way and that, he swam in circles, unable to reach the shore. Summoning his last bit of strength, he lifted his head out of the water and called out to his love, "Ahh, Tamara!" Hearing him at last, she ran to the shore, only to find him sinking beneath the waves, never to surface again. Lovesick and grief-stricken, she threw herself into the sea. It was there that the lifeless bodies of the two met. From then on, locals referred to the island as "Ah, Tamara," and over time, this was shortened to its present Turkish name, "Akdamar."

The Story of Delu Dumrul, Son of Duha Khoja
Legend III from The Book of Dede Korkut

MY KHAN, AMONG THE OGHUZ PEOPLE there was a man by the name of Delu Dumrul, the son of Duha Khoja. He had a bridge built across a dry riverbed. He collected thirty-three akchas from anyone who passed over it, and those who refused to pass over it he beat and charged forty akchas anyway. He did this to challenge anyone who thought he was braver than Delu Dumrul to fight, with the purpose of making his own bravery, heroism and gallantry known even in places as far distant as Anatolia and Syria.

One day it happened that a troop of nomads camped along his bridge. A fine, handsome youth in the nomad troop fell sick and died at the command of Allah. Some cried saying "Son", some cried saying "Brother", and there was great mourning for him.

Delu Dumrul, enhancing to come along, asked: "Why are you crying, cuckolds? What is this noise by my bridge? Why are you mourning?"

They said: "My khan, we lost a fine young man. That is why we are crying."

Delu Dumrul asked: "Who killed your bey?"

They said: "Oh, bey, it was by the order of Almighty Allah. The red-winged Azrail took his life."

"What sort of fellow is this Azrail who takes people's lives? For the sake of your unity and existence, O Almighty Allah, let me see Azrail. Let me fight and scuffle with him to save the life of such a fine youth, so that he never takes a life again," said Delu Dumrul. He then turned away and went home.

Now, Almighty Allah was not pleased with Dumrul's words. He said: "Look at that madman. He does not understand my oneness. He does not express his gratitude to me and dares to behave arrogantly in my mighty presence." He ordered Azrail: "Go and appear before the eyes of that madman. Make his face pale and strangle the life out of him."

While Delu Dumrul was sitting and drinking with his forty companions, Azrail suddenly arrived. Neither the chamberlains nor the wardens had seen Azrail pass. Delu Dumrul's eyes were blinded, his hands paralysed. The entire world was darkened to his eyes. He began to speak. Let us see what he said, my khan.

"What a mighty, big old man you are!
The wardens did not see you come;
The chamberlains did not hear.
My eyes, which could see, now cannot;
My hands, which could grip, now cannot.
My soul trembled and was terrified;
My golden cup fell from my hand.
My mouth is cold as ice;
My bones are turned to dust.
Ho! white-bearded old man,
Cold-eyed old man!
What mighty old man are you?
Go away, or I may hurt you."

Azrail was angry at these remarks. He said:

"Oh, madman,
Do you dislike the cold expression in my eyes?
I have taken the lives of many lovely eyed girls and brides.
Why is it you dislike my white beard?
I have taken the lives of both white-bearded and black-bearded men.
That is why my own beard is white."

He then continued in this way: "Oh, madman! You were boasting and saying that you would kill the red-winged Azrail if you caught him to save the life of the fine young lad. Oh, fool, now I have come to take your life. Will you give it, or will you fight with me?"

Delu Dumrul asked: "Are you the red-winged Azrail?"

"Yes, I am," replied Azrail.

"Are you the one who takes the lives of these fine boys?" asked Dumrul.

"That is so," said Azrail.

Delu Dumrul said, "Ho, wardens, shut the doors." He then turned to Azrail and said: "O Azrail, I was expecting to catch you in a wide open place, but I caught you in a narrow one, did I not? Let me kill you and save the life of that fine young man." He drew his big black sword, held it in his hand and tried to strike Azrail with it, but Azrail became a pigeon and flew out of the window. Delu Dumrul, a monster of a man, clapped his hands and burst out in laughter. He said: "My friends, I frightened Azrail so much that he ran out, not through the wide open door, but through the chimney. To save himself from my hand, he just became a pigeon and flew away. I shall have him caught by my falcon."

He mounted his horse, took his falcon on his wrist and started pursuing Azrail. He killed a few pigeons. On the way home, however, Azrail appeared to the eyes of his horse. The horse was frightened and threw Delu Dumrul off its back to the ground. His poor head grew dizzy, and he became powerless. Azrail came and pressed down upon his white chest. He had been murmuring a short while ago, but now he gasped out through the rattle in his throat:

"O Azrail, have mercy!
There is no doubt about the unity of Allah.
I was uninformed about you.
I did not know you secretly took lives.
We have mountains with large peaks;
We have vineyards on those mountains;
In those vineyards there are vines with bunches of black grapes;
And, when pressed, those grapes make wine, red wine.
A man who drinks that wine grows drunk.
Thus I was drunk, and so I did not hear.
I did not know what I had said.
I have not tired of the role of bey.
I wish to live out more years of my youth.
O Azrail, please spare this life of mine."

Azrail said: "You mad rascal, why do you beg mercy from me? Beg mercy from Almighty Allah. What is in my hands? I am but a servant."

Delu Dumrul said: "Is it, then, Almighty Allah who gives and takes our lives?"

"Of course," said Azrail.

Delu Dumrul then turned to Azrail and said: "You are a cursed fellow. Do not interfere with my business. Let me talk with Almighty Allah myself." Delu Dumrul spoke to Allah. Let us listen, my khan, to what he said.

"You are higher than the highest.
No one knows how high you are,
Allah the Magnificent.
Fools search for you up in the sky and on earth;
You are found in the hearts of the faithful,
Eternal and Almighty Allah.
Immortal, merciful Allah,
If you wish to take my life away,
Then take it by yourself.
Let not Azrail do it."

Almighty Allah was pleased with the way Delu Dumrul addressed him this time. He shouted to Azrail that, because the mad rascal believed in His oneness, he was giving him his blessing and that his life might be spared if he could find another willing to serve as a substitute for him.

Azrail said to Delu Dumrul: "Oh, Delu Dumrul, it is the command of Almighty Allah that you should provide the life of someone else for your own, which will then be spared."

Delu Dumrul said: "How can I find someone else's life? I have no one in the world but an old mother and an old father. Let us go and see if one of them will give his life for me. If so, you can take it, and leave me mine." Delu Dumrul rode to his father's house, kissed his father's hand and spoke to him. Let us see, my khan, what he said to his father.

> *"My white-bearded father, beloved and respected,*
> *Do you know what has happened to me?*
> *I spoke in blasphemy,*
> *And my words made Allah the Almighty angry.*
> *He commanded the red-winged Azrail above*
> *To fly from the sky.*
> *He pressed on my white chest, sitting on me.*
> *He made my throat rattle, almost took my sweet life.*
> *Father, I beg you to give me your life.*
> *Will you give me it, father?*
> *Or would you prefer to weep after me, saying*
> *'My son Delu Dumrul!'?"*

His father answered:

> *"Son, son, oh, my son!*
> *A part of my life, oh, Son.*
> *Lion-like son, for whom I once had slaughtered nine camels,*
> *Backbone of my house with its chimneys of gold,*
> *A flower to my gooselike daughters and brides.*
> *If need be, command the black mountain out yonder*
> *To come here and serve as Azrail's pasture.*

If need be, then let my cool springs be his fountain.
If need be, then give him my stables of beautiful horses to ride.
If need be, my caravan camel can carry his goods.
If need be, the white sheep that stand in my fold
Can be cooked in the kitchen for food at his feast.
If need be, my silver and gold money will be for him.
But the world is too sweet, and living too dear
To spare my own life. So know this.
There remains yet your mother, more dear and beloved than I.
Son, go to your mother."

Refused by his father, Delu Dumrul next rode to his mother and said to her:

"Do you know what has happened to me, my mother?
The red-winged Azrail flew down from the sky
And pressed my white chest as he sat upon me.
He made my throat rattle, almost took away life.
My father denied me the life that I asked from him, mother.
I ask you for yours, now, my mother.
Will you give me your life?
Or would you prefer to weep after me, saying 'My son, Delu Dumrul!'
While scratching your white face with sharp fingernails
And tearing your white spear-like hair?"

Let us hear, my khan, what his mother said.

"Son, son, oh, my son!
Son, whom I carried nine months in my narrow womb,
Whom I bore in the tenth month
And swaddled in the cradle with care,
Whom I fed my abundant white milk.
Son, I wish you had rather been held in a white-towered castle,
Been held there by infidel men with religion so foul,
So that then I might have saved you, using the power of wealth.
But instead, you are sunk to a frightful position

Where I cannot reach you.
The world is too sweet, and the human soul too dear
To spare my own life. So know this."

His mother also refused to give her life for him. Azrail, therefore, came to take Delu Dumrul's life. Delu Dumrul said:

"O Azrail, be not hasty.
There is no doubt about the oneness of Allah.
I was uninformed about you.
I did not know you secretly took lives.
We have mountains with large peaks;
We have vineyards on those mountains;
In those vineyards there are vines with bunches of black grapes;
And, when pressed, those grapes make wine, red wine.
A man who drinks that wine grows drunk.
Thus I was drunk, and so I did not hear.
I did not know what I had said.
I have not tired of the role of bey.
I wish to live out more years of my youth.
O Azrail, please spare this life of mine."

Azrail replied: "Oh, you madman, why do you keep begging for mercy? You went to your white-bearded father, but he refused to give you his life. You then went to your white-haired mother, and she also refused to give you her life. Who do you think will give you his life?"

"I have yet a loved one. Let me go and see her," said Delu Dumrul.

"Who is your loved one, mad fellow?" asked Azrail.

"I have a lawful wife, the daughter of a man from another tribe, and I have two children by her. Take my life after I visit them. I have a few things to say to them." He rode then to his wife and said to her:

"Do you know what has happened to me?
The red-winged Azrail flew down from the sky
And pressed my white chest as he sat upon me.

He almost took away my sweet life.
My father denied me the life that I asked from him.
I went to my mother, but she refused, too.
They said that the world was too sweet and life was too dear.
Let my high black mountains now be your pasture.
Let my cooling springs be your fountain.
Let my stables of beautiful horses be yours now to ride.
Let my beautiful gold-chimneyed house give you shelter.
Let my caravan camels carry your goods.
Let white sheep in my fold be served at your feast.
Go, marry another,
Whomever your heart loves.
Let not our two sons remain orphans."

His wife then spoke. Let us hear, my khan, what she said.

"What is it you say,
My strong ram, my young shah,
Whom I loved at first sight,
And gave all of my heart?
Whom I gave my sweet lips to be kissed;
Whom I slept with upon the same pillow and loved.
What shall I do with the black mountains yonder When you are no
  longer here?
Should I take my flock there, let my grave be there, too?
Should I sip your cool springs, let my blood run like water.
Should I spend your gold coins, let them be for my shroud.
Should I ride on your stables of beautiful horses, let them be my hearse.
Should I love, after you, any other young man
And marry him, lie with him;
Let him turn serpent and then let him bite me.
What is there in life
That your miserable parents
Could spare not their own lives for yours?
Let the heavens, the eight-storied heavens, be witness;

Let the earth and the sky be my witness, as well;
Let Almighty Allah be witness for me:
Let my life be a sacrifice made for the sake of your own."

Saying this, she consented to die, and Azrail came to take the lady's life. But that monster of a man, Delu Dumrul, could not spare his companion. He pleaded with Almighty Allah. Let us hear how he pleaded.

"Thou art higher than the highest;
No one knows how high you are,
Allah the Magnificent!
Fools search for you in the sky and on earth,
But you live in the heart of the faithful.
Eternal and merciful Allah,
Let me build needed homes for the poor
Along the main roads of the land.
Let me feed hungry men for your sake when I see them.
If you take any life, take the lives of us both.
If you spare any life, spare the lives of us both,
Merciful Almighty Allah."

Almighty Allah was pleased with Delu Dumrul's words. He gave his orders to Azrail: "Take the lives of Delu Dumrul's father and mother. I have granted a life of 140 years to this lawfully married couple." Azrail proceeded to take the lives of the father and mother right away, but Delu Dumrul lived with his wife for 140 years more.

Dede Korkut came and told tales and sang legends. He said: "Let this legend be Delu Dumrul's. Let heroic minstrels after me sing it, and let generous men with clean foreheads listen to it."

Let me pray, my khan: may your rugged black mountains never fall down. May your large shade tree never be felled. May your clear running streams never dry up. May Almighty Allah never let you be at the mercy of the base. We have spoken five words of prayer in behalf of your white forehead. May they be accepted. May He clear away your sins and forgive them for the sake of Mohammed with the exalted name.

The Liver and the Cat
(A Nasreddin Hodja Tale)

O NE MORNING, NASREDDIN HODJA went to the market, and while he was there, he purchased two kilograms of liver, which he intended to have that evening for his supper. Upon returning home, he gave the packet of liver to his wife and asked her to prepare it for the family's evening meal. He then left the house on another errand.

While he was away, Nasreddin Hodja's wife cooked the liver and invited over some neighbours. She fed the freshly prepared dish to her guests, not even setting aside a portion for her husband. Several hours later, Nasreddin Hodja came home, looking forward to ending his day with a good meal. "Did you prepare the liver? Is it ready?" the Hodja asked his wife expectantly. "No," she replied. "I'm afraid that the cat has eaten it." Greatly disappointed, Nasreddin Hodja noticed that their old cat was ambling into the room just at that moment. It was a scrawny, mangy thing and not much to look at. Hodja immediately grabbed a scale and quickly put the cat on top of it. The scale showed that the cat weighed about two kilograms. Hodja glared at his wife and exclaimed, "If this is the cat, where is the liver? But if this is the liver, then please tell me, where is the cat?"

Pay to Play
(A Nasreddin Hodja Tale)

O NE DAY, SOME KIDS from the neighbourhood were playing outside and saw Nasreddin Hodja walking down the road. "Hodja," they called, "where are you going?" Hodja replied, "I'm off to the bazaar." The kids gathered around him and asked if he could buy each of them a flute while he was there. Hodja kindly agreed, and a few of the kids gave him money right then and there with which to purchase the flutes while at the bazaar.

Later in the day, Hodja returned, and began to pass the flutes out to the children. Each kid, after receiving their new instrument, began to play it with great vigour and gusto. Their cheerful sounds filled the air. But after passing out instruments to about half the children, Hodja stopped abruptly and began to walk away. The kids who were left standing without flutes were bewildered and called after him, "Hodja, what about us? How come you didn't give us flutes like you did the others?" Hodja responded, "Those who pay money are those who play flutes."

Eat, My Coat, Eat
(A Nasreddin Hodja Tale)

HODJA HAD BEEN INVITED to a special dinner, and when the big evening came, he showed up in the clothes that he had been wearing all day. No one greeted him when he entered the host's marvellous home. No one paid him any attention when he walked through the door to enter the banquet hall where the sumptuous dinner was to be served. And since no one directed him to a seat at the table, he simply found an empty chair on the far side of the room. Though servants brought dishes to the guests, no one offered him so much as a glass of water or a dry cracker.

Without warning, Hodja suddenly got up, left the banquet and returned to his own house. No one noticed him leave. Taking off his frayed garments, he put on his most expensive garment, a fur coat that had hardly ever been worn. He immediately walked back to the host's home and knocked on the door. He was heartily greeted by the head servant, "Good evening, Hodja! Please come right this way, we've been expecting you," and was ushered into the banquet hall. Once there, he was seated to the right of the host, the spot reserved for the guest of honour. Meanwhile, servants scrambled to fill Hodja's glass with wine and delivered a plate spilling over with roasted lamb, sautéed onions, grilled tomatoes and several slices of thick, warm bread just out of the oven. Upon seeing the steaming lentil soup also placed in front of him, Hodja plunged the sleeve of his fur coat into the bowl and exclaimed, "Eat, my coat, eat!"

You're Also Right!
(A Nasreddin Hodja Tale)

TWO TOWNSPEOPLE came to Hodja one day, embroiled in fierce debate. After quieting them down, Hodja had the first man explain his side of the story. "It makes sense," Hodja said, "you are clearly right in this matter."

Hodja then turned to the second man and asked for his side of the story. After hearing his version of the situation, Hodja replied, "Ah! That makes sense, now I see that you are the correct one." Hodja's wife had been listening in the whole time and couldn't stop herself from exclaiming, "Hodja, you simply agree with whomever is the last one to speak!" Hodja looked at her and said, "You know, you are right, too!"

Hodja's Turban
(A Nasreddin Hodja Tale)

HODJA WAS EASILY recognized as a man of learning because he always wore a turban. In those days, only scholars and the few individuals who could read and write wore such head coverings.

One day, a man brought him a letter. "Would you please read it to me, Hodja?" he requested. Hodja unfolded the document, glanced at it, and put it aside. "What's the matter?" asked the man. "Can't you read it?" "No," replied Hodja, "I can't. It's written in Arabic, and I read only Turkish. You will have to find someone else." The man became very angry. "Hodja, you should be ashamed of yourself. And to think that you go around calling yourself a scholar! You should be embarrassed to wear a turban like that." Now it was Hodja's turn to get angry. He ripped off the turban and threw it to the ground. "Go ahead, put it on. If the power is in the turban, then let's see if you can read the letter!" he exclaimed.

The King's Treasure
(Persian)

ALABOURING MAN named Abdul Karim, with his wife Zeeba – "the beautiful one" – lived in a sheltered valley, surrounded by hills, the sides of which were covered with fine gardens, in which the peach, the grape, the mulberry and other delicious fruits grew in great profusion.

Although his wife's name was Zeeba, as a matter of fact, she was very plain in appearance. But from having been named Zeeba, she really thought she was beautiful, and thus it came about that, moved by vanity, her two children were named, the boy, Yusuf, or Joseph, who as you know, was sold by his brethren into Egypt and became next to the King; and the girl, Fatima, after Fatima, the favourite daughter of Mahomet, and the wife of the famous Ali.

Now Abdul Karim was only a labourer on the land, receiving no wages, merely being paid in grain and cloth sufficient for the wants of himself and his family. Of money he knew nothing except by name.

One day his master was so pleased with his work that he actually gave him ten "krans," equivalent to about a dollar of our money. To Abdul

Karim this seemed great wealth, and directly his day's work was done, he ran home to his wife and said: "Look, Zeeba, there's riches for you!" and spread out the money before her. His good wife was delighted, and so were the children.

Then Abdul Karim said, "How shall we spend this great sum? The master has also given me a day's holiday, so if you don't mind, I will go to the famous city of Meshed, which is only twenty miles from here, and after placing two krans on the shrine of the holy Imam, I will then visit the bazaars and buy everything you and the children desire."

"You would better buy me a piece of silk for a new dress," said Zeeba.

"I want a fine horse and a sword," said little Yusuf.

"I would like an Indian handkerchief and a pair of gold slippers," said Fatima.

"They shall be here by tomorrow night," said the father, and taking a big stick, he set off on his journey.

When he had come down from the mountains to the plain below, Abdul Karim saw stretched before him the glorious city, and was lost in wonder at the sight of the splendid domes, where roofs glittered with gold, and the minarets, from the tops of which the priests were calling the people to prayer.

Then, coming to the gate of the shrine, he asked an old priest if he might enter. "Yes, my son," was the reply. "Go in and give what thou canst spare to the mosque, and Allah will reward thee."

So Abdul Karim walked through the great court, amidst worshippers from every city in Asia. With open-mouthed astonishment he gazed on the riches of the temple, the jewels, the lovely carpets, the silks, the golden ornaments, and with humility he placed his two pieces of money on the sacred tomb. Then through the noise and bustle of the crowded streets he went until he found the bazaars.

He found the sellers of fruits in one place, in another those who sold pots and pans, then he came to the jewellers, the bakers, the butchers, each trade having its own part of the bazaar, and so on, until he reached that part where there were only those who sold silks.

He entered one of the shops and asked to see some silks, and after much picking and choosing, fixed upon a superb piece of purple silk with an embroidered border of exquisite design. "I will take this," he said. "What is the price?"

"I shall only ask you two hundred krans, as you are a new customer," said the shopkeeper. "Anybody else but you would have to pay three or four hundred."

"Two hundred krans," repeated Abdul Karim, in astonishment. "Surely you have made a mistake. Do you mean krans like these?" taking one out of his pocket.

"Certainly I do," replied the shopkeeper, "and let me tell you it is very cheap at that price."

Abdul Karim pictured the disappointment of his wife. "Poor Zeeba," he sighed.

"Poor who?" said the silk merchant.

"My wife," said Abdul Karim.

"What have I to do with your wife?" asked the merchant, getting angry because he saw that all his trouble was in vain.

"I will tell you about it," said Abdul Karim. "Because I did my work well, my master gave me ten krans, the first time I ever have had any money. After giving two krans to the shrine, I intended to buy a piece of silk for my wife, a horse and sword for my little boy Yusuf, and an Indian handkerchief and a pair of gold slippers for my little girl Fatima. And here you ask me two hundred krans for one piece of silk. How can I pay you and buy the other things?"

"Here I have been wasting my time and rumpling my beautiful silks for a fool like you," cried the angry merchant. "Get out of my shop! Go home to your stupid Zeeba and your stupid children. Buy them some stale cakes and some black sugar, and don't put your head in my shop again, or it will be worse for you."

Then he took off his slipper, and with many blows drove poor Abdul Karim out into the street. Then Abdul Karim went to the horse market, only to find that the lowest-priced horse would cost two hundred and fifty krans.

The horse dealer mocked him when they found he had only eight krans, and suggested that he buy the sixteenth part of a donkey for his little son. As for a sword, he found that it would cost at least thirty krans; while a pair of golden slippers would run into many hundreds of krans; and for an Indian handkerchief, the price was twelve krans.

As poor Abdul Karim bent his weary way home, he met a beggar crying, "Dear friend, give me something, for tomorrow is Friday" – the Mahommedan Sunday. "He that giveth to the poor, lendeth to the Lord, and of a certainty the Lord will pay him back a hundredfold."

"Of all the men I have met today, you are the only one with whom I can deal," said simple Abdul Karim. "Here are eight krans. Use them in the service of God, and don't forget to pay me back a hundredfold."

Wrapping up the eight krans very carefully, the cunning beggar promised some day to return them a hundredfold.

At last Abdul Karim came in sight of his cottage, and little Yusuf, who had been all day on the lookout for him, ran breathlessly to meet him. "Where's my horse and sword, father?" he cried. And Fatima, who had just come up, called out, "And my handkerchief and golden slippers?" And Zeeba asked for her bit of silk.

Poor Abdul Karim looked so confused that his wife said: "Be quiet, my dears. Your father could not bring them all with him, so he has packed them on Yusuf's horse and left him in charge of a servant, who will be here presently." But when she heard his story, and above all that he had given eight krans to a beggar, she got very angry, and marched off and told the master.

But the master was still more angry, and said: "What! The blockhead gave his eight krans to a beggar? Send him to me." And when Abdul Karim came before him, he said scornfully, "You must fancy yourself a big man, Abdul. I never give more than a copper coin to a beggar, but your Excellency gives them silver. The beggar promised that you should be repaid a hundredfold, did he? And it shall be so, even now." Then as Abdul's face brightened, he laughed and said, "Not in money, but in stripes." And his servants threw Abdul on the ground and gave him one hundred blows on his bare feet.

The next day, Abdul's master sent for him again, and after calling him a fool, said, "I have a nice little job for you, that will bring you to your proper senses. Go into the field and dig for water, day after day until you find it."

So for many days Abdul laboured under the scorching sun, until he had dug down to a depth of about thirty feet, and then he came upon a brass vessel, finely chased, full of round white stones, which fairly dazzled his eyes in the fierce sunlight. He put one in his mouth and tried to break it with his teeth, but could not.

Then he said to himself, "The master has planted some rice and it has turned into stones. Perhaps there are some more." And going down a few feet lower, he found another pot filled with sparkling stones of various colours.

Then he remembered that he had seen pretty pieces of glass like these for sale in Meshed, and made up his mind that at the first opportunity he would again visit the city and take the stones with him. Meanwhile, he would hide them, and say nothing.

Abdul did not have to wait long for a holiday, for on finding water a little lower down, his master was so pleased that he gave him a well-deserved rest, and then Abdul set off for Meshed. But before entering the city, he hid most of the treasure at the foot of a tree under a big stone. Then with still a pocket full, he went straight to the shop where he had seen such stones, and spoke to the shopkeeper who was seated at the entrance to his shop, calmly smoking his water-pipe.

"Do you want to buy any more stones like those?" he asked, pointing to some in a brass tray. "Yes, have you got one?" replied the merchant, for Abdul did not look like a man who was likely to have more than one, if any.

"I have a pocket full of them," said Abdul.

"You have a pocket full of pebbles, more likely," said the jeweller. But when Abdul took out a handful and showed him, he was so astonished that he could hardly speak. Trembling in every limb, he bade Abdul wait a minute and, leaving his apprentice in charge, he hastily left the shop. When he returned, the chief of the police was with him.

"I am innocent," cried the jeweller. "There is the man. His pockets are filled with diamonds, rubies, emeralds and pearls of great price. Without doubt he has found the long-lost treasure of Cyrus."

Then Abdul was searched; the precious stones were found upon him; and when they had brought Zeeba and the children, the whole family were sent under a guard of five hundred soldiers to the capital.

While all these things were taking place, the King saw in his dreams, for three nights, one after the other, the Holy Prophet, who, looking steadfastly at him, exclaimed, "Abbas, protect and favour my friend." And on the third night, the King took courage and said to the Prophet, "And who is thy friend?" And the answer came:

"He is a poor labouring man, Abdul Karim by name, who of his poverty gave one-fifth to the shrine at Meshed, and now, because he has found the King's treasure, they have bound him, and are bringing him to this city to oppress him."

So the King went forth two days' journey to meet Abdul. First came one hundred horsemen. Next, poor Abdul, seated on a camel, with his arms bound tightly. Walking behind the camel were the weeping children and their mother. Then came the foot soldiers guarding the treasure. The King made the camel kneel down, and with his own hands undid the cruel bonds.

Then with tears running down his face, Abdul knelt before the King and pleaded for his dear ones, saying, "If thou slay me, at least let these innocent ones go free!"

Lifting Abdul from the ground, the King then said, "I am come to honour, not to slay thee. When thou hast rested, thou shalt return to thine own province, not as a prisoner, but as the Governor thereof." And smiling, he added, "Already is the silk dress prepared for Zeeba; the horse and sword for Yusuf; and the Indian handkerchief and the golden slippers for Fatima have not been forgotten." For the King had read in the report of the chief of police all the details of Abdul's case.

And so it was that Abdul's piety and gift to the shrine had come back, not a hundredfold, but beyond his wildest dreams, and the shrine and the poor benefitted greatly thereby.

The Story of the Blind Baba-Abdalla
(From One Thousand and One Arabian Nights, of Arabic, Egyptian, Sanskrit, Persian, and Mesopotamian origins)

I WAS BORN Commander of the Faithful, in Bagdad, and was left an orphan while I was yet a very young man, for my parents died within a few days of each other. I had inherited

from them a small fortune, which I worked hard night and day to increase, till at last I found myself the owner of eighty camels. These I hired out to travelling merchants, whom I frequently accompanied on their various journeys, and always returned with large profits.

One day I was coming back from Balsora, whither I had taken a supply of goods, intended for India, and halted at noon in a lonely place, which promised rich pasture for my camels. I was resting in the shade under a tree, when a dervish, going on foot towards Balsora, sat down by my side, and I inquired whence he had come and to what place he was going. We soon made friends, and after we had asked each other the usual questions, we produced the food we had with us, and satisfied our hunger.

While we were eating, the dervish happened to mention that in a spot only a little way off from where we were sitting, there was hidden a treasure so great that if my eighty camels were loaded till they could carry no more, the hiding place would seem as full as if it had never been touched.

At this news I became almost beside myself with joy and greed, and I flung my arms round the neck of the dervish, exclaiming: "Good dervish, I see plainly that the riches of this world are nothing to you, therefore of what use is the knowledge of this treasure to you? Alone and on foot, you could carry away a mere handful. But tell me where it is, and I will load my eighty camels with it, and give you one of them as a token of my gratitude."

Certainly my offer does not sound very magnificent, but it was great to me, for at his words a wave of covetousness had swept over my heart, and I almost felt as if the seventy-nine camels that were left were nothing in comparison.

The dervish saw quite well what was passing in my mind, but he did not show what he thought of my proposal.

"My brother," he answered quietly, "you know as well as I do, that you are behaving unjustly. It was open to me to keep my secret, and to reserve the treasure for myself. But the fact that I have told you of its existence shows that I had confidence in you, and that I hoped to earn your gratitude for ever, by making your fortune as well as mine. But before I reveal to you the secret of the treasure, you must swear that, after we have loaded the camels with as much as they can carry, you will give half to me, and let us go our own ways. I think you will see that this is fair, for if you present me with forty camels, I on my side will give you the means of buying a thousand more."

I could not of course deny that what the dervish said was perfectly reasonable, but, in spite of that, the thought that the dervish would be as rich as I was unbearable to me. Still there was no use in discussing the matter, and I had to accept his conditions or bewail to the end of my life the loss of immense wealth. So I collected my camels and we set out together under the guidance of the dervish. After walking some time, we reached what looked like a valley, but with such a narrow entrance that my camels could only pass one by one. The little valley, or open space, was shut up by two mountains, whose sides were formed of straight cliffs, which no human being could climb.

When we were exactly between these mountains, the dervish stopped.

"Make your camels lie down in this open space," he said, "so that we can easily load them; then we will go to the treasure."

I did what I was bid, and rejoined the dervish, whom I found trying to kindle a fire out of some dry wood. As soon as it was alight, he threw on it a handful of perfumes, and pronounced a few words that I did not understand, and immediately a thick column of smoke rose high into the air. He separated the smoke into two columns, and then I saw a rock, which stood like a pillar between the two mountains, slowly open, and a splendid palace appear within.

But, Commander of the Faithful, the love of gold had taken such possession of my heart, that I could not even stop to examine the riches, but fell upon the first pile of gold within my reach and began to heap it into a sack that I had brought with me. The dervish likewise set to work, but I soon noticed that he confined himself to collecting precious stones, and I felt I should be wise to follow his example. At length the camels were loaded with as much as they could carry, and nothing remained but to seal up the treasure, and go our ways.

Before, however, this was done, the dervish went up to a great golden vase, beautifully chased, and took from it a small wooden box, which he hid in the bosom of his dress, merely saying that it contained a special kind of ointment. Then he once more kindled the fire, threw on the perfume, and murmured the unknown spell, and the rock closed, and stood whole as before.

The next thing was to divide the camels, and to charge them with the treasure, after which we each took command of our own and marched out of the valley, till we reached the place in the high road where the routes diverge, and then we parted, the dervish going towards Balsora, and I to Bagdad. We embraced each other tenderly, and I poured out my gratitude for the honour he had done me, in singling me out for this great wealth, and having said a hearty farewell, we turned our backs, and hastened after our camels.

I had hardly come up with mine when the demon of envy filled my soul. "What does a dervish want with riches like that?" I said to myself. "He alone has the secret of the treasure, and can always get as much as he wants," and I halted my camels by the roadside, and ran back after him.

I was a quick runner, and it did not take me very long to come up with him. "My brother," I exclaimed, as soon as I could speak, "almost at the moment of our leavetaking, a reflection occurred to me, which is perhaps new to you. You are a dervish by profession, and live a very quiet life, only caring to do good, and careless of the things of this world. You do not realise the burden that you lay upon yourself, when you gather into your hands such great wealth, besides the fact that no one, who is not accustomed to camels from his birth, can ever manage the stubborn beasts. If you are wise, you will not encumber yourself with more than thirty, and you will find those trouble enough."

"You are right," replied the dervish, who understood me quite well, but did not wish to fight the matter. "I confess I had not thought about it. Choose any ten you like, and drive them before you."

I selected ten of the best camels, and we proceeded along the road, to rejoin those I had left behind. I had got what I wanted, but I had found the dervish so easy to deal with, that I rather regretted I had not asked for ten more. I looked back. He had only gone a few paces, and I called after him.

"My brother," I said, "I am unwilling to part from you without pointing out what I think you scarcely grasp, that large experience of camel-driving is necessary to anybody who intends to keep together a troop of thirty. In your own interest, I feel sure you would be much happier if you entrusted ten more of them to me, for with my practice it is all one to me if I take two or a hundred."

As before, the dervish made no difficulties, and I drove off my ten camels in triumph, only leaving him with twenty for his share. I had now sixty, and anyone might have imagined that I should be content.

But, Commander of the Faithful, there is a proverb that says, "the more one has, the more one wants." So it was with me. I could not rest as long as one solitary camel remained to the dervish; and returning to him I redoubled my prayers and embraces, and promises of eternal gratitude, till the last twenty were in my hands.

"Make a good use of them, my brother," said the holy man. "Remember riches sometimes have wings if we keep them for ourselves, and the poor are at our gates expressly that we may help them."

My eyes were so blinded by gold, that I paid no heed to his wise counsel, and only looked about for something else to grasp. Suddenly I remembered the little box of ointment that the dervish had hidden, and which most likely contained a treasure more precious than all the rest. Giving him one last embrace, I observed accidentally, "What are you going to do with that little box of ointment? It seems hardly worth taking with you; you might as well let me have it. And really, a dervish who has given up the world has no need of ointment!"

Oh, if he had only refused my request! But then, supposing he had, I should have got possession of it by force, so great was the madness that had laid hold upon me. However, far from refusing it, the dervish at once held it out, saying gracefully, "Take it, my friend, and if there is anything else I can do to make you happy, you must let me know."

Directly the box was in my hands I wrenched off the cover. "As you are so kind," I said, "tell me, I pray you, what are the virtues of this ointment?"

"They are most curious and interesting," replied the dervish. "If you apply a little of it to your left eye you will behold in an instant all the treasures hidden in the bowels of the earth. But beware lest you touch your right eye with it, or your sight will be destroyed for ever."

His words excited my curiosity to the highest pitch. "Make trial on me, I implore you," I cried, holding out the box to the dervish. "You will know how to do it better than I! I am burning with impatience to test its charms."

The dervish took the box I had extended to him, and, bidding me shut my left eye, touched it gently with the ointment. When I opened it again I saw spread out, as it were before me, treasures of every kind and without number. But as all this time I had been obliged to keep my right eye closed, which was very fatiguing, I begged the dervish to apply the ointment to that eye also.

"If you insist upon it I will do it," answered the dervish, "but you must remember what I told you just now – that if it touches your right eye you will become blind on the spot."

Unluckily, in spite of my having proved the truth of the dervish's words in so many instances, I was firmly convinced that he was now keeping concealed from me some hidden and precious virtue of the ointment. So I turned a deaf ear to all he said.

"My brother," I replied, smiling, "I see you are joking. It is not natural that the same ointment should have two such exactly opposite effects."

"It is true all the same," answered the dervish, "and it would be well for you if you believed my word."

But I would not believe, and, dazzled by the greed of avarice, I thought that if one eye could show me riches, the other might teach me how to get possession of them. And I continued to press the dervish to anoint my right eye, but this he resolutely declined to do.

"After having conferred such benefits on you," said he, "I am loth indeed to work you such evil. Think what it is to be blind, and do not force me to do what you will repent as long as you live."

It was of no use. "My brother," I said firmly, "pray say no more, but do what I ask. You have most generously responded to my wishes up to this time, do not spoil my recollection of you for a thing of such little

TURKISH FOLKTALES

consequence. Let what will happen I take it on my own head, and will never reproach you."

"Since you are determined upon it," he answered with a sigh, "there is no use talking," and taking the ointment, he laid some on my right eye, which was tight shut. When I tried to open it heavy clouds of darkness floated before me. I was as blind as you see me now!

"Miserable dervish!" I shrieked, "so it is true after all! Into what a bottomless pit has my lust after gold plunged me. Ah, now that my eyes are closed, they are really opened. I know that all my sufferings are caused by myself alone! But, good brother, you, who are so kind and charitable, and know the secrets of such vast learning, have you nothing that will give me back my sight?"

"Unhappy man," replied the dervish, "it is not my fault that this has befallen you, but it is a just chastisement. The blindness of your heart has wrought the blindness of your body. Yes, I have secrets; that you have seen in the short time that we have known each other. But I have none that will give you back your sight. You have proved yourself unworthy of the riches that were given you. Now they have passed into my hands, whence they will flow into the hands of others less greedy and ungrateful than you."

The dervish said no more and left me, speechless with shame and confusion, and so wretched that I stood rooted to the spot, while he collected the eighty camels and proceeded on his way to Balsora. It was in vain that I entreated him not to leave me, but at least to take me within reach of the first passing caravan. He was deaf to my prayers and cries, and I should soon have been dead of hunger and misery if some merchants had not come along the track the following day and kindly brought me back to Bagdad.

From a rich man I had in one moment become a beggar; and up to this time I have lived solely on the alms that have been bestowed on me. But, in order to expiate the sin of avarice, which was my undoing, I oblige each passer-by to give me a blow.

This, Commander of the Faithful, is my story.

When the blind man had ended, the Caliph addressed him: "Baba-Abdalla, truly your sin is great, but you have suffered enough. Henceforth repent in private, for I will see that enough money is given you day by day for all your wants."

At these words Baba-Abdalla flung himself at the Caliph's feet, and prayed that honour and happiness might be his portion forever.

The Story of Ali Baba and the Forty Thieves
(From One Thousand and One Arabian Nights, of Arabic, Egyptian, Sanskrit, Persian, and Mesopotamian origins)

IN A TOWN IN PERSIA, there lived two brothers, one named Cassim, the other Ali Baba. Their father left them scarcely anything; but as he had divided his little property equally between them, it would seem that their fortune ought to have been equal; but chance determined otherwise.

Cassim married a wife, who soon after became heiress to a large sum, and to a warehouse full of rich goods; so that he all at once became one of the richest and most considerable merchants, and lived at his ease. Ali Baba, on the other hand, who had married a woman as poor as himself, lived in a very wretched habitation, and had no other means to maintain his wife and children but his daily labour of cutting wood, and bringing it to town to sell, upon three asses, which were his whole substance.

One day, when Ali Baba was in the forest, and had just cut wood enough to load his asses, he saw at a distance a great cloud of dust, which seemed to be driven toward him: he observed it very attentively, and distinguished soon after a body of horse. Though there had been no rumour of robbers in that country, Ali Baba began to think that they might prove such, and without considering what might become of his asses, was resolved to save himself. He climbed up a large, thick tree, whose branches, at a little distance from the ground, were so close to one another that there was but little space between them. He placed himself in the middle, from whence he could see all that passed without being discovered; and the tree stood at the base of a single rock, so steep and craggy that nobody could climb up it.

The troop, who were all well mounted and armed, came to the foot of this rock, and there dismounted. Ali Baba counted forty of them, and, from their looks and equipage, was assured that they were robbers. Nor was he mistaken in his opinion; for they were a troop of banditti, who, without doing any harm to the neighbourhood, robbed at a distance, and made that place their rendezvous; but what confirmed him in his opinion was, that every man unbridled his horse, tied him to some shrub, and hung about his neck a bag of corn which they brought behind them. Then each of them took his saddle wallet, which seemed to Ali Baba to be full of gold and silver from its weight. One, who was the most personable amongst them, and whom he took to be their captain, came with his wallet on his back under the tree in which Ali Baba was concealed, and, making his way through some shrubs, pronounced these words so distinctly: "Open, Sesame," that Ali Baba heard him. As soon as the captain of the robbers had uttered these words, a door opened in the rock; and after he had made all his troop enter before him, he followed them, when the door shut again of itself. The robbers stayed some time within the rock, and Ali Baba, who feared that someone, or all of them together, might come out and catch him, if he should endeavour to make his escape, was obliged to sit patiently in the tree. He was nevertheless tempted to get down, mount one of their horses, and lead another, driving his asses before him with all the haste he could to town; but the uncertainty of the event made him choose the safest course.

At last the door opened again, and the forty robbers came out. As the captain went in last, he came out first, and stood to see them all pass by him, when Ali Baba heard him make the door close by pronouncing these words: "Shut, Sesame." Every man went and bridled his horse, fastened his wallet, and mounted again; and when the captain saw them all ready, he put himself at their head, and they returned the way they had come. Ali Baba did not immediately quit his tree; for, said he to himself, they may have forgotten something and may come back again, and then I shall be taken. He followed them with his eyes as far as he could see them; and afterward stayed a considerable time before he descended. Remembering the words the captain of the robbers used to cause the door to open and shut, he had the curiosity to try if his pronouncing them would have the same effect. Accordingly, he went among the shrubs, and, perceiving the door concealed behind them, stood before it, and said: "Open, Sesame!" The door instantly flew wide open. Ali Baba, who expected a dark, dismal cavern, was surprised to see it well lighted and spacious, in the form of a vault, which received the light from an opening at the top of the rock. He saw all sorts of provisions, rich bales of silk stuff, brocade, and valuable carpeting, piled upon one another; gold and silver ingots in great heaps, and money in bags. The sight of all these riches made him suppose that this cave must have been occupied for ages by robbers, who had succeeded one another. Ali Baba did not stand long to consider what he should do, but went immediately into the cave, and as soon as he had entered, the door shut of itself, but this did not disturb him, because he knew the secret to open it again. He never regarded the silver, but made the best use of his time in carrying out as much of the gold coin as he thought his three asses could carry. He collected his asses, which were dispersed, and when he had loaded them with the bags, laid wood over in such a manner that they could not be seen. When he had done, he stood before the door, and pronouncing the words: "Shut, Sesame!" the door closed after him, for it had shut of itself while he was within, but remained open while he was out. He then made the best of his way to town.

When Ali Baba got home, he drove his asses into a little yard, shut the gates very carefully, threw off the wood that covered the bags, carried them into his house, and ranged them in order before his wife, who sat on a sofa. His wife handled the bags, and, finding them full of money, suspected that her husband had been robbing, insomuch that she could not help saying: "Ali Baba, have you been so unhappy as to—" "Be quiet, wife," interrupted Ali Baba, "do not frighten yourself; I am no robber, unless he may be one who steals from robbers. You will no longer entertain an ill opinion of me, when I shall tell you my good fortune." He then emptied the bags, which raised such a great heap of gold as dazzled his wife's eyes; and when he had done, told her the whole adventure from beginning to end; and, above all, recommended her to keep it secret. The wife, cured of her fears, rejoiced with her husband at their good fortune, and would count all the gold piece by piece. "Wife," replied Ali Baba, "you do not know what you undertake, when you pretend to count the money; you will never have done. I will dig a hole, and bury it; there is no time to be lost." "You are in the right, husband," replied she, "but let us know, as nigh as possible, how much we have. I will borrow a small measure in the neighbourhood, and measure it, while you dig the hole." "What you are going to do is to no purpose, wife," said Ali Baba. "If you would take my advice, you had better let it alone; but keep the secret, and do what you please." Away the wife ran to her brother-in-law Cassim, who lived just by, but was not then at home; and addressing herself to his wife, desired her to lend her a measure for a little while. Her sister-in-law asked her, whether she would have a great or a small one. The wife asked for a small one. The sister-in-law agreed to lend one, but as she knew Ali Baba's poverty, she was curious to know what sort of grain his wife wanted to measure, and artfully putting some suet at the bottom of the measure, brought it to her with an excuse, that she was sorry that she had made her stay so long, but that she could not find it sooner. Ali Baba's wife went home, set the measure upon the heap of gold, filled it and emptied it often upon the sofa, till she had done: when she was very well satisfied to find the number of measures amounted to so many as they did, and went to tell her husband, who had almost finished digging the hole. While Ali Baba was burying the gold, his wife, to show her exactness and diligence to her sister-in-law, carried the measure back again, but without taking notice that a piece of gold had stuck to the bottom. "Sister," said she, giving it to her again, "you see that I have not kept your measure long; I am obliged to you for it, and return it with thanks."

As soon as her sister-in-law was gone, Cassim's wife looked at the bottom of the measure, and was inexpressibly surprised to find a piece of gold stuck to it. Envy immediately possessed her breast. "What!" said she, "has Ali Baba gold so plentiful as to measure it? Where has that poor wretch got all this wealth?" Cassim, her husband, was not at home, but at his counting-house, which he left always in the evening. His wife waited for him, and thought the time an age; so great was her impatience to tell him the circumstance, at which she guessed he would be as much surprised as herself.

When Cassim came home, his wife said to him: "Cassim, I know you think yourself rich, but you are much mistaken; Ali Baba is infinitely richer than you; he does not count his money, but measures it." Cassim desired her to explain the riddle, which she did, by telling him the stratagem she had used to make the discovery, and showed him the piece of money, which was so old that they could not tell in what prince's reign it was coined. Cassim, instead of being pleased, conceived a base envy at his brother's prosperity; he could not sleep all that night, and went to him in the morning before sunrise, although after he had married the rich widow, he had never treated him as a brother, but neglected him. "Ali Baba," said he, accosting him, "you are very reserved in your affairs; you pretend to be miserably poor, and yet you measure gold." "How, brother?" replied Ali Baba. "I do not know what you mean: explain yourself." "Do not pretend ignorance," replied Cassim, showing him the piece of gold his wife had given him. "How many of these pieces," added he, "have you? My wife found this at the bottom of the measure you borrowed yesterday."

By this discourse, Ali Baba perceived that Cassim and his wife, through his own wife's folly, knew what they had so much reason to conceal; but what was done could not be recalled; therefore, without shewing the least surprise or trouble, he confessed all, told his brother by what chance he had discovered this retreat of the thieves, in what place it was; and offered him part of his treasure to keep the secret. "I expect as much," replied Cassim haughtily, "but I must know exactly where this treasure is, and how I may visit it myself when I choose; otherwise I will go and inform against you, and then you will not only get no more, but will lose all you have, and I shall have a share for my information."

Ali Baba, more out of his natural good temper, than frightened by the menaces of his unnatural brother, told him all he desired, and even the very words he was to use to gain admission into the cave.

Cassim, who wanted no more of Ali Baba, left him, resolving to be beforehand with him, and hoping to get all the treasure to himself. He rose the next morning long before the sun, and set out for the forest with ten mules bearing great chests, which he designed to fill; and followed the road which Ali Baba had pointed out to him. He was not long before he reached the rock, and found out the place by the tree, and other marks, which his brother had given him. When he reached the entrance of the cavern, he pronounced the words: "Open, Sesame!" and the door immediately opened, and when he was in, closed upon him. In examining the cave, he was in great admiration to find many more riches than he had apprehended from Ali Baba's account. He was so covetous, and greedy of wealth, that he could have spent the whole day in feasting his eyes with so much treasure, if the thought that he came to carry some away had not hindered him. He laid as many bags of gold as he could carry at the door of the cavern, but his thoughts were so full of the great riches he should possess, that he could not think of the necessary word to make it open, but instead of "Sesame," said: "Open, Barley!" and was much amazed to find that the door remained fast shut. He named several sorts of grain, but still the door would not open. Cassim had never expected such an incident, and was so alarmed at the danger he was in, that the more he endeavoured to remember the word "Sesame," the more his memory was confounded, and he had as much forgotten it as if he had never heard it mentioned. He threw down the bags he had loaded himself with and walked distractedly up and down the cave, without having the least regard to the riches that were round him. About noon the robbers chanced to visit their cave, and at some distance from it saw Cassim's mules straggling about the rock, with great chests on their backs. Alarmed at this novelty, they galloped full-speed to the cave. They drove away the mules, which Cassim had neglected to fasten, and they strayed through the forest so far, that they were soon out of sight. The robbers never gave themselves the trouble to pursue them, being more concerned to know to whom they belonged, and while some of them searched about the rock, the captain and the rest went directly to the door, with their naked sabres in their hands, and, pronouncing the proper words, it opened.

Cassim, who heard the noise of the horses' feet from the middle of the cave, never doubted of the arrival of the robbers, and his approaching death; but was resolved to make one effort to escape from them. To this end he rushed to the door, and no sooner heard the word Sesame, which he had forgotten, and saw the door open, than he ran out and threw the leader down, but could not escape the other robbers, who with their sabres soon deprived him of life. The first care of the robbers after this was to examine the cave. They found all the bags which Cassim had brought to the door, to be ready to load his mules, and carried them again to their places, without missing what Ali Baba had taken away before. Then, holding a council, and deliberating upon this occurrence, they guessed that Cassim, when he was in, could not get out again; but could not imagine how he had entered. It came into their heads that he might have got down by the top of the cave; but the aperture by which it received light was so high, and the rocks so inaccessible without, that they gave up this conjecture. That he came in at the door they could not believe, however, unless he had the secret of making it open. In short, none of them could imagine which way he had entered; for they were all persuaded nobody knew their secret, little imagining that Ali Baba had watched them. It was a matter of the greatest importance to them to secure their riches. They agreed therefore to cut Cassim's body into quarters, to hang two on one side and two on the other, within the door of the cave, to terrify any person who should attempt again to enter. They had no sooner taken this resolution than they put it in execution, and when they had nothing more to detain them, left the place of their hoards well closed. They then mounted their horses, went to beat the roads again, and to attack the caravans they might meet.

In the meantime, Cassim's wife was very uneasy when night came, and her husband was not returned. She ran to Ali Baba in alarm, and said: "I believe, brother-in-law, that you know Cassim, your brother, is gone to the forest, and upon what account; it is now night, and he is not returned; I am afraid some misfortune has happened to him." Ali Baba, who had expected that his brother, after what he had said, would go to the forest, had declined going himself that day, for fear of giving him any umbrage; therefore told her, without any reflection upon her husband's unhandsome behaviour, that she need not frighten herself, for that certainly Cassim would not think it proper to come into the town till the night should be pretty far advanced.

Cassim's wife, considering how much it concerned her husband to keep the business secret, was the more easily persuaded to believe her brother-in-law. She went home again, and waited patiently till midnight. She repented of her foolish curiosity, and cursed her desire of penetrating into the affairs of her brother and sister-in-law. She spent all the night in weeping; and as soon as it was day, went to them, telling them, by her tears, the cause of her coming. Ali Baba did not wait for his sister-in-law to desire him to go and see what was become of Cassim, but departed immediately with his three asses, begging of her first to moderate her affliction. He went to the forest, and when he came near the rock, having seen neither his brother nor the mules in his way, was seriously alarmed at finding some blood spilt near the door, which he took for an ill omen; but when he had pronounced the word, and the door had opened, he was struck with horror at the dismal sight of his brother's body. Without adverting to the little fraternal affection his brother had shewn for him, Ali Baba went into the cave to find something to enshroud his remains, and having loaded one of his asses with them, covered them over with wood. The other two asses he loaded with bags of gold, covering them with wood also as before; and then bidding the door shut, came away; but was so cautious as to stop some time at the end of the forest, that he might not go into the town before night. When he came home, he drove the two asses loaded with gold into his little yard, and left the care of unloading them to his wife, while he led the other to his sister-in-law's house.

Ali Baba knocked at the door, which was opened by Morgiana, an intelligent slave, fruitful in inventions to insure success in the most difficult undertakings: and Ali Baba knew her to be such. When he came into the court, he unloaded the ass, and taking Morgiana aside, said to her: "The first thing I ask of you is an inviolable secrecy, both for your mistress's sake and mine. Your master's body is contained in these two bundles, and our business is, to bury him as if he had died a natural death. Go, tell your mistress I want to speak with her; and mind what I have said to you."

Morgiana went to her mistress, and Ali Baba followed her. "Well, brother," said she, with impatience, "what news do you bring me of my husband? I perceive no comfort in your countenance." "Sister," answered Ali Baba, "I cannot satisfy your inquiries unless you hear my story without speaking a word; for it is of as great importance to you as to me to keep what has happened secret." "Alas!" said she, "this preamble lets me know that my husband is not to be found; but at the same time I know the necessity of secrecy, and I must constrain myself: say on, I will hear you."

Ali Baba then detailed the incidents of his journey, till he came to the finding of Cassim's body. "Now," said he, "sister, I have something to relate which will afflict you the more, because it is what you so little expect; but it cannot now be remedied; if my endeavours can comfort you, I offer to put that which God hath sent me to what you have, and marry you: assuring you that my wife will not be jealous, and that we shall live happily together. If this proposal is agreeable to you, we must think of acting so that my brother should appear to have died a natural death. I think you may leave the management of the business to Morgiana, and I will contribute all that lies in my power to your consolation." What could Cassim's widow do better than accept of this proposal? for though her first husband had left behind him a plentiful substance, his brother was now much richer, and by the discovery of this treasure might be still more so. Instead, therefore, of rejecting the offer, she regarded it as the sure means of comfort; and drying up her tears, which had begun to flow abundantly, and suppressing the outcries usual with women who have lost their husbands, showed Ali Baba that she approved of his proposal. Ali Baba left the widow, recommended to Morgiana to act her part well, and then returned home with his ass.

Morgiana went out at the same time to an apothecary, and asked for a sort of lozenges which he prepared, and were very efficacious in the most dangerous disorders. The apothecary inquired who was ill at her master's? She replied with a sigh, her good master Cassim himself: that they knew not what his disorder was, but that he could neither eat nor speak. After these words, Morgiana carried the lozenges home with her, and the next morning went to the same apothecary's again, and with tears in her eyes, asked for an essence which they used to give to sick people only when at the last extremity. "Alas!" said she, taking it from the apothecary, "I am afraid that this remedy will have no better effect than the lozenges; and that I shall lose my good master." On the other hand, as Ali Baba and his wife were often seen to go between Cassim's and their own house all that day, and to seem melancholy, nobody was surprised in the evening to hear the lamentable shrieks and cries of Cassim's wife and Morgiana, who gave out everywhere that her master was dead. The next morning, soon after day appeared, Morgiana, who knew a certain old cobbler that opened his stall early, before other people, went to him, and bidding him good morrow, put a piece of gold into his hand. "Well," said Baba Mustapha, which was his name, and who was a merry old fellow, looking at the gold, "this is good hansel: what must I do for it? I am ready."

"Baba Mustapha," said Morgiana, "you must take with you your sewing tackle, and go with me; but I must tell you, I shall blindfold you when you come to such a place." Baba Mustapha seemed to hesitate a little at these words. "Oh! oh!" replied he, "you would have me do something against my conscience or against my honour?" "God forbid!" said Morgiana, putting another piece of gold into his hand, "that I should ask anything that is contrary to your honour; only come along with me, and fear nothing."

Baba Mustapha went with Morgiana, who, after she had bound his eyes with a handkerchief, conveyed him to her deceased master's house, and never unloosed his eyes till he had entered the room where she had put the corpse together. "Baba Mustapha," said she, "you must make haste and sew these quarters together; and when you have done, I will give you another piece of gold." After Baba Mustapha had finished his task, she blindfolded him again, gave him the third piece of gold as she had promised, and, recommending secrecy to him, carried him back to the place where she first bound his eyes, pulled off the bandage, and let him go home, but watched him that he returned toward his stall, till he was quite out of sight, for fear he should have the curiosity to return and track her.

By the time Morgiana had warmed some water to wash the body, Ali Baba came with incense to embalm it, after which it was sewn up in a winding-sheet. Not long after, the joiner, according to Ali Baba's orders, brought the bier, which Morgiana received at the door, and helped Ali Baba to put the body into it; when she went to the mosque to inform the imaum that they were ready. The people of the mosque, whose business it was to wash the dead, offered to perform their duty, but she told them that it was done already. Morgiana had scarcely got home before the imaum and the other ministers of the mosque arrived. Four neighbours carried the corpse on their shoulders to the burying-ground, following the imaum, who recited some prayers. Morgiana, as a slave to the deceased, followed the corpse, weeping, beating her breast, and tearing her hair; and Ali Baba came after with some neighbours, who often relieved the others in carrying the corpse to the burying-ground. Cassim's wife stayed at home mourning, uttering lamentable cries with the women of the neighbourhood, who came according to custom during the funeral, and, joining their lamentations with hers, filled the quarter far and near with sorrow. In this manner Cassim's melancholy death was concealed and hushed up between Ali Baba, his wife, Cassim's widow, and Morgiana, with so much contrivance, that nobody in the city had the least knowledge or suspicion of the cause of it.

Three or four days after the funeral, Ali Baba removed his few goods openly to the widow's house; but the money he had taken from the robbers he conveyed thither by night: soon after the marriage with his sister-in-law was published, and as these marriages are common in the Mussulman religion, nobody was surprised. As for Cassim's warehouse, Ali Baba gave it to his own eldest son, promising that if he managed it well, he would soon give him a fortune to marry very advantageously according to his situation.

Let us now leave Ali Baba to enjoy the beginning of his good fortune, and return to the forty robbers. They came again at the appointed time to visit their retreat in the forest; but great was their surprise to find Cassim's body taken away, with some of their bags of gold. "We are certainly discovered," said the captain, "and if we do not speedily apply some remedy, shall gradually lose all the riches which we have, with so much pains and danger, been so many years amassing together. All that we can think of the loss which we have sustained is, that the thief whom we surprised had the secret of opening the door, and we arrived luckily as he was coming out: but his body being removed, and with it some of our money, plainly shows that he had an accomplice; and as it is likely that there were but two who had discovered our secret, and one has been caught, we must look narrowly after the other. What say you, my lads?" All the robbers thought the captain's proposal so advisable, that they unanimously approved of it, and agreed that they must lay all other enterprises aside, to follow this closely, and not give it up till they had succeeded.

"I expected no less," said the captain, "from your fidelity: but, first of all, one of you who is artful, and enterprising, must go into the town disguised as a traveller, to try if he can hear any talk of the strange death of the man whom we have killed, as he deserved; and endeavour to find out who he was, and where he lived. This is a matter of the first importance for us to ascertain, that we may do nothing which we may have reason to repent of, by discovering ourselves in a country where we have lived so long unknown. But to warn him who shall take upon himself this commission, and to prevent our being deceived by his giving us a false report, I ask you all, if you do not think that in case of treachery, or even error of judgment, he should suffer death?" Without waiting for the suffrages of his companions, one of the robbers started up, and said: "I submit to this condition, and think it an honour to expose my life, by taking the commission upon me; but remember, at least, if I do not succeed, that I neither wanted courage nor good will to serve the troop." After this robber had received great commendations from the captain, he disguised himself, and, taking his leave of the troop that night, went into the town just at daybreak; and walked up and down, till accidentally he came to Baba Mustapha's stall, which was always open before any of the shops.

Baba Mustapha was seated with an awl in his hand, just going to work. The robber saluted him, bidding him good morrow; and perceiving that he was old, said: "Honest man, you begin to work very early: is it possible that one of your age can see so well? I question, even if it were somewhat lighter, whether you could see to stitch."

"Certainly," replied Baba Mustapha, "you must be a stranger, and do not know me; for old as I am, I have extraordinarily good eyes; and you will not doubt it when I tell you that I sewed a dead body together in a place where I had not so much light as I have now." The robber was overjoyed to think that he had addressed himself, at his first coming into the town, to a man who in all probability could give him the intelligence he wanted. "A dead body!" replied he with affected amazement. "What could you sew up a dead body for? You mean you sewed up his winding-sheet." "No, no," answered Baba Mustapha, "I perceive your meaning; you want to have me speak out, but you shall know no more." The robber wanted no farther assurance to be persuaded that he had discovered what he sought. He pulled out a piece of gold, and putting it into Baba Mustapha's hand, said to him: "I do not want to learn your secret, though I can assure you I would not divulge it, if you trusted me with it; the only thing which I desire of you is, to do me the favour to shew me the house where you stitched up the dead body."

"If I were disposed to do you that favour," replied Baba Mustapha, holding the money in his hand, ready to return it, "I assure you I cannot. I was taken to a certain place, where I was blinded, I was then led to the house, and afterward brought back again in the same manner; you see, therefore, the impossibility of my doing what you desire."

"Well," replied the robber, "you may, however, remember a little of the way that you were led blindfolded. Come, let me blind your eyes at the same place. We will walk together; perhaps you may recognise some part; and as everybody ought to be paid for his trouble, there is another piece of gold for you; gratify me in what I ask you." So saying, he put another piece of gold into his hand.

The two pieces of gold were great temptations to Baba Mustapha. He looked at them a long time in his hand, without saying a word, thinking with himself what he should do; but at last he pulled out his purse, and put them in. "I cannot assure you," said he to the robber, "that I can remember the way exactly; but since you desire, I will try what I can do." At these words Baba Mustapha rose up, to the great joy of the robber, and without shutting his shop, where he had nothing valuable to lose, he led the robber to the place where Morgiana had bound his eyes. "It was here," said Baba Mustapha, "I was blindfolded; and I turned as you see me." The robber, who had his handkerchief ready, tied it over his eyes, walked by him till he stopped, partly leading, and partly guided by him. "I think," said Baba Mustapha, "I went no farther," and he had now stopped directly at Cassim's house, where Ali Baba then lived. The thief, before he pulled off the band, marked the door with a piece of chalk, which he had ready in his hand; and then asked him if he knew whose house that was; to which Baba Mustapha replied, that as he did not live in that neighbourhood, he could not tell. The robber, finding he could discover no more from Baba Mustapha, thanked him for the trouble he had taken, and left him to go back to his stall, while he returned to the forest, persuaded that he should be very well received. A little after the robber and Baba Mustapha had parted, Morgiana went out of Ali Baba's house upon some errand, and upon her return, seeing the mark the robber had made, stopped to observe it. "What can be the meaning of this mark?" said she to herself. "Somebody intends my master no good: however, with whatever intention it was done, it is advisable to guard against the worst." Accordingly, she fetched a piece of chalk, and marked two or three doors on each side in the same manner, without saying a word to her master or mistress.

In the meantime the thief rejoined his troop in the forest, and recounted to them his success. All the robbers listened to him with the utmost satisfaction; when the captain, after commending his diligence, addressing himself to them all, said: "Comrades, we have no time to lose: let us set off well-armed; but that we may not excite any suspicion, let only one or two go into the town together, and join at our rendezvous, which shall be the great square. In the meantime, our comrade who brought us the good news, and I, will go and find out the house, that we may consult what had best be done."

This plan was approved of by all, and they were soon ready. They filed off in parties of two each, and got into the town without being in the least suspected. The captain, and he who had visited the town in the morning as spy, came in the last. He led the captain into the street where he had marked Ali Baba's residence; and when they came to the first of the houses which Morgiana had marked, he pointed it out. But the captain observed that the next door was chalked in the same manner: and shewing it to his guide, asked him which house it was, that, or the first? The guide was so confounded, that he knew not what answer to make; but still more puzzled, when he saw five or six houses similarly marked. He assured the captain, with an oath, that he had marked but one, and could not tell who had chalked the rest so that he could not distinguish the house which the cobbler had stopped at.

The captain, finding that their design had proved abortive, went directly to the place of rendezvous, and told the first of his troop whom he met that they had lost their labour, and must return to their cave. When the troop was all got together, the captain told them the reason of their returning; and presently the conductor was declared by all worthy of death. He condemned himself, acknowledging that he ought to have taken better precaution, and prepared to receive the stroke from him who was appointed to cut off his head. Another of the gang, who promised himself that he should succeed better, immediately presented himself, and his offer being accepted, he went and corrupted Baba Mustapha, as the other had done; and being shewn the house, marked it in a place more remote from sight, with red chalk.

Not long after, Morgiana, whose eyes nothing could escape, went out, and seeing the red chalk, and arguing with herself as she had done before, marked the other neighbours' houses in the same place and manner. The robber, at his return to his company, valued himself much on the precaution he had taken, which he looked upon as an infallible way of distinguishing Ali Baba's house from the others; and the captain and all of them thought it must succeed. They conveyed themselves into the town with the same precaution as before; but when the robber and his captain came to the street, they found the same difficulty: at which the captain was enraged, and the robber in as great confusion as his predecessor. Thus the captain and his troop were forced to retire a second time, and much more dissatisfied; while the unfortunate robber, who had been the author of the mistake, underwent the same punishment; which he willingly submitted to.

The captain, having lost two brave fellows of his troop, was afraid of diminishing it too much by pursuing this plan to get information of the residence of their plunderer. He found by their example that their heads were not so good as their hands on such occasions; and therefore resolved to take upon himself the important commission. Accordingly, he went and addressed himself to Baba Mustapha, who did him the same service he had done to the other robbers. He did not set any particular mark on the house, but examined and observed it so carefully, by passing often by it, that it was impossible for him to mistake it.

The captain, well satisfied with his attempt, and informed of what he wanted to know, returned to the forest; and when he came into the cave, where the troop waited for him, said: "Now, comrades, nothing can prevent our full revenge, as I am certain of the house, and in my way hither I have thought how to put it into execution, but if anyone can form a better expedient, let him communicate it." He then told them his contrivance; and as they approved of it, ordered them to go into the villages about, and buy nineteen mules, with thirty-eight large leather jars, one full of oil, and the others empty. In two or three days' time the robbers had purchased the mules and jars, and as the mouths of the jars were rather too narrow for his purpose, the captain caused them to be widened; and after having put one of his men into each, with the weapons which he thought fit, leaving open the seam which had been undone to leave them room to breathe, he rubbed the jars on the outside with oil from the full vessel. Things being thus prepared, when the nineteen mules were loaded with thirty-seven robbers in jars, and the jar of oil, the captain, as their driver, set out with them, and reached the town by the dusk of the evening, as he had intended. He led them through the streets till he came to Ali Baba's, at whose door he designed to have knocked; but was prevented by his sitting there after supper to take a little fresh air. He stopped his mules, addressed himself to him, and said: "I have brought some oil a great way, to sell at tomorrow's market; and it is now so late that I do not know where to lodge. If I should not be troublesome to you, do me the favour to let me pass the night with you, and I shall be very much obliged by your hospitality."

Though Ali Baba had seen the captain of the robbers in the forest, and had heard him speak, it was hardly possible to know him in the disguise of an oil-merchant. He told him he should be welcome, and immediately opened his gates for the mules to go into the yard. At the same time he called to a slave, and ordered him, when the mules were unloaded, to put them into the stable, and give them fodder; and then went to Morgiana, to bid her get a good supper. He did more. When he saw the captain had unloaded his mules, and that they were put into the stables as he had ordered, and he was looking for a place to pass the night in the air, he brought him into the hall where he received his company, telling him he would not suffer him to be in the court. The captain excused himself on pretence of not being troublesome; but really to have room to execute his design, and it was not till after the most pressing importunity that he yielded. Ali Baba, not content to keep company, till supper was ready, with the man who had a design on his life, continued talking with him till it was ended, and repeating his offer of service. The captain rose up at the same time with his host; and while Ali Baba went to speak to Morgiana he withdrew into the yard, under pretence of looking at his mules. Ali Baba, after charging Morgiana afresh to take care of his guest, said to her: "Tomorrow morning I design to go to the bath before day; take care my bathing linens be ready, give them to Abdoollah," which was the slave's name, "and make me some good broth against I return." After this he went to bed.

In the meantime, the captain went from the stable to give his people orders what to do; and beginning at the first jar, and so on to the last, said to each man: "As soon as I throw some stones out of the chamber window where I lie, do not fail to cut the jar open with the knife you have about you for the purpose, and come out, and I will immediately join you." After this he returned into the house, when Morgiana, taking up a light, conducted him to his chamber, where she left him; and he, to avoid any suspicion, put the light out soon after, and laid himself down in his clothes, that he might be the more ready to rise.

Morgiana, remembering Ali Baba's orders, got his bathing linens ready, and ordered Abdoollah to set on the pot for the broth; but while she was preparing it, the lamp went out, and there was no more oil in the house, nor any candles. What to do she did not know, for the broth must be made. Abdoollah, seeing her very uneasy, said: "Do not fret and tease yourself, but go into the yard, and take some oil out of one of the jars." Morgiana thanked Abdoollah for his advice, took the oil-pot, and went into the yard; when as she came nigh the first jar, the robber within said softly: "Is it time?" Though the robber spoke low, Morgiana was struck with the voice the more, because the captain, when he unloaded the mules, had taken the lids off this and all the other jars to give air to his men, who were ill enough at their ease, almost wanting room to breathe. As much surprised as Morgiana naturally was at finding a man in a jar, instead of the oil she wanted, many would have made such an outcry as to have given an alarm; whereas Morgiana, comprehending immediately the importance of keeping silence, and the necessity of applying a speedy remedy without noise, conceived at once the means, and collecting herself without shewing the least emotion, answered: "Not yet, but presently." She went in this manner to all the jars, giving the same answer, till she came to the jar of oil.

By this means, Morgiana found that her master Ali Baba, who thought that he had entertained an oil merchant, had admitted thirty-eight robbers into his house, regarding this pretended merchant as their captain. She made what haste she could to fill her oil-pot, and returned into her kitchen; where, as soon as she had lighted her lamp, she took a great kettle, went again to the oil-jar, filled the kettle, set it on a large wood-fire, and as soon as it boiled went and poured enough into every jar to stifle and destroy the robber within.

When this action, worthy of the courage of Morgiana, was executed without any noise, she returned into the kitchen with the empty kettle; and having put out the great fire she had made to boil the oil, and leaving just enough to make the broth, put out the lamp also, and remained silent; resolving not to go to rest till she had observed what might follow through a window of the kitchen, which opened into the yard.

She had not waited long before the captain of the robbers got up, opened the window, and finding no light, and hearing no noise, or anyone stirring in the house, gave the appointed signal, by throwing little stones, several of which hit the jars, as he doubted not by the sound they gave. He then listened, but not hearing or perceiving anything whereby he could judge that his companions stirred, he began to grow very uneasy, threw stones again a second and also a third time, and could not comprehend the reason that none of them should answer his signal. Much alarmed, he went softly down into the yard, and going to the first jar, whilst asking the robber, whom he thought alive, if he was in readiness, smelt the hot boiled oil, which sent forth a steam out of the jar. Hence he suspected that his plot to murder Ali Baba and plunder his house was discovered. Examining all the jars one after another, he found that all the members of his gang were dead; and by the oil he missed out of the last jar, guessed the means and manner of their death. Enraged to despair at having failed in his design, he forced the lock of a door that led from the yard to the garden, and, climbing over the walls, made his escape.

When Morgiana heard no noise, and found, after waiting some time, that the captain did not return, she concluded that he had chosen rather to make his escape by the garden than the street door, which was double-locked. Satisfied and pleased to have succeeded so well, in saving her master and family, she went to bed.

Ali Baba rose before day, and, followed by his slave, went to the baths, entirely ignorant of the important event which had happened at home; for Morgiana had not thought it safe to wake him before, for fear of losing her opportunity; and after her successful exploit she thought it needless to disturb him.

When he returned from the baths, the sun was risen; he was very much surprised to see the oil jars and that the merchant was not gone with the mules. He asked Morgiana, who opened the door, and had let all things stand as they were, that he might see them, the reason of it. "My good master," answered she, "God preserve you and all your family; you will be better informed of what you wish to know when you have seen what I have to show you, if you will but give yourself the trouble to follow me."

As soon as Morgiana had shut the door, Ali Baba followed her; when she requested him to look into the first jar and see if there was any oil. Ali Baba did so, and, seeing a man, started back in alarm, and cried out. "Do not be afraid," said Morgiana. "The man you see there can neither do you nor anybody else any harm. He is dead." "Ah, Morgiana!" said Ali Baba, "what is it you show me? Explain yourself." "I will," replied Morgiana. "Moderate your astonishment, and do not excite the curiosity of your neighbours. Look into all the other jars."

Ali Baba examined all the other jars, and when he came to that which had the oil in, found it prodigiously sunk, and stood for some time motionless, sometimes looking at the jars, and sometimes at Morgiana, without saying a word, so great was his surprise: at last, when he had recovered himself, he said: "And what is become of the merchant?"

"Merchant!" answered she. "He is as much one as I am; I will tell you who he is, and what is become of him: but you had better hear the story in your own chamber; for it is time for your health that you had your broth after your bathing."

While Ali Baba retired to his chamber, Morgiana went into the kitchen to fetch the broth, but before he would drink it, he first entreated her to satisfy his impatience, and tell him what had happened, with all the circumstances; and she obeyed him.

"This," she said, when she had completed her story, "is the account you asked of me; and I am convinced it is the consequence of what I observed some days ago, but did not think fit to acquaint you with; for when I came in one morning early I found our street door marked with white chalk, and the next morning with red; upon which, both times without knowing what was the intention of those chalks, I marked two or three neighbours' doors on each side in the same manner. If you reflect on this, and what has since happened, you will find it to be a plot of the robbers of the forest, of whose gang there are two wanting, and now they are reduced to three: all this shows that they had sworn your destruction, and it is proper you should be upon your guard, while there is one of them alive: for my part, I shall neglect nothing necessary to your preservation, as I am in duty bound."

When Morgiana had left off speaking, Ali Baba was so sensible of the great service she had done him, that he said to her: "I will not die without rewarding you as you deserve; I owe my life to you, and for the first token of my acknowledgment, give you your liberty from this moment, till I can complete your recompense as I intend. I am persuaded with you, that the forty robbers have laid snares for my destruction. God, by your means, has delivered me from them as yet, and I hope will continue to preserve me from their wicked designs, and deliver the world from their persecution. All that we have to do is to bury the bodies of these pests of mankind immediately, and with all the secrecy imaginable, that nobody may suspect what is become of them. But that labour Abdoollah and I will undertake."

Ali Baba's garden was very long, and shaded at the farther end by a great number of large trees. Under these he and the slave dug a trench, long and wide enough to hold all the robbers. Afterward they lifted the bodies out of the jars, took away their weapons, carried them to the end of the garden, laid them in the trench, and levelled the ground again. When this was done, Ali Baba hid the jars and weapons; and as he had no occasion for the mules, he sent them at different times to be sold in the market by his slave.

While Ali Baba took these measures to prevent the public from knowing how he came by his riches in so short a time, the captain of the forty robbers returned to the forest with inconceivable mortification; and in his confusion at his ill success, so contrary to what he had promised himself, entered the cave, not being able, all the way from the town, to come to any resolution how to revenge himself of Ali Baba.

The loneliness of the gloomy cavern became frightful to him. "Where are you, my brave lads," cried he, "old companions of my watchings, inroads, and labour? What can I do without you? Did I collect you only to lose you by so base a fate, and so unworthy of your courage! Had you died with your sabres in your hands, like brave men, my regret had been less! When shall I enlist so gallant a troop again? And if I could, can I undertake it without exposing so much gold and treasure to him who hath already enriched himself out of it? I cannot, I ought not to think of it, before I have taken away his life. I will undertake that alone, which I could not accomplish with your powerful assistance; and when I have taken measures to secure this treasure from being pillaged, I will provide for it new masters and successors after me, who shall preserve and augment it to all posterity." This resolution being taken, he was not at a loss how to execute his purpose; but full of hopes, slept all that night very quietly.

When he awoke early next morning, he dressed himself, agreeably to the project he had formed, went to the town, and took a lodging in a khan. As he expected what had happened at Ali Baba's might make a great noise, he asked his host what news there was in the city? Upon which the innkeeper told him a great many circumstances, which did not concern him in the least. He judged by this, that the reason why Ali Baba kept his affairs so secret, was for fear people should know where the treasure lay; and because he knew his life would be sought on account of it. This urged him the more to neglect nothing to rid himself of so cautious an enemy.

The captain now assumed the character of a merchant, and conveyed gradually a great many sorts of rich stuffs and fine linen to his lodging from the cavern, but with all the necessary precautions imaginable to conceal the place whence he brought them. In order to dispose of the merchandise, when he had amassed them together, he took a warehouse, which happened to be opposite to Cassim's, which Ali Baba's son had occupied since the death of his uncle.

He took the name of Khaujeh Houssain, and as a newcomer, was, according to custom, extremely civil and complaisant to all the merchants his neighbours. Ali Baba's son was from his vicinity one of the first to converse with Khaujeh Houssain, who strove to cultivate his friendship more particularly when, two or three days after he was settled, he recognised Ali Baba, who came to see his son, and stopped to talk with him as he was accustomed to do. When he was gone, the impostor learnt from his son who he was. He increased his assiduities, caressed him in the most engaging manner, made him some small presents, and often asked him to dine and sup with him.

Ali Baba's son did not choose to lie under such obligation to Khaujeh Houssain, without making the like return; but was so much straitened for want of room in his house, that he could not entertain him so well as he wished; he therefore acquainted his father Ali Baba with his intention, and told him that it did not look well for him to receive such favours from Khaujeh Houssain without inviting him in return.

Ali Baba, with great pleasure, took the treat upon himself. "Son," said he, "tomorrow being Friday, which is a day that the shops of such great merchants as Khaujeh Houssain and yourself are shut, get him to take a walk with you, and as you come back, pass by my door and call in. It will look better to have it happen accidentally, than if you gave him a formal invitation. I will go and order Morgiana to provide a supper."

The next day Ali Baba's son and Khaujeh Houssain met by appointment, took their walk, and as they returned, Ali Baba's son led Khaujeh Houssain through the street where his father lived; and when they came to the house, stopped and knocked at the door. "This, sir," said he, "is my father's house; who, from the account I have given him of your friendship, charged me to procure him the honour of your acquaintance."

Though it was the sole aim of Khaujeh Houssain to introduce himself into Ali Baba's house, that he might kill him without hazarding his own life or making any noise; yet he excused himself, and offered to take his leave. But a slave having opened the door, Ali Baba's son took him obligingly by the hand, and in a manner forced him in.

Ali Baba received Khaujeh Houssain with a smiling countenance, and in the most obliging manner. He thanked him for all the favours he had done his son; adding withal, the obligation was the greater, as he was a young man not much acquainted with the world.

Khaujeh Houssain returned the compliment, by assuring Ali Baba, that though his son might not have acquired the experience of older men, he had good sense equal to the knowledge of many others. After a little more conversation on different subjects, he offered again to take his leave; when Ali Baba, stopping him, said: "Where are you going, sir, in so much haste? I beg you would do me the honour to sup with me, though what I have to give you is not worth your acceptance; but such as it is, I hope you will accept it as heartily as I give it." "Sir," replied Khaujeh Houssain, "I am thoroughly persuaded of your good will; and if I ask the favour of you not to take it ill that I do not accept your obliging invitation, I beg of you to believe that it does not proceed from any slight or intention to affront, but from a reason which you would approve if you knew it.

"And what may that reason be, sir," replied Ali Baba, "if I may be so bold as to ask you?" "It is," answered Khaujeh Houssain, "that I can eat no victuals that have any salt in them; therefore judge how I should feel at your table." "If that is the only reason," said Ali Baba, "it ought not to deprive me of the honour of your company at supper; for, in the first place, there is no salt ever put into my bread, and as to the meat we shall have tonight, I promise you there shall be none in that. Therefore you must do me the favour to stay. I will return immediately."

Ali Baba went into the kitchen, and ordered Morgiana to put no salt to the meat that was to be dressed that night; and to make quickly two or three ragouts besides what he had ordered, but be sure to put no salt in them.

Morgiana, who was always ready to obey her master, could not help seeming somewhat dissatisfied at his strange order. "Who is this difficult man," said she, "who eats no salt with his meat? Your supper will be spoiled, if I keep it back so long." "Do not be angry, Morgiana," replied Ali Baba; "he is an honest man; therefore do as I bid you."

Morgiana obeyed, though with no little reluctance, and had a curiosity to see this man who ate no salt. To this end, when she had finished what she had to do in the kitchen, she helped Abdoollah to carry up the dishes; and looking at Khaujeh Houssain, knew him at first sight, notwithstanding his disguise, to be the captain of the robbers, and examining him very carefully, perceived that he had a dagger under his garment. "I am not in the least amazed," said she to herself, "that this wicked wretch, who is my master's greatest enemy, would eat no salt with him, since he intends to assassinate him; but I will prevent him."

Morgiana, while they were eating, made the necessary preparations for executing one of the boldest acts ever meditated, and had just determined, when Abdoollah came for the dessert of fruit, which she carried up, and as soon as he had taken the meat away, set upon the table; after that, she placed three glasses by Ali Baba, and going out, took Abdoollah with her to sup, and to give Ali Baba the more liberty of conversation with his guest.

Khaujeh Houssain, or rather the captain of the robbers, thought he had now a favourable opportunity of being revenged on Ali Baba. "I will," said he to himself, "make the father and son both drunk: the son, whose life I intend to spare, will not be able to prevent my stabbing his father to the heart; and while the slaves are at supper, or asleep in the kitchen, I can make my escape over the gardens as before."

Instead of going to supper, Morgiana, who had penetrated the intentions of the counterfeit Khaujeh Houssain, would not give him time to put his villainous design into execution, but dressed herself neatly with a suitable head-dress like a dancer, girded her waist with a silver-gilt girdle, to which there hung a poniard with a hilt and guard of the same metal, and put a handsome mask on her face. When she had thus disguised herself, she said to Abdoollah: "Take your tabor, and let us go and divert our master and his son's guest, as we do sometimes when he is alone."

Abdoollah took his tabor and played all the way into the hall before Morgiana, who, when she came to the door, made a low obeisance, with a deliberate air, in order to draw attention, and by way of asking leave to exhibit her skill. Abdoollah, seeing that his master had a mind to say something, left off playing. "Come in, Morgiana," said Ali Baba, "and let Khaujeh Houssain see what you can do, that he may tell us what he thinks of you. But, sir," said he, turning toward his guest, "do not think that I put myself to any expense to give you this diversion, since these are my slave and my cook and housekeeper; and I hope you will not find the entertainment they give us disagreeable."

Khaujeh Houssain, who did not expect this diversion after supper, began to fear he should not be able to improve the opportunity he thought he had found: but hoped, if he now missed his aim, to secure it another time, by keeping up a friendly correspondence with the father and son; therefore, though he could have wished Ali Baba would have declined the dance, he had the complaisance to express his satisfaction at what he saw pleased his host.

As soon as Abdoollah saw that Ali Baba and Khaujeh Houssain had done talking, he began to play on the tabor, and accompanied it with an air; to which Morgiana, who was an excellent performer, danced in such a manner as would have created admiration in any other company besides that before which she now exhibited, among whom, perhaps, none but the false Khaujeh Houssain was in the least attentive to her, the rest having seen her so frequently.

After she had danced several dances with equal propriety and grace, she drew the poniard, and holding it in her hand, began a dance, in which she outdid herself, by the many different figures, light movements, and the surprising leaps and wonderful exertions with which she accompanied it. Sometimes she presented the poniard to one person's breast, sometimes to another's, and oftentimes seemed to strike her own. At last, as if she was out of breath, she snatched the tabor from Abdoollah with her left hand, and, holding the dagger in her right, presented the other side of the tabor, after the manner of those who get a livelihood by dancing and solicit the liberality of the spectators.

Ali Baba put a piece of gold into the tabor, as did also his son: and Khaujeh Houssain, seeing that she was coming to him, had pulled his purse out of his bosom to make her a present; but while he was putting his hand into it, Morgiana, with a courage and resolution worthy of herself, plunged the poniard into his heart. Ali Baba and his son, shocked at this action, cried out aloud. "Unhappy wretch!" exclaimed Ali Baba. "What have you done to ruin me and my family?" "It was to preserve, not to ruin you," answered Morgiana, "for see here," continued she (opening the pretended Khaujeh Houssain's garment, and showing the dagger), "what an enemy you had entertained! Look well at him, and you will find him to be both the fictitious oil-merchant, and the captain of the gang of forty robbers. Remember, too, that he would eat no salt with you; and what would you have more to persuade you of his wicked design? Before I saw him, I suspected him as soon as you told me you had such a guest. I knew him, and you now find that my suspicion was not groundless."

Ali Baba, who immediately felt the new obligation he had to Morgiana for saving his life a second time, embraced her: "Morgiana," said he, "I gave you your liberty, and then promised you that my gratitude should not stop there, but that I would soon give you higher proofs of its sincerity, which I now do by making you my daughter-in-law." Then addressing himself to his son, he said: "I believe you, son, to be so dutiful a child, that you will not refuse Morgiana for your wife. You see that Khaujeh Houssain sought your friendship with a treacherous design to take away my life; and, if he had succeeded, there is no doubt but he would have sacrificed you also to his revenge. Consider, that by marrying Morgiana you marry the preserver of my family and your own."

The son, far from showing any dislike, readily consented to the marriage; not only because he would not disobey his father, but also because it was agreeable to his inclination.

After this, they thought of burying the captain of the robbers with his comrades, and did it so privately that nobody discovered their bones till many years after, when no one had any concern in the publication of this remarkable history.

A few days afterward, Ali Baba celebrated the nuptials of his son and Morgiana with great solemnity, a sumptuous feast, and the usual dancing and spectacles; and had the satisfaction to see that his friends and neighbours, whom he invited, had no knowledge of the true motives of the marriage; but that those who were not unacquainted with Morgiana's good qualities commended his generosity and goodness of heart.

Ali Baba forbore, after this marriage, from going again to the robbers' cave, as he had done, for fear of being surprised, from the time he had brought away his brother Cassim's mangled remains. He had kept away after the death of the thirtyseven robbers and their captain, supposing the other two, whom he could get no account of, might be alive.

At the year's end, when he found that they had not made any attempt to disturb him, he had the curiosity to make another journey, taking the necessary precautions for his safety. He mounted his horse, and when he came to the cave, and saw no footsteps of men or beasts, looked upon it as a good sign. He alighted, tied his horse to a tree, then approaching the entrance and pronouncing the words, Open, Sesame! the door opened. He entered the cavern, and by the condition he found things in, judged that nobody had been there since the false Khaujeh Houssain, when he had fetched the goods for his shop; that the gang of forty robbers was completely destroyed, and no longer doubted that he was the only person in the world who had the secret of opening the cave, so that all the treasure was at his sole disposal. Having brought with him a wallet, he put into it as much gold as his horse would carry, and returned to town.

Afterward Ali Baba carried his son to the cave, and taught him the secret, which they handed down to their posterity, who, using their good fortune with moderation, lived in great honour and splendour.